Praise for Glen Duncan and

## *By Blood We Live*

"Duncan writes with caustic edge and pop-culturally relevant humor."
                                        —*The Dallas Morning News*

"The horror genre at its best—wildly imaginative, written with wit and intelligence, wickedly entertaining."
                                        —*The Times* (London)

"There are plenty of battles, blood, and sexy escapades; but the real treat continues to be Duncan's beautifully twisted way with language and the profound thesis he poses about humanity."
                                        —*Booklist*

"Horror fiction at its best."                  —*The Oregonian*

"A page turner with heft. . . . Storytelling to chill the blood."
                                        —*Sunday Herald* (Glasgow)

"Vigorous, funny, sexy and necessary at a time when so much genre fiction is drowning in melancholy vampires and self-serious teen dystopias."                  —*Kirkus Reviews*

GLEN DUNCAN

*By Blood We Live*

Glen Duncan is the author of nine previous novels.
He lives in London.

# By Blood
# We Live

A NOVEL

*Glen Duncan*

VINTAGE BOOKS
*A Division of Random House LLC*
*New York*

FIRST VINTAGE BOOKS EDITION, OCTOBER 2014

The Cataloging-in-Publication Data is on file at the Library of Congress:
LLCN2013044988

Vintage Trade Paperback ISBN: 978-0-307-74219-3
eBook ISBN: 978-0-385-35038-9

*Book design by Michael Collica*

www.vintagebooks.com

146056540

*By blood we live, the hot, the cold,*
*To ravage and redeem the world:*
*There is no bloodless myth will hold.*

—Geoffrey Hill, "Genesis"

# Part One

# The Beguiled

# 1

# *Remshi*

IT'S BETTER TO kill people at the end of their psychology. They have nothing left to offer themselves or the world.

Not that I should have been killing anyone just then. Having fed less than twenty hours ago I should have woken slaked and mellow, indifferent to blood for at least a week. Instead I'd woken in a state of—not to put too fine a point on it—complete fucking pandemonium. Voices in the head (repeating, God only knew why, *He lied in every word . . . He lied in every word . . .*), earthquake in the heart, Sartrean nausea in the soul—and *thirst* such as I hadn't felt in centuries. Not the domesticated version, to be fobbed off with a half-dozen pouches from the fridge. No. This was The Lash, old school, non-negotiable, the red chorus that deafened the capillaries with its single moronic imperative: *GET LIVING BLOOD NOW, OR DIE*.

Traumatically baffling though all this was it wasn't the main mystery. The main mystery was the dream I'd had. Do *not* start with a murder. Do *not* start with a dream. I know. But my defence is two-pronged: One, I'm a murderer. Two, the dream was a colossal anomaly. Not the content. Just the fact of it. I don't, you see, dream. At all. Ever. Not since Vali died. And that was a long, *long* time ago.

No chance to consider that now, however. The thirst's virtue is that next to the need to satisfy it everything else becomes laughably secondary. It gives you, as would a gun pointed at your head, focus.

So here I was.

The house of Randolf Moyser, pornographer, was, not surprisingly, the pornographer's house: Milanese sofas in cream leather, jade side tables, cowhide rugs, chandeliers, planes of carpet the colour of Bahamian sand, mirrors it would've needed a crane to hang. I'd chosen it for its location, a mile northwest of Malibu Springs, high on an unoverlooked hill with pinewoods cover on the eastern side to within fifty yards of the ground floor terrace, and on the west uninhabited scrub all the way to the nearest neighbour's tree line a quarter of a mile away. I say "chosen," but that's not true. The Lash applies suave guidance, finds the ether's invisible vectors and drifts, the spaces in space that lead to fulfilment. The blood's dialogue—yours and theirs (or rather mine and yours)—starts before you've quite set eyes on each other. Like a love story. Like the moments just before I first saw Vali, seventeen thousand years ago.

(Yes, you read that right.)

I left the car in a lay-by on the country road and walked up through the woods.

Randolf, known in the industry as E. Wrecked (and known to me ever since a production company I own made a documentary about him), was at the end of his psychology. He'd just turned fifty-eight, and for more than two decades had been rich enough for it not to matter what he looked like. Letting himself go, physically, had been part of the psychology: there mustn't be the slightest chance that the twenty-two-year-old on her knees with his cock in her mouth could possibly want to be on her knees with his cock in her mouth. Therefore unkempt toenails. Therefore waxy belly and flaccid bubs. Therefore yawning pores. It was quite something to be able to go bald not only without anxiety, but with satisfaction.

Yet his psychology had betrayed him. His psychology had said that if he got enough women to do things they didn't want to do—no force (force was cheating), just persuasion, seduction, money, *psychology*—then the great burning formless question of his being would be answered. He didn't know where this equation had come from—that the degradation of women was the doorway to revelation—only that it was his and that it was beyond contradiction or doubt. He hadn't shirked it. After thirty-five years in the business there wasn't much he could think of that a woman wouldn't want to do that he hadn't got a woman to do. But his psychology had lied. His psychology had been like the Devil, full of false promises. Leaving aside the problem of the small number of women who, for what-ever reason, *wanted* to do all the things all the other women didn't (in their performances you could glimpse impatience or irritation that they weren't degrading themselves enough, a frantic desperation at the limits), leaving aside this small number of women who were useless to his psychology (and who were frankly ruining the industry for everyone else), leaving these aside, the fundamental problem didn't alter: degrading women or getting women to degrade themselves did not, in fact, answer the burning formless question of his being. It was Eve biting into the apple to discover only that it was an apple and she could bite into it. His psychology had no other methods on offer. His psychology was a one-trick pony, and the trick had failed, every time.

Randolf, or E., wasn't alone. His gofer was on the phone in the downstairs office, and two sharp-kneed escorts in bikinis and strappy stilettos were drinking mojitos by the opalescent moon-pool. Randolf was in one of the upstairs bedrooms (Corinthian pillars, a fireplace like a wedding cake) shouting at his web manager about problems with the recently launched site, imsorrydaddy.com. His production company was facing legal action from a Christian counselling service who—courtesy of domain registration meltdown—had a site of the same name devoted to reconciling rebellious daughters with their churchgoing fathers. "I don't fucking care what fucking Anthony fucking told you," he was saying, while examining a possibly cancerous mole on his Tiresian chest. "I'm telling you we get *those* assholes to change the name. What? No, imsorrymommy.com *isn't* a viable fucking alternative. Jesus fucking Christ. Why doesn't any—What the fuck—"

He was having the moment of disbelief. That he hadn't seen or heard me come in. But there I was. His mouth was open, breath a hot mix of Booker's Bourbon and a meat-packed bowel.

"You're on CCTV," Randolf said. I didn't contradict him, though it had taken me less than a minute to disable the system. I didn't speak at all. There was nothing for me to say. At this moment there never is. He found himself on his back on the floor, with me on top of him. He didn't know how that had happened. It was an awful magic, the blur, the compression, the two states—upright/on the floor—with no causal apparatus between them. And of course he knew what I was. Humans always do, when the time comes. *Vampire. Vampires. In spite of governments and Christmas and Microsoft. Well, I'll be.* When their time comes there's always a disinterested part of them ravished by such things being real after all. They think: Damn, this would've made quite a difference to my life. It wouldn't, in Randolf's case, but there was no point going into it with him.

I hoofed him in the balls and broke his left arm.

The last moment before the bite is like the last moment before coming: stopped time and shrugged-off space, an instant of seeing how it is for God. It's why people in sexual extremis say *Oh, God*. It's not a cry to the Divine, it's a recognition of their own divinity. I was very aware of my mouth open, my heartbeat in my teeth, the obscene ease with which I held him, the room like a frozen grin around us, and beyond it the Californian night and the orange blossom and the desert and the sprawling dark continent's indifferent consciousness gathering to a kind of Meaning. All Randolf's details huddled in him like a terrified village crammed inside its church. This is what happens: the particulars gather, exude their fraught vibe like an odour and before you bite, before you drink, you get an inkling of what it's going to give you, the base notes, the exploded secrets, the finish. All your victim's decisions and imprecisions and crimes and losses gather and sing—in this moment—of the tiny and unique ways in which this life will, once you've drunk it down, change you.

He was trying to say something, but my hand around his throat reduced it to abortive sibilants and fricatives. He was struggling, I suppose, but he might as well have been a sack of oatmeal for all the good it did him. I shifted my grip to cover his mouth, lay fully on top of him, looked him in the eyes, once—then sank my fangs into his throat.

Dark and sweet and total. Surrender like the guillotine's drop. The universe comes in through those eye-teeth as it does to a suckling babe through the nipples of its mother. You want more, you want it all. So you take more, you take it all. Randolf's life.

*If I'd got a woman to kill her own child while I fucked her in the ass—*

This was one of his last thoughts, unfortunately. It was unavoidable, once he knew he was dying. In the wake of every failure his psychology had said it was his fault, he hadn't gone far enough, and he'd thought that would be about as far as you could possibly go. Only he'd never gone that far, and now he was dying this thought along with others (his mother's powdery face, the Jersey tenement stoop, the hot flank of a big dog that had knocked him down when he was small, a million TV fragments and hoarding slogans and women's faces spattered with come) flashed brief and vivid against the wall of fear. He'd thought he'd known fear. But I showed him the end of his psychology—worse even than a handful of dust—and he realised he'd never known fear before.

You don't let the heart stop. Anne Rice got that right. But I know when there are a dozen beats left. Ten. Six. Three. Two . . . Naturally you push it. Naturally the last draughts are precious, carry the yolky taste of the soul's torn caul, the residue of its confused farewell. The swallowed life fans out in your blood, exhales its wisdoms and losses, its poignant incidentals that enlarge you, force you to find shelf-space in the groaning stacks. Your heart's library, whether you like it or not, expands. I used to see it as a woeful irony that murdering humans increased my love for humanity. Now I accept it, drink, make room, get bigger, love them, go my ways. *Because someone has to bear witness*, the voice of my maker had said, long ago, in the darkness of the cave.

I sucked hard, went wholly seduced—went *wantonly* into the drink. If the soul was immortal it left its memories behind in the blood, shed consciousness and passed on, naked and pure, to the realm beyond image and word, to be wrangled over by God and the Devil, or to reach final dissolution in the void. But I didn't need the soul. Only the blood. Always and always and always the blood. I drank and felt the rhythm of the drinking in my eyelids and fingertips and nipples and feet. I drank and swam down into Randolf's goodbye pulse, softened into the beat, systole, diastole, systole, diastole, at last lost myself, went, for a time, out of time.

But the sixth sense hauls you back. I stopped with two heartbeats left. Watched his eyes flutter, observed the last moments. His psychology had brought him all the way to death then turned and left him with nothing. Now he was going, desperate, terrified, unready, like the last grains of sand sucked through the hourglass's dainty midriff. Gone.

Randolf's life had woken the other lives in me and my heart was a rose of fire. Cells bloomed, the song of my dead throbbed in the tissues. The universe's half-revealed Meaning surrounded me. The busy clues to the grand architecture that was like an irresistible enigmatic smile.

I stood up, hilariously strong, a glut of sly power in the shoulders, the thighs. You forgot how good it was. You forgot it was everything. You forgot it took possession from soles to scalp, refreshed fingerprints, eyelashes, pubes, the queer little papillae of the tongue. You forgot it let Meaning bleed back in like colour returning to a monochrome world. You forgot it was something perfect, and in the way of perfect things—the pole-vaulter's flawless clearance, for example, the skater's nailed triple salchow—made you want to laugh. I might have laughed, too, had the memory of the dream not suddenly flashed and fractured me again, had *He lied in every word* not buzzed like a wasp in my ear then whizzed away, leaving behind in me a feeling of knowing that I knew something without knowing what it was.

Downstairs, the gofer dropped ice cubes into a glass. I took a last look at Randolph's shocked face (his formidable head was the centre of an expanding Rorschach butterfly of blood), wished, briefly, that I could always take the lousy ones, pick the human race clean of its wretches like oxpeckers rid Cape buffalo of their parasites, then I leaped across the room to the window, slid it open and jumped. One of the angular escorts looked up, thought, Jesus that was some fucking . . . Do eagles fly at night? No, that's . . . that's owls. Anyway, whatever . . .

# 2

STUNNED AND SYMPHONIC with new blood, I retraced my steps through the woods to the car, a humble Mitsubishi (the trophy vehicles went years ago, novelty exhausted; I regretted it just then, remembering the lurch and grip of the bronze '68 Camaro, its smell of gasoline and vinyl and the stoned end of the decade, Jimi on the eight-track) and within minutes was heading east on the 101. The moment—rolling darkness and the empty LA hills, me wide-eyed and stinking rich with stolen life—needed music ("O Fortuna" from Orff's *Carmina Burana* and Guns N' Roses' "Welcome to the Jungle" both sprang to mind), or rather, it would have needed music, had not the quenched thirst left me at dreadful liberty to consider the madness of everything that had happened since I'd opened my eyes in the vault less than three hours ago.

The inexplicable thirst.

*He lied in every word.*

The dream.

Oh, yes. While I'd slept. As opposed to the flashbacks and fugues my head goes in for when I'm awake.

A dream?

Impossible.

Im*possible*.

It might not seem much to you, but I have to repeat: I don't dream. Categorically: I *do not* dream.

Not since . . .

*Not since you were very young. Not since Vali died . . .*

Sadness swelled, suddenly—and I knew if I let myself I'd start crying. (I'd been prone to little weeps, of late. You're a bit fragile, Fluff, Justine had said, not long ago, having discovered me in tears in front of a TV movie starring Lindsay Wagner dying of leukaemia . . . )

I didn't dream.

I did *not* dream.

But there it was. Last night, I'd dreamed.

*In* the dream I was walking barefoot on an empty beach. It was twilight and the sea was black. There were a few lonely stars in the sky, as if the bulk of the constellations had been swept away. I was walking towards . . .

Towards what?

*He lied in every word.*

Someone else was there, close behind me.

That was all.

Was that all? Wasn't there something else . . . ?

My face tingled and my hands tightened on the Mitsubishi's steering wheel. This had, actually, happened, no matter how much it seemed it couldn't have. Millennia of empty sleep—now this. The last dream *before* this—seventeen thousand years ago (or was it sixteen? precision goes; epoch-edges blur)—had been of Vali. The night Vali died she appeared to me in a dream and said: *I will come back to you. And you will come back to me. Wait for me.*

Tears welled again. Stunned and symphonic with new blood I might have been, but it made the feeling of forlornness worse, and before I knew it, there I was—yes, ridiculous, ridiculous—weeping. I imagined Justine saying, as she had when Lindsay Wagner had upset me, *Don't cry, Stonk.* I liked it when she said that. I liked it when she put her hand in my hair or wrapped her limbs around me like a monkey. There were so many things I liked. That was the awful thing about being alive: there were so many things one liked. The awful thing about life was that there were so many *things*, full stop. You're not waiting for Vali's return, Mahmoud had bitched to me, shortly before his suicide, you're just addicted to *life*. You're not a romantic. You're a junkie.

I dried my tears with the heel of my hand, like a woman in a movie driving away sadly but bravely from a break-up, and forced myself to think back. With every hero from every pre-Seventies horror film I said to myself: Now just calm down. There has to be a perfectly rational explanation for all this . . .

Last night had been, as far as I could remember, unexceptional. Justine and I had watched *The Graduate* and *A League of Their Own* (Geena

Davis's smile is one of the things I stay alive for, I'd said. Do you think that makes me an emotional moron?) then she'd gone out to the club and I'd gone down to the vault, drunk six O positive MREs from the cooler and read *Don Juan* for the last two hours of darkness until sleep took me just before dawn. That was all. Nothing unusual. Nothing to explain the dream, the wake-up panic, the pounding thirst, the conviction that I knew something without knowing what it was. Nothing, in short, to explain the overwhelming feeling that either I or the world had gone completely insane.

Desert night flowed over the car. I was aware of my face, thudding, and of the Mitsubishi's instrument panel attending to my mental wrestle with a kind of sympathetic innocence. The dream's images tantalised: the empty beach, the sparse stars, the black water, the unknown someone walking behind me. Naturally I'd forgotten what this was like, the way a dream's churned wake or slipstream left you groping after the dissolving fragments, what they meant, what they seemed to mean. They don't mean shit, Oscar the analyst had said to me one night in Alexandria. Dreams are prick-teasers *non pareil*. They promise and promise but they never put out. Don't waste your time on dreams. Oscar was dead, too, it must be seventy years. So many dead. I had not known death had . . .

And, yes, back came the tears. Accompanied, this time, by the beginning of real fear, because what, what, *what* the fuck was wrong with me?

I spent the rest of the journey going through the same amnesiac loop, but I was none the wiser by the time I made it—precarious, tender, horribly alive to my own confusion—home.

Nor was home an end to the madness.

Having parked the car out front I paused, arrested in spite of the unhinged nature of things by the Californian night, the scents of orange blossom and bougainvillea and the lovely odour of damp travertine where the sprinklers' arc had rinsed the drive. My memory being what it is I got by way of association an open mass grave at Auschwitz, thrilled rats rummaging the pale limbs as if for valuables long since purloined by the master race. I stood still for a moment to let the vision fade. There's nothing to do with these headflashes but wait them out. Which is what I would have done, had the reverie not been interrupted by a sudden human whiff, rich as a cured meats and pickles counter, that compelled me to turn and look back down the drive.

It didn't need night sight.

He was standing between the gateposts, illuminated by the two outdoor lamps that sit atop them like twin full moons, a beggarly old man leaning on a single crutch. His bulk, I knew, came not from protein but from a dozen never-removed layers of clothing with an eco-system of their own. His face was gaunt—what there was to see of it amid the matted hair and health-hazard beard—and one of his large eyes was dramatically blood-shot. His hands were tanned and filthy. If one of my neighbours had seen him the cops were probably already on their way.

He was staring at me, smiling.

"You're going the wrong way," he said.

For what felt like a long time I just stood there, looking at him. Then I said: "What?"

But he swivelled on his crutch and hurried away.

Angry now (too much bafflement eventually just makes you want to hit someone), I set off down the drive after him.

But there was a delayed effect, apparently of his non sequitur, because after a few paces I stopped. I'm not sure why. A feeble but comprehensive intuition—that following him was not a good idea.

Instead, throbbing, delicate, afraid, I turned and went back to the house.

# 3

JUSTINE WAS STILL out. I spent a wearying time locating my cellphone, which for some reason she'd locked in the study desk drawer. The phone had been switched off. Waiting the few seconds for it to power-up exposed the raw fact of my existence, terribly, as does standing waiting for an elevator with strangers. I had the feeling of just realising I was the subject of a reality show, imagined an invisible audience of millions thinking, Poor bugger, he hasn't got a clue . . . *He lied in every* . . .

Huge relief when I got the power symbol, the AT&T bars, the home screen (Botticelli's *Primavera*, which in spite of everything—things of beauty, joys forever—still stole a vivid second to beguile my 24/7 aesthete). I called her cell.

Voicemail. She'd changed her greeting. Gone was Bette Davis saying: *I've been drinking all the way from California—and I'm* drunk! Replaced by Justine herself, sounding remote: "You've reached Justine Cavell. Leave a message."

It occurred to me, as it has countless times before, that you can't take your eye off this world for a moment. Smoke signals. You blink. Cellphones. Six thousand years of foot messengers—now this: instant access, everywhere. FaceTime. I wish they hadn't called it that. Face Time. I can't help seeing it as an implacable *instruction*.

"For fuck's sake, Justine," I said. "Call me, will you? It's important. Something's going on. I'm a bit . . . Just call me as soon as you get this."

It calmed me, slightly, to be under my own roof, but the house felt subtly altered. I'd left in such a rush three hours ago I hadn't noticed. Now here were my sweet walnut floors and high ceilings, the study's amber lamps and red velvet drapes and twenty thousand books (one for each year of my life, I quip to after-dark guests) the hallway's green and gold Persian runner and the kitchen's copper splash-backs and black slate tops—but all possessed of a taut sentience, as if they didn't know whether to let me in on what they knew, whatever the hell it was they *did* know. Justine had tidied the TV room since our movie double bill. She'd washed and put away the glasses, got rid of the spent bottles, emptied the ashtrays, plumped up the cushions. Incredibly, it looked as if she might have vacuumed. My nostrils said recent frangipani incense and Pledge floorwax. Why? Had she thrown up somewhere? Were it anyone else I might have supposed a lover's visit, room-hopping sex, stains to mop, odours to expunge. But this was Justine, therefore that wasn't a possibility.

There was nothing to do but wait for her. I took a consolation shower in the vault. Not very consoling, since the dream leftovers wouldn't stop burgeoning and vanishing in my head, with a little more—but no less maddening—detail. On the empty beach we'd walked until we'd found a small wooden rowing boat in the shadow of a wall of black rocks, blistered and barnacled and half-covered in sand and sun-dried seaweed. (We? Me and whoever was with me. The liar in every word, presumably.) When we found the boat I said: "It's happening. Just as in the dream. I know what it means. Of course. I know now what it means."

Yes, well, I didn't know *now* what it meant.

Naked, towelled dry, I stood in front of the full-length mirror. (Reflections? Yes. We show up on film, too, don't let anyone tell you different.) Courtesy of the blood booze-up on Randolf's tab I looked ludicrously healthy. My skin, currently the colour of a double-shot latte, was tight and smooth. I used to be darker. Much darker, long ago. I reached up to touch the little carved stone Oa that hung on a chain around my neck. Its small weight was a comfort, as was the image it conjured, of my father's hands working it in the light of the cooking fire, his dark eyes full of calm knowledge, the smell of roasting meat, my mother digging a hole nearby for the offering . . .

It's a terrible thing to see yourself start to cry, as I did, just then. Not least because in spite of your misery there's how funny your face looks. But here were the tears—dear *God*—again, and the feeling of something big and obvious infuriatingly just out of view—

At which point I heard the door upstairs open and close. Justine was back.

# 4

IT'S MY NATURE to move silently. Therefore she got an almighty fright. She was standing in the study by the desk with her cellphone in her hand, staring into space with the look of someone trying to assimilate a shock. She was dressed in a short black suede jacket, red t-shirt, tight white jeans and red suede clogs. It's taken her years to wear anything on her feet other than running shoes. Naturally. Her world being for so long a place where she had to be ready to run.

"Jesus *Christ*."

"Sorry," I said. "I didn't mean to startle you. You've had your hair cut." The centre-parted jaw-length bob had been replaced by something short and snazzily chopped. She looked like the world's prettiest schoolboy.

"Oh my God," she said. "Fuck."

"What's wrong?"

She sat down in the desk's swivel chair, a cream leather ergonomic thing that would've been at home in the cockpit of the *Millennium Falcon*. The room was lit only by the Tiffany desk lamp, a delicate trapezoid of stained glass in green, gold and peach that threw a soft light on her pale hands and face. Turquoise nail polish. A big amber ring I didn't recognise. She smelled, deliciously, of cigarette smoke and booze and dry ice. She'd been to the club, TCOS, three floors on Sunset Boulevard, which I'd given her as a twenty-third birthday present five years ago. The world having nothing better to do, there was endless online speculation about what TCOS stood for. Only Justine and I knew. The Comfort Of Strangers. Her choice.

"You look different," I said to her. "It's not just the hair."

She let out the breath she'd been holding. "Yeah," she said. "I would . . . Fuck."

"Will you for the love of Thoth tell me what is going on?"

Pause.

"Have you fed?" she asked.

"Yes. Something's wrong with me. I don't . . . How come you vacuumed?"

"What?"

"The place has been cleaned since last night. How come?"

She sat back in the chair, which received her with a maidenly sigh. Three floor-to-ceiling walls of books attended in silence. A little bubble of Randolf burst in me: him six years old, falling for the tenth time off a bike he was trying to learn to ride in the yard. His father's big beer-flavoured mouth laughing. I had a feeling of something catching up with me.

"That wasn't last night," Justine said. "That was two years ago."

# 5

A CONFESSION: MY memory isn't exactly the Rolls-Royce of memories. *Memory full*, the computers say, managing with machine pathos to make you feel you've force fed them, like those poor *foie gras* geese. But my memory's never full. My memory goes in for violent clear-outs. My memory self-harms. It also makes wild boasts and risible claims, sends me absurd snapshots and improbable clips: the bodies of Amenhotep's murdered tomb builders in a moonlit heap, for example, a poignant assembly of nipples and feet and grinning faces, covered in dust. Or Niccolo Linario on a red damask couch looking up at me and saying in Latin: *They've arrested Machiavelli. Did you hear?* Or my own hands, darker-skinned, thicker-fingernailed, winding gut around a worked flint. Oh yes, *flint*. I don't expect you to believe it. For myself I'm beyond believing or not believing. For myself I just—as my darling and religiously commercial Americans say—*deal*. I decided long ago that the far from total recall is a coping mechanism. Who, after all, is built to carry twenty thousand years' worth of recollections? Too much luggage for the hold. Therefore bags and cases must be continually jettisoned and replaced, jettisoned and replaced. Otherwise flight would be impossible. Otherwise we'd crash. Only yesterday I'd said to Justine: You know, Juss, I sometimes think that if I remembered everything that's happened to me, I'd simply die. And she'd looked at me with disturbing gentle exhaustion and said: I know, Fluff. You've told me.

Except of course it turns out that *wasn't* only yesterday.

*Los Angeles Times. Monday, 27 August 2012*. There were the facts, in black and white. I'd slept for twenty-one months. The better part of two years—gone.

Justine had made me sit down in one of the study's two obese armchairs—cowhide Thomasvilles decadently left behind by Las Rosas' former owners—while she'd gone to the kitchen to fix herself a drink. (Eagle Rare seventeen-year-old single-barrel bourbon, my nose said. She's come a long way from her days of Jack Daniel's and Coke.) Now she perched on the edge of the desk facing me, tinkling tumbler in one hand, American Spirit in the other. I'd found the softpack stuffed down the side of the cushion and lit one up myself. Blood-drink your fill and nothing rewards like nicotine. I remembered seeing the first colour billboards go up: MORE DOCTORS SMOKE CAMELS THAN ANY OTHER CIGARETTE! Which detonated—along with chrome and fins and Elvis and ferocious canned laughter and Budweiser neons and the lady-shaped Coke bottle—the memory of a buxom stenographer's dewey nape smelling of Elnett hair-spray and Pond's cold cream, her tough-bra'd breasts filling my hands. Her apartment had a fold-out bed and an Alba record-player. In the bath-room cabinet hidden behind cosmetics and Band-Aids a flesh-coloured diaphragm in a plastic case like a scallop shell. She'd thought it was going to be a seduction. She'd thought it was going to be sex.

"What do you remember?" Justine said.

I felt the room tilt, intimate its mountains, cliffs of fall, got an inkling of how sick all this might make me feel, while all the Lears I'd ever seen went O, *let me not be mad, not mad sweet heaven* . . . So I said, out of my dry mouth: "Well, thanks for easing me in gently."

"This is what you told me to do if this happened. You told me . . . Jesus, I can't fucking believe this."

I didn't blame her. Every morning for twenty-one months she'd woken up hoping the coming night would restore me. Every night for twenty-one months been denied. The study's book-surrounded atmosphere bris-tled with how tightly that had wound her.

"Are you even *here*?" she said. "I can't believe it. Fuck."

I was very aware of my face, hot and overfull. In spite of the shock of twenty-one months gone I was still being ravished by the in-creeping sense of things meaning things. This is the gift of the blood: Slake the thirst and the world gestures beyond itself to an underlying blueprint. The world is a series of vivid clues to the riddle beyond appearances. The world has a purpose, a pattern, a story, a plot. The world has Meaning. Even Justine, standing there with the chunky tumbler and smouldering cigarette, backed by Tiffany lamplight and red drapes, her dark eyes and her mouth like a bruise, the schoolboy haircut . . .

"For fuck's *sake*," she said. "Hello?"

"I'm sorry. You look like a Vermeer. Girl with Drink and Cigarette." Which winked its connection to the memory of the stenographer's diaphragm. Vermeer, Dutch, Dutch cap, diaphragm. It wasn't continuous, this blood-joke of design, but it was, once you were back on The Lash, continu*al*.

Justine shook her head. Feelings jammed. Too much, too fast. Meanwhile I blew the rich smoke bullishly through my nose. The thought of sitting still and letting all this take shape around me made me queasy. All this? All what? What *was* this?

"Did you move out?" I asked her.

"Of course I didn't move out. Do you have any idea what this has been like? You told me you'd know if a long sleep was coming. You remember telling me you'd know, right?"

"I imagine I would have told you," I said. "I've always known before."

"Well, you didn't know this time. I've been out of my goddamned mind. Two *years*. I thought you weren't coming back." Suddenly she got really angry: "You fucking *promised* me you'd know when it was coming."

"I'm sorry," I said. "I truly am. I *have* always known before. I would never have promised, otherwise. You know that. This must have been awful for you. I'm so sorry." It was a relief to concentrate on the way she was feeling instead of the way I was. I stood up and went to her. "May I?" I asked. She didn't respond. She hadn't decided if she was letting me back in. Me. This. All of it. "Please," I said.

She put the drink down and laid the cigarette in the desk's onyx ashtray. Her hair smelled of Flex shampoo. She had a lot of mascara on. Black eyes full of her mutilated history, full of everything she'd wrapped around her past to make it survivable. I'd saved her and damned her. Therefore with her love for me was always a little hate, with the hate always a little love.

Very gently I put my arms around her. She let herself be embraced without fully softening. She was still angry. I could feel how much she wanted to rest her forehead on my clavicle. But she didn't do it. I loved her for that, her loyalty to how angry she was. The small muscles of her back were determined. I wanted to say to her: I'll do everything in my power to prevent anything bad happening to you ever again. But I didn't say that. She doesn't trust words. Actions got there first with her, violently, prematurely, indelibly. (I had a memory of Niccolo Linario saying: Is it like owning a pet, then, this business of having a human in your life? Like keeping a dog or a talking bird? We were in the low-life streets off the Mercato Vecchio, the air warm and choked with the smell of raw sewage and foully smoking oil lamps. He was new to The Lash, and flabbergasted that I enjoyed a close friendship with an old blind harper I'd picked up from the street and taken to my house, where I cared for him. I'd said to Niccolo: Do you know what it is to embrace a human in tenderness? To feel the racing blood of a body ruled by time? But he'd barely been listening. Too busy eyeing up the laced breasts and ribboned thighs of the night's blood buffet.)

"*Are* you all right?" I asked her.

She didn't answer.

"It's been vile for you. I'm so sorry."

She remained resistant in my arms. She was angry with herself for the relief she felt now I was back. In joining her life to mine she'd cut the ties to her kind. It had taken losing me to bring that severance home. It had aged her. She used to run on anger and damage. Now there was sadness, too.

I kissed her small forehead. She yielded a fraction, but then extricated herself. It was a soft tearing pain to lose the flicker of her mortality, the fluttering angels in her wrists and throat and groin. She retrieved the cigarette and the tumbler and moved out of my reach. Paced away. Halted and turned with her back to one of the bookcases.

"Do you want me to ask you the questions or not?" she said. Her face was directly parallel to the Grasset first edition of *A la recherche du temps perdu* in thirteen volumes. Of course it was.

"What is it?" she asked, seeing me registering it.

"Nothing," I said. I sat down in the armchair again. "It doesn't matter."

The dark eyes calculated. "Is it the connection thing?"

"What?"

"You told me when you drink from someone like that you see connections between things." Then, with a note of disgust: "The meaning of things." It had annoyed her when I'd first told her about it, the gift of The Lash, and I could see it still annoyed her now. If true it meant that everything that had happened to her had happened for a reason. In accordance with a design. It's the same thing that makes her furious with me every time the book of prophecies comes up. (Yes. I'm afraid there's a book of prophecies. I know. I can only apologise.)

"It's nothing," I said.

She looked at me. Then away. Then back at me. In those three looks was the pattern of our relationship. Not my daughter, not my sister, not my lover. More than any or all of them. Everything between the two of us rejects all the names for it the world has to offer. This is the strange contract between life and language: language keeps naming and life, like a woman seductively escaping her seducer's caress, keeps just a little beyond its names.

"Do you want me to ask you the questions?" she repeated.

"Yes."

"Okay. Where are we?"

"Las Rosas. 2208 Carmine Drive, Hollywood Hills, Los Angeles, California. You're Justine Cavell. I met you eight—no ten, I suppose it'll have to be, ten years ago in Manhattan. Your knee was bleeding. You were ready for something extraordinary."

"What's the IRIBD?"

"International Research Institute for Blood Disorders. Established and funded by yours truly longer ago than I care to remember. Centres in thirty countries, linked to hospitals, morgues, donor programs, universities. A meal in every port. You see? I'm up to date."

"A midwinter night's dream?"

"Midsummer. Procedural and declarative memory's intact. I can still drive, thank God. I feel multiple musical instruments in my fingertips and too many languages in my tongue."

*And fear in my heart.*

"What's the last thing you remember?"

"You and me watching *A League of Their Own* and *The Graduate*. I'm not sure about this new hairdo, by the way. You've lost some of your edge."

She was already halfway through the bourbon, and now tossed the rest of it back. Rose-gold hoop earrings. The pretty throat I'd never laid a lip on. I've always had a talent for random exemption. Except of course they're never random. On The Lash, nothing's random.

"Do you remember . . ." Hesitation. Difficult territory. She was treading carefully. "Do you remember being in Europe?"

"Before Geena and Dustin?"

"After."

Ah. So the last thing I remembered wasn't the last thing that happened. Amnesiacs seized on something safe and happy and made it their last memory, the first big breadcrumb on the trail that would lead them home.

"Tell me," I said.

She mashed the American Spirit in the ashtray, lips like a flautist's for the downwardly exhaled and always slightly disgusting final lungful. "In a minute," she said, eyelashes lowered. "It might not . . ." She shook her head, corrected herself. "Marco Ferrara," she said. Her little face was warm and full of calculations.

"What?"

"Does the name mean anything to you?"

"No."

"Vaughn Brock?"

"One of my aliases. God knows what I was thinking."

"Emilio Rodriguez?"

"Another. Latin was cool in the Eighties. The *nine*teen Eighties."

"Carter Marsh?"

"Juss, there's no need for this. I remember. Seriously. I know who I am. You'd better tell me about Marco Ferrara and Europe. Did I disgrace myself in some way?"

The feed-glow had deepened. The room's colours thudded. Justine's microclimate was dense, sunned melanin and Dior Chérie and bitter nail polish, flashed through by the dash of whiskey loucheness on her breath, a little cooled sweat, the sweet-salt tang of her cunt. And of course the blood, young, human, packed with her wounded and racing life. The force that through the red fuse drives the flower.

"Oh God," she said, tipping her head back. "I don't know what to tell you. I don't know whether it'll . . ."

"What?"

She thought for a moment. Then her shoulders went slack. A decision.

"Before you fell asleep," she began—then stopped, reassaulted, I knew, by the bare fact of my being there, real, with her again. "Sorry," she said. "This is just so fucking bizarre."

"Tell me what happened."

"I need another drink," she said—and oddly, it sounded a false note between us. The Lash gives bright clues to the elusive truth, yes, but vivid flashes when lies are flying too. Her dark eyes flicked away. I didn't say anything about it. She went to the kitchen and came back with her glass refreshed. I lit us another American Spirit each.

"Before you fell asleep," she began again, "you got sick. We were in Europe. You don't remember any of that?"

Well? Did I?

Something. On the periphery, until I tried to focus on it—then it whisked away. The study was live with currents of déjà vu. Shocking recognition was somewhere near, a sheer drop you wouldn't see until you were falling through it.

"It's in there somewhere," I said. "Go on."

"Okay. We were in England. You left me in London and went to Crete."

Each place name a recognition test. So far nothing.

Or rather not quite nothing. The faintest synaptic twinge. London. Crete.

"What was I doing on Crete?"

"You were . . . I don't even know. You wouldn't tell me. You left me in London for weeks. You came back from Crete, then we were in England together, but while we were there you got ill. Don't you remember? I had to get us home."

"From England?"

"We had Damien. The jet."

"Jesus Christ."

"You really don't remember?"

She was incredulous, but there was something else underneath it. Relief.

"I got you back here," she went on. "You couldn't drink. You had a temperature. And your mind was . . . You were forgetting things. And remembering things. You said you thought if you remembered everything that had happened . . . Anyway, you were a mess. You kept telling me things you'd already told me. It was like you had fucking Alzheimer's."

"I'm sorry," I said.

"Stop saying sorry."

"It's hard not to. You've suffered."

She shook her head, impatient. She'd felt pity for herself alone here in Las Rosas while I'd slept, and now the memory of it disgusted her. Her default was to be brutal with herself. When I'd seen her standing by the dumpster that night in Manhattan I'd recognised someone who could only ever take solace in the world when it was obvious the world was offering none.

"Okay," I said. "I don't remember Europe. Crete. London. I don't remember being ill. And I don't remember losing my marbles either. What happened after we got back to LA?"

"We had about a week of you getting more and more sick and confused and me getting more and more freaked out. You were in and out of fever. You couldn't feed. You couldn't do *any*thing. You were weak and rambling and fucking green in the face."

"Green?"

"Then it seemed to break. You seemed better. Clearer. You said you realised you hadn't been well. We watched the movies. Then you went down to the vault and never fucking came out." Saying it brought her loneliness back. Her eyes filled, but she didn't, quite, cry. To Justine her own tears are unforgivable. Which makes her irresistible to me. Nothing draws me to humans like the absence of self-pity. For a while we remained in silence. A police siren went *boowepp?* half a mile away. I wanted to tell her about the dream but I knew it wouldn't help. *He lied in every word* earbuzzed me again, then veered away.

I got to my feet. I didn't want to. Nor did I want the recollection of the false note when she'd said she needed another drink. Right up until I opened my mouth I wasn't sure what I was going to say.

"It's all right," I said. "It's me. I know who I am."

"Who are you?"

In a cod Transylvanian accent I said: "My name is Remshi and I am the world's oldest vampire. Radio carbon dates this little Oa around my neck to eighteen thousand BC. I remember watching my father carve it." This last sentence shed the comedy accent. Again I saw my father in the firelight, my mother digging the offering hole. Two dark-skinned, long-haired people with bright black eyes and thinly muscled bodies. I was sitting between them. Peace. The last time I remembered feeling peace.

"Or I don't remember that," I said. "It's possible I have a condition. They're memories or they're not. Either way I don't want to die. Not while you're around."

This little speech steadied her. She looked at me with a flash of allegiance.

And I knew for certain there was something she wasn't telling me.

"Granted, I've forgotten things," I said, while The Lash lit the lights of deceit around her head. "But I know we have a life together. I know I care more for you than for anything else on earth. I know *you*."

"Do you?"

"Yes.

Her finiteness gathered, drew the mortal details together: the small body, the dark-eyed head, the heartbeat. Humans, you have no idea how deeply and finely not living forever is inscribed in your every moment.

"I thought you weren't coming back," she said, very quietly.

"I'm here," I said. "I'm not going anywhere."

"You can't know that. You could go down there now and not come out again for fifty years. I could be fucking dead."

I don't know what I would have said in reply to that—since she was right—but I never got the chance.

Something sharp hit me from behind and spectacular pain exploded under my ribs.

# 6

I LOOKED DOWN to see seven or eight inches of a precision-pointed wooden javelin protruding from my gut. Lignum vitae. Second in hardness only to Australian buloke. In the moment it took me to turn around, I thought: This fucker isn't taking any chances, whoever he is. Then I *had* turned around (if someone had been standing next to me I would've clouted them with the other end of the thing sticking out of my back, like a slapstick idiot carrying a ladder) to discover it wasn't a him, but a them, and two of them were female.

The man was in his early forties, with a large, tough, mongolian head and owlish eyebrows. To his left was a tall young woman with tied-back red hair and green eyes. She was flanked by a dark, taut girl of perhaps twenty with a satiny burn scar disfiguring the lower left quarter of her face. All three wore light combat gear and were heavily armed—I saw what looked like a nail gun, mini-crossbows, cartridges, stakes—but the redhead was wielding a sword.

"You missed," she said, to the dark girl, quietly.

Too much was happening. Pain, first. It wasn't a stake through the heart but the heart wasn't stupid; it screamed the nearness of the miss. Its blared panic deafened the nerves, turned up the fire in my gut where the javelin had gone in—in spite of which a big share of consciousness was still staring moronically at whatever it was Justine hadn't told me, and the dream, and *He lied in every word*, and *What do you remember?* Meanwhile Justine was moving towards me and the redhead had taken two more paces into the room. The study was tropical. The books were in shock.

"Get out of here," I said to Justine.

"Let me pull it out," she said. But I was ahead of her. I reached around (thinking, in the doolally way of such moments, of a woman reaching around to unhook her bra) and yanked the shaft as hard as I could. Appalling violation. Neurons roared. The weapon came free with a comedy squelch. Followed immediately by the inner hiss of molecular repair, the furious cellular regroup. (Pain? Yes. Fatality? No. Stake in the heart. Beheading. Fire if you get it hot enough. Nothing else. Anything else, you better run.)

"Get out," I repeated to Justine. But she didn't move.

Everyone else did.

Contemptuous of Hollywood, all three of them attacked at once. Four rounds from the nail gun hit me in the shoulder, buloke bullets, two of which went straight through; the other two set my heart's klaxon off again.

Nonetheless sly joy warmed me. Because they had no idea, these over-equipped hopefuls. They had *no idea*.

Wrong.

*I* had no idea.

The dark girl went past me towards Justine, and my lunge to intercept her took me off-balance. There ought to have been plenty of time. We ought to have been operating according to the usual farcical discrepancy. (I watch humans trying to kill me the way McEnroe watched Connors trying to play him in the '84 Wimbledon final, with a sort of incredulous pity.) But that's not the way it was. The way it was was that whoever these three were someone had used them to take combat training to a new level. I got the dark girl off her feet, yes, but not before taking a deep cut across the chest and four more rounds in my left leg. She got, kicking, away from me. I could smell Justine behind me. I ducked under the redhead's sword and broke her left femur with a single chop (a *haito uchi*, to be precise. It was good to feel my assault options wide awake, restive; briefly brought back Atsutomo's training compound in Kikaijima, the damp hot mornings, the mountains like slumped heavyweights themselves.) Her odour was delicious: adrenal sweat and apricot hand cream and the fatigues' whiff of clean canvas. Also, bizarrely, incense. Her breath said tuna Niçoise less than five hours ago. She went down in silence, mouth open. The lamplight caught her eyelashes. The guy's hand gripping a stake whipped past my face. He was heavy but fast, with experience deep in the muscles, a useful familiarity with violence. AB negative, my nose reported (shrugging, doing its duty) fried onions, coconut Radox shower gel and roll-up smokes—and, again, incense. The hand holding the stake was broad-fingered, with discernible dark hairs. It would look dashing, Rolexed, coming out of a crisp white cuff.

The redhead speed-rolled away, still holding the sword. She had an intriguing Celtic face, broad-cheekboned and wide-mouthed, and the milky green eyes like a flash of faerie. Meantime I head-butted the guy from underneath, a sharp drive upward that cracked his bottom jaw (I heard the absurd clack of his teeth hitting each other) and snapped his neck back into his shoulders. He didn't fall, but it was all the time I needed. I wrenched the stake from him and jabbed it hard and fast into his throat, felt the trachea's cartilage split and three or four internal carotids rupture. The incorrigible bloodstink touched me, lewdly, but I was still full from Randolf. It brought a note of disgust, and in any case to drink again so soon would be dangerous. (Stake through the heart, beheading, fire—and overdose.) All the while some backroom boys of consciousness were going through the motions of wondering who these people were, but without much conviction: You're a vampire. Someone's always trying to kill you. After a while it doesn't matter who or why—only *that*. The dark girl had got out of my sight. I let go of the guy, who dropped first to his knees then onto his side, both hands around the stake in his throat. He was making a depressing soft gargling sound. I was thinking—above or below or alongside the combat-maths—that Justine and I would have to use what remained of the night to Get Rid Of The Bodies and proof the room against the real world's satirically unglamorous CSI squad. I turned to make sure she was all right—and a lignum vitae bolt hit me in the chest.

Not the heart. But this time less than an inch away. The dark girl had got behind one of the Thomasvilles and lined me up in the crosshairs.

The heart, in shock, went still.

It sprang a lock in me. I leaped, took the armchair and the girl twenty feet across the floor to crash against one of the stacks. Books toppled and fell. I pulled her out by her hair. She wriggled extraordinarily, and twice I almost lost my grip. But the heat coming off her now spoke of resignation. Her soul had turned to the exit, was already murmuring the first words of its prayer.

In fact, no: *she* was murmuring a prayer. The Lord's Prayer. In Latin.

"*Pater noster, qui es in cælis,*" she said, while blood ran from her nose.

*"Sanctificetur nomen tuum; adveniat regnum tuum; fiat voluntas tua, sicut in caelo et in terra."*

"Who are you?" I said.

*"Panem nostrum cotidianum—"*

"Who *are* you? Speak now or you—"

I don't know how she did what she did next. I had her by the hair. Her back was arched, her feet flat on the floor. I felt her thrust backwards against me, then her weight shifted—and her legs were around my neck.

There was, I knew, very little time. Her hands were free and already busy with a holstered stake. Heat pounded out of her. Her tiny armpits were drenched. The small, frenetic reality of her made me feel tender towards her, as did the inevitable realisation that we were in the sixty-nine position, albeit vertically, followed by the intuition that she was a virgin.

However, I broke her neck, cleanly and quickly, then let her slide to the floor, where she lay, one hand trapped beneath her, the other on one of the toppled books. It was open, face-down. An 1894 edition of Browning's *Collected Works*. Something else fell, too. A first edition of Sylvia Plath's *The Colossus*. I thought, I bet that's open at "Black Rook in Rainy Weather."

At which moment the light in the room shifted, and Justine screamed.

# 7

She was on her back on the floor in front of the desk. She'd pulled the Tiffany lamp off the table by its cord. The redhead stood over her, leaning on the sword as if to provide support to her broken leg.

But the sword was buried in Justine's guts.

Although a single leap took me back across the room, there was plenty of time. Time does you this perverse service of expansion when all you've got to fill it with is horror. Time to begin the relevant calculation of how long Justine might have left, of how quickly an ambulance could get here, of how I'd have to move her to another room—or better still outdoors—*I came home and found her on the lawn like this*—and how soon, since it was a stabbing, the police would show up. But time for questions, too: What would I do if she died? How would I stand being alone? Where, since Las Rosas would die for me with her, would I go? Time for whatever it was she hadn't told me, the lacuna she might take to the grave, and for the dream, and for the beginning of the sense that I knew something, I *knew* something if only I could reach it . . . Time, too—how not?—for the perennially available option—to Turn her—and the irony that after all these years of her postponing it, choosing it now might kill us both.

The redhead had one of her own stakes buried in her thigh. Good girl, Justine. It had hit the femoral artery, and even before I landed on her she was slipping to her knees. I had to take hold of the sword lest it tilt and make the wound worse—at which point I perceived it had gone all the way through my girl and deep into the walnut floor.

"Keep still," I said to her. I pulled the stake from the redhead's leg—her pale green eyes had closed, she didn't make a sound—and drove it hard and fast through her sternum into her heart. Her mouth opened and I got a glimpse of her shrimp-pink tongue and one charmingly overlapping tooth. Then she was gone. The room was soupy with death. I imagined Sylvia Plath witnessing it all through the portal of *The Colossus* and not being the least surprised. Ted Hughes, on the other hand, for all his hawks and foxes and crows, would be agog.

"Do it," Justine said, when I looked at her. Life was faint in her face. Wrists and neck and groin spoke of an equivocal pulse.

"I can get you to a hospital."

"I want you to do it."

I looked at the amount of blood she'd lost. There was no way of knowing. The air between us jammed with all the dialogue we didn't have time for.

"I want you to," Justine said, then her face twisted in pain. When it went back to normal she looked at me again. "I mean it, Fluff," she said.

"It might not work."

*And it might kill me*, I didn't add. But the momentum was established. The alternative future—of ambulances and doctors and elaborate false testimony and separation and possible flight—dissolved in both of us with the mental equivalent of a sigh. We let it. We'd always known this time would come, and here it was. She'd had ten years of self-debate; now chance had forced the issue. It's what chance is for. As with all such surrenders, it was a relief.

Which is not to say she wasn't afraid. I felt her fear. She was leaving behind the biggest thing she had. She was going into the darkness. This was what she'd been thinking of, all alone in Las Rosas, for almost two years.

"Promise me you won't leave me."

"I won't leave you, angel."

"Promise."

"I promise I won't leave you."

The room bore witness. The world registers promises.

"Are you ready?" I asked her.

She said, "Please," and turned her face away, the way people do before the needle goes in.

I took one last look at her, the person she would never be again.

Then I pulled the sword out of her in one quick motion and began to drink.

# 8

IT WAS VERY bad. As bad as I thought it would be. Less than a quarter of the way through draining her the over-oxygenation started. Blood packed, hardened, became a warning throb: *Stop drinking. Stop drinking. Stop drinking.* Yet there was nothing to do but keep drinking, keep increasing the pain, keep bearing it. My eyeballs were big. I thought: warm hardboiled eggs. I had these thoughts. A capillary tearing. A soft inner explosion. Blood suffocated by blood. You can't do this. You can't do this. Stop drinking. Stop now. You can't go on, so you go on. I thought of Paul Newman's egg-eating scene in *Cool Hand Luke*, George Kennedy squeezing them past his lips, saying, them's little eggs, *quail's* eggs, really . . . Eggs again. Symbol of the soul . . . Or you do the Hemingway thing, promise yourself you'll hold on for just one more second, then one more, then one more—and the seconds become hours, days. Like that, I thought, just do that, one more suck, one more swallow. Trick your own courage, your own cowardice. The Old Man and the Blood.

I saw what I didn't want to see. The girl of five or six, her face too warm. The low-ceilinged room with a knocked-over table lamp throwing a stretched ellipse on a stained wall. The woman and the men like dark giants to her. Mommy, I don't like it. The men's massed concentration, their intent. The child's world contained these fun-house distentions and drops that were the opposite of fun, these invisible mirrors that turned people into monsters. Her mother's face was moist, with a look sometimes of frowning irritation, sometimes of giddy disbelief. In herself. In being able to do this. One of the men said, Come here. There was always thereafter a man saying, Come here. I saw what I didn't want to see. The young girl, the teenager, the young woman, the religion of self-hatred, the men, always and deliberately the wrong men. The endlessly renewable contract with her own brokenness. The deep reassurance of their contempt. You like that, don't you? Tell me you like it, you little cunt. *I like it.* Easier to say the more it was a lie. A pure inversion she could hold on to like a talisman.

But the destruction wasn't complete. There were bright fragments. I saw her standing alone on the edge of a wood in falling snow, face upturned for the sacramental flakes. I saw her sitting in an apartment, hands wrapped around a mug of hot tea, at something like peace, maybe just a break in her identity, an accidental transcendence. I saw her opening a front door suddenly and unintentionally giving the FedEx girl a fright, and the two of them laughing. Laughter was absent from her life. Unless strategic or issued in triumph at some further depth she'd managed to go down to. I saw her seeing a bare tree against the sky and thinking, That's like the cross-section of a lung . . . trees give oxygen, lungs need oxygen, a connection . . . But the thought overtaken by her habitual self, whose job it was to piss on such thoughts. I saw her seeing me in the freezing lot and, after a brief intuitive stumble and leap, knowing what I was. I saw her set down one by one the invisible burnings she carried and walk towards me. Inflamed. Scarred. Too far past everything to be afraid . . .

I couldn't go on.

I went on.

Muhammad Ali said the third fight with Frazier in Manila was the closest he'd come to death. The closest he believed it was possible to come to death without dying. They call us the undead. It's not true. We're born. We live. We can die and so we can come close to death. I was close to death. The blood was a deafening totality. Like the scream of God. I wouldn't be able to go on drinking. I would die.

I went on drinking.

Ten beats of the heart. Seven. Five. Four—

I tried to say to her, "Drink," but there was no room in me for speech to come out of, no place words could have been kept. The blood was stone. I was stone. For a moment I went completely into darkness. I thought: Is this it? Is this death . . . ? Then I came out. I opened my left wrist with the edge of the sword and pressed the wound to Justine's lips.

The pause before the connection, before the wavering magnet snaps to the metal. Darkness came close a second time. If I went in again I knew I wouldn't come out.

Then I felt her. Not the little mouth and teeth, not the hot face, but the first tiny shift in the weight, from blood coming in to blood going out. In Kenya two hundred years ago I'd seen a doctor lance a man's infected foot. With the first expression of sepsis the man wept. The joy of passing from pain to relief. He'd held the doctor's hands and kissed them. It had made them intimate, like loving brothers.

Justine drank. Hard. Rushed the conversion with the weight of her need, the way nurses squeeze the drip bag to hurry fluids in. The receiving veins ache, you imagine. These were the giving veins, however. Mine. And they didn't ache, they felt like they were haemorrhaging powdered glass.

The progression would be from slight relief, to relief, to deep relief, to the bliss of blood equilibrium. Then, since she would have to drink on, since it would be murder to stop her, from blood equilibrium to slight discomfort, to pain, to agony. Finally the fear, like a vast soft darkness edging near, that she would drink me to death.

And if I got it right, stopped her when she'd drunk enough to Turn her without killing me, we still had three bodies to dispose of—and not a half hour of the night left to do it.

There were these thoughts. But they were frail or faint next to the other thing.

The thing that had gone into me from her at the very edge of her death.

The thing she hadn't told me but that her blood couldn't hide: that in the werewolf, Talulla Demetriou, the spirit of my beloved Vali was alive and well and waiting for me to fulfil the prophecy.

# 9

I REMEMBERED.

I'd had the dream of the deserted beach before. Had been having it, in fact, since That Night almost three years ago in Big Sur. (I have a house there. One of the dozen or so sub–Frank Lloyd Wright luxury bunkers, formerly owned, though rarely lived in, by lovely and mysteriously deceased Natalie Wood.) I remember I slept late That Night, too, and woke not long after moonrise . . .

. . . A full moon.

No coincidence.

The dream had shocked me. Of course it had. The beach. The twilight. The poor-show sprinkle of stars. The someone walking behind me. *He lied in every word.*

That Night, when I came up from the basement, Justine was on the couch in the TV room, meticulously painting her toenails pale blue. *A Day at the Races* was on the plasma screen. My hands were shaking, so I stuffed them in my pockets. "Jesus, Norm, you look terrible," she said.

"I'm fine," I said. "Oversleep headache. I'm just going out for some air. Back in a bit." I couldn't tell her. Partly because the shock of having dreamed was still too giant and raw for language—I could barely stand up straight, let alone discuss it—but mainly because it would alarm her. I'd worked so hard to make her feel safe in our world. She wouldn't like this. A dream. Fluff—*dreaming*? It would seem ominous to her. It *was* ominous.

"Don't be ages," she said. "I need to talk to you about the club."

I walked. Staggered, rather, once I was out of sight of the house and free of the need to dissemble. I chased the dream images, never quite . . . never *quite* . . . My hands and feet and face had discrete little fevers. The world's gears had shifted while I slept. A dream! All these years. All these *years.*

The first dream since Vali died.

*I will come back to you. And you will come back to me. Wait for me.*

I had waited.

Hadn't I?

The footage threatened. The dense montage of my life that was like a cliff-face uprushing past because you'd fallen and were now plummeting down the sickening drop. More sickening still, you were abruptly and randomly stopped and forced for a split second that opened onto infinity to confront something vivid—your neck craned to see Michelangelo's bare paint-spattered foot poking over the edge of the scaffold and the chapel's contained heights filled with the smell of oils and plaster; a mob-capped young housemaid with red curls and a copper warming pan looking up and seeing you, her blue eyes fractured by the understanding that this was her death; Viking longships on the black Volga in the small hours, helmets and spears moonlit, one—just one—of them seeing you standing and observing from the bank, the curiously tender exchange of consciousness, then the window of connection closed; sodden soldiers in a trench full of blood, the stink of wet leather and rotting flesh, a rat swimming, chevron ripples from the lovely little head; a toilet in Rwanda with a Tutsi baby cut in half and shoved in it—before being just as violently yanked back into gravity's grip and the nausea of all the time and weather and extremes and approximations—

I stopped and lay down on the forest floor. Sometimes lying down is just the thing. (Millions of people's bad days would be improved if they listened to the impulse to lie down for a few minutes on the office carpet or bathroom tiles or pleasantly chilled pavement. Drunks and children know the wisdom of this—but who listens to them?) I lay down on the forest floor and the softness of the ferns and the odours of earth and evergreens gave me solace. Don't be ages, Justine had said; but it was very hard to imagine moving anytime soon. Empty sleep for millennia, now this: a dream like a furious disease, an inverted plague that had swept life instead of death across my inner continent in a single night. I turned my head to the left and for no reason (no reason except the currently flashing narrative insistence) parted the undergrowth and looked down the slightly inclined forest floor.

Which is when I saw her.

Them, rather.

Two werewolves, a female in front, a male a dozen paces behind. They were thirty metres away, downwind—

Her scent hit me. Eliminated all time and space between now and then. Tipped the world like a kids' ball-bearing puzzle and dropped me back to where . . . to when it had . . . Oh God. Oh *God*.

It was Vali's scent.

Which was impossible.

*I will come back to you. And you will come back to me. Wait for me.*

For a moment I think I lost consciousness. At any rate I had, a few seconds later, the feeling of emerging from profound darkness, a feeling of shocked, sudden birth. Or rather, *re*birth.

*I will come back to you.*

The female—Vali, Vali, *Vali*—stopped and lifted her elegant muzzle to the moon. Light silvered the long throat, the wet eyes and snout.

My heart almost refused. Even in the midst of its own upheaval my heart knew what was at stake and tried to refuse. If it's not . . . If it's a trick, if it's an illusion—

But a thread of blood in my cock twitched. My cock! Which, since her death, had been of no more consequence to me than the fluff in the seam of my pocket.

Desire. *Desire.*

Was it possible?

I breathed the carried scent of her and my cock leaped. The smell couldn't lie. Her smell. *Her.* My eyes filled. Joy for the return, sorrow for the years of loss. It was an eviscerating happiness, left me empty and frail with hope. Left me with all but disbelief in my own hands and feet and teeth, in the forest and the night, in the real, solid world.

Moonlight salved her hard breasts and lean belly. Her navel was a well of shadow.

Just as I remembered. Just as it had been. Vali. My beloved.

The joy moved up into my mouth, which opened involuntarily to call to her.

But at that moment the male came close behind her and wrapped his arms around her and she tilted her head back so their muzzles and tongues could touch.

·

I followed them. With sickness expanding. With sickness making me giant. They couldn't keep their hands off each other. Of course they couldn't. I knew how it was for her. I knew how it was for her because with her that was how it had been for me. For us. Killing. Together.

Their victim was a neighbour of mine, a music producer, Drew Hillyard. I climbed a plane tree at the edge of his high-walled front yard and watched. Grabbed my own giant sick head and rubbed my own giant sick nose in it. *America's Next Top Model* played on the flatscreen to a room wild with blood. Hillyard's white leather couch became a canvas for his frantic red swipes. Vali opened his chest and rammed her snout in. Her hindquarters shivered as the male entered her, his hands roaming over her flanks and belly and breasts. The open chest was mine. The sternum cracked cleanly and prised apart, the heart plucked out and tossed in the dirt. A thing of no importance. A negligible thing. A joke.

It seemed to last a long time. It occurred to me that if the wind shifted slightly they'd catch my scent. There was an appeal in that, the rushed confrontation, the surrender to chaos, the relief of rushing the male, of killing or being killed. It would consume me, at least, eclipse the unspeakable wealth of detail, of sordid, brilliant particulars, of her tongue curled in martial or erotic delight, his dark moist cock giving rhythm to my misery, in, out, in, out, her body warm and full of cunning welcome. I knew how it was. I knew, I knew, I knew.

*He lied in every word.*

The dream images burgeoned and died, repeatedly, bled through by the other dream, sent to me by Vali or the liar in every word the night she died. *I will come back to you. And you will come back to me. Wait for me.*

And here she was, and I had waited, and now become a giant, laughable sickness. Because apparently it wasn't me she'd come back for after all.

·

I tailed them, unseen, all the way to where they'd left their gear hanging high in a tree, the packed rucksacks, the clean-up products, the car keys. Justine would be pissed—but there was no going back until I'd seen it, seen her, in human form. Short window between moonset and sunrise. I'd have to move fast when it was over—but I wasn't thinking about that. I wasn't *thinking*, period. I was caught in the slipstream of the living dream.

They lay a little apart on the ground. Here were shivering ferns, nodding bluebells, the tree roots' knuckles breaking the earth. The scene had a quality of appalling familiarity. Hadn't I been here before? Those three small pale rocks there, blotched with yellow lichen? Those twittering leaf-shadows?

She regained her human form quicker than he did his. Hers was seamless CGI, his clumsy stop-motion. I watched her skeleton's fluid shrinkage, the impossible resizing of muscle and skin, the human head resolved out of the lupine's compressed implosions. Her hands were the lovely hands I remembered, touching me, idling on my chest, tracing the outline of my jaw, buried in my hair. The body was the body I knew, the pale breasts and belly, the small shoulders, the tenderly functional knees. Her shins were wet with dew. The last phase of the transformation turned her face-down in the ferns. Her spine rippled, hooked—half a dozen vertebrae bulged like buboes, then settled, straightened, found their place, stopped their squabble—and there was the smooth and deep-grooved back I'd run my fingers down a thousand thousand times (the journey never got old, renewed its mystery with each passage of discovery) and the sacrum's flare, and the beautiful rear, upthrust in fabulous diptych, as it had been for me, for me, for me.

She lifted her head. I saw her face. The dark hair and self-accommodating eyes. The full mouth.

I knew her.

It was Vali.

It *was* Vali.

# 10

## *Justine*

I woke up in the vault, in bed with the vampire.

I woke up in the vault—a vampire.

A vampire.

You can't imagine what it feels like.

No matter how much you've talked about it or thought about it. You really can't.

The weird thing (like there's one weird thing; like the whole *thing* isn't the weird thing)—the weird thing is you know straight away how soon it'll feel completely normal. Like the first time I drove a car I knew that by the third or fourth time it would feel totally familiar. My hands on the wheel remembering something from a former life. Second nature.

This is my second nature.

I didn't like my first, so I changed.

Vampire. Vampire. *Vampire.*

That thing where if you keep repeating the same word it just becomes meaningless sound.

No going back.

Ever.

There were empty MRE bags scattered around. Spots of blood on the sheets. Fluff told me once that in the old days they used to hang the new bride's bloody sheets out the window to prove she'd been a virgin. And the ones who weren't virgins used to shove pellets of goat's blood up themselves to fool everyone.

I sat up, slowly. Thought back to what had happened. Tried to put it together.

Last night I'd woken in the study to find Stonk slumped across me. White, cold, not dead—but dying. I could tell. It wasn't just the way he was breathing. There was something else, like I could feel his life inside mine.

It took a weird effort to feel it. Like the effort you have to make with those Magic Eye pictures, the trick of sort of looking and not looking at the same time. I can't describe it. It was like there was a bigger body squeezed inside mine that any second was going to tear through, like the Hulk ripping through his clothes. All my sensations were big and soft and heavy. Everything—the chair, the rug, the lamp on the floor—was somehow too much itself, like all the dials had been forced up past max.

I seemed to get to my feet without getting to my feet.

Then I felt it.

Sunrise.

Minutes away.

I didn't know how I knew, since the drapes were closed, but I did. You just do. You feel it inside. It's like a shadow made of pure light rushing towards your heart.

I had to get blood into him. Hide the bodies. Get us underground. I knew I had to do these things and I knew there wasn't time. There just wasn't. It was impossible.

When I moved it was like I was constantly catching up with my body. I kept finding myself doing things: running through the hall; opening the fridge; carrying him over my shoulder (he weighed nothing) down the vault stairs. And the whole time the sun was coming. I pictured myself caught by daylight halfway to the garage, dragging three corpses out to the cars. *You'll burn.* Your skin knows. Your skin screams when you even think of it.

I managed to find four pouches. I laid him on the bed. Raced back upstairs—but moving got harder. Space went syrupy, like in those dreams where you're running but it feels like you're wading through treacle. The sun loved it. The sun wanted me slow. I was thinking how weird it was that the sun straight away became your enemy, really an enemy, like an evil old man, like a god who hated you.

Two minutes till it came up.

One minute.

Thirty seconds.

My head and arms and legs were hot and everything had a confused edge. All I could do was throw the corpses into the hidden place that led down to the vault. I couldn't stand the thought of bringing them *into* the vault, to spend the night with us. There was nothing I could do about the blood all over the study. Just had to hope no one came snooping.

I got the doors locked and sealed. All the system lights were green. I'd never felt the vault like this before, all that snug concrete and fat steel no amount of sun could get through. I'd never felt the *goodness* of that until now.

On the bed I had to hold him up and pour the MREs into his mouth. His breath totally stank. The pouches wouldn't be enough. I knew that, too. I could feel he'd drifted far away. I thought I heard his voice saying: No, don't, angel. I won't be able to stop. But I blanked that out and bit into my wrist. I felt the blood rush up and something like a big rubber band in my heart snap. Then I forced the punctures up against his mouth.

Dark and heavy and blurry after that. Except for one image: him trying to keep my wrist there and me grabbing him by the throat and squeezing and strangling until he let go.

Then I guess I must have passed out.

I sat up now in bed in the vault and looked at him. Still sleeping. His body was calm in the wrong way. Like in a film when someone's sitting there smiling and peaceful but it's shock because their entire family's just been hacked up in front of them. Inside myself I could feel a sort of faint copy of what he'd been through. He'd been to the edge of death. A blackness like deep space where even the stars have run out. For a moment I got scared: What if it was like before and he didn't wake up for years? All those nights I'd come down and tried to wake him (I burned the back of his hand with a cigarette one time; it didn't make any difference. The skin just healed in front of my eyes)—but the moment passed. He was coming back. I could feel him hauling himself on my blood like someone going hand-over-hand up a rope. My blood. Our blood. His before it turned into mine. Mine before it turned back into his.

If I wanted you to Turn me one day, I'd always asked him, would you do it?

He'd always said: If I believed it's what you really wanted, yes.

*If I wanted you to Turn me.*

Not if. *When.* That first night in New York I stood there looking at him and I knew what he was and the voice in my head said: This is the way for you. It's the only way. It's just a matter of time.

Now I've done it. Now there's no way back. Ever.

*No way back* reminded me of something: last night, standing in the study listening to his voicemail just before he walked in I'd noticed the title of one of the books on the shelf in front of me. It was called *You Can't Go Home Again.*

Was this what he'd told me about, the way things started to connect? Signs. Coincidences. He said you had to be careful of it. He said it was a . . . what was the word?

Beguilement.

I lifted my hands and looked at them. My skin was whiter. Fingernails grey glass. The turquoise nail polish was gone, even though I didn't take it off. Fingernails. I've seen him open a can of cherries with his. You feel what your new fingernails can do. You feel what the new all of you can do.

I ran my tongue over my teeth. Nearly laughed. *Fangs.* The movies. *True Blood.* What the movies and TV don't show is the way fangs *feel.* Like they're little alive things in your mouth. If someone pulled them out—

*Ohmygod.*

Blood-rush. Puke coming up. A scream trapped in my skull.

I grabbed the edge of the bed and held on. Breathed through it.

Fuck. Lesson one: You don't want your fangs pulled out. And not—another blood-rush, barf-rising—your fingernails, either.

I put my feet on the floor. Stood.

Stupid strength. *Sick* strength. This time I did laugh. I could feel it in my shins and thighs and butt and shoulders. Crazy power. *You could pick that up with one hand. Punch through that. Pull that off like a button.* Objects told me what I could do to them now. There were a lot of things I'd be able to do, now.

As long as I didn't mind being a murderer.

That had been in me from the second I woke up. Like a new person living inside my body who was more alive than I was, someone I had to catch up with. Now she was there I realised I'd been waiting for her ever since. Ever since all of it.

*All of it* was the other thing that had been in me from the second I woke up.

I'd thought it might be gone, but it wasn't.

I used to know this crackhead on the street, Toby Dreds. Mentally fucked, but harmless. His thing was philosophical questions. Suppose you got a car, right? Like it's a Lexus, right? And every now and then something on it breaks and you have to replace it. You go on replacing parts as they wear out. Years, right? But at some point, if enough of its parts have been replaced, isn't it true that it's a different car? It can't be the same car if all the parts have been replaced. It's still a Lexus, but it's not the Lexus you started with. It's *notionally* the same car, right? But it's not *materially* the same car. He knew big words. Notionally. That killed me. I'd never heard it before, but I got what it meant. Like a notion. Like an idea.

All of me had been replaced—except the one thing that was still there.

Her face sweaty and her eyes wide. Looking at me to show me she couldn't see me.

You get the body restart for free. The rest you have to earn.

I put my hand gently on Stonk's forehead. (I don't know why I call him these things. Stonk. Fluff. Frankie. Norman. He doesn't mind. He says he likes it.) His life came to me through my fingertips. There's species understanding, he'd told me. Telepathy *ish*. But you have to learn to control it, to be selective. Like screening calls. It was one of the things that had always put me off. Too late now. I knew if he woke up he'd be able to see everything, go into my mind like a burglar wandering through a house and the owner has to just sit there watching, horrified. Which would mean he'd see all of it.

As soon as I had this thought I knew he'd already seen all of it. When he drank from me. Maybe I thought he'd drink it out of me for good.

It doesn't matter. He's always known anyway. He's always imagined. Everyone always does. It comes off me like a smell. (One of them, the one they called "Pinch," had said: Honey, I'm gonna make you so dirty you won't *never* scrub clean again.)

I know what you're thinking. You're thinking: So what? It's not a big deal for anyone, apart from the ones who feel insecure and useless so they become social workers or therapists so they can be around fuck-ups who make them feel competent and normal. But for most people when they get the smell off me it's just a drag they know they'll have to deal with sooner or later because I'll turn out to be a wacko or whatever. To most people what happened to me is just that thing that can happen, that happens. They're right. That's all it is. A thing that can happen, that happens. That's all anything that happens is.

I was still in last night's clothes, covered in blood. We both were. I lifted my t-shirt to see the place where the Cate Blanchett bitch's sword had gone into me. Nothing. Completely healed. Not even a scar.

Fluff's eyeballs moved behind his eyelids. REM sleep. When you're supposed to dream. He doesn't dream, he says. Not a vampire thing. Just him. Remshi, whose REM's for shit, I'd said to him. He'd said: Juss, if you ever become like me, you're going to have to do better with the jokes.

Would I stop dreaming now? Sleep without dreams would be like something cool resting on me. Like that time in kindergarten when the Sri Lankan nurse put her hand on my forehead and I hadn't known how hot I was until I felt her cool palm on my skin.

*Every now and then, Justine, I'll take a longer than usual sleep. There will be disorientation when I wake up. There are things you'll need to ask me to jog my memory. Don't worry. I'll write them down. I'll know when it's coming, so you'll have time to prepare.* Except I didn't. One minute he was there, the next he was gone, out like a light for two years. Two years in Las Rosas alone. Hours and days and weeks and months. I lay curled up on the bathroom floor. I felt safest between the base of the washbasin and the side of the tub. I wrapped myself in a blanket and slept there, eventually. Slept during the day. Nights at the club. Two thousand strangers. You go into them, you imagine their lives. I don't know how much longer I would've lasted if he hadn't woken up.

And now that he had I was going to lose him all over again.

Either because the werewolf was who he thought she was, and if he found her he wouldn't want me around.

Or because finding her would kill him, just like it nearly did the last time.

# Part Two

# The Fairy Tale

# 22

# *Talulla*

MY CELLPHONE RANG. Factory setting ringtone. Our days of thinking it a hoot to have "Bad Moon Rising" and "Werewolves of London" are over.

"Talulla?" a man's voice said.

It was just after sunrise. I was standing, naked, in the kitchen of the falling apart villa we'd taken in the hills outside Terracina. The window showed a coarse back garden of long grass and peach trees and sunlit floating dandelion seeds. My phone had been left out on the dining table (Jesus, woman, shape *up*) amid empties and ashtrays and the remains of Cloquet's *blanquette de veau*. The table itself looked like a post-apocalyptic city.

I felt terrible. Less than seventy hours to transformation *wulf* was all muscle-jab and neural snap, the peppy violence to remind me, redundantly, who'd be running the upcoming lunar show. Walker and I had got smashed on tequila and grass last night to take the edge off. Bludgeoned awake by dehydration (and the now predictable dreams of misbehaviour) I'd come down for water.

To this. A stranger's voice. Adrenal flash-flood and the hangover's blur washed away, instantly. Even with the sweat coming out in my palms like stars I thought: Serves you right: All this and it's not enough.

"Who is this?" I said.

"There's a package for you. If you go to the front hall you'll see it on the doormat."

I scrolled the known voices, got nothing. The accent might've started in the Middle East but it had picked up tonal inflections on promiscuous travels.

"Happily," he went on, "it fit through the letter-box. Otherwise we would have had, God help us, *logistics* to negotiate."

*Wulf* thickened in my wrists, the ghost-claws split my nails. *Trying it on.* This close to full moon, my girl took any heightened state as an invitation.

"Hello?" the voice said.

I ran for the stairs.

"Are you in the hall yet?"

"Shut the fuck up."

"Oh. You'll be worried about the children. I understand. But can you at least *see* the package?"

I had, in fact, glimpsed a small Jiffy bag on the front doormat, but panic owned all of me. Actually not quite all. The voice had conjured, whether I liked it or not, Omar Sharif, Persian carpets, mint tea, a perfumed moustache, that big male ease that looks genial but is really just a habitually gratified ego on autopilot. Years ago when we were teenagers my friend Lauren had said: My mom likes this guy, Omar Sharif? He's one of those guys looks like he's got an invisible woman permanently sucking his cock.

"I'll give you a minute," the voice said. "But if it's any comfort I'm several thousand miles away as we speak. I promise you, no one in your house has anything to fear from me."

My tongue was dry, knees liquid. Lose possession of your child once and the fear it'll happen again becomes your resident hair-trigger insomniac. Once a bad mother, always a bad mother. It's like being an alcoholic: you only ever haven't fallen off the wagon *yet*.

"What?" Walker said, when I arrived, hot, at the top of the stairs. He was standing—also naked—in our bedroom doorway, scratching his lean belly. Lycanthropy hasn't touched his human charms, green-eyed dark blond boyishness, the look of readiness to laugh at himself. (I've wondered when it was I first saw the finiteness of us, us as a specific portion of wealth to be gone through. Maybe from the beginning. Certainly from the night two years back when the vampire came to call. The vampire came to call and left behind him spores of sadness, irritation, desire.) Beyond Walker the curtained window was an oblong of sunlight. The room had the fatigued smell of the night's drunk and silently argumentative sex, shot through with the ribald stink of our share in imminent *wulf*.

"Lula?"

I ignored him and went straight to the twins next door. Zoë and Lorcan were both in their beds, sleeping, Lorcan (whose pre-transformation symptoms were getting worse: nightmares, tantrums, a shocking malice towards everyone except his sister) with unchildlike composure, arms by his sides, Zoë with hers up above her head, as if someone had just relieved her of a little dumbbell. Both here. Both safe. Thank God. Gods. Ex-gods. Nothingness.

"Stay with them," I told Walker, unnecessarily, since species telepathy was giving him the gist. He grabbed a Beretta from under our mattress and went to the window between the children's beds, cracked it an inch to check for scent, peeked round the edge of the curtain for a sweep of the back garden. Throbbing blue sky and an anarchy of birdsong. All clear. He nodded: I've got this. Be careful. I clamped the phone between my shoulder and chin (thinking, since consciousness can't help it: violinists must really fuck their necks up), pulled on last night's jeans and shirt and plucked the Smith & Wesson from my purse.

"Who is this?" I said into the phone. "Answer me or I'm hanging up right now." In the old life I would've been wondering how a stranger had got my number. Not anymore. Privacy's an illusion. In my world it's always only a matter of time. Yours too, if you want the truth.

"My name is Olek," he said. "I'm a vampire—but please try not to hold that against me. I'm not your enemy. I have a mutually beneficial business proposal I'd like to discuss."

I was hurrying on tense bare feet back down the stairs, hugging the wall. Kept hugging it all the way to the locked front door, which was oak, thick enough, I reminded myself, to stop a bullet, silver or otherwise. The Jiffy bag was addressed simply to "Talulla" in black italic marker. Neat, perfectly straight printing.

"Do you have the package?" he said.

"Do you seriously think I'm just going to pick it up and open it?"

A pause. A cigarette being lit. Again the image of Omar Sharif, the cuboid head and plump black eyes and gap-toothed smile. "Well," he said, exhaling. "I'll leave that to you. I imagine your instincts are good. Consult them. It's not a bomb, or silver, or anything that will do you or anyone you love any kind of harm. I can only give you my word, but believe me, I'm old enough for that to mean something. If it helps I can tell you it's a document. One Jake would have wanted you to see."

Lucy and Trish had appeared at the top of the stairs, Lucy in a pale green silk nightie, Trish in boy-cut panties and Red Hot Chili Peppers t-shirt. Both slapped awake by my fear. Cloquet, my familiar and the only human member of the household, hadn't stirred.

*A document. One Jake would have wanted you to see.* Jake Marlowe. My ex. My late ex. My late werewolf ex. The love against which all others were measured. Ask Walker.

"Take your time," Olek said. "I'm not going anywhere. In the package you'll find a note from me and a number to call when you're ready to talk. And again, I swear to you: you have nothing to fear."

The line went dead.

Look at her, I imagined my Aunt Theresa saying, disgusted. She's *excited*. Like when the Twin Towers went down. Like with the riots in those ugly English towns. She sees another serial killer victim in the newspaper and it gives her a sick thrill. She's not normal. (Well, Aunt, no, she's not. Not *now*.)

"What the fuck?" Trish said, starting down the stairs. At twenty-four she's the youngest of the pack, not counting the twins. Short, punkily chopped maroon hair and big green eyes and a supple little body full of delighted and occasionally catastrophic energy. I motioned her to stay put. Caught myself thinking: It doesn't *look* like a bomb—followed immediately by the admission that aside from cartoons and war footage I had no clue what a bomb looked like. For all I knew they could be making them the size of postage stamps these days. A werewolf can survive a lot of damage, but I doubted I'd come back from being blown to pieces. I had a vivid image of myself in bits, one severed hand walking on its fingers to find my eyeballs, a doomed attempt to put myself back together. Like the beginning of *Iron Man*. Or that scene in *The Thing*. Or was it *The Faculty?* Whatever it was it was like something I'd already seen. Four hundred more years of things being like other things you'd already seen. The effort finding the new would demand. I could see how Jake ended up the way he had: tired. Ready for death. Until he found love. At which point death was ready for *him*.

"Who was that?" Lucy asked, holding her elbows, hip bones pressing against the pale green silk of her nightie. She's an angle-poise English-woman of forty-three with dark auburn bangs and a broad delicate freckled face which in the absence of make-up her features are in danger of dissolving into. She would have been voted by all her (Cheltenham Ladies' College) school friends pupil least likely to become a werewolf. I've seen her punch through a man's sternum, rip out his heart and gobble it in two bloody bites. It's quite something to be able to say that and not be speaking figuratively.

"Lu?" she said, since I remained static, staring at the package. "Who was that on the phone?"

"A vampire," I said. "Nobody do anything for a minute. We need to think about this."

# 12

Something like this happens and you realise you've been waiting for something like this to happen. It turns out things can't go on as they have been and you admit you'd been thinking things couldn't go on as they had been. At which point you can yield or fight. Wars start like this. Cultures gamble decadence and death will win them rebirth, watch themselves sliding into it, knowing it's an all-or-nothing bet. Last night I'd felt Walker thinking, while I changed positions so we wouldn't be face to face: *Why are you wrecking this a little more every day?*

Half an hour after the call I sat on the bottom stair, smoking a Camel, alone. The Jiffy bag remained where it had dropped on the doormat. The hallway was still and cool and delicately conscious: white floorboards; round convex mirror; hat stand. I'd sent the household—Cloquet, Lucy, Trish and the twins (Lorcan protesting, violently rejecting every adult's helping hands)—out to what I judged safe distance at the bottom of the back garden seventy metres away. Walker had tried to stay with me. A calm argument, same outcome every time: No. It's got my name on it. Whatever it is I'm not exposing anyone else. Certainly not you. And besides . . . No need to complete the sentence. *And besides, if I get blown up, who else will take care of the kids?* He wasn't their father (that would be the late Jake Marlowe) but he was the closest thing they had to one. That love had knit easily, even if ours hadn't. It was a deep pleasure to me to watch them with him, clambering, pestering, yanking his hand to come and *look* at something. They didn't call him Dad. They called him—as everyone did, including me—Walker.

*I'm a vampire—but please try not to hold that against me.*

Species enmity. Mutually Assured Detestation at the cellular level. To the werewolf the vampire smells, as Jake was wont to put it, like a vat of pigshit and rotten meat. God only knows what our kind smells like to theirs. But circumstances had forced me to spend time close to them. Two years ago a lunatic vampire religious sect kidnapped my son for use in an idiotic ritual. In the struggle to get him back I was captured, incarcerated and tortured, not by vamps, but by the all too human WOCOP (World Organisation for the Control of Occult Phenomena); one of my fellow inmates was a vampire boy, Caleb, Turned when he was twelve years old. For the first twenty-four hours in prison the stink of each other had made us both violently sick. But over time the effect had lessened.

And then of course there was the *other* vampire. Yes. The one who'd been watching me in Alaska the night I gave birth to the twins. The one who'd come to see me, briefly, two years ago, then disappeared. The one who'd been alive, allegedly (hard to think this with a straight face; to think it was to more or less dismiss it), for *twenty thousand years.* The one who, according to (his own) ancient prophecy, would reach apotheosis when—and I quote, kidding you not—"he joined the blood of the were-wolf."

The one I couldn't get out of my head.

Remshi.

I'd dreamed about him last night. Again. Always the same dream: Impossible protracted transcendent sex that morphed into the two of us walking on a beach at twilight. With a feeling of seeing the dismal punch-line of a long-winded joke.

For a moment on the phone I'd thought it was him. But the voice was different. I remembered his voice very clearly. I remembered all of him very clearly, skin the colour of milky coffee, dark eyes and unkempt hair, an expression of chimpish mischief, battered clothes, the look of having just done five thousand miles on a motorbike. Beautiful hands and filthy fingernails. (What are you thinking about? Walker still annoyingly asked. Too easy lately to lie. A couple of times, fascinated by my knack for casual bankruptcy, I'd answered, "Jake." Which did its job. Closed the subject. For a while. Walker loves me but the in-awe days are over. Sooner or later he'll get tired of ghosts. Or shadows. Or secrets. Or the growing conviction that not all of me belongs to him, and never will. *The lover's tragedy and triumph,* Jake wrote, *is that he is always bigger than love.* So is she, Jacob. So is she.)

The hallway held its portion of light and silence very still.

Cognitive dissonance because a Jiffy bag on the doormat in the old life meant a gift, an Amazon order, Greek sweets from my dad.

I'll finish this cigarette, then I'll open it.

I finished the cigarette.

There was no decision. In the abstracted way of these things I found myself getting to my bare feet (toenails last night painted L'Oreal "Scarlet Vamp," since there's no end to one's tawdry acts of self-collusion), walking the dozen paces, bending, and, with only the slightest delirium in my fingertips, picking up the packet.

Not heavy.

A book?

In a few seconds of near complete blankness I tore it open.

A book.

Diary, rather. Old-fashioned. And in fact old. Soft pale calfskin stained and scratched, damp-buckled pages with green marbling. A gap between the last sheet and the back cover said some were missing. Exposed binding where the excision had been made. My nose expected mould, the sour of old leather. Instead got pharmacy. Medicine. Chemical.

*A document Jake would have wanted you to see.*

For a few moments I stood there on mindless pause.

Then all my abstractedness shrank back to sudden, tight, bristling consciousness. My skin livened. I was very aware of the dimensions my body occupied, standing in the hall, the villa, the town, the hills, boot-shaped Italy, the big aching curve of the planet, space and time that used to dissolve into God but now went eventually via the Large Hadron Collider into a pointless looped nowhere and nothingness. I was very aware of stilled, wide-eyed *wulf*'s for once almost perfect fit inside me.

Because in an intuitive leap I'd realised (plot-addicted Life hopped from foot to foot with excitement) whose diary this was.

# 13

QUINN'S.

Impossible.

I wanted to sit down. Didn't. Just stood there, holding it in both hands as if I were about to make a presentation of it to an invisible dignitary.

*It's a ridiculous story*, Jake had written, *but history's full of ridiculous stories*.

The story of Alexander Quinn, an amateur archeologist who went to Mesopotamia in 1863 and discovered, by accident, the oldest account of the origin of a near worldwide myth—the men who became wolves. Told to him by a dying man, translated by Quinn's guide, recorded by Quinn in his journal. But Quinn had been killed by bandits in the desert and his journal lost. Jake had spent forty years searching for it. In the end gave up. In the end told himself finding it wouldn't make any difference: *Suppose I found it and it said werewolves came on a silver ship out of the sky five thousand years ago*, he wrote in his own journal, *or were magicked up out of a burning hole in the ground by a Sumerian wizard, or were bred by impregnating women with lupine seed—so what? Whatever the origin of my species it would make no more cosmic sense than the origin of any other. The days of making sense, cosmic or otherwise, are long over. For the monster as for the earthworm as for the man the world hath really neither joy, nor love, nor light, nor certitude, nor peace, nor help for pain, and we are here as on a darkling plain . . .*

By the time I met him it had petrified into dogma: Don't bother looking for the meaning of it all, Lu, he said. There isn't one. I'd inherited it. Repeated it verbatim to Walker when he was still new to the Curse.

But as soon as I'd pulled the book from the Jiffy bag I'd known. Quinn's journal. Maybe the truth of how it all began. Maybe the truth of what it all *meant*. A dizzying rush, and under the rush, boredom: This was Life, at it again, trying to flog you connectedness, pattern, structure, trying to flog you a plot. (It's Life's suppressed Tourette's: months, years, decades of clean contingent smalltalk—then a sudden foul-mouthed explosion of X-rated coincidences and symbols and narrative hooks, a frantic and ludicrous claim for *story*.) But I repeat: the boredom was *under* the rush. The rush was no less real. My hands were nerve-rich, face full of soft heat. I'd grown up Catholic, and though the Curse doth make existentialists of us all (monthly murder will do that; watching your victims' lives end, feeling all their lights go out in the darkness, all their hopes of heaven met by . . . by the vast mathematical silence) my childhood self kept its stubborn flame burning. Suppose Quinn's book reopened the questions? Suppose there was a magical architecture, transcendence, a supernatural scheme of things? Design, intent, meaning. Morality. Suppose there would be, after all, *consequences*?

There was a folded slip of paper sticking out from between the pages like a bookmark, about a third of the way in. I opened it there. Forced myself to avoid what was on the diary pages (in spite of which I registered beautiful sloped handwriting in sepia ink and the words "Enkil" and "in tents" and "sacrificed to the gods") and focused on the sender's note:

*Dear Talulla,*

*Here, believe it or not, is the last journal of Alexander Quinn, and in it is contained the oldest known account of your species' beginnings. It isn't complete. As you can see I've removed some of the pages and retained them—for reasons which will become clear when we next speak. I have, as you will by now know, a mutually profitable proposal to put to you, but it won't make much sense until you've had a chance to read this.*

*I suppose it's possible you'll doubt the authenticity of the document—yet something tells me you won't. A superficial examination by an antiquarian will at least confirm it fits the period, and more rigorous analysis will only strengthen its claim. But my gut tells me you won't need any of that. Let me at least tell you that the previous owner—Mme Jacqueline Delon (who is well known to you, I realise)—has no idea she's been relieved of it. I have no love for her, but that's another story, and really, if you don't believe me about the book, why should you believe me about anything else? Let me nonetheless also tell you that with this book belongs a stone tablet, the second part of Quinn's strange legacy. This I also have in my keeping. Fortunately for both of us.*

*Listen to my idiom! I sound like a solicitor. God only knows why. Pre-sumably the content determines the style. Anyway, I don't sound like this at all, normally. As you'll discover if and when we meet.*

*Call the number below when you've read the journal. Keep this to your-self. It isn't meant for anyone else. Not yet, at any rate.*

*Yours,*

*Olek*

Keep this to yourself.

Impossible. Everyone had seen the package. And even if they hadn't there's only so much *wulf* telepathy will miss. Details, yes, but not the *fact* of the thing. Plus there was Walker. I might scam pack consciousness, but there'd be no fooling him. Keep fucking the same werewolf and mental privacy suffers.

And wherefore, dear Lula, I could imagine Jake saying, all this talk of fooling and scamming and keeping it to yourself?

Yes. Thank you, Mr. Marlowe. Because I had to be in control of it. Whatever it was. And it was something. My nose for Life's addiction to plot insisted: This is something. This is dangerous. This will throw out effects like the spars of a spiral galaxy. Be careful. Knowledge is power, someone said. (Who? Jake would've known.) *Knowledge is power.* Yes. And if there was power to be had it was better to have it than not.

But there was more to it than that. Irrationally more, nonsense more— but nonetheless, *more.* I believed—why? *why?*—it was connected to Remshi. Wishful thinking. Desperate thinking, derived from nothing more than him saying *I'll see you again* and then not seeing me again. Two years, the repeated dream, this. *This has something to do with him.* Me and my savvy rational self sneered at our intuitive partner (bagged with astrology, dowsing, faith healing, crystals) but we both knew she'd win this one.

My phone rang again.

"So?" Walker said.

"Well, it's not a bomb."

I could hear Lorcan kicking-off in the background.

"Great. We're coming in."

"Wait."

He didn't ask why. He'd already heard it in my voice. The appeal to collusion. The appeal for a partner in crime. My heart softened. It wasn't perfect between us, but it was very, *very* good. It needed a specially perverse soul for it not to be enough. At which thought I pictured Jake and my mother watching me from the afterlife (for the two of them a place like a Vegas casino, bottle blonde waitresses, booths, the murmur of happy gambling) smiling and shaking their heads. A specially perverse soul? Oh, Lula!

"Whatever I say to the others," I instructed Walker, "go along with it. I'll explain later."

"Whatever you say, Miss D."

Miss D. It was what he used to call me. It hurt my heart to hear it now. It hurt my heart not enough.

# 14

IT WASN'T EASY. Doubly difficult since I mixed truth with lies.

"It's one of Jake's journals," I said. "I thought I had them all, but apparently not. There are at least another half dozen."

We'd gathered in what we called—since it had an untuned old upright piano in it—the Music Room. Seating was two cream corduroy sofas and a wicker rocker. Eggshell walls, a black cast-iron fireplace, an odour of patchouli and fresh air and dust. The big bay window looked out into a front garden as beardily overgrown as the one at the rear, with the added attraction of a pond of thick dark green water watched over by two lichened demurely kneeling stone Nereids, one with a missing nose. Zoë had calmed Lorcan down, though he sat under the piano with a face of compressed fury. Two nights ago, in a rage, he'd put his bare foot through the conservatory's glass door. I'd had to hold him down while Walker tweezered the shards from his flesh.

"God knows how this Olek character's got them, but he's offering them in exchange for something. I don't know what yet. Probably just money. He sounds a little desperate. He wants to meet."

The *wulf* in Lucy and Trish was trying to get hold of whatever it was I wasn't saying, the other thing . . . something . . . But I kept it moving, just out of reach. The room's atmosphere was dense.

"You're not going to meet him, obviously," Lucy said. She was in the rocker, not rocking but tipped forward, elbows on knees. She'd changed into black jeans and an olive green blouse. Any green set off the auburn hair and hazel eyes. She'd put on mascara and eyeliner and warm peach lipstick. The Curse had rebooted her interest in the way she looked, now that she was never going to look any older.

"No. Not yet."

"Not yet?"

"I'm thinking about it."

Trish, who'd been looking out the window at two scuffling feral puppies (our canine vibe kept the grounds full of them), turned. The Chili Peppers t-shirt had been replaced by a white cheesecloth *kurta* and sawn-off 501s. Bare legs of lovely Gaelic whiteness. But her *wulf*'s irritation (this thing I wasn't saying was like the comedy bar of soap every grab flipped from one hand to the other) had reddened her small face.

"How can you be thinking about it?" she said. "Thinking about going to meet a vampire? It's a trap. It can *only* be a trap."

"I'm not so sure," I said. I had Quinn's book in my hand. My hand pulsed, surely visibly. I thought: Any minute one of them's just going to snatch it from me.

"Look, I don't want to make a big thing out of it," I said. "It's not something . . . I don't have to decide anything right now. Besides, we've got Saturday to get through."

Saturday. Full moon. The kill. And everything that went with it. Only the fourth time we'd be going as a pack. It had become an occasional necessity. Not every month, and not on any recognisable cycle; but when the need spoke none of us argued. None of us except Madeline, who went her own way, who had fuckkilleat partners queueing, who had honourable reasons for staying out of mine and Walker's way that one night of the month. She was stopping by tomorrow en route to Spain, where she had arrangements in place. She would land early in Rome, spend the day with us and the night fucking Cloquet's brains out (it had become a pre-Transformation ritual for her, a last hit of human warmth before the beast got out) then leave on Friday. She had to keep their encounters brief. It was bad enough he was in love with her. If she fell in love with him, she'd end up killing and eating him. Since that would be the worst thing she could do to a human. Since doing the worst thing to humans is the thing we do. Hot tip: If you're a human having a fling with a werewolf, break it off. Now.

"I don't like it, either, *chérie*," Cloquet said to me. He was still in green silk pyjama bottoms and black towelling robe, nursing a claret hangover of his own, albeit with the aid of a bloody mary and a Gauloise. His bony face with its large mouth and big black eyes was crimped with morning-after misery. His dark hair looked like a mouse had spent a rough night in it. "He phoned you," he said. "He had a package delivered. He knows where we are. We're going to have to fucking *move* again. *Merde*." It had been our intention—mine, Walker's and Cloquet's—to stay here for six months. We were sick of perpetual flight. Transit lounges and hotels and border controls and time zones and languages and currencies; continual adjustment breeds deep fatigue. But the equation doesn't change: Stillness is death. Keep killing on the same patch and watch the investigation noose tighten. Rudy Kovatch, the documents and ID specialist I'd inherited from Jake, had furnished us all with several EU passports to complement the U.S. fakes; either side of the Atlantic, that gave us a lot of room to hunt. Europe made more sense: you could be in and out of three countries a day. Tough to track.

"Lula, this is bollocks," Trish said. "I can't believe you're talking about going to meet a fucking vampire, after what you've been through—after what we've *all* been through with those arsewipes."

*What we've all been through.* Quite. When the vampire religious nuts had kidnapped Lorcan, Lucy and Trish had been two of the team that had helped me get him back. At mortal risk to themselves. Partly pack gravity, yes (no one ever referred to me as being any kind of leader, but I was the one they'd constellated around; there was something, some latent power), but partly because they were generous beings. Unless you happened to be one of their victims. In which case generosity wouldn't be the first of their personal qualities that sprang to your mind.

"And while we're at it," Lucy said, "aren't you remotely curious as to how he got your mobile number?"

Walker was negotiating quiet angry agony. He knew about the night two years ago when the vampire Remshi had made ambiguous contact with me. He knew because I'd told him. I'd told him because nothing had happened. Nothing had happened and I had nothing to confess. Nothing had happened and I had nothing to confess except that from that night the vague expectation that I'd see Remshi again had grown into an insistent mental mass. Now here was another vampire seeking me out. Another—or the same? *When he joins the blood of the werewolf.* I'd forced myself to tell Walker that, too. Made a joke of it, the phrase's B-movie portentousness, the surely bogus archaism. Once or twice we'd tried to make it a private language idiom for anything that was never going to happen, as in, *when hell freezes over, when he joins the blood of the werewolf—* but the words had hung awkwardly in the air and we'd stopped trying.

"Mike and Natasha will help," Walker said, forcing himself into practicalities. "If we take this any further it should be with them as back-up."

I hadn't thought of that, but he was right. Mikhail Konstantinov, Walker's former colleague, and his wife Natasha Alexandrova. Natasha had been made a vampire against her will. Mikhail had made her Turn him so they could be together. Outdoors, with ten feet between us, we could bear each other's odour. We had to. We were friends. They *would* help.

"I'm not taking it further," Trish said. "Your kids, Lu, that's one thing. But I'm not walking into a vamp trap for half a dozen books, even if they did belong to Jake. Sorry."

"Please," I said. "Can we just forget this for now? I'm not asking anyone to do anything. The likelihood is I *won't* take it any further. If you hadn't all already seen the goddamned package I wouldn't even have mentioned it. Seriously. Forget this. It's no one else's problem."

*Unless we're being watched.* Lucy didn't say it. Didn't have to. Instead she said: "It's a bad time to be getting involved in anything we don't have to. The way things are out there."

"Out there" was the world, which, courtesy of our population explosion, wasn't what it used to be. Full moon these days you couldn't open a cupboard without a howler jumping out at you, if Internet gossip was to be believed. The virus that had brought the species to near extinction had died at last in me, and Jake too, by the end. Every werewolf since could trace its infection to either him or me. The good or bad old days were back: Survive the bite and the Curse was yours. Estimates ranged from six hundred to ten or twenty thousand monsters roaming the earth. No one really knew. Transformations were all over YouTube. Demand for werewolf porn, which, since it invariably centred on fuckkilleat, was also snuff porn, was growing, according to *Playboy* magazine, "at an exponential rate." Governments had taken the line of lumping us in with crop circles and the Loch Ness Monster. The U.S., UK, German and Russian administrations had posted counter-videos online, "showing" the alleged transformations were cleverly manipulated effects and props. "Hoaxers" had "confessed." Up until two weeks ago the Christian Churches had sung the politicians' song. Then the Vatican had volte-faced and stunned the world: Not only are werewolves and vampires real, their statement said, but Rome is secretly training an army of warriors to destroy them. The announcement launched an all-platforms ad campaign, a TV, print and online assault on the faithful's credulity, filled with testimonials from believers—and more importantly former *non*-believers, now converts—who'd been attacked by one of these abominations but "saved" by the intervention of God's holy soldiers, the *Militi Christi*, whom everyone (except, officially, the Catholic Church itself) was now calling "the Angels."

"I know," I said. "I get it. Don't worry. I'm not going to do anything without discussing it with you. But can we just agree to shelve it until after Saturday?"

In the end we let it go, with some abrasion. The temptation was to change the arrangements for Saturday. But as Walker pointed out: If someone was watching us now with a view to following us they could follow us wherever we went. Changing the kill wouldn't make any difference. Besides, we only had two and a half days. Not enough time to orchestrate an alternative. The only alternative, in fact, would be to abandon the pack kill, go our separate ways and take our chances with victims as and where we found them. None of us wanted to do that.

Lucy took the local train to Rome to spend the day at the Villa Borghese. Trish went to the beach. Cloquet, who'd evolved a second or meta-hangover, went back to bed.

As soon as Walker and I were alone with the kids I told him the truth: Quinn's journal. The possible origin of the species. Olek's note.

He was underwhelmed.

"I wouldn't get too excited," he said. We were in the kitchen. Zoë and Lorcan were under the table, Lorcan aggressively colouring a picture of the Three Little Pigs (God being dead, irony still rollickingly alive), Zoë building a precarious tower with empty cotton spools she'd found somewhere. I had maybe six months before the thrill-discrepancy between things like cotton spools and Xboxes registered.

"Don't get excited?" I said. "Are you serious?"

"Just because there's a story doesn't mean it's true."

I managed not to say: "Jake thought it was." Too much Jake, lately. Jake too often invoked. Instead, I said: "I know that. But wouldn't you rather know the story and disregard it than not know it and spend your life wondering?"

"I won't be spending my life wondering," he said. "I'm not the wondering kind."

Zoë said, apropos of nothing (except to a three-year-old everything is apropos of something): "Elephants don't eat beans." She doesn't like beans. Especially kidney beans, which she calls "bugs."

In spite of everything else going on it made Walker and me laugh. Then made us infer a kid's instinct for when the adults need help, which made us both sad again.

"Whatever the origins are," he said, "we're here now, two arms, two legs, full moon every month, life to live. It's different for you. You had the Catholic childhood. You're hardwired to think there's got to be something up there, out there, wherever, some meaning to it all, no matter how many times you quote Jake. I didn't grow up with any of that. I grew up with McDonald's and *Pets Do the Craziest Things*."

Every so often he said something like this and I realised I'd forgotten his past, the tumour around which his character had formed. When he was seven years old he'd killed his father, an NYPD cop. *I shot him with his own gun. Standard issue Glock nine-millimetre. He was smashing my mother's face into the television.* I remembered the way he'd told me. In a tone that conceded that his horror story—any horror story—was only ever one among many. Especially to me, multiple murderer, eater of human beings, werewolf. *It can't be anything other than minor to you*, he'd said. It wasn't minor. Nor was it his only horror story. It was the told one. There was also the untold one. The story of what had happened to him when he'd been captured with me by WOCOP two years ago. Inside the detention facility they'd kept us apart. We'd never spoken about what they'd done to him. Torture was a given, but we'd never used the word "rape." All this had happened to him before he'd been Turned. His embrace of *wulf* had been (amongst other things) an attempt to shed the dirty skin. *Expect the absurd*, Jake had written. *It's the werewolf's lot.* And since he was right, here was someone who'd chosen one monstrosity to blot out another, the principle of violent eclipse. Not total. The seven-year-old boy was still in there, the raped man, all the shadowy selves that even in the blood din of the Curse could still, at moments, be heard. I felt sorry for him, loved him afresh—but felt too my heart's appalling approximateness, its devious generosity, its room for other things.

The journal was in my left hand. I hadn't put it down the whole time. Couldn't. Had to know. True or not.

Lorcan, whose "colouring" had evolved into gouging holes in the pages, got up and stormed out of the room.

"Go ahead," Walker said. "I'll keep an eye on these two. I'll read it when you're done."

# 15

Long ago, long before Hattia and Assyria, before Sumeru, before the Pharaohs raised their big stones, palm shadows danced on the waters of Iteru under the eyes of the gods. These were the old gods, before Ra and Horus and Zeus and Hera, before young Yaweh and gentle Yeshua. Before An and Enlil, before Nin-khursag and Enkil, before even Taimat and Abʒu, who were not the first. Before all these a travelling people stopped for a season by Iteru, thousands of years before it became the Nile. They built no stones, but lived in tents of skin and fur. Thin strong men and women. They loved the desert sky at night, where the gods wrote in stars that touched the earth's face. They ate the meat of goat, cow and pig. They ate the date and the fig. They sacrificed to their gods.

The people were the Maru.

Edu was their king, and his wife was Liku, the queen. They had a three-year-old son, Imut.

In those days there were passages from the Middle world to the Upper and the Lower Realms. It was given to some among the Maru to open these passages. They opened them with songs and with the blood of the living and with the smoke and fire of burning. They were called, in their tongue, the Anum, the Guardians, and mightiest among them was Lehek-shi.

Lehek-shi was enamoured of Liku, the queen, and she of him. They became lovers. Lehek-shi made a drink of the bark of the aho tree and the berries of the nawar sweetened with dates and coconut milk, and in the evening Liku gave the drink to Edu, her husband, and made love to him. Then when he slept she stole from the tent and went through the darkness to meet Lehek-shi.

This went on for five moons, and the king never suspected. His wife worked with great care to give him pleasure and his sleep was deep. He confided to *his closest friends that he was the luckiest of all the Maru, to know such wifely devotion and to sleep such untroubled sleep.*

*But Liku and Lehek-shi were not content. Stolen hours by the grace of drug and darkness were not enough. Their passion was rare and real and fiercer than the sacrificial fire, and its patience with secrecy was at an end. Therefore they resolved between the kisses of their mouths to kill Edu. After the period given for mourning, Liku would be free to choose a new husband—and naturally she would choose Lehek-shi.*

*But Lehek-shi was full of foreboding. He knew the ways of the Upper and Lower realms. When a Maru of pure heart died, the gods of the Upper realm sent down to earth one of their servants—the Kamu—to put its mouth upon the mouth of the corpse and breathe in the soul for its passage to the Upper realm. Released in the Upper realm the soul would tell its story—and the gods would take vengeance on the murderers.*

*"There is an another way," Lehek-shi told Liku, with his arms wrapped around her in the darkness. "But it is a risk."*

*"What other way?" Liku asked. Her hair was full of the scent of oranges.*

*"We can send his soul to the Lower realm. Amaȝ will take it. But Amaȝ is a hard god to bargain with."*

*"If Amaȝ is a risk," Liku said, climbing astride her lover, "the wrath of the Upper gods is a certainty."*

*Lehek-shi entered her, and the decision was made.*

*Lehek-shi sacrificed and made a burning and inhaled the smoke of the branch that gave sight and sang the song that opened the way to the Lower realm and let his spirit go out to seek audience with Amaȝ.*

*The threshold of Amaȝ's kingdom was guarded by three of his messengers, those dark opposites of the blessed Kamu, the Iȝul. Invisible in the Middle realm, in the Lower they were terrible to behold.*

*Lehek-shi was a diviner, one of the Anum, and had by birth the right to hold discourse with the beings of the other realms, but still, this was the kingdom of Amaȝ, and he was afraid.*

*One of the Iȝul carried his message to the demon god, and eventually Amaȝ himself came to the threshold.*

## By Blood We Live

"I will do as you ask," Amaz said, after Lehek-shi had told him what he wanted. "In return for what issues from your first coupling with the queen after the king's death. Understand me. If there is a child, its soul must come down to me. Thereafter I will hold our pact fulfilled."

Lehek-shi vowed inside himself that there would be no child—even in those days there were the ways and means to make the chances of new life slight, and they had only to avoid conception once—and so he agreed to Amaz's terms. (And even if there is a child, he thought, Liku will relinquish it if our happiness is at stake.) With the bargain sealed, therefore, Lehek-shi's spirit took its leave of Amaz and returned to his body in the Middle realm.

The lovers had to wait. Even with the dark god's bargain sealed Edu's murder must have no earthly witnesses. So Liku began to beguile her husband.

"I never have you to myself," she complained, sweetly. "Even at night there are guards outside the tent, listening to us."

Edu was puzzled. "They are for our safety," he said. "They are spears and shields. They aren't listening to us! And what if they are? They are servants!"

But Liku persisted. "But don't you understand that sometimes I want you simply, as a man, as my husband, just the two of us, alone under the stars?"

For a while Edu made light of it, but eventually Liku's pleading prevailed, and he agreed to spend one night with her away from the camp, alone, man and woman, husband and wife, together under the stars.

"The soul has understanding," Lehek-shi had warned Liku. "If it senses death near it will rush up into the head to be ready for the Kamu's kiss. Therefore we must surprise the soul. You must keep the soul distracted."

Liku kept the soul distracted. She even had thought for the approach of Lehek-shi's shadow, and made Edu lie on his back with the low full moon in front of him so Lehek-shi, approaching with the long, sharpened flint stone from behind the king's head, would make no change in the light.

*Edu's soul, at the moment of joy, knew nothing of what fell.*

*Lehek-shi struck hard and fast, and in three blows severed Edu's head from his shoulders.*

*Amaʒ, the lord of the Lower realm, sent one of the Iʒul to claim the king's soul. Not from the mouth, into which the soul in its ignorant bliss had had no chance to flee, but from the mouth between the buttocks, the speaker of filth. The soul had no choice. It could not remain in the body after death. It could not resist the indrawn breath of the Iʒul. The Iʒul swallowed it and carried it down to Amaʒ.*

*One moon later, the lovers were married. Imut was too young to take up the throne, so Liku ruled as queen until he should come of age. Lehek-shi was her consort.*

*But in the Lower realm, the soul of Edu would not cease its lamentations.*

*When Lehek-shi told Liku of the price of the bargain, she was not very afraid. She knew her monthly bleed well enough, and when the chances of conceiving were slim. She and Lehek-shi waited. And when they did come together the first time after Edu's death, Lehek-shi made an offering in the fire to Nendai, the god of prudence, and wore on his manhood the dried skin of pig-gut to prevent any seed from entering Liku's womb.*

*But a splinter from the wood he'd cut for the burning lodged under Lehek-shi's thumbnail, and tore a small hole in the minnan—and though the lovers willed it not, Liku was made with child.*

*In the Lower realm, the demon god Amaʒ felt the new life stir.*

*When Liku realised what had happened, she was afraid. By the third moon without her bleed she could feel love wrapped around the child inside her. Lehek-shi knew he would never get her to relinquish their baby of her own free will. Nor, as her belly grew bigger and she put his hands on her to feel the first kicks of life, could he bear the thought of sending his son or daughter down to the kingdom of Amaʒ. The lovers had murdered together*

*and bargained with a demon god—and the passion and understanding
between them was stronger than ever.*

*The Maru numbered little over two thousand, and among that number
were some dozen women at the same stage of their carrying as Liku. But
all the women gave birth before the queen, despite the drugs and songs of
the wise women, and between Liku's baby—a boy, whom they named
Tahek—and the latest born to the tribe was almost one whole moon.*

*Nonetheless, the substitution was made, the mother bribed (Lehek-shi
would deal with her if she made trouble) and the replacement child—
rubbed in the blood and birth fluids of Liku for disguise—beheaded in
Tahek's place.*

*The Izul came up and sucked out the soul from the tiny mouth between
the buttocks and carried it down to Amaz.*

*Three years passed. Liku and Lehek-shi believed their trick had worked.
Their son Tahek grew strong and healthy. The Maru moved north, but the
cold weather stayed close behind them.*

*One day a great snowstorm caught them. The winds blew and a noon
darkness fell. Liku and Lehek-shi became separated from the tribe. In the
gloom, they heard the howling of wolves.*

*They seemed to be in nothingness. There were no trees, no rocks. The
division of land and sky had vanished. The snow drove hard and plied
deep. The wind was cruel. Liku's fur tore from her and went up into the
sky. They tried to catch it—but it was gone. Lehek-shi made her wear his.*

*For hours they could not count, for a time that might have been days they
struggled through the storm, with no knowledge of where they were going,
only with the hope of finding shelter. Lehek-shi grew very weak from the
cold. At last, exhausted, he fell.*

*When Liku knelt to try to warm him, she gave a cry. There, not twenty
paces away, was the edge of a forest.*

*With what little strength that remained to her she dragged Lehek-shi
into the shelter of the trees. The wind died, suddenly. For a few moments
the lovers lay together, unable to move. Darkness came over them.*

•

"Come with me," a voice said. "If you do not get warmth and food, you will both die."

Liku opened her eyes.

Standing over her was a dark-eyed man, great in height, wrapped in the skin of a wolf. He bore a bloody spear and around his neck a long loop of animal teeth. A red birth mark stained half his face.

"Come," he repeated. "I will carry him. Be swift. He has not much time."

Not knowing if she was awake or dreaming, Liku followed the man, who bore Lehek-shi over his shoulder as though his weight were no more than a child's. She was near death herself, from hunger and cold.

"Here," the man said. "I have food and warmth for you both."

Under two mighty trees lay the body of a giant wolf, slain. The beast was bigger than three men. It had been slit from its throat to its loins and its innards cleanly removed.

"I have not means to make the fire," the man said, "but if you are willing to pay my small price you can eat of the animal's meat and shelter in his skin, and in the morning the storm will have passed, and your people will find you. They are coming this way, but will not get here before the sun rises."

Liku, frozen and starving and weak, reached for the animal's hide— but the stranger stopped her.

"You have not agreed, freely, to pay my small price," he said.

"What is your price?" Liku asked. "I am a leader of my people. I can give you all that I have!"

The stranger shook his head. "I ask very little," he said. "A drop of blood from each of you, and the animal's warmth and meat is yours. Give me this courtesy offering freely, and you will live to see the sunrise."

At that moment the clouds tore a little, and the full moon sailed free on a field of black.

Liku's heart misgave her, but she knew that without food and shelter the stranger's words would be proved true before morning. "Very well," she gasped. "A drop from each of us. But hurry! I feel death near me!"

The stranger took one of the teeth from around his neck and gave it to

*Liku. "Do it freely," he repeated. "Because your life and the life of your beloved is precious to you."*

*Liku took the tooth and saw that it was sharp. Quickly, too cold to feel the pain, she made a tiny cut on her thumb and did the same for Lehek-shi.*

*"Very well," the stranger said, and lifting open the belly of the wolf, he cut several pieces of the animal's flesh. Liku, driven by her need, ate, and fed Lehek-shi, though Lehek-shi could barely open his eyes, and seemed still to be wandering in death's country. The meat tasted sweet and tender, and Liku was surprised.*

*"Now hurry," the stranger said. "Into the beast. There is a second storm coming from which the trees will not be shelter enough."*

*Liku dragged herself and Lehek-shi into the warmth of the wolf's body while the stranger watched. Again Liku was surprised that there was no smell of death in the animal, only the feeling of warmth and succour. The stranger watched, and, when the lovers were settled, he smiled and spoke:*

*"I bring you greetings from Amaz, god of the Lower Realm," he said. "The meat you have eaten was human flesh, and your blood is mingled with the blood of the beast. Now every time the moon is full, the wolf will take shelter in you, and your craving for that same human flesh will be more than you can bear. Those who survive your bite will carry the same curse. You do not cheat my master and go unrepaid. Farewell!"*

*And with that, the stranger walked away and was swallowed by the darkness.*

*So it was that the races of wolves and men were mixed. In the years that followed many tried to free themselves from the Curse, but it was not until people returned to the banks of Iteru that*

I stopped reading. I didn't have a choice. The remainder of the page had been torn away, along with all the other remaining pages.

*. . . but it was not until people returned to the banks of Iteru that*

The implication—Olek's editorial implication—was clear: someone, eventually, had found a cure.

# 16

WALKER FINISHED READING and laid the book down on the night-stand. We were in the bedroom. Bed unmade (*love* unmade, my nasty inner voice said), each of the two big windows full of afternoon sunlight. Across the hall, the twins were trying to wake Cloquet up. Cloquet wasn't enjoying the experience.

"So?" I said.

I was sitting on the floor by the open door across from him, smoking a Camel filter. Last night's hangover had talked itself into wanting another drink. My copy of Byron's *Don Juan* was open face down on the floor by Walker's foot. I remembered exactly where I'd stopped reading last night. Before we'd had the sex that had felt like an argument:

*There's doubtless something in domestic doings,/Which forms, in fact, true love's antithesis.*

He shook his head. "What do you want me to say?"

Wait. Count to five. Don't snap at him.

"Well, do you think it's genuine, for starters?" I said.

"Do you mean do I think this is really Quinn's journal, or do I think this story has any basis in fact?"

Count to five again. Pointless, since my irritation contained was just as visible as it would have been let out.

"Okay," he said, exhaling, seeing it. "I think there's every chance the journal's the real deal. As for the story . . ." he laughed. Shook his head again. No.

"Just like that," I said. "Amazing."

"Jesus Christ," he said. "Lu, are you serious? *Gods of the Lower Realm?* Are you fucking kidding me?"

"I'm aware of what it sounds like."

"Apparently not, if you're taking it seriously. Who knew demons could suck some poor bastard's soul out of his ass!"

My face was hot. Because of course he was right. Of course. Of *course*.

"Please," he said. "*Please* tell me you're not . . ." He couldn't finish. Incredulity was getting the better of him.

"Doesn't something resonate?" I asked. "I mean not the details, necessarily. I mean the . . . I don't know."

Across the hall, Cloquet said: "Zoë, *mon ange*, that is really annoying. I am not well."

Delighted giggles from the twins. Zoë had a funny little old lady laugh.

"No," Walker said, with his own forced calm. "Nothing resonates. It's a *fairy* story, for Christ's sake."

"What are *we*, then?" I asked him. "*We're* a fucking fairy story."

Awkward silence. For the two readings of that sentence. I'd meant we, werewolves, are a fairy story. But the opportunist subconscious never sleeps. He'd heard we as in me and him, *we* were a fairy story. A relationship not to be believed in.

"*Mes enfants*," Cloquet groaned. "There is going to be violence here if you keep doing that."

More fiendish cackling from the twins. I wondered how long we'd have before Lorcan's next rage, or nightmare, or worrying trick of picking an adult and staring expressionlessly at them until they got mad.

"You know what you're pissed about?" Walker said. "You're pissed because it *doesn't* resonate. You were expecting some big revelation. Instead you get this horseshit. It's just another story. I mean why stop here? If a story's all we need let's have the little baby Jesus and the Tooth Fairy and fucking Santa Claus."

I didn't say anything. Because again, he was right. He got up from the bed, went to the window and looked down into the softly blazing garden, hands in his back pockets. I thought how much I'd loved the shape of him. Lean, economically muscled. The pretty profile. Loved. Past tense. What happened? What happens?

A vampire comes to call.

"Let me ask you one thing," I said. "If there was a cure, would you take it?"

This, I knew, was also what had vexed him. The suggestion of return. Which brought the absence of anything to return *to*.

He didn't answer straight away. His face was calm and golden in the sunlight.

"There's no going back," he said. "Not for me."

At which moment my phone rang. Again.

# 17

"FORGIVE MY IMPATIENCE," Olek said, "but I'm on tenterhooks here. Have you read Quinn's journal?"

I got to my feet and stepped out onto the landing. Walker turned and watched, but didn't follow. Through the door opposite I could see into Cloquet's room. The twins had found an assortment of hats and gloves and shoes in the downstairs closet. They were putting them on Cloquet, who was still half asleep. He was currently wearing a bicycle helmet, an oven mitt and a pair of battered dress shoes much too big for him.

"Yes," I said. "So what?"

"So what, Miss Talulla, is that I know what the people who returned to the banks of Iteru—or the Nile as we now call it—knew. I know the way out of the Curse."

"I repeat," I said: "So what?"

If you can hear a smile, I heard his.

"I knew you were going to say that."

"Who the fuck *are* you?"

"Who am I? I've told you. My name is Olek. I'm a vampire. I have an interest in science. And *I* repeat: I have a proposition of potential benefit to us both."

"Not if I don't want what you're offering."

"You might not want it for yourself," he said. "But you'll want it for your children. Do you have access to a computer?"

*For your children.* It sounded like a threat. Then I thought of Lorcan's problems around full moon. Could the vampire know about that?

"Yes," I said. I could feel more of what there was between me and Walker tearing. He hadn't moved from the window. Was letting himself imagine the future without me.

"Stay on the line. Go to your computer. Open your web browser."

The laptop was in the en suite, half-buried under a pile of laundry. Lycanthropy hadn't made me any tidier. I went back through the bedroom—Walker gave me a now what? look to which I raised a hand: Hang on. I sat down on the bathroom floor and powered-up the laptop.

"Okay," I said. "I'm online."

"Good. There's something you need to see. Go to Google. Sign in to Mail with the following address. Don't worry. It's an account I've set up just for this." He gave me a sequence of letters which didn't spell anything in English, at gmail.com. The password was numbers and letters that meant nothing to me. Naturally the thought that this was being traced or hacked—or that the entry would set a time bomb under the villa ticking—occurred to me, but I dismissed it. Not with good reason. Just out of impatience. I was doing this, whatever the fuck it was.

An inbox opened, with one mail item.

"Open the email and click on the link," Olek said. "It's secure, I promise you. When the link page opens, it'll ask you for another password. You there?"

"Yes. Page open."

More numbers and letters.

I hit enter.

"What you're about to see is a real event," Olek said. "I'll stay on the line. Just watch. I'll explain when it's run."

Video clip. Very high resolution. No sound. Timecode in the bottom left corner. Another sequence of numbers on the right.

Blue sky. Sunshine. A long line of what appeared to be Chinese people filing into a solitary low-lying white building with no windows set in manicured grounds. Heavily armed military everywhere.

Cut to inside.

Processing. Desks with more military personnel. People one by one presenting driver's licences, passports, documents—and being issued in return with numbered paper wristbands of the kind used at music festivals.

Cut to: An overhead shot of a room the size of a soccer pitch, divided into rows of concrete cubicles, several hundred, each with a set of steel bars down one side and another set across the roof.

The people in the holding cells, looking scared shitless. Some of them in tears. Families incarcerated together, single people alone. One armed soldier per three or four cells. Men and women in civilian dress with iPads and walkie-talkies.

Cut to: A large digital stadium clock. Counting down.

Cut to: Wide angle. Twenty or thirty of the cells visible. A sudden silent flurry of activity. Soldiers and iPad personnel moving. Prisoners screaming—all with the terrible visual intimacy of silent film.

Jerky zoom in.

In one of the cells, a woman of around twenty years old is turning into a werewolf.

Because, I now realise, the countdown has reached zero—and the full moon, though we can't see it, is up.

Two soldiers empty magazines into her.

Silver, manifestly, since she falls, immediately.

# 18

"THAT WAS SHOT in secret three months ago at Zanghye, Gansu Province, in the People's Republic of China," Olek said. "It was one of dozens of such actions currently being carried out by the Chinese government. They're starting small."

I was still, absurdly, sitting on the bathroom floor. I was thinking three things. First, that the footage was genuine. Second, that it wouldn't be possible to roll out extermination like that openly and nationally—to industrialise it. Third, that that was naive. It had been done before. Many times. Which gave birth to a fourth naive thought: In China, maybe, but not at home. Not in the U.S.

Wrong. *It couldn't happen here* was exactly the thinking that made it happening here possible. Wherever "here" was and whatever "it" might be.

"You're thinking, perhaps," Olek said, "that even if what you've just seen is genuine, it'll be confined to places like China. Places without what the West likes to call freedom."

"I'm a little ahead of you, thanks," I said.

He laughed. A sound of genuine delight. "A pupil of Mr. Marlowe's," he said. "Of course. And perhaps his Conradian namesake. 'And this also has been one of the dark places of the earth.' Very good. This saves us time. We have a sensibility in common. I'm so much looking forward to meeting you."

"Now you're ahead of *your*self," I said.

"You wouldn't want to spare your children extermination?"

"It's going to be a long time before they're at risk."

"You *have* a long time. All of you. Four hundred years, give or take. The writing's on the wall, Talulla, and people with a big simple enemy will have no trouble reading it. Extend logically from what you've just seen. Extend twenty years. Fifty. A hundred. Your species—and ours—is living in the last days of its liminality. China is the New Inquisition's first whisper in secret. But soon the whisper will be a proud global shout. Genocide has always depended on getting people to see the enemy as not human. A redundancy, if the enemy *isn't* human."

Walker had appeared in the bathroom doorway. I hit the video's Play button and handed the laptop to him.

"I'm offering a way out for you, for your children, for any of your kind who want it," Olek said. "You're too smart to dismiss it out of hand."

"What makes you think we're going to line up for this?" I said. "You think this is going to happen without a fight?"

"Of course not," Olek said. "I imagine you'll raise an army. Turn as many as you can. Maybe you'll win. Maybe you'll become the new master race."

I had a vision of myself and the pack going through city after city, biting or scratching everyone we could. News reports of escalating panic. A world map showing a werewolf population exploding. But it was followed by a vision of the Chinese model turned into a primetime game show, bets placed, just another outlet for the viewing world's already rapt boredom.

"Maybe you'll elect to roll the dice of all-out war," Olek said. "If anyone could lead a species . . . Well, you'll think this is just flattery. But I think the truth is you know they'll win. They have that thing. They have collective durability. It's a sort of stupidity, really, a lack of refinement, but it keeps them going."

I felt tired, suddenly. Claustrophobically irritated. Questions I hadn't wanted to ask myself were here now whether I liked it or not, petitioners who, once they were in, simply wouldn't go away. Even the sunlight and the garden's sleepiness felt like the soft edge of the world's incipient threat. It's coming for you. They're coming for you. It's only a matter of time.

"Why don't you tell me what it is you want from me," I said. "Because I'm pretty sure whatever it is it's something I'm not going to give you."

"Talulla, I promise you, it's nothing that will harm you. But I don't want you to make a decision until you've seen the proof."

"The proof of what?"

"The proof that the cure works."

"Which you have."

"Which I have. I want you to come and see him."

Walker had watched the video. He set the laptop down, open, on the bed, and returned to his objectless vigil at the window. I knew it wouldn't have made any difference to him. I knew he wasn't, under any circumstances, going back.

"Fine," I said to Olek. "Let me think about it. I have your number. Don't call me again."

"But you mu—"

I hung up.

"Don't say anything," I said to Walker.

He didn't, but he didn't stop staring out the window either. I kept telling myself to get up off the floor, and kept failing to get up off the floor. The bathroom smelled of unwashed laundry and the villa's lousy drains. I thought: Symbolic—then was immediately pissed at myself for thinking it. It was an annoying habit I'd acquired, of looking for signs, correspondences, metaphors, the goddamned pointless tic of finding things behind things, things connected to things, things *in* things. *Don't bother looking for the meaning of it all, Lu. There isn't one.* But ever since the vampire sought me out . . . Ever since the recurring dream . . .

The self-disgust was enough, at least, to get me up off the floor. I was about to go to Walker and stand close behind him and wrap my arms around his chest and haul whatever was left of love up into my heart and be thankful, when he said: "That's becoming the thing you say to me."

I'd lost track in the reverie.

"What is?" I asked him.

"'Don't say anything,'" he said.

# 19

THE NEXT MORNING I picked Madeline up from Fiumicino in the rented Cherokee. I was tired. Lorcan had had a wretched night. Dreams that woke him screaming in a sweat. He wakes and doesn't seem to recognise me. *Fights* me, initially. It's only after I've gone and got Zoë and put her in bed with him that he calms, focuses, realises that for better or worse it's me, his disappointing mother. I hadn't slept much after that. *You might not want it for yourself, but you'll want it for your children.*

"It's official," Madeline said, before she'd even got her seat belt on. "WOCOP's gone bust."

I was nervous. She and I were close. I wasn't confident I'd be able to screen my thoughts. She looked, as usual, hilariously attractive: blonde hair pulled back in a ponytail, catty little green-eyed face precisely cosmeticised, signature French manicured nails. She was dressed in a pink boob-hugging t-shirt, skin-tight Prada bluejeans and a pair of tan suede Giuseppe Zanotti ankle boots. A soft little aura of Shalimar by Geurlain surrounded her, flashed through—to my kindred nose—by two-days-pre-Transformation *wulf*. She and Fergus had made fast money on European foreclosures over the last two years, courtesy of my ten-million-dollar investment for a thirty per cent stake. Natural born capitalists. Resign yourself to killing and eating someone once a month and there's not much point being anything else.

"The whole organisation's been running on empty for the last three years, apparently," she said. "Not helped by the top brass using every trick in the book to line their pockets." She took a softpack of Winstons from her purse (a small Chloé Elsie python-leather shoulder, about two grand) and lit us one each. *Running on empty. Every trick in the book. Line their pockets.* I thought of Jake wincing at the clichés. Then letting the irritation morph into desire. No end to sexual cunning. Who knew that if not me? Madeline and I hadn't slept together but the possibility was always there, a sinuous current that slipped around and between us like a fascinated snake. In her human life she'd been Jake's London escort of choice. Eventually Turned, accidentally, by him giving her a sharper than usual lovebite. This was before he'd met me. Now she and I had him dirtily in common. And not only Jake. It was Madeline who'd turned Walker. Because Walker was in love with me and I'd been in something like love with him. Because I'd been scared that if I did it myself he'd hate me for it somewhere down the line. Oh, forget it, she'd said, when I'd tried to thank her and the two of us had ended up in ridiculous tears. You would've gone on agonising forever. He wanted it. You wanted it. I could do it, so I did. Job done, everyone's happy. Now for fuck's sake get on with being together, will you?

Every time I thought of how simply and generously she'd behaved it made me feel tender towards her. Followed lately by a dash of sad selfishness, since having been given what I thought I wanted I'd discovered it wasn't enough.

"Not, frankly, that it makes any difference," she said, exhaling smoke, "what with these fucking *religious* nutters taking over the show. Did you see that Cardinal on Sky? They're like pigs in shit." The Catholic Church, she meant, thrilled with what the actual existence of diabolical critters was doing for their investment portfolios. "They've raised close to fifty million already," Madeline said. "In this climate! You can't believe people are that stupid. Except of course you *can*." She cracked the window, through which the airport's smell of baked asphalt and jet fuel and ready meals rushed in. The sky was turquoise. I'd been in Italy two months and the country's casually piled-up history still made my American reel. The Colosseum like a giant half-eaten cake, its ghost-odours of big cats and urine and death, blood puddles in the hot sand. In Rome a tour guide dressed as a centurion had walked past me outside Burger King in a whiff of sweat and leather and for a moment it all slipped back. I'd thought of the vampire, Remshi. *Twenty thousand years,* he'd said, *you think you've seen it all.*

"It's the Catholics now," Madeline said, "but Fergus says the Russian and Greek Orthodox aren't going to be far behind. Once the American Fundamentalists and Africans join in there's going to be billions in it. Careful!"

I should've known there'd be no evading her. She'd probably sensed I was hiding something from the moment she got in the car. A few minutes' misdirect with the WOCOP/Vatican update—then a swift, effective rush in. I'd felt her, a sudden tingling or effervescence in the shoulders and scalp, the so much stranger feeling of someone moving like cold air over your thoughts. I'd nearly rolled the Cherokee. An outraged Fiat driver leaned on his horn. In the stream of Italian that went with it I caught, not surprisingly, *vaffanculo* and *pucchiacca*.

"Sorry," she said, grinning. "Why don't you tell me all about it?"

"Jesus Christ."

"Sorry," she repeated, laughing, retrieving my cigarette from the floor where I'd dropped it. "Should've just asked. But for fuck's sake, Lu, you've got to get better at this."

"I *am* getting better at it," I said. "With everyone else. Fuck."

"Who's Quinn, anyway?"

There was nothing else for it. I told her. All of it.

"So what's the cure?" she asked, when I'd finished. We were on the coast road heading south, just passing the Lido di Capo Portiere on our left. On our right the umbrella'd beach and sunlit Mediterranean. Blue and gold. Colours of the Renaissance. She hadn't sounded particularly interested.

"No idea," I said. "And I don't know what it is he wants, either. That's the whole point. I have to go there to find out. You obviously don't think it's for real."

She was searching in the Chloé Elsie for something. Her hands were white, lovely, quick-moving. I thought of all the men she'd touched, professionally. Jake, foremost, naturally. There was a line in one of his journals: *Madeline's hand, French manicured, was warm, lotioned and even in its moist fingerprints promissory of transactional sex.*

"Oh no," she said (ignoring the sly shared heat Jake in my head had bred between us), "it might be totally genuine for all I know. But I mean, what's the point?"

I was going in and out of being able to read her—she wasn't screening—but it was tough to concentrate on driving at the same time. I'd got: WHO WANTS TO BE CURED?—then withdrawn.

"Not me," she said, knowing I'd picked it up. She'd said it with a brightness that touched the place guilt or shame ought to be. Not wanting to be cured was, after all, wanting to go on killing and eating people once a month. She felt me thinking this and it did hold her still for an honest moment. There were vestiges yet to be burned through. But only by way of formality. The new version of herself was up and running. I could feel *wulf* at smug athletic ease in her, expansive and secure, at home among the victims babbling in her blood. It drew my own wronged dead up, an icy itch in the flesh, a swelling ache. "I mean there's no going back for me, now," she said. "I can't. The old life. I just can't." The reality of which pressed on us: the warm wet weight of future meat, the frantic hearts and fraught faces we'd get to know through the obscene intimacy of murder. You want disgust, but that's not what the Curse gives you. The Curse gives you the cunning to find room for the Curse. To welcome it. To love it. You contort and manoeuvre but eventually despite your wriggling its dirty truth holds you still: It's only the best for us if it's the worst for them.

"Is that what this is really about?" Madeline said, having found the sunglasses she was looking for in her purse, Bulgari wraparounds, gunmetal grey.

"What?"

"Is this what you really want to change?"

Walker, she meant. She saw so far into me I thought for the umpteenth time the sanest thing would just be for her and me to become lovers. It's the inner life that fucks up relationships: with her I wouldn't have one. My hands on the Cherokee's wheel felt heavy and electric and tired.

"There's something wrong with me," I said.

"There's nothing wrong with you."

"I've got everything I want."

"Wan*ted*. Wan*ted*. It's not going to stay the same, is it? If it did you might as well drop dead."

She put her booted foot up on the dash and stretched her arms back over her head. Glimpse through the t-shirt sleeve of nude white armpit, scent of floral deodorant, deeper sweet stink of *wulf*. Mischievous twinge in my clit. Jake's ghost pulling up its chair and reaching for the remote. I knew she was feeling it. Mentally I sent: Just ignore me. I'm a fucking mess.

She closed her eyes behind the shades. Had put them on, I now realised, to make the Walker conversation easier for me. Kindness was one of the dozens of the things Jake's skewed portrayal of this woman had missed.

"It's not even that," I said. "Or it's not just that. I love him. I mean I do, I *love* him."

"I know you're still thinking about him," she said.

Him.

Not Walker.

Remshi.

I released a breath I didn't know I'd been holding.

"Feel free to laugh," I said. "I know it's ridiculous."

"D'you think this other thing's connected with him? All this stuff with the book and a cure and all that?" Then she made the predictable leap: "Wait. You think it's the same person? You think Olek *is* Remshi?"

"No," I said. "The voice was different, and I don't know why he'd bother pretending to be someone else, since I know who he is. But I can't help thinking there's a connection. That's really what this is, if you want the truth. Christ, this is more embarrassing than having a crush on a fucking vampire. Are you ready? Ever since I met him I've had this feeling that there's something going on. That there's a kind of . . ."

"What?"

I could barely bring myself to say it. Wished for a moment she was reading me again, so I wouldn't have to.

"A kind of meaning to it," I said, feeling slightly sick.

After a few moments Maddy said: "No, you're right. It's not."

*Not Madeline's department*, was what I'd been thinking.

"Don't be offended," I said. "It's not mine, either. In fact it's a sort of retardedness. I thought I was done with all that crap. Jake's probably turning in his grave. Except he never got one. I don't even know what happened to his body. What the fuck is *wrong* with me?" Because suddenly I was on the verge of tears.

"Here," Madeline said, producing a quarter bottle of Bacardi from her purse, unscrewing the cap and passing it to me. "For God's sake, have a drink."

I took a pull. The shock and shudder (last night's tequila had thought it was being left to rest in peace) did actually help, short-circuited the tears, or at least took the emotion out of them.

"Ever since I met him I've had this feeling," I repeated, determined to get it out without fuss, "that this isn't just all random crap. It's as if someone's watching it all, or making it up."

"Like we're in a TV series."

"Exactly. Ex*actly*."

She took a drink, thought about it. Shook her head. "See that's the difference between you and me," she said. "I don't care if we're in a TV series as long as it's good. As long as I get . . . you know, a good part."

"Seriously? You wouldn't care? You wouldn't want to know?"

More thought. "It's like . . ."

*Madeline isn't used to framing similes and metaphors*, Jake had written. *But she can blow her nail polish dry with unparalleled eloquence.*

"Like when you watch the extras on a DVD, behind the scenes and all that. I don't watch those bits anymore. It ruins it for me."

I started thinking: That's not the same, that's not analogous—but let it go. The precision of the analogy didn't matter. I knew what she meant. And it *was* a fundamental difference between us. In college there'd been a band called Miserable Socrates and the Happy Pigs.

"Well, either way," I said, "I can't get him out of my head. I'm *dreaming* about him, if you can believe that."

"Sex dreams?"

"Yes. And then we're walking on a beach at dusk, looking for something."

"What?"

"I don't know. I wake up."

She handed me the Bacardi and I took another bracing pull. "Anyway, fuck it," I said. "I can't start living life according to dreams at my age. Tell me how the Last Resort's going. It must be nearly finished by now."

Not a very convincing segue, but she let it go, for now. "Be finished in three weeks," she said. "All the electronics are in. Steels. Floors are done. You wouldn't recognise it."

The Last Resort—Fergus had called it that, jokingly, and the name had stuck—was a bunker in Croatia, designed by Walker and Konstantinov, project-managed by Madeline, built by a hand-picked team who'd been made to understand what breaking confidentiality would cost them and kitted-out with state-of-the-art security systems to be supported, eventually, by enough hardware to deal with a small army. Financed by the ludicrous fortune I'd inherited from Jake. We were all resigned to a life more or less on the run, but ever since what had happened two years ago I'd been determined to have a place of my own to die in, if it came to dying. Somewhere to put your back against the wall, as Fergus said.

"The upper floors are habitable," Maddy said. "But I should warn you now I've ignored your paint-everything-white crap. With all the steel it'd look like a bloody hospital. And don't have a benny. It's not floral wallpaper or anything. It's *nice*."

It was just after noon when we arrived at the villa. I'd been telling her about Trish's planned Harley trip around the Southern U.S.—but stopped mid-sentence as we pulled up at the end of the drive. She'd felt it, too.

Something was wrong.

"Wait! Lu! Wait!"

But I was already out of the car, blood loud, limbs dreaming, sprinting up the steps to the open front door.

# 20

DEATH VIVIFIES DETAIL despite the blur. The hallway's white floor and maple hatstand, the convex mirror that suddenly evoked the one in Van Eyck's *Arnolfini Marriage*, the red and green tricycles I'd bought the twins when we got here.

The twins. The twins. The twins. My sick heart was ahead of me, nosing the rank air beyond their loss/death/mutilation while the rest of me flung up like a black wall simply *No . . . No . . . No . . .*

There was the stink of blood, giant, unarguable with, mixed with the smell of meat cooked in wine. Onions. Fresh peaches, cut. Cigarette smoke. A human scent I didn't recognise.

You should've taken them with you to the airport. But they were so weary of airports. Now they're dead. And all the labour for nothing. Nothing.

But the blood was human. Only human. And Jacques Brel's "Amsterdam" was playing on the CD in the kitchen.

I knew before seeing.

He liked to kick us all out so he could cook and sing along in peace. I felt precisely the little portion of time left between my realisation and what would be Madeline's. Collective intuition had been part of the reason for her visit. The other part was here, on the floor, butchered, in a pool of blood.

Cloquet.

You don't speak. You don't go "Oh God." Not straight away. In the first pure moment of comprehension you simply dissolve into the reality of what you're seeing. It's transcendence, of a kind.

Then the same reality forces you out again, separate, compelled to negotiate, compelled to accept.

I ran to him, aware as I did so of Madeline arriving in the doorway behind me.

He'd been shot in the head then hacked with what must have been a hatchet or a machete. Or hacked first then finished with the bullet. Either way it was over. Either way he was gone. The solid fact—he's dead— expanded, filled the room, continued expanding. In spite of which, thanks to Hollywood, a part of me was waiting for the rasp, the gasp, the cough and flutter back into life. All the life we'd shared rushed up like a crowd that couldn't believe it wasn't going to be let in. The crowd that didn't realise the thing it had come to see was already over. I was imagining the twins' faces when I told them. *Cloquet has had to . . . Cloquet has gone to . . .* Old habits. My children didn't need euphemisms. Not for death, at any rate. They knew what death was. They watched their mother deal it. *Cloquet is dead.* Zoë would cry. She loved him. She *had* loved him. Lorcan wouldn't cry. Lorcan didn't cry. He was too curious for tears. My fault. The ordeal of his infancy I'd failed to prevent. He'd been introduced too early to loss, isolation, betrayal. He'd been introduced too early to not being able to count on anyone. Not even his mother.

Madeline put her bag on one of the kitchen chairs, very carefully, as if it contained a bomb. She stood over me, looking down at the body. She didn't touch him. They'd been occasional lovers for almost two years. Against all expectations something intense and quiet existed between them. Had existed between them. To me it was as if she'd given him a part of her old self, her human self, for safe-keeping. Only a human would be able to keep it safe. Only a human would want it.

I took out my cell and dialled Walker.

"Hey."

"Are the kids with you?"

"Yeah, we're at the beach. What's—"

"You need to get back here. Something's happened. Someone's been here." Pause, to give reality a chance to change its mind. Reality declined. "Cloquet's dead."

Irreversible now. I'd said it. I felt Madeline hearing the words. Involuntarily looked down at Cloquet's face. It was turned to the left, eyes (thank God) closed. His mouth was open. I thought of all the times he'd done small things for me. Lit my cigarette, handed me a cup of coffee, fastened the kids' shoes or hassled them to brush their teeth. He insisted on a cooked breakfast, for the two weeks in the month we ate regular food, whipped-up fresh herb omelettes, mackerel paté, soft-boiled eggs and soldiers for the twins. It was good to come downstairs in the mornings and find him, tow-haired, scowling, barefoot, making coffee, smoking. Sometimes with Zoë sitting up on the counter, talking to him, sharing the momentous business of her life.

"Are Lucy and Trish with you?" I asked.

"Lucy's here," he said. "Trish is shopping. Christ. Is Madeline there?"

His maker. For a second or two I hated him. For the connection. For how much the kids loved him. For not being, in spite of love, enough for me.

Then I wanted him there with me, the casual strength in his arms, the familiarity.

"She's here," I said. "We just got back from the airport and he was . . ." It was only now I noticed the Le Creuset casserole dish upturned on the floor, the food spattered, the sauce nudging the edge of his blood. Madeline reached over and turned the range's burning gas ring off.

"Take the kids straight upstairs when you get here," I said. "They can't see him like this."

"Have you checked the house?"

Idiot. Idiots, both of us. We should be better than this by now.

"Get Lorcan and Zoë in the car," I said. "You and Lucy stay with them. And call Trish. Don't move until I've called you back." I hung up, knowing he was going to say something else, issue some warning or advice, the male habit. Madeline was still standing, staring down at the corpse. Blood had gathered around my knees, her booted feet. My head felt hot, suddenly. *Wulf* had livened at the whiff of carnage. The hunger flickered, shrank back at the smell of the *bourguignon*.

I got to my feet.

WE HAVE TO CHECK THE—

I KNOW.

It was a relief to her, to have to do something. Her allowance of deferral was nearly spent. I could feel the reality coming to her: *Never hear hold feel his voice laugh life again. Never. Dead. Gone.* Her force field was heavy. The longer she stood still the worse it would be.

There was a Luger on the third shelf of the crockery cupboard and a Colt behind *Uncle Vanya* in the lounge. We moved silently, room by room.

Nothing. Sunlight on the waxed floors. Languid mote-galaxies. The odours of old rugs, crayons, mould, the kids' clothes, Lucy's new leather coat and faint whiff of Chanel No.19; the edgy sex Walker and I had had this morning, before the twins were awake. All the smells and colours of the life that no longer had Cloquet in it. The life that was nothing to him now. The house, the daylight, the hills that led eventually to the clamour of the world—all of it would go on without him. *We* would go on without him. That was how we honoured and disgraced the dead. And if there was an afterlife? A place of comeuppance or reward? Neither his love for us nor ours for him would count. Thanks to the arrogance that came with being (until recently) top of the food chain, betrayal of your species didn't feature in any of the human world's moral codes. But it wouldn't be a head-scratcher for heaven. Conspirator and accessory to murder. If there was a hell, he was going there. With which realisation, as usual, the ghost of my childhood faith withdrew. That hell was for people like Cloquet meant there was no such place.

I called Walker and told him the house was clear.

"Look at this," Madeline said. We were back in the kitchen. She'd put a cushion under Cloquet's head, closed his mouth. There was a precision to her movements. Death so close and ugly recharged her beauty, her finite perfections. She was in a different phase of shock, balanced between denial and belief. There was a lightness to it. I knew the feeling. "What does this mean?"

She was looking at a mark on one of the kitchen cabinets, drawn by a finger evidently dipped in Cloquet's blood. A vertical line with a small circle on top. Something that looked like the symbol for pi next to it. Something else that might be a crescent moon. It meant nothing to me.

"I don't know," I said. "But whoever did this knows we're not going to the police. There are fingerprints everywhere."

Your voice coming out is an offence, a blatant demonstration of your continuing life. Thinking, fingerprints, cause, effect, strategy, action. Life. Consciousness. Every time it registered it refreshed the fact of his death. It's one of the things that drives the impulse to remove the corpse, burn it, bury it, give it to the sea. The dead body makes the living one obscene. It's why we close the eyes, too. The dead shouldn't have to look on the lewd aliveness of the living.

"It's a religious thing," Madeline said.

"Is it? How do you know?"

"It's the fucking Angels. I've seen this sign in the ads."

"The Catholics?"

"They're killing familiars. Not just us. Everyone who helps——" Her voice cracked slightly on the word "helps." The balance between denial and belief was tipping. Belief. He's dead. Thinking of what losing him meant to her postponed what it meant to me. *Mon ange. Chèrie.* The casual endearments taken for granted. The life taken for granted.

"It doesn't make sense," I said. "If they knew he was here they'd know we were here. Why give themselves away?"

She shook her head, let the theory go. Let the thinking go. I knew what she was realising.

LOVE.

She closed her eyes. Swallowed. Didn't cry.

# 21

IT TOOK WALKER a lot of calls to get a boat at short notice. High season, everything booked. Eventually he told the hire company to call anyone they thought might be willing to return their vessel early for a fee. Which the hire company did, as well as translating it into an opportunity to slap on an extra twenty per cent. Even in our state the little rip-off registered, dismal, reliable, an affirmation of the world's shrugging, grinning continuance. Blackly funny, in fact, if you let yourself see it that way.

These and other practicalities (wrapping and tying the body, finding stones and junk to weight it, downloading the shipping lanes and working out where to make the drop) did what it's their job to do in the face of death: demanded small actions that stopped you giving yourself entirely to the loss. Nonetheless reality kept refreshing its page for me, this new version without Cloquet in it. There's nothing so mundane it can't speak the new absence: a teaspoon; a TV ad; the shadow of a bird passing overhead. For a short while a sore formed where murder rubbed against bereavement. Vestigial circuitry said killing and eating people disqualified me from grief. But *wulf* did what it does: Simply insisted. Simply burned through. Simply defied. The same shrugging, grinning continuance. The nature of life. The nature of the beast.

We waited until after midnight then took the *Sirius* (a thirty-five-foot cabin cruiser cop-show education said was normally home to bikini'd escorts tanning between drug lord blow-jobs) out into the Tyrrhenian Sea. Lucy, whose Henley-on-Thames family had had boats, drove, though Walker had been given the basics by the bandit at the rental office. Trish was with me, Madeline and the kids in the stern, a luxurious snug of waxed walnut and cream leather, chrome fittings and trim. Madeline hadn't officially cancelled her Spanish arrangements but it was known between us she'd stay with us now for the kill. (The kill? Oh, yes. Have no illusions. The hunger treats everything apart from its own gratification with egalitarian indifference. Depressed? Heartbroken? Bereaved? It's all one to *wulf.* Full moon rises. You change. You need what you need, so you do what you do. The kill—like the show—must go on.)

"D'you think he'd hate being buried at sea?" Madeline asked me. It was much cooler on the water, half an hour out from the harbour. We'd passed the dark little islands: Zannone, Ponza, Palmarola, Ventotene and tiny Santo Stefano. The sky was black and star-crammed and low. It felt artificial, like a planetarium. The sudden nearness to it and the smell of the water had woken us back up to the honourable alive finiteness of our bodies, bare hands and throats and faces and the fresh salt air around them. "I mean I know it's the safest thing," Madeline said, "but it seems so fucking lonely."

I'd had the same thought. I didn't recall Cloquet ever stating burial preferences, but the sea seemed wrong for him, somehow. You tell yourself not to be stupid—the dead don't care because the dead can't care (unless of course they're the dead you've eaten, who find a curious cramped afterlife in you)—but still, some people you can imagine happy enough in a coffin being gradually reclaimed for the earth by bugs, others going into the fire and sighing away in a quick consummation, some— equipped with robust atheism or black humour—content to become the freshman prank-fodder of medical science. What I couldn't imagine was Cloquet being okay all alone in billions of tons of dark water, the prey of fish, big and small.

Which thinking brought Quinn's book back. Death. Spirits. Gods. Underworlds. Afterlives. The possibility of someone, somewhere, knowing what it was all about. The hope of seeing Jake again, albeit in hell.

"I don't like it, either," I said to Madeline. "But I don't think we have a choice." A land burial was too risky. Bodies got found. Inquests got opened. Questions got asked. And we didn't have time.

"I know it's not going to make any difference to him," Madeline said, lighting a Winston for something to do. "I know that. I just . . . I don't like the thought of him all alone down there. In the dark."

Lucy had said it would take us a couple of hours to reach the coordinates Walker had picked, almost equidistant from the Italian mainland, Sardinia to the northwest and Sicily to the southeast, but the whole day since the morning had hung in dream or imaginal time. The twins were quiet again, after the brief excitement of Going On The Boat. It had sidelined the other fact, temporarily. But the pack mood had dragged them back to it. When I'd told them Cloquet was gone—*dead*, I made myself use the word—they'd both wanted to see him. Maddy and I cleaned and covered him as best we could but there was no disguising the violence of his death. Zoë didn't cry until she took his hand and found it cold. She knows what death is, of course. She's watched me kill. She's eaten the flesh, lapped the blood, gnawed the bones. But that's *them*. The humans. I doubt she'd ever had Cloquet in the same category, even though that's what he was. We're like those racists who exempt their favourite Indian waiter: No, not *you*, Raj. *You're* all right. Lorcan had startled me by asking: Where will he go?—until I realised it wasn't a metaphysical question. He meant: Where will you put him? He's a very practical child—but he's not altogether cold. Denial kept coming and going in his face like the sun going in and out of cloud.

Now, as Lucy cut the engine and the boat came to unrestful rest on the swell, both children drew close to me, one at each leg. Walker and Lucy came down from the upper deck. Madeline tossed her cigarette into the water. Comedy, of course, lives for serious moments. Manhandling the corpse with its weights onto the gunwale we could feel the sprites of farce dying to get a look-in, the misbalance that would see us dropping him prematurely, or one of the chained stones crashing onto someone's foot.

"Does anyone want to say anything?" Walker asked. He, Trish and Lucy had stepped back a little. Only Maddy and I held the body in place. What was there to say? *Here we commit to the waves the body of Paul Cloquet, abused child, former male model, drug-addict, lately human familiar and conspirator to werewolf murder . . .*

"I know it doesn't count for much," Lucy said, "but at least it's a beautiful night."

Which turned out to be all the eulogy he needed. For a few moments Madeline and I kept our hands on the body, then, feeling each other knowing it was now, now, let's let him go, oh God, goodbye, goodbye, sorry, sorry, I love you (impossible in the moment's meld to separate our thoughts or the feeling of fracture in her my our chest)—we let him go. Pushed gently, firmly, until the weight rolled, passed its fulcrum (we shared a horror-flash of his eyes suddenly opening under the tarp, Where am I? What the fuck)—then dropped the dozen feet into the sea.

# 22

THE OBSCENITY AND sadness and inevitability over the next two days was that we didn't talk about what it could or would or did mean that Madeline was sticking around for the kill. She tried. Not out loud, not even face to face. I was in the bath the morning after the "funeral" (*wulf* drives me there with its lashings-out and rakings and swipes) dosed up with codeine and grass and scotch. I felt her outside the door. She had her back and palms flush to the wall. I thought how good her trim waist would feel to Walker in his hands.

HEY.

HEY.

YOU'VE GOT NOTHING TO—

I KNOW. IT'S OKAY. PLEASE LET'S NOT.

The problem was she knew there was no promise she could make and keep. Promises get sucked into fuckkilleat like paper scraps into a furnace. For a while she stood there, thinking: *I'll go. I should go. I can't.* She'd worn this loop out. Pack gravity compelled us, now. No argument. Without the weakness of grief she might've been able to break free, but Cloquet's death had gone deep. For both of us.

•

"Where did you get the information?" I asked Fergus.

"Come on, Lu," he said. "I don't take risks. Trust me. It's watertight. Although you've got to wonder how tough this was before people decided to start living their lives on fucking Facebook."

Fergus, fifty-three and a functioning alcoholic sales rep for Toyota with a physique like Baloo the bear when he was Turned, had lost weight and improved his wardrobe. Gone the womanish butt and pendulous paunch, gone the machine washable suit. Money and the prospect of a four-hundred-year lifespan had bucked his aesthetic ideas up. He'd put some time in at the gym, shaved off the perennial stubble, got a trendy haircut and kitted himself out with smart dark casuals that actually fit. I was round his Fulham flat the other day, Madeline had told me with delighted distaste. You should see the bathroom cabinet. It's like the fucking Avon Lady lives there. Seriously, right, he goes, Mads, these pore minimisers—do they work?

We'd met him at Grenoble as planned. What would *not* be as planned— sans Cloquet—was the absence of a getaway driver. Which would mean killing late and travelling fast. Fergus, who took a weird delight in the logistics, had had very little time to rearrange.

"This is the way it works," he said, unfolding a Google map satellite printout. "The house is here, five miles from Charmes sur-l'Herbasse. We leave the vehicles here"—he pointed with a propelling pencil; I noticed he'd had a manicure—"where this trail comes off the road into the woods. One mile in: change site. You know the drill. Moonrise is at 2108. That's going to mean sitting on our feckin hands for . . . I'm saying four hours to be on the safe side. Which leaves two hours to get there, make the kill, get back to the site. We've got to time it right. Once we leave the house we don't want to be in the vicinity any longer than we have to."

We were sitting in the back of a three-year-old Fleetwood RV in a rest area just outside Le Chalon. (I was imagining its former owners as silver-haired retirees in golf slacks. Or a Middle American family the economic meltdown had smashed, all the barbecues and Xboxes and kids' bikes and bonuses and healthcare gone, all the minor irritations magnified by suddenly not having money. Having money now—a *lot* of money—I knew one thing for sure: If you had a lot of money and you were miserable, you'd be miserable poor. You'd be miserable, just without the consolation of quality towels and thirty-dollar cocktails.) Second and third vehicles were lined up between Grenoble and Geneva, from whence . . . Well, that wasn't decided. It seemed madness to go back to the villa at Terracina since someone—presumably the goddamned *Militi Christi*—knew we were there, though it was understood between Maddy and me that finding Cloquet's killers was loud on the inner list. If it hadn't been for the kids we'd have gone back there and waited for them to try again. Fergus was returning to London to oversee half a dozen land deals, then on to Croatia to push the completion of the Last Resort through. Lucy had planned to come back to Italy with me for a week (there remained two or three Roman galleries she hadn't seen; the woman was obsessive) and Trish was supposed to go to the U.S., where she had a Harley rented for a two-week road trip around the Southern states. Walker, I'd supposed (in a knot of love and claustrophobia) would come with me, wherever I went. I'd supposed. I *had* supposed. We hadn't spoken properly since Cloquet's death. I could feel him thinking it had accelerated our disease. My disease. My room for other things. *I'll see you again . . .*

From the upper bunk on the left, Lucy groaned. The last few hours before Transformation laid her low. Trish, too; she was in the second bunk, knees drawn up to her chest, cold-sweating, shivering. Walker was on his feet but visibly suffering, face thin-skinned and grey, thread veins you never saw at any other time of the month, cramps and spasms he rode with jaws clenched, shuddering. I wasn't much better off. Blisters of *wulf* swelled and burst in my blood, the monster's idiot insistence that its will could break the moon's rules. The big skull seemed to form at moments like a leaden helmet around my own. It was a surprise to put your hand up and not feel the snout there, the muzzle, the broad cheekbones, the huge breath. I wandered in and out of the negligible effects of codeine and ibuprofen. Booze would've helped—but it would also have made me drunk, and there was too much at stake not to go in sober. Only Madeline, Fergus and Zoë—blessed, randomly—remained pre-Transformation symptom free. Poor Lorcan lay in the fetal position, very still, eyes wide, breathing through his nose, holding Zoë's hand.

"Everyone clear?" Fergus asked. His Chanel *pour homme* wasn't doing Walker and me any olfactory favours.

"For fuck's sake, Ferg, we've got it," Trish said. "Let's *go* already. I can't stand this waiting."

It was an hour's drive to Charmes sur-l'Herbasse. Another half-hour down single-width lanes inadequately supplied with passing bays to the trailhead. By the time we got there I was in my full-of-beans stage. It's what happens: gastric, osteo and muscular misery morphs into inane energy and the attention span of a gnat. The Curse has a thing for contrast: frivolity one minute, homicide the next. I sat up front with Fergus, who drove, the hunger pounding in both of us. The hunger speaks with diminishing sophistication: starts with glimpses and hints, echoes of previous kills, the multiple accents and notes, snatches of swallowed lives shot from arty angles, a complex prose poem or post-modern score. But the moon insists on simplicity. The free-verse epic becomes a sonnet, the sonnet a limerick, the limerick babytalk, the babytalk the beat of a drum. Eventually there's nothing but the rhythm of blind and deafened need. It's peace, of a sort, a return to original silence.

We parked the RV at the trailhead, took our knapsacks and clean-up kits, our liquid soap and our wet wipes. Went into the forest, selected our spots. Walker came with me and the twins, though the vibe between us was strained. The evening was warm and still and smell of the trees gave us the feeling of being in a friendly labyrinthine wardrobe. We settled under an enormous horse chestnut. I was thinking of a line I'd read (*1984?*): *Under the spreading chestnut tree, I sold you and you sold me . . .* Moonrise was fifteen minutes away. Fergus's arrangements never went wrong. I could hear him and Maddy talking softly nearby about an industrial coatings company they were thinking of buying.

When Walker spoke, I knew a split second before what he was going to say.

"Have you seen him again?"

Weeks without going anywhere near it and now, out of nowhere, this: "Him." The vampire. Remshi. No point pretending I didn't know who we were talking about.

"No," I said, my face warming.

"But you're waiting to." Statement, not question. We weren't looking at each other. Amongst other things I was thinking it was a relief to have done with secrecy. It was like taking off a too-tight shoe.

"It feels inevitable," I said. "I know that sounds stupid."

For a few moments he tossed a pine cone back and forth with Lorcan, who threw it back harder every time, as if the game were an argument. Zoë had climbed into the lower branches of the horse chestnut tree. The moon was touching me, a little lozenge of cold heat under the roof of my skull. Another between my legs. In spite of everything I thought of how its salving and seductive light would feel on my bare nipples and a circuit of pleasure lit up for a moment across my chest.

Walker said: "Is it like that?"

*Like that.* Is it a sexual attraction.

Lie? (Dream footage flashed.) Walker felt it, picked it up, though he was trying to have this conversation the honourable old-fashioned way.

"Yes," I said. "But that's not the . . . That's not important."

IT IS TO ME.

"We're doing this *now?*" I said. Relief or not, moonrise was close enough to make a domestic heart-to-heart absurd.

Walker didn't answer, though I could feel him turning emotional options over like coins of different currencies: anger; jealousy; desire; curiosity; sadness; liberation.

"It doesn't have to mean any more than it does," I said, but the moon was losing patience; the moon was getting a little annoyed. "Zoë, honey, come here. Lorcan? Come on."

Walker was on his feet, leaning against the tree, breathing hard. The twins were crouched next to each other, almost touching. The change drove them close, a reminder perhaps of their days coiled together in my womb.

*You may not want this for yourself, but you'll want it for your children. Because if you don't act now, they'll die . . .*

Walker sank to his knees, then onto all-fours.

# 23

OUR VICTIMS' HOUSE was a run-down T-shaped chateau set in seven acres—meadow, woodland, orchard, scrub—and we formed a loose circle around it. Zoë stayed close behind me, as she'd been taught (I could feel her half a yard off my right heel), but Lorcan disobeyed me and went with Walker. It was one of many small acts of contempt the boy performed, one of many small punishments: he'd been only minutes old when the vampires kidnapped him, and I'd got him back before he turned three months; too young to remember the details, you'd think. But the grammar of the thing had gone into him, that I'd failed him, that I'd let them take him, that Mother's first act was to demonstrate she couldn't be counted on. In the years to come he would refine these punishments, I knew. It would be a rationed violence I'd have to bear. I would bear it, but not, my heart had already told me, forever. I had, whether I liked it or not, the sort of self that would eventually decide enough was enough. He'd have to either forgive me or go his way. My mother's ghost smiled. Hard Colleen Gilaley, they'd called her.

The occupants (Fergus's intelligence is infallible) were two couples, Alan and Sue Yates, sixty-three and sixty-one, respectively, their daughter, Carmel, and their son-in-law, Rory. Carmel and Rory were both thirty-four.

Sue was in love with her husband, Alan. Or rather Sue was terrified of Alan leaving her. Alan was in love with his daughter, Carmel. Rory had thought he was in love with Carmel when they first met but he wasn't in love with her anymore. He was simply afraid of her. Carmel was in love with herself. No one, sadly, was in love with Sue, although Rory had surprised himself by having the occasional startlingly satisfying mother-and-daughter fantasy (the woman was *sixty-one*, for fuck's sake), usually with Sue being forced by Carmel to go down on her, which she did (in Rory's fantasy) with visible and arousing reluctance.

The Restoration (upper-cased in the minds of all four, since it had taken over their lives) was Alan's idea. He'd made a little money. Two lucky London house moves in the price-hiking Nineties—Denmark Hill, Balham—had left him with a £400,000 profit, and hundreds of episodes of *Grand Designs* and *A Place in the Sun* had left him with a vision of himself in benign lordship over a quality B&B—the word *gîte* was rarely off the familial lips—in France. Which vision might never have progressed beyond idle fantasy had it not been for Rory losing (a) his job and (b) all the money he had in a string of wretched investments. Of course this was the global economic clusterfuck—*everyone* lost money (even Jake's satirically huge fortune took a thirty per cent hit)—but what made it tough for Rory was that he didn't have much to lose in the first place, and he lost the lot, as well as racking up a hundred grand's worth of debt. In a way it was a relief to him. He'd painted a completely false picture of their affluence for Carmel, for the simple reason that Carmel insisted on a certain level of affluence. There was Bose in the lounge, Prada in the walk-in, Audi in the garage. And more or less permanent fire in Rory's armpits, livened by the arrival of every windowed envelope. By rights, on full disclosure, Carmel ought to have ditched him—a development which would have been a large part of Rory's relief—but she didn't. Who knew why? Well, oddly, in her timid and denied heart, *Sue* knew why. Because without anything being said between them Alan and Carmel, father and daughter, saw it would be pleasurable to keep Rory around for a little while to make him suffer. Punishment for Lying was Carmel's superficial rationalisation, while Alan (who had an impregnable image of himself as a Decent Bloke, and began most of his sentences "To be fair . . .") went for Giving the Lad a Second Chance. Therefore Rory was, with a sort of stern magnanimity, *spoken to* by Alan. Carmel, in Alan's idiom, was invariably "my Carmel" (pronounced "mar Carmel") and when she was in his thoughts he was never far from intense emotion. He was in unembarrassed tears by the end of the talk with Rory, overwhelmed by the ferocity of his, Alan's, love for his daughter and by his, Alan's, financial and spiritual largesse. By the end of what he'd assumed would be a merciless dressing down Rory found himself tremulously—and indeed terrifyingly, Alan being a big, solid man, at that moment radiant with paternal heat—embraced.

And so The Restoration had begun. Rory was given responsibilities which, being incompetent, he failed to discharge, drawing sighs from

Alan, scoffs from Carmel and winces (off-stage) from Sue. It was all grist to the father-daughter mill. Not, of course, that anything improper had ever *happened* between father and daughter (Alan, quivering with disgust, would do violence to you for thinking it), which was a pity; its simmering latency was nauseating.

When we entered the building, Carmel was sitting on her bed painting her toenails and listening to Rihanna. Alan and Sue were in the kitchen, Sue preparing the evening's casserole, Alan going over the paperwork detailing Rory's latest mismanagements, shaking his head with sad delight and mentally rehearsing his tone of near-exhausted patience: Rory . . . Rory. These are elemental mistakes, mate. Ele*mental* . . . Rory meanwhile was simply standing in what would, when it was Restored, be the laundry room, wondering for the $n$th time how his life had so quickly turned so much to shit and how long it would be before he got his next weary drubbing from Alan and whether he didn't yet have the courage to tell them all to go and fuck themselves and walk out. Or better still slip away without a word in the middle of the night—

Sue, midway between countertop and range, saw us first.

Us. Me and Walker. (Zoë and Lorcan under strict telepathic instruction to stay put in the hall until called to feed; Lorcan not ready to push his luck with me on this one.) So Sue saw us. Me and Walker, two werewolves, standing there *looking at her.*

"I mean for Christ's sake, Rory," Alan said, momentarily forgetting to keep the rehearsals in his head, "this is fifteen-hundred quid here, mate. It's not like we can afford—fuck!"

Sue had, after what seemed an extraordinarily long time, dropped the casserole dish, which had exploded on the stone floor. She didn't scream. It's amazing how often people don't scream. Instead her mouth lost its shape and let out a very quiet, wobbling "ohhhh" which, left unchecked, I knew would just keep repeating, indefinitely.

"What the—" Alan started but then saw Sue was looking at something behind him—and turned.

Upstairs, Carmel *did* scream. Fergus and Trish (who sometimes got it on together in lupine form but never in human) had introduced themselves. A clatter and crash from the laundry room (I pictured Rory backing into a bucket and mop) said Madeline and Lucy had arrived, too.

# 24

IT'S A THING of beauty to see your victim in perfected extremis like that, maximally himself, all his life's forgotten details recalled in a rush, as if for the first time since birth every cell's at full, living attention. The individual's odour at this moment—your odour *facing death*—is cruelly sweet, an ecstatic tension before the snap that throws us into attack.

I leaped over the table, over agog Alan's head, and at the end of my parabola opened Sue's belly with a contemptuously casual downward swipe. She sank to her knees—oven-mitted arms still weirdly holding the ghost of the dish—then fell against my legs as if in confused supplication. I grabbed her by the hair, tugged her head back, dropped and sank my teeth into her throat, sensing, as I did, Lorcan peeking round the kitchen door—NOT YET NOT SAFE YET STAY THERE—and Zoë's little tremor of guilt and excitement because she wasn't far behind him, while Walker punched through open-mouthed Alan's chest and laid giant fingers around his hot and haywire heart and upstairs Fergus entered Trish from behind as she pinned Carmel (legs and arms flailing, face fat with backed-up blood) to the bed by her throat and Lucy lifted Rory off his feet by his hair and the house filled with the concussive smell of traumatised flesh and blood and the condensed quiet music of death.

*It's only the best for us if it's the worst for them.*

The central truth of the Curse, as succinctly put by one Jacob Marlowe, deceased. No one wants it to be true. But the truth doesn't care what anyone wants. The truth is innocent. You can't blame the truth.

Walker had a huge erection. (Yes, I'm afraid this is precisely what the Curse means by "the best for us." Long ago in a fetid and poorly lit cellar of the universe a wretched marriage ceremony took place between our arousal and your suffering. God gave you away. No pre-nup: divorce was never an option.) I was in a state myself, but not an uncomplicated one. *Wulf*'s desire was there, deep and dumb and reliable, but so, undeniably, was the dismal impulse to shit on love's altar, to force through the bill of betrayal. Once when I was small my mother had found me in the yard in tears because I'd trod on a snail and half mashed it. She'd said: It's very simple, Lulu. If you know something's dying in pain, kill it. Then she'd stomped on it and whisked away to answer the phone.

The last of Sue's life was going. I'd had her liver and kidneys and several big chunks from her midriff and haunch. In with the meat had gone the frail fragments of a life lived on tiptoe, a few big moments like standing stones—the day at St. Catherine's when she'd got her first period in the middle of hockey and run from the pitch in tears; breaking her leg when Jane Radcliffe's swing collapsed; the surreal afternoon when, knowing it was insane, she'd gone down by the river with the boy from the fair and he'd got angry when she wouldn't and she'd thought she was going to get raped; her first time—with Alan, the appalled intimation that it might be better, *much* better, with someone else, but letting the idea go, like a bird released from her hands that would never come home; giving birth to Carmel, seeing Alan's solar glow when he held her; her demented father in the nursing home not recognising her, accusing her of stealing his cardigan. The World was the ITN News and the *Daily Telegraph* and Carmel's i-gadgets and wars always with some foreigners and toothless old women in burkas always screaming over someone's body and even though she knew it was terrible imagine if your son had been killed she wished they wouldn't scream and wail like that with no teeth and the men were no better screaming and carrying on and wrapping their arms around the coffin Alan said our immigration's the laughing stock of the world and not enough whites having kids now because of women having careers and the Muslims breed like rats and pretty soon they'll outnumber us ten to one and it did seem like they were everywhere now there was a *weather* girl in a burka the other day . . .

NO. I CAN'T.

Walker, bloody up to the elbows, had put his hands on my hips.

I WANT YOU.

I CAN'T. THE OTHERS.

*Go* to the others, I meant. Trish. Lucy.

Madeline.

YOU.

IT'S OKAY. I WANT YOU TO.

Lorcan and Zoë were in the room. I hadn't called them, exactly, but the mental restriction had slackened. They were waiting for permission to feed. When I gave it, neither of them hesitated. Zoë scampered to the wounds in Sue's midriff, but Lorcan leaped up onto the table and began tearing at Alan's corpse. We didn't operate a not-in-front-of-the-children policy (they'd seen what adulthood added to the kill, but they didn't understand it; it was already a nagging tumour, the question of what I'd do with them when puberty kicked in) but their presence this time confirmed me.

I CAN'T. PLEASE. DON'T.

Pause.

It seemed to last a long time, that pause. In it, I felt him taking it completely into himself that I was leaving him. Had been for months. Maybe years. Maybe two years. Maybe since the night the vampire came to call. It shocked me. As long as Walker hadn't believed it there was room for a little denial in me. But now he did—and it was like sudden cold air coming up from a sheer drop behind me. Immediately I wanted to undo it, to tell him he was wrong, that we'd stay together, that whatever this was it wasn't the end of us, that I loved him, of course I did, my God this was *us*—

But at that moment bullets shattered the kitchen window and I realised we were under attack.

# 25

WALKER HAD LORCAN safe. Not safe, but out of the kitchen and into the stairwell, walled on both sides. Original walls, two and a half feet thick. I hadn't been aware of grabbing Zoë, nor of leaping for the stairs after Walker—but there we were. He and Lorcan were already on the first-floor landing. I could hear windows smashing. Searchlights swivelled. I was conscious of some brain department riffling through calculations—*two points of attack so far; how many miles to the RV? why hadn't we arranged a contingency rendezvous?*—while the big engines of panic churned blood and haemorrhaged adrenaline and moving was a thing of slow delicious vividness—here's my enormous leaden leg bending its knee to climb another step . . . and here's my giant head lunging through the molasses of emptiness . . . The chateau breathed its odour of damp plaster and dust, avowed in a sad silent way its harmless existence here for two hundred years; it was like a gentle old person forced to witness some modern obscenity in the street. Sue's spilled blood and beef and onion casserole brought Cloquet's death back along with the certainty that these were the same assassins. It irritated me, in the midst of all this physical immediacy, that the world had to interfere with us, that the world couldn't leave well alone.

But of course as far as the world was concerned we weren't well, we couldn't be left alone.

Walker shoo'd Lorcan back down to me as an explosion did big damage to the building's fabric somewhere on the first floor. Incredibly, a severed human foot flew past Walker's shoulder, struck the wall beside me and bounced down the stairs. Painted toenails (a colour very close to "Scarlet Vamp," my disinterested ironist observed); Carmel.

Madeline, snout and hands and arms jewelled with winking gore, appeared in the doorway that led from the kitchen into the hall. A huge shard of glass was sticking out of her back. She didn't seem to know it was there.

LUCY?

I LOST HER TOO MANY OF THEM SILVER SILVER SILVER—

I could feel it, too, on my tongue, in the roof of my mouth. Lorcan and Zoë had their hands over their ears, not understanding it was too late for that, that the metal's threat and promise was already in the air, in their heads, their lungs, their blood.

Madeline reached out as if to fend off a negligible invisible blow—then sank to her knees.

At which point I saw the two men behind her.

Both young, trim, fair-haired, giddy with health and taut with training. Light combat fatigues in dull grey, niftily designed to accommodate the silver-delivery gadgetry. One of them held what looked like a scimitar. Not silver (only an idiot would make a sword out of silver) but that wouldn't matter, since its purpose was to separate werewolf head from werewolf body, werewolf life from the universe.

DON'T MOVE DON'T MOVE WALKER THE KIDS—

Since if I didn't move myself Madeline would die and the instruction to Walker and the imperative to Zoë and Lorcan were left behind like a bright smudge in my slipstream because I was flying through the air—in slow motion, always in slow motion, with time to feel three, four, five silver bullets cut my aura but not my flesh, leisure to see Sue's moist guts like something her body had heaved out with the very last of its strength and Alan's head all but severed, eyes open, tongue trapped between his teeth and the windows shattered and figures moving outside and a female voice screaming *Gloria Patri! et Filio! et Spiritui Sancto!*—time to take in all this (and to examine from all angles what might be the last shape of my life: besotted with a vampire; hurting my lover; distracted from my kids; infected again with the suspicion of a plot and simultaneously a little sick of myself, my greed, my promiscuous curiosity, my nothing ever being quite enough so perhaps this is what gives you the courage to risk death—time for all this before, with a detonation of blood that speeded time and space back up to normal, I landed hands-first on the guy with the scimitar, the blade of which went with extraordinary ease, with a delight in performing its function, clean through my lower left abdominals and out the back of me with a feeling of ice that I knew within seconds would become fire.

I ignored it. First contact had buried the claws of my right hand in his throat just above the Adam's apple. I tightened my grip and pulled. Out came the trachea and a fistful of blood vessels. Sufficient damage—but there was no time for self-congratulation. Nor was there time to pull the sword out of my guts. I looked up to see the second guy standing over me. He'd learned a valuable lesson: Don't fuck around trying to cut heads off when you've got a holy .44 Magnum with a chamber full of silver bullets at your disposal. The gun was pointed directly at my head.

# 26

THE BRAIN'S AN honest organ. It began the avoidance calculations—time, mass, speed, energy, angles, trajectories—but couldn't disguise their pointlessness. The gunman's finger already had the trigger halfway through its spring. I was going to die. I felt the future like a vast dark landscape full of huge sharp things and my children being blown and tumbled around in it alone, lost.

I'M SORRY, I sent them. I'M SO—

Then something smashed into the gunman's face and knocked him off his feet.

A piece of rubble the size of a bowling ball. Flung by Walker. An explosion had wrecked the room opposite the head of the stairs. In one move I pulled the scimitar out—felt the tissues scream—and thrust it straight through the assassin's midriff and into the wooden floor.

OUT! NOW!

Madeline had struggled to her feet and Walker had come back down the stairs and pulled the glass shard out of her. The twins were huddled between the two of them. My most perverse self said: That's the proper picture. That's how it should have been. Walker and Maddy and the twins. You don't love anyone enough. You don't have love. Just fucking curiosity. Like your mother.

NOW!

But all the ground-floor exits were covered. The house was encircled by thirty Angels at least, and *all* the ammunition was silver. Even with our speed we'd be hit. The woods beyond had a beautiful darkness and large, indifferent sentience.

FUCK! *FUCK!*

ROOF. THEY'RE CLOSE ENOUGH. OVER THEM.

If we could get up on the roof there was a chance we'd be able to jump clear of their perimeter. It wouldn't guarantee not getting hit, but they were less likely to be looking over their own heads than at the building's obvious exits.

We went back to the stairs, Zoë on my hip, Lorcan clinging to Walker's back. Madeline had recovered from whatever had debilitated her. Plaster and brick dust swirled.

OH GOD.

Half the front wall of Carmel and Rory's room had been blown away and the fresh smell of the night came in mixed with the stink of gunfire. Carmel's body had been ripped in half—though by the explosion or by Trish and Fergus it was impossible to tell.

OH GOD.

We'd all felt it, a moment before seeing it. Trish's body, splayed, dead. One arm was bent awkwardly under her, her head twisted to the left, mouth open, fat tongue lolling. Thirty or forty bullet-holes, the ether still migrained from where the silver had gone into her, the terrible reaction that touched all of us in our mouths and nostrils, bittered our saliva, turned our guts.

There was no time. There was the fact of the death—everything that was Trish—that had *been* Trish—began the rush together, the panicked gathering in us so we would know all that we'd lost—but there was no time, no time—bullets spattered the wall behind my head and a searchlight's beam swung—

THIS WAY!

Down the landing a second flight led up to another floor. Four more bedrooms, a half-plumbed bathroom, a tiny water-closet, ladders and tarps, bare plaster, an exercise bike, a brass curtain rod . . . Zoë, clinging tight to me, was trying to find room to accommodate Trish, lying like that with her tongue out it meant it meant that thing that happens to the humans that happens but and what will where will she go—

HERE. UP.

Walker had found the hatch in the ceiling that led up into the attic or loft. He set Lorcan down, bent his knees, leaped, straight up. The hatch crashed open. He got a purchase and hoisted himself up.

KIDS.

Lorcan first, tossed up by Madeline. Then Zoë, full of gossiping adren-

aline. IT'S ALL RIGHT, ANGEL, WE'RE GETTING OUT OF
HERE.

Three skylights. We would have very little time. No time, really. Three
or four seconds, maybe, before the first shooter spotted us.

Madeline was first out. I passed Zoë up to her (felt her LIE FLAT ON
YOUR TUMMY, SWEETHEART) then Lorcan.

GO!

Walker. I didn't argue. A second later I'd joined Madeline and the kids,
prostrate on the cold shingles. It was better than it might have been: two
of the house's half-dozen chimney stacks shielded us on two sides. We
had to go simultaneously. Fast, high, hard. Three at once (and the twins)
would be more confusing. Spread their fire. Make them miss. The lies you
tell yourself. The necessary lies.

YOU HOLD *VERY TIGHT*. BOTH OF YOU—UNDERSTAND?

Walker took Lorcan again. Zoë scrambled onto my back, wrapped her
arms around me. It was a fifty- or sixty-foot jump. Hit the ground running.
Eighty yards to the trees. And then? And *then*? The RV was no good to us
in this state, and there were still two hours to moonset. Two options: get
back to the change site, pick up the clothes and get as far away as possible,
or fuck the change site (which they'd more than likely have covered), hit
the nearest house and take our chances killing the inhabitants and stealing *their* clothes. Clothes. The inability to drive with these hands and feet.
Practicalities. Like a group of happy idiots you could never ditch. You've
got to laugh. Except when you've got two three-year-olds laughing's not
always an option.

READY?

YES.

NOW!

We jumped.

As with all actions performed because other options have ceased to
exist, it was a relief. I had time to notice a torn sheet of hurrying cloud
just below the moon (while the moon reminded me I hadn't eaten enough),
and, glancing down, to pick out the upturned face of one of the Angels, a
young man not more than twenty, wearing some sort of protective head-
gear (a cross between a boxer's headguard and a cycle helmet) that framed

a sweet, sharp-featured, androgynous face. He was looking up in just the way he would've looked up—freckled, wide-eyed—at a spectacular firework when he was little.

Walker hit the ground a split-second before me. Madeline landed close. The forest rushed towards us like a crowd storming a barricade, full of love. Gunfire and wildly swung searchlights and a voice screaming some order over and over in Italian that mine wasn't good enough to catch.

Then the tiny detail of something sharp going into the back of my left thigh—before everything went black.

# Part Three

# The Prophecy

# 27
## *Remshi*

WHICH WAS WHY my sweet Justine had kept shtoom. If I found love again, she thought, there would be no room in my life for her. And what would finding Talulla—Vali reborn—be if not love?

"I know why you didn't tell me what we were doing in Europe," I said to her, when I came up from the vault, when I came back from death. "What *I* was doing in Europe. I know why you didn't tell me about Talulla."

She was in the study, naked, on her hands and knees, scrubbing at the bloodstains with bleach and a brutal-looking brush I didn't even know we owned. It was just after one a.m. There was no sign of last night's bodies. Without looking up, she tossed me a roll of garbage bags, which I caught. We don't drop catches, especially when thrown by one of our own.

"Strip off and put your clothes in there," she said. "We're going to have to burn them."

"Justine, I—"

"We don't have much time. Go take a shower, then get dressed in something you don't like because we'll have to burn that as well. And don't track back through here when you're clean. Go around through the lounge. Wait for me in the garage."

"The garage?"

"They're in there. We're going to have to bury them somewhere, right?"

The three from last night. For a moment I stood watching her, full of love. It's terrible the way someone intently doing a crossword or tying their shoelace or scrubbing a floor can ambush you with the whole weight of your tenderness. When she'd drunk from me I'd felt death very close. A huge soft darkness. Then her blood had come to me like a rope. And in spite of myself I'd grabbed it. Oh, *hadn't* I just. That wretched moment when I realised I couldn't stop, that she'd have to make me stop. And she had. It was a delight to me to know she'd had the strength and instinct to do that.

"Justine, angel, listen—"

"Look, we have to deal with this," she said. "*This*. Now. Okay?"

It was very, *very* difficult not to pour out reassurance. My heart ached with the need to tell her she was wrong, she was worrying for nothing. But her force field made it plain: Don't. Don't. Don't.

Very well. Let the practicalities do what practicalities could: provide a distraction until she was ready. It was why she'd begun the clean-up without me.

"Thank you," I said.

"What for?"

"You saved my life."

She didn't look up. Her little breasts bobbed, prettily, as she scrubbed. Then she said: "Yeah, well, you did the same for me. Now will you for Christ's sake hurry up?"

"Is this how it's going to be now?" I asked her, desperate to put my arms around her.

"What?"

"You barking orders at me all the time?"

"Yes. Get out of here. Go shower."

Under the jets (set to massage, striking my head and shoulders with a hail of soft bullets) I realised I'd had the dream again. (Coming back from death it's light-years of void, void, void, but eventually the void morphs into the ocean of sleep, and sleep into the shore of waking.) The memory hit me like the smell of the sea: the deserted beach at twilight, someone walking behind me, the abandoned rowing boat. The terrible feeling of being on the edge of a profound and simple truth. And the maddening familiarity of *He lied in every word* circling my head like cartoon concussion birds when I woke.

Again, fear was very available, if I were only willing to turn and face it.

But I'm no coward when it comes to cowardice. I concentrated instead on soaping my genitals and wondering how long it would take me to pick up Talulla's trail.

Vali's trail.

# 28

"Look at the tattoos," Justine said. "They're Angels."

We were in the garage, getting the bodies ready. The two women each had a black sigil above and to the right of the navel. The man had one on his right bicep.

"Angels?" I said.

Justine had seen these marks before. Angelic script. Revived by the Vatican's marketing gurus and flashed in every ad. Apparently, while I'd been asleep, the Catholic Church had not only shed its have-your-cake-and-eat-it coyness about the supernatural (yes, the Devil exists, but please don't embarrass us by asking us to go into detail) but had introduced the world to the fighting force it had been secretly training to deal with it, namely, the *Militi Christi*, the Soldiers of Christ. Known in the optimistic vernacular as "the Angels."

"Well, it was only a matter of time," I said. "What's rather more worrying is how the fuck did they know where to find us?"

We had to take both cars, the guy squeezed into the Mitsubishi's trunk, the two women (wrapped in the hall's Persian runner) in the Jeep's. Los Angeles' twinkling darkness had seen all this before, many times. Bodies. Trunks. The innocent practicalities of murder.

Justine was full of glamorous energy. Her new nature flashed and glimmered. All her years of wondering. I could feel the delight. A smile kept coming. She kept suppressing it. But also kept coming moments of residual disbelief that made her go briefly blank, the system trying to reboot past its astonishment at the new software.

We drove inland on the 10. Desert. Sky rich with stars. Murder someone in England or Luxembourg and sooner or later a jogger or dog-walker stumbles on the buried remains. Small countries keep the moral world at your shoulder. The American desert spaces, it's different. You bury a body, the empty land shrugs and says, Fine with me, Jack.

Six miles east of Joshua Tree there's a road south that runs for a mile and comes to nothing, just peters out into sand and scrub. Not far enough from civilisation, but there wouldn't be enough night to get back safe if we went on. Thanks to the new blood, The Lash gratified for the second night in a row, a saguaro cactus stood with its head and three big out-stretched arms each lined up with a bristling star. A gesture. One of the infinite number of gestures. Through The Lash's mischievous grace the shape said absurd balance. The balance you needed to accept the insistent meaningfulness and meaninglessness of things.

We worked in silence under the mighty constellations. Strength came back to me, gently, through the digging. The bodies were forlorn and pathetic. There was no connection with them. We hadn't drunk from them. Nothing of them had passed to us. They were strangers. I thought (and felt Justine thinking the same) of the people they must have had in their lives who loved them. People to whom their details were precious. It was ugly, to have killed them with no memorial trace in our blood.

We got home an hour from dawn. Obviously there was an argument for not going back to Las Rosas at all, but it didn't hold. If they knew about that place there was no reason they wouldn't know about any of the others within a couple of hundred miles, and none of those had a vault to compare. They'd have to *find* the vault, for starters (it's hidden) and if they did find it nothing short of demolition explosives would get them in. All, if it were to take place in the next fourteen hours, in broad Californian daylight. I doubted even the messengers of God had the requisite mad-ness or chutzpah for that.

Neither of us needed to feed. Not, in my case, because I was full, but because my system was still raw from the Turning. Justine would need blood three nights from now. Her first human.

With the vault door locked, we showered (there's a walk-in down here) and got ready for bed. Justine's face, scrubbed of its make-up, looked young and surprised and tired. Without the practicalities to distract us what she'd kept her mouth shut about was between us like an embarrassed third person, shuffling and clearing its throat. The longer we ignored it now, the worse it would get.

"I know what you're afraid of, angel," I said. I was lying on the vault's bed, undressed but for a pair of black Calvins. She was in crisp white t-shirt and panties, sitting on the edge with her back to me. We've seen each other naked often enough (she knows there's no sex in me, knew it from that first moment in Manhattan; it was what tipped her scales) and we've always been physically affectionate, but the secret she'd kept from me had thrown up tension around her body. I'd stayed out of her mind so far, but she knew that had been my choice, not hers. Now there was defeat in her small shoulder blades. "It's all right," I said. "I understand. But you're worrying needlessly."

"Am I?" she said.

"You think I'm going to leave you."

"You are."

"Listen to me. I'll never leave you. Not like that."

"Not like *that*." Sarcastic emphasis. She sounded exhausted. Torn by regret already, only twenty-four hours old.

"Listen to me," I said. "I'll be in your life, with you, living with you for as long as you want me."

"No, you won't. Three's a crowd."

"That's not it. That's not—"

"It won't work anyway if you can't fuck her. I don't know much but I know *that*."

"Justine, listen to me. It's not about that." (It's not *only* about that, I should have said. And besides, apparently . . . No. Better not go into that.)

"Right. I forgot. It's about 'the prophecy.' The big fulfilment. And by the way how exactly are you going to 'join the blood of the werewolf'? Just following her around gave you dementia and nearly fucking killed you. Some fulfilment."

She got down off the edge of the mattress and went to the vault door. For a second I thought she was going to walk out. Daylight fear rushed my skin. I opened my mouth to say "Don't!" But she reached for her leather jacket hanging there and went into one of the pockets. Took out a pack of American Spirits and lit one. Then lit another for me. Smoking's integrity: Two people, mid-combat, the etiquette of shared vice endures.

"Look what happened," she said, handing me the cigarette. "As soon as she came on the scene everything started going wrong. You disappear for days on end. I get a phone call from fucking *Alaska*. You were so sick I thought you were going to fucking die. It was like dealing with . . ." She turned away. "Actually forget it."

"I'm aware of how insane it must seem."

"No, you're not." Very rational. Very subdued. "You're really not."

*Vor kleʒ fanim va gargim din gammou-jhi.* Translation: "When he joins the blood of the werewolf." One of the prophecies. One of *my* prophecies. Written down in *The Book of Remshi*. The only prophecy that mattered to me anymore.

"Do you really believe it?" Justine asked. Her little face looked drained. "Just tell me, honestly, that you believe, I mean *really believe*, that a woman—a werewolf you were in love with thousands of years ago, who died, has come back as . . . I mean can you *hear* this? Can you hear what this *sounds* like?"

"Yes, angel, I can hear what it sounds like."

"Do you believe it?"

I wanted, you've no idea how much, to give her a simple yes or no. But either would have been a lie. "It's something I have to do," I said. "It's . . . I've been waiting for this for a long time, Juss. One doesn't like the word 'destiny,' but . . ."

There's that phrase you have: Someone walked over my grave. For when the future's cold ether reaches back into your warm present and touches your shrinking skin. Years ago, when I'd kept journals to pass the time I'd written: *It's either/or. Either the world contains magic—dreams, portents, visions, signs, clues, synchronicities, maddening oblique gestures to a hidden meaning—or it does not. There are no grey areas. It's one or the other . . .*

"Destiny," Justine repeated, then laughed, sans amusement. "Fluff, it's just the same *face*, that's all. Everyone's got a double walking around, even in their own lifetime. We've probably both got doubles right here in L.A. In five hundred years the same face must turn up . . . I don't know. In a thousand years? Ten thousand?"

"I know," I said, with a gentleness I knew would only make her more desperate. "I've seen them."

"So why this time? Why her?"

There was nothing to tell her except the feeble truth. My hands filled with weakness at the thought. "I felt it," I said. "That night in Big Sur. I felt it. And I started having the dream."

"What dream?"

Ah. Shouldn't have said that. It wouldn't help. Nothing by way of explanation would help. She didn't want explanation. She wanted me to forget the whole thing.

"What dream?" More exhaustion. And a hint of derision. Dreams! she was thinking. Destiny, prophecies, dreams. Sure, why not?

"You *don't* dream, you said."

"Forget it. It's not—"

"Tell me."

It would be worse not to, now. Now that I'd opened my big mouth that's learned nothing in twenty millennia.

"I've been having this dream," I said. "When I woke up last night I thought it was the first time I'd had it, but now I know I've had it before. I've been having it since I saw Talulla. Before that I hadn't dreamed since Vali died."

I was ready for her to ask what the dream was, but she didn't. The fact of a dream, the fact that a dream was *involved*, disgusted her. Dreams were in the same bag as Meaning and Things Happening For A Reason and God. And yet now that I had opened my big mouth, I felt relieved. "I know it's something," I said. "This beach I've been dreaming about. I know I have to find it. It's a real place, though I haven't the faintest idea where it is. I thought you might help me look for it. I thought we might travel together. It'll be different for you, now we're the same. There are so many places I want to show you."

It didn't help. Visibly it didn't help.

"There's something I've never got," she said, with unnerving evenness.

I had a terrible feeling of energy leaving me. "What?"

She paused. Wanted to get it right. Wanted to make it as hard for me as possible.

"Why don't you drink from people all the time?"

Ah.

"I mean, if blood from the living lets you . . . I mean if you can see the meaning of things, the connections . . . If you can see the goddamned *story* life's supposed to be, why stop? Why not live like that all the time?"

Ah, again.

I took a moment myself. There are moments when twenty thousand years catch up with you.

"It's unbearable," I said.

She looked at the floor, jaws bitterly clamped.

"It's too much," I said. "We can't stand it. Why do people who read Shakespeare still spend hours watching shitty TV or staring out of the window or arguing about whose dinner party to go to? Seeing what we see brings . . . It brings the reality of life too close. It brings death too close. You can't live with the reality of death at the centre."

I remembered the stone circles going up. One night in Britain in spring I came to an encampment. Humans had spent the day dragging a stone that must have weighed seventy tons. Now they lay by their fires, exhausted, breath going up in clouds, hands and feet bloody and scraped, eyes bright with the inscrutable purpose that had been revealed to them. They call the place Avebury now. There's a pub and a car park and t-shirts. There are dozens of books in the gift shop. All with the same conclusion: We no longer know what purpose these megaliths had. We no longer know what they mean. Forgetting hadn't even taken very long. I'd gone back there four hundred years later and people were already vague. Smiling, but vague.

"It makes you too curious about who's writing the story," I said, regretting it even as I said it. My mouth felt like a handful of dead grass. "It makes you too curious about death."

There are these utterances that still and silence a room at the molecular level.

"There's something going on here, Justine," I said. "There's a confluence, don't you see?"

Justine shook her head. Not disagreement. Surfeit. Refusal. Annoyance.

"It's just your thing," she said. "It's just your word, *beguilement*. It's your word and you can't even see it. You can't even see you're falling for it." She walked over to the refrigerator and opened it, stood looking inside. Displacement activity. "It doesn't matter," she said. "You go and do what you have to do." Then after a pause: "I've got things I have to do, too."

The priority, immediately she'd said this, was to avoid making her do something rash. If I obeyed my impulse, which was to wrap her in my arms and tell her that we'd work things out and that I'd never do anything to hurt her and that I'd never go near Vali again, there was every chance I'd wake to find her gone.

"Can we agree something?" I said, quietly.

She didn't answer, but thought IT DOESN'T MATTER, which, since she'd half-thought it *at* me, I got.

"It does matter," I said—and felt the little thrill in her. First flash of invasive telepathy. FUCK FUCK THAT'S WEIRD BUT HOW BUT HE MUSTN'T DON'T DON'T—

I withdrew. I can turn it off. Perk of age.

"Listen," I said. "All I want you to agree is that we don't discuss this any more right now. It's my stupid fat-head fault for bringing it up. I'm exhausted. I still feel like shit from last night. And whatever you say I know you're tired too. We have this conversation now, it's going to be pointless."

"You wrote it as a bet," she said, still calm, still staring into the fridge. "You wrote a bunch of prophecies as a joke, stoned, in a hut in the middle of nowhere."

The image detonated: Me and Amlek, heads thick from the *fazurya*, cold dirt floor, curved walls of baked dung, firelight and the body of the witch-doctor we'd fed on. We'd been laughing (difficult not to) at the poor old fellow's last thought: "I didn't see this." Amlek, between laughing fits, had said, I bet you I can see more of the future than you can. Which, whether I like it or not, *was* how it started. We began that night.

*I see a mighty people from the north with yellow hair like rope.*

*I see sickness and death and rats fifteen thousand summers from now.*

*I see a leader of this country who eats babies for breakfast and his name is Jehengast Ka.*

*I see a man making visions on the ceiling of a cave like no other. There are white clouds and blue sky and naked humans.*

*I see a silver spear taller than the tallest tree with a tail of fire and smoke rising up into the air. There are humans inside it.*

*I see a thin man stuck with big thorns to a tree.*

All those were mine. Amlek soon got bored. I don't know why I didn't. I started writing them down. One day I wrote: *And in time Vali will come back to him and he will achieve fulfilment when he joins the blood of the werewolf.* "He" was me, obviously. "He" featured in the prophecies, from time to time. I met Amlek in Jerusalem the night Christ was arrested. That's another of mine, I told him. He's the thin man. You watch. Not thorns, *nails.* Close enough, though, right? Don't like to say I told you so, but . . .

I've counted them up, the ones that have come true. Less than a third. Just enough to keep the belief alive that I'm living in a story—the greatest detective mystery story ever written—that I've been given clues, that it'll mean something, in the end. Just enough for that—and just not enough to do away with the thought that the whole thing's complete random meaningless bullshit and that any village idiot could've cooked up prophecies so vague that some of them were bound to come true. Or rather "true."

Just enough to keep the faith in Vali's return alive.

Just not enough to stop me conceding my own idiocy in keeping it.

"Please," I said to Justine. "Can't we sleep first?"

She closed the fridge door, gently. More calm defeat.

"Come on, sweetpea, turn out the light."

She stared at me. It didn't need telepathy. What I'd said to her last night: I promise I won't leave you.

# 29
## *Justine*

NIGHT AGAIN. DARKNESS goes into you like ink into water. *Like.* I keep seeing the ways things are *like* other things. Since Turning.

I thought Fluff would've been awake before me, but he wasn't. I sat up and looked down at him. He was frowning, slightly. Sometimes, asleep, he looks about five years old.

Five years.

Twenty thousand.

One night, a few months after we met, he took me to a self-storage place out in Pasadena. U-STASH. It's a chain. He owns it. A hundred facilities, nationwide. You've probably seen them: logo's a big red packing crate on a yellow background. We went in and he took me to one of the units and opened it up. It was full of Egyptian treasure. Gold. So much gold. He said it was only a small part of it. Amenhotep the First. His tomb was never found. The tomb builders were kept in isolation in special villages so no one would find out where the king and his treasure was going to be buried. Sometimes, when the tomb was finished, the Pharaoh would have them killed to make sure. Stonk said he got the information from one of the workers in exchange for his life.

I left him sleeping in the vault, got dressed and went upstairs. The house knew I'd changed. The floor and the walls and the furniture. They were in on it.

There was something else. A faint throbbing I hadn't felt last night. I stood still. It was a good, warm feeling now but I knew it wouldn't feel good later, in a few days if I didn't . . . if I didn't . . .

Drink.

The thirst. For years the thirst meant him. Now it meant me. My skin prickled. I thought of the blood bags in the fridge—but that wouldn't work yet. He'd told me it took years to make the shift. And even the thought of MREs sort of annoyed the thirst, put an edge on it like the smell of electrical burning. I tried to remember drinking *his* blood, but I couldn't, even though my body knew it had happened. Instead of a memory of it there was just a massive red blackness. Just nothing.

For a while I stood in the kitchen doorway thinking about what I was, now. The reality of it. *A vampire feeds on the blood of humans. Drinks it. Swallows it down.* In the world I grew up in blood was something to be scared of. Hepatitis. HIV. (Stonk had shaken his head when I asked him. No, sweetpea, we don't get diseases. Diseases can't live in us.) In the world I grew up in blood was practically the dirtiest thing around.

I thought I'd got used to the idea. *Drinking blood.* But when I thought of myself doing it it made me dizzy and hot. Disgusted, too, a little. I told myself not to be shocked. It was stupid to be shocked. I'd known this was what it was, what it would be. I'd always known.

The study still smelled of bleach but there were no other signs of what had happened, what we'd done. I turned the desk lamp on and woke my laptop.

Finder.

Documents.

Files.

Encryption.

Enter password.

My hands didn't move. The book title I'd noticed yesterday came back to me: *You Can't Go Home Again.* It meant something different now. It made me doubt myself. I saw what Fluff had meant, that you couldn't trust it, the feeling of things seeming to mean things. Or what he'd actually said was you had to trust it and mistrust it, to keep bouncing between the two. *Be the loving servant of two masters*, was the phrase he used.

Yeah, well, physician heal thy fucking self.

I entered the password.

The faces came up, the information.

# 30
## Remshi

WHOEVER LOVED THAT loved not at first sight?

I loved Vali. But you'll have worked that out by now.

All of it, once I was in it, felt as if it had happened before.

Naturally. Love being indefinite déjà vu.

•

The humans, in lousy furs, rattling with trinkets of teeth and bone, had been following the retreating ice north, and I'd been following the humans. Not just me. Fellow vampires Amlek, Mim, Una and Gabil were travelling more or less with me, though they were elsewhere that night. We were governed by an irregular familial gravity. We gathered for a while, lived and hunted as a group, separated, came together again. No obligations, no see you Friday or I'll be back around seven. I'd made Amlek. Amlek had made Mim. Una and Gabil, two and three hundred years old respectively, had their own makers, but they'd have to trace back to me in the end. (The first question I asked any vampire I met was: How old are you? So far no one counted as many winters as I did.) But that particular night I'd felt like being alone, and I'd been around long enough to know when to follow my inclinations.

As I entered the clearing a gang of *Homo sapiens* were just about to hack the werewolf's head off. She was impaled on a low tree branch, stuck with at least a dozen spears, one through the throat. (Not looking where I was going, she fessed-up afterwards. My own stupid fault. If I hadn't stuck myself on that tree they'd never have got the spears into me.) Her hands, huge and elegantly clawed, had been cut off and lay among the frozen leaves on the ground.

Two humans with flint hatchets had climbed up (had been *ordered* to climb up, their wobbling faces said) into the tree above her and now stood, or rather crouched, ostensibly ready to deliver the decapitative *coup de grâce*, in fact wishing they were far away. The remaining fifteen ringed her, the boldest darting close—grinning and screeching and tongue-flapping and mooning—to add wounds with knives and darts, with which latter her torso was already liberally quilled. The full moon—the heavenly one—lit the forest's slivers and gashes of stubborn snow. Lit too Vali's wet snout and bloodied fangs, her glistening pelt, her hard bare breasts and flat, deep-naveled belly . . .

I can tell you what I did next. I can tell you exactly what I did next. But I can't tell you why. Divine whim? A determined universe? Aesthetic indignation? Desperate boredom? Sheer randomness? Take your pick. These days my preference is for Mysterious Moments of Pure Being, wherein perhaps all the above meet in paradoxical simultaneity and you find yourself doing something with both a deep sense of inevitability and absolutely no clue why you're doing it.

The two shivering ninnies in the tree first. She wouldn't die from her wounds, but she would certainly die from having her head cut—or, as it would have been with these halfwits, bludgeoned—off. (These were pre-silver days, or at least, pre-*worked* silver; a handful of smarter-than-average primitives had found certain rocks gave the creatures trouble—argentine and chlorargyrite we now know, though at the time your grandsires simply called them "wolf rocks" or "monster rocks"—but bullets and blades were millennia away.) The forest was cold and crisp and full of dark consciousness. It had been a long time since I'd seen this sort of action, but there were my energies like loyal horses, rearing and snorting and pounding the earth. I held them for a moment (a long time since I'd felt this sort of physical self-delight, too, outside feeding) then released them, with a thirty-foot leap into the tree, where a nifty spring and flip had me hanging like a bat in front of human Tweedles Dum and Dee. There was of course the stretched moment of stunned introduction. Their faces, swiped with paint, achieved a lovely nude look of surprise that had the briefest moment to switch to one of terror and certainty of death before I despatched them with a pair of tracheal slashes. A moment later my lady's would-be decapitators went sailing over their companions' heads and disappeared into the darkness on the other side of the clearing.

High human spirits dropped a little. Dropped further when the assailants found four more of their number dead, suddenly, throats ripped out or bellies opened, when they hadn't actually seen how that was possible, when they were forced to concede that they hadn't, actually, *seen that happen*.

Mooning and tongue-flapping ceased. Celebratory gibbering petered out. One of your lot, wearing feathers in his hair and a necklace of small bird skulls, flung his spear at me. I caught it, cheerleader twirled it, then sent it back at him with such force that it went straight through *his* skull, splitting his forehead and cleaving his affronted brain, nicely, en route. Group shock. Perhaps because the feathers testified to chieftainship the bisection of this particular noggin produced a pivotal dip in morale. The remaining humans fled, some blubbering, some screaming, some in bug-eyed silence.

I turned to see the werewolf forcing herself backwards off the snapped tree limb that had pierced her just beneath the ribs and come through slightly to the right of her spine. With a moan, she collapsed on her back then rolled onto her side, gasping. I went to her as if in fluid obedience to an inevitable choreography. With, I imagine, an inane or beatific smile on my face. I felt—in those rare split seconds when I wasn't wholly dissolved into the experience—full of uncomplicated warm innocence.

"It's okay," I said to her in my own language, despite knowing she wouldn't understand me, while the ghostly collective of my vampire peers went: *What the fuck are you doing?* "The humans have gone. Let me help you."

(We didn't stink to each other in those days. That came later, when the species war was already a thousand years old and the vampire ruler Hin Kahur implemented howler aversion therapy: Newly turned vampires were tortured for weeks and months; each time something excruciating was done to them they were gagged and hooded with *gammou-jhi* hide, saturated and coated with the creature's urine, faeces and the fluids from the sex organs and scent glands. Within a hundred years the therapy was no longer necessary. Even brand-new vampires found the smell of a werewolf unbearable. Conditioned response morphed into sensory hardwiring—go figure. There's plenty of *post hoc* vamp science that attempts to explain it—my friend Olek, the oldest vampire egghead, has a theory that it's like the experiential formation of neural pathways in the brains of newborn human infants—but whatever the explanation, there the phenomenon unequivocally is: to vampires, werewolves absolutely fucking stink. And though the blood-drinkers' *gammou-jhi* stereotype is a moron, it didn't take his species long to copy the aversion method, rendering the olfactory feelings mutual. However, when I met Vali all that was still in the future. Our races didn't socialise with each other, and there was natural competition for prey, but we managed as best we could simply to keep out of each other's way.)

"I know you can't talk," I said. "And I know your wounds will heal. But we should move in case they come back in greater numbers. Can you walk?"

She couldn't. She'd lost a lot of blood through the big wound, and by the time I was done pulling out the spears and darts she'd lost more—along with consciousness. I wondered what language she spoke in her human form, what tribe she was from, how long she'd had the Curse. I wondered—astonished at myself, since it was risibly irrelevant—what she'd look like when the moon set. What she'd look like as a woman.

I tore a leg off one of the humans, plucked a couple of hearts and tongues and stuffed them into one of their furs. I debated taking her own severed hands, but closer examination revealed they were decomposing already, and besides, it was common knowledge that *gammou-jhi*, like vampires, could regrow anything (apart, obviously, from a head) overnight. So I left the forlorn things where they were. (Later she said to me: I think there must be a place all the parts go, all the hands and feet and hearts and eyes. They're put together to make whole creatures, who carry the confused memories of all their original owners . . . )

The sky said seven hours till sunrise. Two hours less to the setting of the moon. There would be a second and possibly more awkward introduction.

I picked her up, slung her over my shoulders and set off.

# 31

MY NEAREST EARTH was four miles away in a cave in the hills. Unburdened and going at a sprint (we'll have to talk about flight later, though I already know I'm going to make a devil's arse of explaining it, and in any case these were the days before I could do it) a journey of a few minutes. Going carefully with a nine-foot *gammou-jhi* across my shoulders it seemed to take forever. I wasn't tired when we got there, but small muscles I'd forgotten about had woken up and were stretching and blinking, astonished they'd slept so long. When I laid her down on her side her eyes opened. They were dark, their lights still a little adrift. I knelt beside her.

"You're in a cave in the hills on the side of the river where the sun goes down," I told her, this time in the tongue of the tribe who'd been chasing her. "You've been hurt, but as you know, you'll live. I brought meat. It's here if you need it."

The cave was dry, and smelled of icy stone and the wild sage that grew over the entrance. Now of her, too, a complicated odour: her bitter canine blood, yes, but also something that just when you thought it was sly and fruit-sour hit you with a dash of brine—then astonished the back of your throat with maddening sweetness, like too much honey, so that you could hardly breathe. I'd never smelled anything like it. It sensitised my face. My idiot face. My tranced, beguiled, undone face.

Nonetheless the long moment of pure being was passing and the strangeness of what I was doing was beginning to assert itself. I'd never been this close to one of her kind before. The big totemic head looked bizarre lying still, blinking, jaws open. I looked down to where her hands had been lopped from her wrists. Two new nubs were sprouting already. Even with my hearing I'm sure I only *imagined* catching the whisper of furious cellular repair. I'd lost a hand more than once down the centuries (although never both together) and supposed regeneration to be the same for her as it was for me, a sensation as of millions of tiny insects hurrying to form a very specific complex cluster . . .

"I can't explain this," I said to her. I felt hyperreal and precarious, repeatedly close to laughter. I'd been picturing myself trying to explain it to Amlek and the others. *I don't know what made me help her. I just found myself helping her.*

Her eyes closed again. The bleeding had slowed. Phlegm rattled in her chest when she exhaled. I realised I was looking—a flower of absurdity opened in my heart—at her breasts, which were small and hard, nipples dark as blackberries.

I felt very rich in the body and confused in the head.

"You have nothing to fear from me," I said, pointlessly. For a moment her eyes focused and I saw all her dreadful power, the monthly rhythm of her need for living meat, the work it had been to find room for the beast. The souls of her dead babbled in her blood, not knowing if her dying would release them. My own dead stirred, wondered how it was for these others suddenly close by. "Something's happening," I said. To her, to myself, to the universe—or was it the universe saying it through me, matter-of-factly? Something's *happening*.

By accident or her own intention her giant knee relaxed and touched mine where I knelt. Then her eyes closed again.

# 32

A LONG AND unhinged night for me, walking up and down outside the cave telling myself what was happening wasn't possible. I kept laughing out loud. The sound of which frightened me and made everything worse. Details were urgent and vivified: a bare white-branched tree; the shadows of small stones; the odour of snow. The moon sailed by slowly like a delighted intelligence, faceless yet somehow grinning, somehow *in on it*. My guest's breathing sounded as if she had a slight cold. I kept going back to her—(Her! Upper case was ten thousand years in the future but she'd acquired its mental equivalent)—ostensibly to see if she was awake or to check on the progress of her budding palms and fingers. In fact to keep feeling what I was, against all reason, feeling.

What I was feeling.

Yes.

I laughed again, and again it made me feel worse. I lost my balance— actually found myself falling sideways and reaching out; I would've fallen over—fallen over! Me!—if I hadn't been so close to the sheer side of the hill. Instead I leaned there, imbecilic, incredulous, full of dumb certainty. The blood in my head was colossal and unruly, a giant who'd drunk too much.

I know what you're thinking. You're thinking the shock derived from the hilariously inappropriate *object* of my desire. (I could see the faces of my vampire friends going from plain surprise to crimped bafflement to wrinkled disgust. Really? A *gammou-jhi*? A *dog*? Gods, Rem, you're sick in the blood!) But you're wrong. It wasn't the object of my desire. It was the fact of desire itself.

Desire.

After a thousand years.

(Or two thousand. One loses count.)

I'd passed thirty-nine summers before I became a vampire. I'd fathered several children. My equipment had, back in the human days, worked. Splendidly, on occasion, if the shrieks and teethmarks and flailing not-quite-knowing-what-to-do-with-themselves limbs of my various lady friends were to be believed. But since my Turning, nothing. Not impotence. Just a complete absence of desire. It's common knowledge in modern times (thanks not least to peskily scribbling Jacob Marlowe) but back then we had to make the wretched discovery for ourselves: The Lash murders libido.

But here I was . . . Here *I* was . . .

Nor was it merely desire. Desire alone would have cracked the paradigm's egg and scrambled it. But I repeat: It wasn't merely desire. Every time I went within range of her scent reality's tectonic plates shifted, threatened to come apart entirely. Because here, along with desire, was an unbalancing recognition. I knew her. I *knew* her. The ether between us shivered with dark remembered joy. *Remembered* joy. It wasn't perversion. It wasn't—I searched myself thoroughly for this—the titillation of taboo. It was . . . It was . . .

A burst of laughter from the moon smashed the reverie and I looked up to see it was almost below the horizon.

# 33

*IT'S NOT SOMETHING they want you to watch.*

So said the lore, and my roused shame as I approached the cave endorsed it. But I had to see. Had to.

She was on her feet, leaning back against the left-hand wall of the cave, head lowered, jaws open, panting. Her tongue went back and forth with each pant. The wounds had healed. Only the claws on the regrown hands hadn't yet arrived. The smell of her dizzied me. Its soft kernel was in her somewhere, an infinite source. I wanted to find it. Go into it. Lose myself.

I stepped inside the cave. She knew I was there, of course, could have snarled or chased me out, made a need for privacy plain. But she didn't. Instead she turned her magnificent head and looked at me.

I know you. You know me.

How?

All my past gathered, as if it knew what was about to happen would draw a line marking the beginning of a New Age.

Then with a strangled sound she grabbed her belly, doubled up, and crashed forward onto her knees.

It was compelling and ugly to watch. After that first choked gargle she didn't utter a sound. Which made her body's mad monologue of bone-squeak and muscle-crunch loud. A jerky series of implosions, the beast done bit by bit out of its molecular rights as the long femurs shuddered through their appalling compression and the head thrashed from side to side as if the inner skull were trying to shake off the outer. Her odour bloomed, swelled for a moment at the edge of rottenness, then in an instant atomised around her and hung, suspended, waiting to resettle in its human version. And all the while my baffled certainty grew, reached a warm fullness as all but the now resting head returned in three, four, five slow spasms (she would climax with these same pretty convulsions, I knew) to its human form. She turned her face away for the last and most intimate part of the transformation, though I watched the scalp's short fur hurry out as thick dark human hair, one long wave curved as if by design over the breast nearest me.

Moments. Her face turned away, her breathing slowing. Our mutual awareness naked. I thought: Was I mistaken? Am I mistaken?

Then she turned her face to me, and I knew I wasn't.

# 34

IN THE LANGUAGE of the upper river people, she said: "I'm freezing." Her voice was low and soft and confident and the colour of the river at night.

I answered her in her own tongue: "Take these. I'll make a fire."

"These" were the fur, emptied of its human remains, plus my own bear-skin cloak. When she wriggled into them giant desire uncoiled in me. Laughter rushed up immediately, made itself available. I only just resisted it. The vastness and simplicity of wanting her in that way—of wanting anyone in that way—was *so* vast and simple laughter seemed inevitable. It was as if someone had lifted the sky like a lid to reveal a completely different wonderful realm beyond, one that made everything we thought we knew redundant—and hilarious. Every drop of my blood stared at its new reflection, scared to recognise itself, convinced that to accept this gift would be to lose it.

"Hurry," she said. "The sun'll be good for me but not for you."

I'd known from the start she knew what I was, but to have it casually confirmed like this was another sweet shock. I thought: Has she been with *other* vampires?

"If you have to dig, I can help you. That'll give us more time."

She spoke with such swift control, as if we'd known each other for years, as if she knew just the sort of moronic dazes I was liable to fall into. She was as tall as me, supple, dark-eyed. She'd seen thirty winters in her human life and now would never look a minute older. Her face—the bold eyes and wide mouth ready to find delight—said she was at fierce peace with what she was. Whatever terms her condition demanded she'd met them long ago. The thought that monstrosity had stripped her of a right to live had never crossed her mind. She'd had her teeth and nails in life's pelt from birth; *this* wasn't going to make her let go.

"It won't hurt you, will it?"

The fire, she meant.

"No. I'll be as quick as I can."

Modernity tells you vampires are afraid of fire. Well, that's true, but only in the way you're afraid of it: we don't, any more than you do, want to get burned. We don't much fancy, you know, *going up in flames*. We're certainly not impervious to the charm of its warmth. We feel the cold and the heat much less than you do, but that's not to say we don't feel them at all. I was cooler without the bearskin, but I could have gone out—as the modern idiom has it—stark bollock naked and wandered in the snow for several hours without much more than minor discomfort. (The more delicious and immediate discomfort—and speaking of bollocks—was that sans cloak I was left in only footwear and a doeskin loincloth, loose enough to make my feelings apparent.) The fixings for fire were—to my luck, or in accordance with the forces softly engineering this encounter—available. Amlek and Mim had slept here with me not long ago. We'd fed early and come back to the cave hours before dawn. Amlek had found flint and lit a fire, more for aesthetics than warmth, since the night had taken a reminiscent turn, and the scar of the burning near the cave mouth was still visible. There was very little dry stuff, but I found the flint and did what I could, and in a few minutes had a dozen small flames frolicking. Fir trees growing fifty feet below the cave supplied pine cones, which, together with what dead wood I could find, would be fuel enough till sunrise. I busied myself with the flames, poking and prodding and blowing, conscious all the while of her watching me, the space between us rich with our potential movement through it, to each other. The ghost of myself was already moving through it, an erotic whole-body version of the phantom limb. And still the fever of incredulous certainty enriched the thud of every passing second.

Then, suddenly, I stood up and turned, and there we were. Looking at each other. The fire marked her with little wings of light: cheekbones, knees, one bare shoulder. We didn't speak. Her face was full of knowledge of me. The lights in her dark eyes were steady. We didn't speak. It was a concussive pleasure, the not speaking. I only realised I'd been thinking: *You're not alone anymore* when I felt coming from her: *No, we're not*.

There was no decision. One minute we stood facing each other, the next I felt the little distance between us going, going, dissolving into fluid warm nothing, until our arms were around each other and there was the shape of her perfectly fitting my own.

# 35

THE MYTH OF male and female as an originally single hermaphrodite being survives, even now. *My other half,* you say. Read literally it short-changes homosexuals—which ought to be more than enough to let literalists know their reading needs work. Genitals aren't the issue. The issue is the feeling of homecoming. Of recognition. Of re-encounter. Of knowing that you knew each other once, were forced into separated forgetfulness, mistook others for each other (wilful myopia or innocent near-misses) but now, by sheer chance or ineffable design, you've found the *real* each other again. Thank the gods. Thank accident. Thank the determined universe. At any rate the impulse (endearing, if you think about it) is to thank *some*thing.

And my cup, obviously, ran over. A brand-new sex life and a life-changing lover to share it with. We didn't congratulate ourselves. Shared intuition said it would be asking for trouble. We were very quiet and careful, going about our loving business. We didn't want to attract the universe's attention. We didn't want the universe noticing it had made an obscene mistake and, appalled at its negligence, *rectifying* it at a brutal, hurried stroke.

"How is this possible?" I whispered to her (since the universe might be listening) in the firelight. We'd made the cave home, temporarily. Clearly the cave was ours. Clearly the world was ours. We were deep in the mesmerised phase of quiet entitlement. I'd often wondered about the point of the everything. Well, here it was.

"I don't care how," she whispered back, clambering onto me. "Only *that.*"

"I love you."

"I know."

She did know. She was delighted and appalled at her greed for it. If she hadn't loved me my love would have invited her cruelty. If she hadn't loved me my love would have made a tyrant of her. Fortunately, she did love me.

"That's it, just like that. Oh God, that's good. That's what good means."

I'd never known peace and pleasure and profound necessity as I knew when I was inside her. She liked to sit astride me ("cowgirl," as contemporary pornography has it, in one of its rare female-friendly coinages), said I hit her in just the right place like that. (The G-spot was thousands of years in the future. But just as people knew sound reasoning before Aristotle formalised logic . . . ) She liked to sit astride me with my hands on her hips, occasionally lowering her mouth to mine for kisses that took us both out into the void. There were these dips into darkness which momentarily solved our selves' separateness. But the real sweetness— you'd say the *human* sweetness—was in the moments either side of transcendence, the frenzied attempt to get all, enough, everything of each other, the delighted disbelief in what we were experiencing, the outrageous undeserved gift of it. Oh, we made rare pigs of ourselves! We often fell asleep having just come, in whatever position we'd ended up in. And yet there was a little infallible gravity of tenderness that always drew us, half-asleep, back into each other's arms. Sometimes we'd become aware that we'd both woken, and were thinking.

"Stop thinking," she said, when this happened.

"*You're* thinking," I answered.

"I'll stop. You stop, too."

"Okay."

Once—and only once—she said: "My lifetime will be the blink of an eye next to yours."

I almost said: "I won't go on without you." But didn't. Because even though I believed it I knew it would annoy her. She knew I was thinking it, anyway. We were in the cave, lying naked on the bearskin. The fire was low, but we were flushed from lovemaking. She was on her side, one leg bent. I was lying with my head resting on her thigh, breathing the smell of her cunt, which to me had become (had always been; I'd just forgotten it, along with all the other things I'd forgotten and was now being given back) the smell of love. The thought of losing her filled me with frantic energy. Energy that didn't know what to do, but couldn't stop believing there was something it *could* do.

"Promise me something," she said.

"What."

"Promise me you'll live as long as you can."

I didn't answer. Nothing I could say seemed right. She was aware of *that*, too.

"Just promise me," she said.

After a long time breathing the smell of her and trying to imagine existence without it, I said, "All right. I promise I'll live as long as I can."

It shouldn't have felt such a difficult promise to make.


I told Amlek about her, but not the others.

"And you're saying . . . With her it's . . . ?"

Naturally this was the big thing. Naturally this was what he couldn't get over.

"Yes," I told him. "Everything. As when we were human."

It was just after sunset on my farewell night. Vali was waiting for me in the cave three miles away. Amlek and I sat in a plane tree overhanging the river. The water was a large peacefully moving intelligence. He knew I was leaving with her. I hadn't needed to tell him.

"How long will she live?"

He regretted it immediately.

"Not forever," I said.

"I'm sorry."

"For a little while."

"Really, I'm sorry."

"But she's alive now."

"Of course."

For a few minutes we sat in silence. In silence saying goodbye. I felt him thinking of the time and space immediately ahead of him without me in it. Sadness, yes, but also his self's excitement to be free of anything against which to measure itself. To be the only answer to his own questions.

We didn't arrange anything. Time, place. We shared blood. We'd see each other again.

"Rem?" he called, when I was moving off in the darkness.

"What?"

I felt him grinning.

"She doesn't have a sister, does she?"

When I got to the cave Vali wasn't in it. Its smell had changed, too. Hers was still there, but mixed with a human's, raw and acrid, discharged in fear or rage. I realised, as I followed both odours back down towards the river, that I was trembling. Here was the cruel joke: We give you bliss then take it away. I'd been right all along.

But I found her, alive, unharmed, less than a mile away. A shallow valley of turf and pale stones descended to a narrow stream with thorn trees growing on its banks. She was kneeling over the body of a man and she was holding a rock in her right hand. The man was face-down. His head was bleeding. The smell of which, though I didn't need to drink until tomorrow night, pulled on my instinct like a child tugging its mother's hand.

"He's not dead," Vali said.

I knew that from the blood. We can't drink from the dead.

"Who is he?" I asked her. She looked beautiful. The warmth of what had happened still in her.

"His name's Mabon. He's from my tribe. I can't believe he followed me all this way."

I understood. He wanted her.

"If he's come this far," I told her, "he won't stop now. Does he know?"

What you are.

"Yes."

A little flicker of respect for poor Mabon, desire to rip his head off notwithstanding.

"I can't kill him," she said. "I won't kill him." Which meant: And I don't want you to kill him, either.

"Tomorrow's full moon," she said. "I'll be able to travel as fast as you. Soon we'll be far from here. Too far for him to follow. He's not a bad person."

"He doesn't have to be a bad person to be a dangerous one."

"I don't care. We're not killing him."

"Okay. You're the boss."

Pause.

"Am I?"

Said with just enough play to stir my cock.

"*You* are a bad person," I said, moving towards her.

We kissed, and felt the option of fucking here, by poor prostrate Mabon—on top of him, why not? But she rejected it. Trivial piquancy. The sort of mean symbolic gesture someone smaller might need. Not her. Little cruelties suggested she still needed help to be reconciled to the big ones. She didn't.

Mabon, in any case, was showing signs of consciousness, so we took our leave. It was my plan to travel east by the river, skirting the mountains. Water meant people, and the mountains meant easy concealment.

Tomorrow, it had passed between us, we would hunt together.

# *36*

WE HADN'T TALKED about it. We'd known not to. It was the only thing we were uncertain of. She was afraid I'd forgotten what she turned into. I hadn't, but still, I didn't know: that first night in the cave, if she hadn't returned to her human form, would I have lain with her?

"How far is the camp?" she said. It was almost moonrise. We were in a cave I'd kicked a mountain lion out of the day before. He'd put up a fight for a while, but I was too fast. I'd said to him: Look, give up, will you? You've lost a lot of blood. It's only going to get worse for you. And with what was unmistakably a sigh, followed by a roll of the neck and a stretch that was meant to make it look as if boredom had got the better of him, he'd turned and slouched away.

"Less than a mile," I told her. "Is it always this bad?"

She smiled. Stupid question. She was pale and shivering and wet with sweat. I couldn't touch her. When it had first started I had very gently put my hand between her shoulder blades. She said: "I love you, but if you do that or anything else to my skin I'll kill you."

"Do you want water?" I asked her now.

She shook her head, no. When she swallowed her throat swelled for a moment—then returned to normal.

"I wish I could help you."

"Shshsh. It's . . . Oh fuck, it's coming. Move."

Again, I watched. The same process in reverse. More alarming this time: The beast becoming beauty relieves. Beauty becoming the beast unnerves. Her skull shuddered. Her jaw leaped forward with a wet crunch. Her legs lengthened before her arms and torso, so for a moment her head was a remote spectacle the way a stilt-walker's is. Her dark eyes darkened. Hair hurried out with a sound like distant burning. She fell onto all-fours, rolled onto her side, clutched her gut, convulsed. Her scent pounded out of her, filled my face and limbs with wealth. The soft kernel of that smell was between her legs. I'd found it that first time, kissing her there in her human shape. Now at the first inhalation my cock rose. At the same time I imagined Amlek saying: *It's still basically a dog, Rem. A big dog walking on its hind legs.* Of course the romantic antidote was that it was my beloved on the *inside*—but that wasn't true. I didn't want the woman inside the beast. Nor did I want the beast around the woman. I wanted Vali, all of what she was, every point on the scale of her nature. This was her and the dark-eyed woman ready to laugh and kiss and see through you and fuck you was her. They weren't divisible. Nor, it turned out, was my desire. This revelation was a warmth spreading through me. I could feel happiness in my face. *There is nothing of you I don't want.*

There would be a discrepancy . . . There would be practical . . . The discrepancy would leave us with certain practical . . . I laughed, quietly, seeing in her eyes she'd picked this up and was thinking, *me on all-fours, of course*, was seeing us in that position, her snout buried under the burst ribs of a victim.

The image gave her hunger a final push, and the last vestiges of her human shape surrendered.

My thirst didn't need a push. It had been three days. One more and it would start to hurt. I kept swallowing. My fangs were live, my blood loud with the murmur of my countless drunk-down dead. You'd think it'd get old, wouldn't you? But it doesn't. Every victim's unique, quenches in its own way and adds its way of being to yours.

They'd posted lookouts. Two, within shouting distance of the camp.

We took one each.

They didn't get to shout.

I hadn't known how it would be. Only that it would be unlike anything else.

Which it was.

I drank a lot, fast, alone with my drink. Partly because the thirst was three days old and at the first spurt and whiff of blood (my guard was a young man, leanly muscled, full of strength and as yet undischarged love; love was there in him, waiting, almost ready—and now would never find its way to anyone) took away everything but the need to satisfy it. Partly too (the intractable logistics, which as much as love or art or imagination make the world what it is) because I daren't risk a draught from her victim: if his lights went out while I was drinking, mine would too, and his lights were in her hands. But partly—let me be scrupulously honest—because now that we'd come to it I didn't know what she'd want. We hadn't, I repeat, talked about it. Only moved towards it via irresistible gravity.

I rose, slaked, inwardly aswirl with my young guard's life: the dizziness when he first saw the sea, his child's mind imagining it pouring off the edge of the earth in a giant dark green waterfall but where did the water go? He was almost sucked over the edge with it, he'd felt himself fighting its terrible pull, actually turned away and put his arms around his mother's hips and pressed his face to her thighs, though the big open salt air of the shore was also calming, an offer of love, like his mother's love but too big—

Vali was down on all-fours, looking back over her shoulder at me, legs spread, backside thrust up. Her muzzle winked and dripped gore. Her blood-scented breath went up in rhythmic signals, contemptuous of all restraint. It was an appallingly recognisable version of the way she looked at me when she was in human form, in that same position of brazen, insistent availability. A look of dark understanding. I know you. You know me. This. This. *This.*

Her body's aliveness when I went, cock blood-packed and aching, into her was an all but unbearable sweet assault. She was full of sly power. Drownable in. Her victim's life flailed in her. Her greed was there in the pulse of her cunt that my own pulse rushed to join, until we were in thudding synchronicity I'd never felt before, something in time with the heart of . . . Of what? The universe. Life. Everything. The glimmering lode or stubborn tremor of corruption was essential, the awful fact of pleasure that increased proportional to her victim's suffering, a relation I—lustless for centuries until now—had in my mortal days only ever glimpsed, as a ghost through smoke. But it was there with us (as the divisions between things dissolved, and the full moon swam in the river above us and the mountain opened on a vault of stars), the great spirit of cruelty, of enlargement by theft, that whether we liked it or not was close to the heart of what we were. This was what she'd had to find room for. The monster gave, if nothing else, an honest ultimatum: Find room for this or die. And she *had* found room. She'd forced her own growth to accommodate it, let the moon month by month shrink guilt and sadness until they were only two forlorn rooms in the house of many mansions. Rooms she went to less, would go to less, would revisit with diminishing nostalgia. This, I now knew, was why we hadn't talked about it. She hadn't known (intimations, yes, but not certainty) whether it would be this way for me, whether *I* would find room for it.

But with her, like this, with manhood (as it were) restored, there was no room for anything else. I knew—with the negligible part of me not unstrung by ecstasy—that I would have to spend some energy after this convincing her she hadn't done me an injury of initiation. It would take all her cunning courage to rise above *that* fear, *that* guilt. And yet I knew she would. It was the last gap in intimacy between us bridged, that she loved me and wanted me enough to risk turning herself into something I'd resent. I loved her for it.

# 37

THREE YEARS LATER, we came back.

Three years. Approximately. In how many thousands?

Nothing had dulled. *Nothing* had dulled. The world was still ours. Giant skies, glamorous constellations. The sound of the sea on the shore. That mist-rain that doesn't fall but materialises in soft suspension in the air around you. The kills knitted us. The profane matrimonial rite, renewed every month, deepening our monstrous cahoots. Only species exigencies rucked the silk. Most obviously, that I was confined to the hours of darkness. Of course she adjusted her sleep pattern and became mostly nocturnal, but it wasn't easy. For a start, the week either side of full moon, her sleep was all over the place. But more than that, she missed the light. Of course she did. *I* missed the light, and I'd had centuries to get used to it. We had, effectively, weeks apart. Naturally, just after sunset was our window. Even if she was sleeping nights we still had hours, and the restriction made them precious.

"How was the light today?"

"Big. Hot. Broad. Yellow-white. The sky's blue was like a drumbeat. I watched the black tree shadows revolve. When the sun went down it was like someone's hand was pulling it, very gently. It was soft-edged and orange. The land went purple, then dark blue and grey, then black. Then you opened your eyes."

Sometimes, kissing her, I could smell the sun and the air on her skin. It aroused me beyond reason.

The other discrepancy was that I had to feed every fourth or fifth day. But killing with her had made killing *without* her an enraging chore. I pushed it. Six days, seven, eight. It was the one thing she scolded me for. But when I timed it just right—starved myself so that the thirst reached a debilitating intensity on full moon—the reward was unholily sweet. There was nothing—*nothing*—like our union then, wedded in blood, a lawless law unto ourselves.

"We go at night," I said. "I come with you."

"I don't want you to come with me."

We'd come back because she'd dreamed of her mother, dying. Her human mother. Whom she hadn't seen since the tribe had driven her out. Her mother had fought for her to be allowed to stay. Until her father had beaten her into silence—and near death. Now, because of the dream, my beloved wanted to see the old woman again, one last time.

Once, I said to her: "Vali, it's just a dream."

Only once, because when she answered "I have to do this," and looked at me, I knew it would be pointless to argue. She believed in dreams. Not comprehensively. Perhaps five or six times since I'd known her she'd dreamed something and been unable to ignore it.

*We should go south tomorrow.*

*Why?*

*I dreamed it. There's something bad waiting in this direction.*

*You dreamed it?*

*Yes.*

I didn't argue. She was so unsuperstitious in all other respects it left the value of the exceptions high. And who was I, after all, to argue with dreams? I had none. Had had none since my Turning. Sleep was an uninterrupted blackout. Sometimes I woke with the vague feeling that something had been going on—that my slurped-down dead had been boisterously up all day—but there was never any content. Waking then was like coming home to a house perfectly in order and nonetheless knowing the kids had had a party while you were away.

"I'll come with you as far as the edge of the camp," I said. "I won't come in with you. No one will even know I'm there."

We were still a day's journey from her tribe, whose annual peregrinations she was assuming unchanged. A dangerous assumption, I thought. For all she really knew there would be no one there. Or a different tribe altogether. A hostile one. A *more* hostile one.

"Vali?"

"We'll talk about it tomorrow. Come on, it's getting late."

Early, she meant. We were in a mossy forest of giant trees and tiny bluebells with a green-and-black stream running through it like liquid malachite. No cave. I'd dug out an earth in the bank under a dying oak, half the roots of which emerged from the turf like a wizened hand. (Daylight protection in those days was a drag. Stones, brushwood, skins, logs, holes in the fucking ground.) I'd fed, joylessly, three days ago, and in anticipation of coming deprivation—Vali wouldn't need to eat for another eight days, and I wanted to wait—the thirst had started a preemptive protest in my chest and calves.

"Don't go far," I said to her.

"Calm down," she said. "This forest is going to be pretty in the sunlight. Besides, I'm exhausted. Give me a kiss."

I remember that kiss. Soft and lingering and tender. Her hand wrapped in my hair, one fierce squeeze. The smell of her skin, the dark glimmer of her eyes.

That day, that sleep, *I* had a dream.

I was in a meadow, just after sunset. Daisies and buttercups like shy little spirits in the dusk. A line of dark trees to my left, rolling hills to my right. I didn't recognise the place. I was looking for Vali. Every blade of grass said she'd been this way, recently; the land was rich with her scent. But something resisted me. My legs laboured, weakened with each trembling step. The air was first soupy, then pliable, then quagmire. Eventually, I lay down on the ground, utterly exhausted. I seemed to lie there for a long time, watching the stars, wondering what would happen when the night was gone and the sun rose. Or rather, knowing what would happen, but wondering how it would feel. The sadness of not seeing Vali again before I died kept expanding in me. It kept reaching what I thought must be the limit of what I could feel and still go on existing. But the sadness just kept getting bigger.

Then I felt her, next to me. It seemed impossible that I hadn't heard (or smelled) her coming near, but I turned, and there she was, lying next to me. She was naked, but her skin was warm.

"I will come back to you," she said. "And you will come back to me. Wait for me."

When I woke, I knew she'd gone to her tribe without me.

# 38

I DID THE twenty-hour journey in six.

When I got to the camp, daylight was less than two hours away. Skin tents, cooking sticks, a few women already awake, lighting the fires. A sleepy lookout, leaning on his spear, standing with his left foot on top of his right, a little way beyond the perimeter.

He didn't see me coming. Didn't hear me. Didn't smell me. Instead found himself lifted by the throat and whisked with marvellous mystery into the cover of the trees. He'd dropped his spear (needing two hands for the pointless attempt to dislodge my one, which was cutting off his air) but there was a sharpened flint at his hip that would do. I pinned him, sat on him, showed him the flint, let him feel it at his throat. He grasped the situation immediately.

"Cry out and you die," I said to him, in his own tongue, Vali's tongue. "Understand?"

He nodded, eyes bugging from the choking. He was a long-bodied fellow with a big head of thick, matted black hair like a large fur hat. I put my finger to my lips—breathe, but do it quietly—then released the pressure on his windpipe. Much gurning and wincing as he struggled to keep the noise of recovering from near-strangulation down. The flint had already drawn a little blood from his neck. He swallowed and gasped, gasped and swallowed. I gave him a moment. He smelled of river water and cured skins and some animal fat they rubbed into their hair.

"The woman who came here," I said, pressing on the flint. "Where is she?"

"She's . . . She's here."

"Where?"

"The big tent. Fa's tent. Fa and Mabon's."

Mabon. The spurned lover who'd followed her. Whose head she'd biffed with a rock. My blood rustled, a nervy herd about to be panicked into a stampede.

I knocked the lookout unconscious and went in silence back to the camp. (Strictly I ought to have slit his throat, but the possibility he was kin to Vali stopped me.) Thirty or so tents, no mistaking the biggest. Two spear-equipped guards and a fire already going outside. You'd think I'd have thought out what I was going to do. But having the capabilities I had, I hadn't. Human resistance, to me, was like the resistance of straw to fire.

The guards were awfully surprised when I morphed out of the firelight.

"Greetings," I said, palms raised. "Peace. I'm here to speak with your chief."

From their reaction I might as well have said: *Die screaming, motherfuckers, I've come to kill you all!* They both assumed a combat stance, spears hoisted, and simultaneously released a strange, warbling, falsetto cry—something like, *mooloomooloomooloo*—which, I knew, with a sort of weariness, was the raised alarm. Women shrieked and dropped their firewood. Tents stirred. Feet scurried. Within a few moments I was surrounded by gawping humans in varying states of dress and consciousness. The old, the women, the children, mainly. Perhaps a dozen men under twenty-five, armed with spears, flints, bows and arrows, the string-and-rocks caboodle with which their most skilled hunters could niftily trip and hobble an antelope from fifty paces. (The masculine cream of the tribal crop away on the hunt, obviously.) The sweet stink of roused human blood roused *my* blood, lashed the already restive thirst into prancing delight. But that wasn't what I was here for.

The flap on the main tent whipped open and a young woman of dark, bitchy prettiness emerged, a-jangle with beads and teeth. Firm little breasts and a taut belly. Her black hair hung in thick ripples down to her trim waist. Tribal psyche hushed, more in fear of her than they were of me. Mabon and Fa. This was Fa, evidently. Chief's wife. Mabon had sought solace in the arms of another. I doubted he was entirely happy.

"Greetings," I repeated. "I'm here for the woman, Vali. Let me speak with her and we'll be on our way."

Mistress bitchy looked me up and down. She had a fiery, perpetually calculating little brain. Very few men would be her match, I thought.

"Hold him, idiots!" she barked.

Muscled arms found me, established what they thought would be an undislodgable grip on my wrists and biceps and neck. Removing them would be a moment's trifle, once I'd decided on it.

"What do you want with her?"

"To escort her from your camp, quietly."

"She's your woman?"

"My companion."

"Ha!"

She had very white teeth, plump lips but a small mouth. Her face was too easily and too much animated. She wanted power. She was devoted to it.

"She's not your woman," she said, grinning. "She's not a woman at all. She's a traitor and a murderer and a stinking *malek-hin*!"

"I'd like to see her, please," I said. "Perhaps I could speak to Mabon?"

Crowd murmur. The very slightest hint of uncertainty in Fa.

"Mabon is not here," she said. "I speak for him in his absence. However, we will give you your 'companion,' so you can 'escort her' from our camp safely. Bring her!"

One knows, of course.

Always, with the big things, one knows just a moment ahead.

*I will come back to you. And you will come back to me. Wait for me.*

The two guards disappeared behind the tent. Then returned with what they had to show me. The first was dragging Vali's naked, decapitated body. The second bore a wooden pole, with her head jammed onto its sharpened end.

I don't know how many of them I killed. Not all, since most of them began running once they saw what they were up against. I don't remember killing any children (though I can hardly swear to it) but I certainly killed several women, starting with Fa, whose guts I opened with a single swipe. That image, actually—her looking down to see her abdomen yawning, emptying its contents like someone opening his mouth and letting half-masticated food fall out—was the last clear snapshot. Everything after that swims red. Rage (the dark twin of ecstasy) is transcendent, in that you only know you were gone in it by virtue of coming back to yourself. It's a blank Somewhere Else defined by the return to the all too vivid Here and Now, where you find yourself still saddled with insufficient finiteness, still in dismal possession of fingertips and eyebrows, a face, hands, legs, the whole maddening corporeal package. Maddening because every cell speaks the reality, the new reality—in this case the reality of what I'd lost. Forever.

The disgust was unbearable. The disgust at what they'd done to her, yes, the violent demonstration that her body obeyed the physical laws, but disgust too at the thought that as far as the world was concerned this couldn't be anything other than justice. If there was to be a notion of justice it would have to entail this. And who—millennia before poor Socrates asked his suicidal question—did not have an intuitive notion of justice? Here was the core of monstrosity: If you were a monster the human world had nothing to offer you but the just demand for your death. And since they were, in the last analysis, your food and drink, what could they be but right? There was no argument you could bring against them. All you could bring was your monstrous enmity. Irreconcilable differences, as the divorce laws would have it, far in the future.

I buried her a mile away, in the forest, since forests were her favourite, in either form. *I buried her a mile away.* Let me not exclude the vicious, innocent practicalities, that I had to cradle her body in my arms with her severed head resting on her own soft midriff. There are things you think you won't be able to do, that need the actual to become possible. There are things that only become thinkable once you're already doing them. And even then perhaps not. I performed the actions in a self-averted trance, not really taking it in, not really accepting it. Thinking all the while, in fact, that I would discuss the horror and absurdity of it with her later.

*Promise me you'll live as long as you can.*

I nearly broke the promise there and then, sitting by the freshly filled grave while the world without her in it boomed against me like an ocean. An ocean going about its vast, repetitive, pointless business. The temptation to simply wait for the sun was full of warm comfort. It would be so easy. Just don't move. Just. Don't. Move.

But I imagined her face, smiling with a forgiveness that was also a demand at the exposed cowardice. I felt the calm force of her. You can't. You have to live. You promised. I will come back to you. And you will come back to me. Wait for me.

I didn't decide to live.

I just postponed killing myself.

It began to rain. I knelt, kissed the cold earth of her grave (still, *still* thinking, with the idiot part of myself, with all the stubborn stupidity of love, that I would see her when I woke) then rose, turned, and headed deeper into the forest.

# 39
## *Justine*

STUPID FUCKING IDIOT.

All these years and everything he's told me and I still do the dumbest fucking thing. I can't be this stupid again. *You think it through, Justine,* he told me, God knows how many times. *Because if you stop thinking it through, you die. It's as simple as that.*

Well, maybe I'll die. Maybe I've fucked it up for both of us.

*Dear Fluff,*
   *Please don't worry about me. I have to do this. And I can't do it with you. Don't come after me.*
   *Go and find her. I'm sorry for what I said. I'm sorry for everything.*
*Love,*
*J*

I left the note at the top of the stairs that lead down to the vault. I dressed upstairs, in my room, threw a few clothes into a bag, licence, passport, cash, cards, then went down to the garage. Unlocked the fake plates strongbox and found a Texas registration. Swapped it up for the Jeep's locals and slipped two more (Wyoming and New Jersey) under the spare wheel. I was so busy congratulating myself on how smart I was to remember to do this that it wasn't until I'd been driving for an hour that I realised I should never have taken the Jeep in the first place: It didn't matter what state the car was from if forensics swept it and found traces of the body we'd had in the trunk.

I pulled over. Hands shaking. Knees unravelling.

And the thirst like a wasps' nest I'd just jabbed with a stick.

I leaned against the side of the car, breathing, thinking: You're on the freeway. You can't stop. Cameras. Cops. There was a piece of graffiti I'd seen somewhere that said: ONE NATION UNDER CCTV.

I got back in. I told myself there was no reason for the cops to stop me. Anyway the bodies were wrapped and we'd bleached the trunk. Stop being an idiot. Stop panicking and think it through. You stop thinking it through and you die. It's as simple as that.

Deep breath. I put it in drive. Signalled. Gas. Gently. If they'd seen me pull over I'd say I wasn't feeling well. That's what it would've looked like. That's what it *was*.

Two hundred and fifty miles to Vegas. Eight hours till sunrise. Plenty of time. I'd just drive normally. I'd stick to the speed limit. Nothing would happen.

But my hands felt empty, and the stirred-up swarm of flies around my heart wouldn't settle.

A McDonald's M rose up on the left. A Subway. A KFC. Like flags waving from the old life. That book title. *You Can't Go Home Again*.

# 40

I REACHED NORTH Vegas just after three in the morning. The air was hot and damp and full of low clouds. Soft empty greyness. I sat there, hands on the wheel, engine off, feeling sick with aliveness.

1388 Balzar Avenue. A one-storey shithole. Dirt front yard with a broken laundry spinner and a solitary trash barrel. Empty beer cans and a shattered box crate. A screen door with half the mesh gone. All the lights out. Looking at the house a phrase of Fluff's came back to me. *Objective correlative.* What? I'd asked him. He'd said: It's some object in the physical world that corresponds, symbolically, with something non-physical or inner. (He'd said: You see them all the time on The Lash. On The Lash, everything's— Then he'd remembered it was me, and what I thought about all that.) Now I looked at the filthy, broken-down house and thought: That's him. That house is Karl Leath's objective correlative.

Then I thought: No, it's not.

It's mine.

I knew he was inside. I would've known anyway, even without the new version of myself. This wasn't the first time I'd been here. I had an apartment forty miles away in Boulder City. Rented a year ago under a false name. Nothing fancy, barely furnished. I didn't need furniture, except for appearances. Everything was for appearances. The only thing not for appearances was the bathroom without a window and with a heavier than usual door. And locks. Lots of locks. Because I'd known that by the time I came here to do this, that's what I'd need. I was supposed to go there now. Rest. Get it together. Come back tomorrow night at sunset. That was the plan. This was supposed to be scoping. I wasn't supposed to do anything now.

I hit the button that rolled the driver's window down. The smell of warm asphalt and garbage came in. Leaked fuel somewhere. Stale Chinese take-out and hash. A big sudden whiff of piss-soaked concrete. A block away someone was playing rap with too much bass. An annoying thud through everything. Like a heartbeat. Like their heartbeats. I remembered the heat and heaviness and smell of burped whiskey and his heartbeat like something hitting me. It had made me think of the Tin Man, who didn't have a heart. And the horrible disappointment when the Mighty Oz turned out to be that little old guy with white hair. Their heartbeats against me felt like the dirtiest thing.

You won't need to feed until Saturday, Fluff had told me. Saturday was tomorrow. He should know, I guess, but it was there in me already, right now, and had been since yesterday, a feeling like a million tiny teeth biting my blood.

Scoping only. Nothing yet.

But it was as if the space around me in the car wasn't empty. It felt like soft arms and hands prompting me, little pressures at my elbows and wrists, the small of my back, behind my knees. Some part of my brain was grabbing at questions about what if someone sees the car and if he's not alone and a neighbour or there's not enough time and the car breaks down and the sun and you're there in the middle of the highway— But my body, moved by the soft invisible hands and arms, felt like a calm smile. All the things around me—the car's dials and smell of vinyl, the low-rise houses and the stink of waste and the asphalt's slight curve and even the spilled trash from a torn garbage bag smiled with me, as if I'd found the one thing that they'd been waiting for to make them perfect and happy.

I got out of the Jeep and closed the door behind me.

# 41

SOMEONE HAD SCRAPED the "L" from his name on the mailbox and scribbled in a "D." Leath had become Death. It was just random shit. The sort of thing you'd expect kids to do. *Except on The Lash, nothing's random*. I could hear Fluff saying it, shrugging, apologising, half-laughing. It prickled my face. Not excitement. Irritation. As if someone had turned the heating on on an already too hot day. It could become like claustrophobia, if you let it, this beguilement.

My nails and teeth throbbed. The darkness was like goodwill from the world. The darkness was on my side. I went around the house, silently, looking in the windows. There were things I could've accidentally kicked or tripped over, but I didn't. I realised I'd probably never do anything like that again.

Four rooms. Tiny bathroom. Dirty kitchen with unwashed dishes and a microwave with a dark brown burn on its door and a drop-leaf table covered in take-out cartons. A lounge with a too big fake leather couch and armchair and a bookcase with what looked like car engine parts on it instead of books. TV still on, muted.

One bedroom at the front with a bare mattress on the floor.

The other at the back, a double bed.

With him on it.

Lying uncovered on his back in boxer shorts, a stripe of streetlight across his white paunch. Breathing. The paunch went up and down. Something in his nose whistled.

For a few seconds everything went black. Just nothingness. I thought I'd died.

Then I came back, as if every tiny particle of myself started speaking at the same time. I thought: I'm dreaming. I'll wake up. But moments passed and I knew I wasn't dreaming. I was awake right into my fingerprints and eyelashes.

I wasn't aware of deciding anything. But I found myself moving, doing things.

Getting into the house wasn't difficult. I took hold of the kitchen door handle, twisted and just gently pushed until the lock snapped. Like a perforated join in a sheet of cardboard. Big heavy things were nothing. When I put my hands on them I could feel how easy it would be to break them. I stepped into the kitchen. I thought the house felt sorry for him, the way he lived. Now I was inside, his breathing was louder. He sounded older. He was older. It made me feel sick again for a few seconds, thinking of him alive all these years, walking around and talking and drinking coffee and smoking cigarettes and watching TV. I had a clear image of him sitting on the toilet, staring at the floor—and suddenly felt so sure I was going to throw up I had to lean on the table. I focused on a Domino's pizza box on the floor to stop the room heaving and spinning.

But in a few moments everything around me went still and gathered again, the soft invisible arms holding me, moving me, gently, and the nausea passed.

I checked my jacket pockets, even though I didn't need to. Duct tape and Tuff Ties in the left, gun in the right. I walked down the hall to the bedroom. The door was open.

A smell of socks and stale bedding and cigarette smoke and spilled beer. There was enough light to see his face. It looked small. Because in my head it was always huge. He'd lost a lot of hair. Still oiled what was left, back, off the tough greasy forehead. Open your eyes, they always said. *Open your eyes.* And when I did the faces were like giants, the smell of hair oil and whiskey breath and cigarette smoke and the pores with little worms of dirt and the eyeballs like planets. The laughter and the heartbeat against me the dirtiest thing. The bigness and heat of the heartbeat against me.

I stood at the bottom of the bed, looking down at him, amazed at how small he seemed. His legs were thin. He had varicose veins.

One of the things that could happen was that because of how small and insignificant he was now I could just turn and walk away and never go anywhere near him again. I'd seen this in movies. It was mixed up with the way people always said something like two wrongs don't make a right or if you resort to violence they've won or you're just as bad as they are and in *Schindler's List* the way Liam Neeson said to Ralph Fiennes that the real way to exert power over someone was to forgive them. I was aware of this like a kind of glittery lightness somewhere near me.

Then he opened his eyes.

He saw me straight away. Started, with a small cry. Tried to get up.

"Don't move," I said.

I didn't remember pulling out the gun or stepping into the light where he could see it. But I must have, because there I was. He was suddenly very alive, up on one elbow. His paunch quivered. His mouth was open. He was squinting to see me properly. Waking up like that his body had pushed out its stink of beer and pizza and coffee and sweat.

"Don't move," I said again. I thought the floor was tilting. I put a hand out to steady myself. But it was an illusion.

"Who the fu—"

"Shut up. Shut the fuck up."

"What do—"

"*Shut up!*"

I hadn't known the voice would be like that. The same voice. I couldn't stand it. I couldn't stand it because it was like being hit with a fascination. Like someone pulling a soft dark bag over my head.

The gun had gone big and heavy in my hand. In my mind was a mish-mash of all the times I'd imagined this with me saying *Don't you know who I am* and *Do you remember telling me to open my eyes* and *You're going to keep your eyes open* and *All you'll want is to die quickly but you won't you're going to die very slowly* and *Look at me look at me open your fucking eyes.* But it was hard to imagine saying any of those things now. Now that he was there saying those things would . . . It was as if those things weren't big enough. Nothing I could say would be big enough.

A feeling of tiredness and disgust came over me. I had this image of dragging him outside the house and a crowd of people all standing around staring, amazed, because by the time I got him out he'd be this tiny, shrivelled thing, not like a man at all but like a little piece of dried up meat like that thing biltong they sell in the delis now and it wouldn't be enough, just like nothing I could say would be enough.

Then he said "Jesus," and I knew he'd figured out who I was.

I remembered his hand, sour and hot and moist over my mouth and nose. I remembered him saying You keep that wriggling up you're gonna make me come and the one called Pinch laughing and her face staring at me and not seeing me showing me she couldn't see me.

I had the gun pointed right at his face.

And when he flung his arm out and knocked it from my hand, it seemed to happen in slow motion. It was as if I'd wanted him to do that. It was as if I'd asked him to.

# 42

FOR A SPLIT-SECOND I knew everything up to now had been a dream and the reality was that *I* was the tiny one and that I had no power and that I'd come back to him willingly so it could all happen again. So he could do it all again. For a moment it was a relief to know I was nothing. Not even disgusting. Not even shit. Just nothing.

Then all the soft invisible arms in the air that had been guiding me hardened and coiled and released—and suddenly in place of nothingness was something dark red and full of energy and laughter and lightness, and when I looked again at his face I saw that my fist had smashed through his mouth, smashed clean through. Most of his teeth were gone and his bottom jaw was hanging from where my nails had sliced the muscle on their way out. He was making a weird *gah, gah* sound in the back of his throat, trying to get his legs off the bed.

I grabbed his loose jaw. *You could pick that up with one hand. Punch through that. Pull that off like a button.* When I yanked it came away from his head. I held it up for a moment, felt him not believing it, not believing what was happening—then dropped it on his chest. His tongue, left behind, looked huge hanging there, like an ox tongue on a meat counter.

He rolled onto the floor at my feet with a soft thud. He was trying to work out where the gun had gone. He got up onto his hands and knees. I let him move a couple of feet because I was hypnotised by the sight of it.

Then suddenly I was impatient and I reached down, took hold of his throat, lifted him to his feet—felt his hands on my wrist like nothing, like butterflies, like paper bracelets—and dumped him back onto the bed.

I wasn't thinking. This was something else. Time wasn't passing. Instead it was just Now . . . Now . . . Now, like a flower opening wider and wider.

He tried to speak again, but it was just soft sounds and dark blood. It made me feel peaceful that he couldn't speak. Then he tried to grab me, and as soon as he did that the impatience and disgust rushed back up in me and I smacked him hard in the middle of his chest. The big bone there cracked. I felt it. *Heard* it. I pictured the bone like a white wall protecting his heart—but now with a huge crack in it. I imagined myself pulling the two broken halves apart and seeing his heart, like Jesus's in the Sacred Heart painting our neighbour Mrs. Clemence had in her hallway. *Bless Our Home*. It always made me think of *our* home. Jesus watching everything that happened in the living room, with the big, uneven blue curtains drawn and the bare overhead bulb lighting everything too much, the hair on their shins, their thick toenails, my mother's face shiny with sweat.

Gasping and making a gargling sound, he struggled up again onto his left elbow. He reached for the nightstand. Missed. Tried again. It exhausted me even more, that he was still trying to come up with something, trying to help his situation. It made me angry because I knew he'd keep on trying to stay alive. It made me angry because a part of me was standing to one side saying it's not enough it's never going to be enough it's too small it's too ordinary ordinary bones and falling on the floor and his tongue hanging like that and how can it ever be enough?

Without thinking about it, I slashed my fingernails across his throat.

Blood sprayed my face.

Touched my eyes, my lips.

My tongue.

Which changed everything.

# 43

*YOU WON'T NEED to feed till Saturday.*

Wrong. The flower that had been opening all this time turned into a black red hole that sucked me in, head-first, a long fall that ended when I felt the bump of my teeth in his throat and the first warm spurt of his blood going into my mouth.

At first there was . . .

I felt myself thinking: I've never had to use this word before . . .

Joy.

*Joy.* This is what joy is. Like those flying dreams the moment you first realise you can do it . . . At first it was simple. Three, four, five seconds the blood was just goodness. The goodness was immense and nothing to do with him. He was just a funnel for the blood that was coming from somewhere else, from the universe, and the blood went into me and forced delicious warmth through my shoulders and face and breasts and belly and legs and feet. It was as if the blood was in a mad rush to map every part of me, to get all of me. And from the first swallow I was in a mad rush to get it in me, all of me. We were like two animals, me and the blood, two animals who loved each other but had been kept apart for years.

Then on the third or fourth or fifth swallow it turned into *his* blood—and I saw him, maybe eight years old, and a basketball hit him full in the face and broke his nose (I felt some tiny echo of the bone going in my own nose) and the kid who'd thrown it laughing and the force of the blow knocked him onto his ass and they laughed harder because he sat down in a shallow puddle on the uneven court and I could feel his face hot and big and his heart full of something like shame. I thought: You can't stop. Once you start drinking you can't stop. You don't suck the blood, the blood sucks you. Video-game footage raced, trolls and marines and things that looked like they were made of mud and it gave him not peace but took his memory away for the hours days months years that the explosion graphics and death screams filled him though it was also a kind of boredom like too much food. There was a girl and the two of them in a bar that looked like a ski-lodge but it was hot and I could feel the air like soup because the air-conditioning had gone and he was feeling that it was going okay with her (I saw her moist, big face and heavy blonde bob like a helmet and her hands were a little cracked with eczema but with fat red fingernails) and she's laughed a couple of times but then time speeds up and he's holding her elbow and trying to force her away from the bar and people are looking and she yanks her arm free and knocks a pitcher of some red cocktail from the counter and it hits the floor and bursts. The familiarity of this is like more heat on him, as if someone's holding an electric fire close to his face on top of how hot it is already in the bar. It's so familiar to him, this moment when it goes from going well to them not wanting his hand on them and one minute they're laughing the next it's get your fucking hands off me and they're all the fucking same fucking cunts and it's like a bored relief for him to have this thought, fucking *cunts*, and it *is* a relief because the truth is he doesn't want them and I wanted to stop but I didn't want the blood to stop it was so good so good and then I knew what was coming, what was coming through the blur of surfed channels and image after image of children's small half-undressed bodies and confused or terrified faces and each image brings the same claustrophobia, the space they're trapped in and the big heat of unfamiliar bodies and someone shouting orders or silently positioning them with a focus and farawayness that's more terrifying than the shouts and slaps. Oh please let me stop but I couldn't. Every ounce given over to the rhythm of the sucking, the gulping, the swallowing in time with his heartbeat—which brought the other heartbeat, his beating into my back and I saw myself from his point of view and when I saw the back of my head and the yellow t-shirt and felt myself through him crying I tried to shut my eyes shut my eyes block it out but I couldn't because the blood kept coming and it was in my head whether I shut my eyes or not and it broke my own chest like I'd broken his and I felt all the time I'd lived since then and was saying sorry, sorry, sorry to the little girl I was as if she was someone I'd abandoned and never gone back for and it wasn't her fault it wasn't her fault it was mine.

*Don't let the heart stop, angel! If the heart stops you'll go with it!*

From somewhere. Maybe I remembered him telling me or maybe he was in my head right then but I knew I had to stop and the hearts were close and only in the last moment before I pulled my mouth away did I see the final image of the little boy, four or five years old, and the man with his trousers down and his cock exposed and I felt Leath always trying to get away from it and it always dragged him back and I knew it had happened to him. It had happened to him, too.

I thought I was getting to my feet, but I found I'd fallen, crashed to the floor. For a moment everything went black again. I could feel the room swinging. The blood was heavy on my chest and in my limbs, but as soon as I started to move, started to get to my knees, I could feel it changing, dissolving into an energy I'd never, ever run out of. I ran for the door—but found I'd got there in one huge high stride, as if the invisible soft arms had lifted me there. All I could think of was getting as far away from his body as fast as possible.

The house seemed to shrink behind me. A dog barked three times somewhere close. A mile away a truck downshifted. My hands were hot and wet with blood. There was blood all over me. I was soaked with it.

I got to the Jeep, got in, slammed the door. I'd left the keys in the ignition. Stupid. So stupid. But in those moments my stupidity and the risks I'd taken seemed like small things. Little objects far away.

Ten miles from Boulder City I realised I'd left the gun in the house, and fingerprints—in his blood—everywhere.

# 44
## *Remshi*

I KNEW SHE'D gone before I opened my eyes. A rip in the newly visceral fabric, a hole in the weave of shared blood.

Fear for her went through me like a delirious disease. *I promise I'll never leave you.* As far as she was concerned I already had. The lines of the note she'd left me like grit in my blood:

*Go and find her. I'm sorry for what I said. I'm sorry for everything.*

Go and find her. Talulla. Vali reborn. The prophecy awaiting fulfilment. All reduced, as I stood in the study with the note in my hand, to the risible American pop ethic: *Follow your dream.* Naturally I'd *had* the dream, again. The twilit beach, the boat, the someone walking behind me. Naturally *He lied in every word* had woken me with its tongue in my ear. Naturally I'd sat up in the basement bed sickened and thrilled by the feeling of knowing something without knowing what it was.

Go and find her. Go and find the werewolf you believe to be the reincarnation of your lover of seventeen thousand years ago? Go and find her. Because after all, you've had a couple of dreams and scribbled down a prophecy or two, stoned out of your mind in a witch-doctor's hut. Because after all you've had the beginnings of a hard-on after millennia of your dick being as much use as tits on a boar.

The full absurdity of it hit me, settled on me like a giant . . . Like a *giant vampire bat*. (Why not?) I saw myself for what I was: a confused fool. A *pitiful* fool. And there's no fool like an old fool, the saying goes. Which made me the biggest fool in history. Only God could be a bigger one.

Not, of course, that the full giant vampire-bat weight of absurdity was the whole story. (Nothing is the whole story. The self's curse—and the writer's.) Yes, there was the concession to the pitiful old fool and his *dreams*—but there remained, whether I liked it or not, the prickle of meaning on the ether, the design-wink of the world, the story-glimmer that wouldn't be denied. There remained, stubbornly smiling, the beguilement.

Go after Talulla.

Go after Justine.

There was an old philosophical chestnut, Buridan's Ass. Faced with two identically appealing haystacks—and therefore unable to prefer one to the other—the donkey starves to death.

But donkeys, of course, lack whim and intuition. More importantly, they don't smoke. I reached for the almost empty pack of American Spirits on the desk (one left, slightly crumpled) and found that they were right next to Justine's laptop.

I opened it and powered-up. Justine's desktop image is the Apple logo. She doesn't feel entitled to the personalisation of her technology. Even the former recorded Bette Davis greeting on her phone had been my doing.

Finder.

Documents.

File.

Encryption.

Password.

I rummaged in the blood. Dissolved myself internally and swam in the red dark. It's not the same ease of access as when the other person's nearby. It's like holding your breath underwater. Sooner or later you have to come up.

I came up. The external world shivered back into authority.

My fingers didn't hesitate.

The document opened.

Blank.

She'd deleted everything.

I loved her for her precautions, her stubbornness, her decision to be strong enough to do it all on her own. That was Justine: she *decided* how much strength she would have, then acted as if she had it. And in doing so, had it.

I took a deep drag on the cigarette, exhaled. Try again. Browning's *Collected Works*, I noticed, was still lying where it had fallen the other night. I ignored it—though the act of ignoring it made the ether shudder for a moment. I ignored *that*, too.

Tougher this time. Facts occluded by feelings. Heavier water choked with weeds. It began to hurt.

I surfaced a second time.

Not much. Karl Leath was still in North Vegas. The other man, the one they called "Pinch" (his actual name eluded me, but I knew it sounded odd . . . I struggled . . . Dale . . . Wayne . . . Schrutt) had won $814,000 in the Texas state lottery. Retired early. Gone to live in Thailand.

That was all. The house addresses were beyond me—though Leath's and Pinch's faces were in her like bloated twin suns, her system's colossal binary star.

She'd go after Leath first, closest to home.

I looked at the clock; it was just after midnight. I'd slept so late again. A little portion of consciousness like a lone schoolboy at a solitary desk had been busy fretting about these lie-ins, this pissing away of darkness I'd been guilty of. I ignored it. In the VanHome I could make North Vegas in three and a half hours. If she was there, I'd find her.

# 45
## *Justine*

IN THE BOULDER City apartment I lay on the bathroom floor in the dark, the door locked with all its locks, the little gap at the bottom blocked with a rolled-up towel. Leath's life going into mine was like flashes of fire and sudden sheer drops and a sick feeling of certainty that it was in me forever now and what happens is that inside you make room somehow you have to make room and it hurts but you know that one day it won't, one day it'll be totally familiar the way like I said before you know driving a car will be. I didn't want it. The image of the little boy pressing himself awkwardly into the corner of a big green velour couch and the sudden switch to his point of view seeing the big pale penis and snuff-coloured pubic hair and a tiny yellow-headed pimple buried in the hair on a man's thigh. And like a reflex to it all the video-game footage and the peace of the intricacy of muscle car engines the peace of the cold grease smell of the workshop and the tools in your hands like friends. But the peace never lasted because you went back and those first pictures were when he was fifteen and he thought it was buried but the pictures when he saw them were like a warmth going through him and it was like the warmth of coming home and his face had felt so full and tender with this feeling of ashamed homecoming that even then he'd known would never be free of rage and boredom and sadness and he'd never be anything except alone and what he was.

I was lying on my side on a doubled comforter and pillow, knees drawn up, next to the base of the washbasin, which every now and then I would reach out and touch because my palms were hot and the coldness of the porcelain felt good. I was remembering something Fluff had said. He was always teasing me about not reading books, but one day he said: *Reading a book is a dangerous thing, Justine. A book can make you find room in yourself for something you never thought you'd understand. Or worse, something you never wanted to understand.* I thought now: He wasn't just talking about books. He was talking about this. He said: *You know the people who dread getting called for jury duty? Big readers. The more you read, the harder it is to condemn.* Then he'd frowned and added: *Assuming, that is, you're not reading execrable pap.*

Execrable pap. He uses words and I don't know what they mean, except the context makes it obvious. I missed him, suddenly, really badly. The last couple of nights it had been nice falling asleep and waking up next to him. I felt sad that I'd left him such a short note. I felt sad that I hadn't told him how much I loved him. I don't know why it suddenly felt like I was never going to see him again, but it did. I felt it so strongly that if it hadn't been daylight outside I would've jumped in the Jeep and driven back to Las Rosas right then.

Thinking of the Jeep brought up all the unbelievably stupid things I'd done, all the ways I'd fucked this up. The Jeep itself, for starters. Should've used a rental. The gun. Fingerprints, sneaker prints. There were probably tyre prints in the spilled oil. I'd driven out of the city breaking every speed limit. In clothes covered in blood. I hadn't even changed. Just driven to the building, put the Jeep in the underground lot and taken the elevator up to Four. It wasn't that I was trusting to luck not to run into anyone. I wasn't trusting to anything. I wasn't thinking. I was just blind soft heat, and the first violent movement of the new blood finding room in me. If the police acted fast I'd probably left enough evidence for them to be here before sundown tonight. Practically a trail of goddamned footprints in blood. Weirdly, there was a sort of comfort in knowing that even if that were true, there was nothing I could do about it now, and nowhere I could go.

I realised I still had my socks on, so I pulled them off. Underneath the raging sort of enrichment I was deadly tired. Obviously I couldn't see the daylight, but I could feel the four hours the sun had already been up. *We can stay awake*, Stonker had explained, *but it's not much fun.* It wasn't. There was a dry, hard ache behind my eyes. It was like the blood couldn't settle or knit properly until I slept and let it. Until I stopped watching it.

*The harder it is to condemn.*

That was the thing keeping me awake, of course. Like a snake trying to unknot itself. A blood snake jerking and writhing. It had happened to him. Shouldn't that make a difference? Didn't it?

*You keep wriggling like that you're gonna make me come.*

I turned and rested my face against the cold of the porcelain. It felt so good. That was something you could say about the world, that some things didn't change, that if you were hot it was nice to feel something cool against you.

# 46
## Remshi

THERE WERE CALLS to make en route. I have relationships with people such that when I call, they answer. Even in the early hours. They answer because each of them carries a phone on whom I'm the only person who calls. For some humans money and a dedicated phone makes any relationship possible.

First, Olly Maher, of the Amner-DeVere International Private Bank. He wasn't asleep. He was at a party of what sounded like restrained indulgence. There were glasses clinking. There was music playing. Bowie from the live *Ziggy Stardust* album. "My Death." Hardly party music. But this, I reminded myself, was the twenty-first century.

"Norman," he said.

I was on the hands-free in the VanHome, heading east on the 10. Ontario Mills. Hotels and retail parks. Neoned slabs and slivers that reminded me of the days when there was nothing but dust and sage scrub and giant wildrye and mallards quacking with a kind of dour introversion on the river. You blink, you miss it. A long time ago, in a cave, in the darkness, I'd said: "Why?" and the voice had answered: "Someone must bear witness."

"Justine Cavell," I said. "I need to know as soon as she uses any of the cards." She has half a dozen, and only one of them is Amner-DeVere, but that presents only modest difficulty to Olly.

"No problem," Olly said.

"You call me anytime, day or night."

"*Day* or night?"

I'd be sleeping with the cell right next to my ear.

"Day or night, Olly."

"Will do."

Next I called my girl at the FBI, Hannah Willard.

She *was* asleep.

"Jesus Christ," she said. But even in the Jesus Christ I could hear her money-self waking up, eyes wide.

"Two people," I said. "First, Dale Schrutt. Or possibly Wayne Schrutt. In any case Schrutt. U.S. national, now resident in Thailand. Start in Bangkok."

"Look," Hannah began.

"Double," I said. "Start now."

There was a pause. "This has to be the last time," she said. She says this every time. She says this for herself. Three or four more jobs like this, she knows, she'll be able to quit the Bureau for good. She'll be able to quit doing anything she doesn't want to do for good. Which, by and large, is all any human wants. Or thinks they want.

"Spell the last name," she said. Which I did. "You got anything else on this guy?"

"Spent some time in North Vegas. Nickname 'Pinch.' Lottery winner sometime within the last ten years. This is easy money, Han."

"None of it's easy," she said. "This isn't the movies. And the other?"

"Talulla Demetriou."

"Are you kidding?"

"No."

*"Again?"*

"What do you mean, 'again'?"

I could hear her adjusting her position. Sitting further up in bed. She lives alone. She has a hard blonde face and an impatience with idiots. She's waiting to be rich enough to really pick and choose.

"I mean I already found her for you. You lost her again?"

My foot came off the gas a little. Images tumbled: the Forum in Rome at night, torchlit, crowded and vivified because Cleopatra had entered the city that afternoon. Three soldiers with their sandals off at a bar's outside table, drinking cheap wine from wooden cups. A pretty twelve-year-old girl with starved dark eyes huddled in the doorway of a Saffron Hill slum, her legs covered in syphilitic sores. A young woman with her clothes ripped and half her hair pulled out tied to a stake atop a pile of brush and firewood, the lantern-lit faces of a large crowd, some rapt, some jabbering, some bored, the terrible distinctness of teeth and fingers and eyeballs.

A car I'd nearly hit honked, protractedly.

"Explain," I said to Hannah.

Pause. Recalibration. She was wondering if this would compromise my ability to pay her.

"Three years ago," she said. "Alaska. You don't remember?"

I remembered Alaska. The lodge. Talulla. Vali. But I had no memory of how I'd known she was there. The driver of the car I'd just missed, having stopped honking, realised he hadn't vented sufficient spleen, and honked again.

"You traced her?"

"Yeah, and I don't want to have to do it again. The woman has aliases like fucking Imelda Marcos had shoes. I don't know who's doing her IDs, but whoever he is, he's the best in the business."

I clamped my jaws together for a moment, let the fact sink in. You forgot.

"Be that as it may," I said. "Same job. Do what you can."

"For God's—"

"Get me what I need and I promise you can retire."

Silence. She knew enough to know I had it within my power.

"Call me as soon as you have anything," I said, and hung up. Justine's face flashed. *Just following her around gave you dementia and nearly fucking killed you. Some fulfilment.*

I called my chief pilot and transportation logistics guru, Damien. He, too, had been sleeping. He cleared his throat. "Sir?"

"Has Justine asked you to prep the jet?"

"No, sir."

"Nothing about flying to Thailand?"

"No, sir."

"What about Detroit?"

"No, sir. I haven't heard from Ms. Cavell since you were . . . Since we got back from Europe."

Since you were doolally. Since chasing that werewolf gal nearly killed you.

"Listen carefully. If she contacts you, you are to let me know immediately. Without her knowing. Understood?"

"Understood, sir."

"She may want to fly at short notice," I said. "But *do not* go anywhere until you've checked with me. Make up a problem with the plane. But stay on the ground until I get there. Okay?"

"Absolutely, sir."

"I'll be contacting Seth and Veejay with the same instruction, just in case. If you hear from either of them—anything unusual at all—you must also report it to me straight away. I know you're fond of her, Damien, but you have to trust me, this is for her own protection."

"Sir, if she comes to me in person, do you want me to keep her with me?"

"Not by force. And in any case, you wouldn't be able to do anything like that. Not anymore. Just call me straight away. Delay tactics only. Understood?"

"Absolutely, sir."

"We're going to be travelling soon, one way or another. You up to snuff?"

"Absolutely, sir. You can count on me."

"Good man. Everything all right in your world?"

"Peachy, sir. Couldn't be better."

"Call me as soon as you hear anything."

"Standing by, sir."

Very well. She wasn't going to Thailand first. That made Vegas favourite. She wouldn't go to her mother.

Not yet.

# 47

NORTH VEGAS TOLD me she'd been here but I'd missed her. I nosed the VanHome around for more than an hour before I caught (windows down, the city's smells a stadium crowd I was searching for the one beloved face) the first strand on the ether, a psychic stink like the odour of cordite after a gunshot.

Elusive, though. I had it and lost it. I stopped the VanHome and got out. Urban deadspot. Three empty, garbage-strewn lots between an out-of-business repairs garage and a cluster of one-storey homes that were barely more than shotgun shacks. A small freight trailer lying on its side, covered in graffiti. A couch reduced by weather and fire to its rusted sprung frame. A butchered space-hopper. A defeated army of filthy plastic carrier bags. One gets used to these occasional anti-oases in American cities, with their inexplicable inhabitants and remains (I once saw a live parrot sitting in the mouth of an abandoned tumble dryer) but even I was surprised when I noticed the horse.

Not least because it had taken me this long *to* notice him. He limped out of the shadow by the overturned trailer, took a half-dozen unsteady steps, then stood, trembling. He didn't appear to be tethered.

He didn't move when I approached him. (Not knowing, quite, why I was approaching him. Except at the soft insistence—Lash-enriched—of the air around me, that even in its reek of engine oil and human shit *said* to approach him.) It was very quiet. One of the street lights buzzed. I was aware of time, of wasting valuable seconds and minutes in which Justine's trail could only be cooling—but I couldn't help it. My practical self was working through the understandable questions: *How could a horse be . . . ? Whose . . . ? Surely a permit . . . And not even tied . . . How could . . . ?* While the rest of me had accepted the moment's obscure gravity.

I couldn't remember when I'd seen an animal in worse shape. Aside from his grotesque thinness and distended belly there were unhealed gashes all over him. His left eye was swollen shut by a hot, delighted infection. There were maggots in one wound on his right foreleg. Sepsis oozing from another on his haunch. When I put my hand gently on his quivering neck, he urinated, a hot arrow of blood. Via an impenetrable association he reminded me of the old beggar man I'd seen on the drive at Las Rosas. I'd forgotten about that. The crutch, the grinning face, the cryptic remark: You're going the wrong way.

"Shshsh," I said, though the horse hadn't, beyond his laboured breathing, made a sound. I rested my forehead against his muzzle. His shivering was almost a thing of disgust.

I don't quite know how long we stood together like that, out of time. I was thinking of the scene in *Crime and Punishment* that never failed to wreck my heart, the milk-cart horse whipped to death by his driver, the crowd laughing, egging the driver on—but there was something else it reminded me of, something . . .

It didn't matter. I fetched the pistol, a Glock 32, from the VanHome's glovebox (Justine insisted on a gun in every vehicle) and drew his head down and placed the barrel in his ear. I worried for a moment that the noise would attract attention. But the area had already made it clear that gunshots weren't rarities here. In any case, I was resolved.

His big skull was full of exhaustion. I embraced him, gently.

Then stood back and pulled the trigger.

•

I picked up Justine's scent again thirty minutes later. West on West Carey Boulevard, south on Martin Luther King, west on Balzar Avenue. Warm. Warmer. Hot. Red hot. 1388. By which time I didn't need her scar on the atmosphere. By which time the spilled blood was blaring.

Sunrise eighty-two minutes away. I wasn't worried. The VanHome had a built-in blackout compartment. (Justine should have taken this instead of her Jeep.) I'd go to one of the underground casino lots. There was time.

I found Karl Leath as she'd left him (aside from the glut of circumstantial evidence there was no mistaking either my girl's physical scent or its soul's correlate), on his back on the bed, one pale and varicosed leg hanging over the edge, bottom jaw missing, throat torn open. His eyes were wide, showing mostly whites. His tongue lolled, lewd and frank as an Aztec god's.

"She made quite a mess," a female voice said.

At the risk of redundancy, let me tell you I'm not easily startled. It had probably been a thousand years since anyone had given me a fright. But I'd poured all my consciousness into Justine's slipstream and left none for what was going on in my own. Therefore I started—and turned.

"She's new, obviously," the vampire said.

She was standing in the bedroom doorway, hands by her sides. Tied back blonde hair, glacier-blue eyes, white skin and a full red mouth. Red, white and blue so vivid the Tricolour flashed in my memory. Dark jeans, riding boots, black leather motorbike jacket. All of which had seen better days. She'd fed, recently. The blood-glut's throb came through her body's aura of dust and gasoline and burnt flesh. She wasn't alone. Someone else was in the kitchen.

It took me a moment—memory wobbled and flailed and wrenched itself back into balance—then I knew her: Mia Tourisheva.

There was history. Three years ago her vampire son, Caleb, had been captured by WOCOP and incarcerated. Talulla, held at the same facility, had escaped and taken the boy with her, saving his life. Which would have left Ms Tourisheva in her debt, had Talulla not done what she did next. What she did next was threaten to torture and kill Caleb herself unless his mother infiltrated the vampire cult holding *Talulla's* son and helped her rescue him. Mia had had no choice. In the rescue operation that followed (I was there—Justine had filled me in—as Marco Ferrara) relations between the two women were further complicated by Talulla saving *Mia's* life—and returning Caleb to her unharmed.

"Is she all right?" I asked her. "Do you have her?"

"Have her? Why would I have her? We just happened to be passing. I was curious. I observed."

"Do you know where she went?"

"Southeast."

"How long since?"

"Two hours, perhaps."

"You remember me?"

"Of course. Though I don't believe the name Marco Ferrara is yours."

"It's one of mine," I said. "You have no idea where she was going beyond the direction?"

Mia shook her head. She looked tired. Sensing I meant her no harm, she stepped into the room. Light from the streetlamp showed dried blood on her hands. There were holes in the jeans. One side of the bike jacket was heavily scuffed.

"Trouble?" I asked. She'd been screening, but understood now it wasn't necessary. I wasn't trying. We know when someone is.

Her smile said yes, trouble. The latest in a long run of troubles. "Idiot driver," she said. "There's a wrecked Harley in the desert."

A child's voice said "I found some" a moment before a boy with a human age of perhaps twelve appeared in the doorway. White-blonde nest of hair, gaunt, androgynous little face, large green eyes. Also in torn jeans and scorched leather jacket—a blood-red one that set his hair and eyes off beautifully. He had an open pack of Lucky Strikes in his hand. I found some. Cigarettes.

"We're not that broke," Mia said to him. Then to me: "They went up in the bike fire. With other things."

The boy stared at me.

"Hello, Caleb," I said. I felt sorry for him. I've seen it before: Turned before adulthood. It never works out, the body that never catches up, the body fundamentally deprived, the body that becomes a joke at the immortal soul's expense. It was palpable between them, that he had the power to punish her for doing it to him. Palpable, too, was the love. There was nothing she wouldn't do for him. And to her nothing she could do for him would ever be enough. Looking at them was like looking at someone resigned to a deformity.

"How do you know who I am?" he said. He'd pocketed the cigarettes, quickly. To leave both hands free. I recognised in him Justine's reflex readiness for flight. Or fight.

"Your mother and I have met before," I said.

"Are you . . . ?" Mia asked me.

*Who they say you are.*

"I think so," I said.

"You think so?"

"It's the only answer I have." I felt suddenly tired myself.

"Do you—"

"No."

I interrupted her quietly, but with finality. Our eyes met. *No, I don't have any answers. I don't know why. I don't know what it means. Only that the conviction that it means something is a necessary disease. Not sure which sense of the word necessary.* The room bristled. It had been waiting for this. The corpse wasn't its nucleus. This was.

Mia looked at me. I wasn't trying to summon the length of my life for her. It came up on its own. It comes up in my eyes. In the space immediately around me. People feel it and it's like stepping into a tomb unopened for twenty thousand years. In which there may or may not be treasure.

"The prophecy?" she said.

I shook my head. I knew which version of the prophecy she meant. The wrong one. The mistranslation. Not "when he joins the blood of the werewolf" but "when he *sheds* the blood of the werewolf." Jacqueline Delon had been working from a (conveniently) corrupted text, one which suggested that Remshi (that would be me, yes, don't laugh) would return and raise the vampire race to global supremacy in a midwinter ritual that demanded not the betrothal but the *sacrifice* of a lycanthrope.

"I was looking for Talulla at the time," I said. "But not for the reason you think. Not for the Disciples' nonsense."

"Are you—"

"Be quiet!"

Are you still looking for her? Caleb had been going to say. His screen was hopeless. Stunted. Another juvenile disadvantage. As soon as he'd begun "Are—" the room's latent store of meaning had surged. Every atom opened its mouth to say: This. Now. Pick this thread up and follow it. It leads. It leads. Mia had cut him off in Russian. But since Russian is one of the countless languages I speak, the werewolf was out of the bag. You see? It's this story after all.

For a moment, I remained silent. Then I said to Caleb, "Could I have one of those?"

He looked at his mother. There was a raggedness to both of them beyond the bike accident and the ruined clothes. In Mia, particularly, the exhausted ghost of entitlement. She was almost—almost—past raging against the pain of whatever it was she'd lost. She'd almost accepted it. She looked at me. Every remaining ounce of her instinct and judgement rose up, leaned against me like a host of the dead. I remained passive. She knew I could get into her son's head if I wanted to. She knew I was refraining. I gave it to her: I WON'T. NOT BY FORCE. LET US UNDERSTAND ONE ANOTHER.

Her shoulders relaxed slightly. Her face said she was getting used to these capitulations, these relinquishments of authority. Caleb, taking his cue from her, extracted the pack of Lucky Strikes and brought them over to me. Lit up me, his mother, himself. All vampires smoke. Smoking's high on the list of Things You Take Up To Pass The Time.

"What happened to you?" I asked, very gently. It was a wretched effort not to dash off there and then in a southeasterly direction. Justine had only two hours on me, after all. But the chances of finding her before sun-up without a city to go on were risibly small. "Southeast" was still a quarter of the available compass. Which was another way of saying she could be a quarter of anywhere.

Mia took a deep drag, rolled her lovely, cold, jewel-eyed head on its flawless neck, exhaled through her nostrils. "We fend for ourselves," she said. "That's all. We have no choice."

NOT IN FRONT OF.

I understood. There was no way of telling their story without it sounding like it was at least partly the boy's fault. She opened enough for me to see: She'd broken the long-standing Fifty Families law by Turning a child. And the child had got himself captured. The Family had found out. She'd been stripped of her assets. Cast out. Effectively excommunicated. There were, of course, other pariah vampires in the world, but she'd get short shrift from them: as a former member of the House of Petrov (one of the oldest and most powerful of the elite—and elit*ist*—Fifty) she'd probably spent years scorning them. She was the bankrupt aristocrat suddenly in jail with the mob. We're not that broke, she'd said. But you can tell a lot about a vampire's bank balance by where she hunts, and if Balzar Avenue was any indicator, *flat* broke wasn't far away. The Harley was probably the last thing of material value. Now gone. A great deal of her weariness had come from having to adjust to the loss of the countless ways wealth removes obstacles. The loss of the unimpeded exercise of the will. It had probably been hundreds of years since the world had said No to her. Now the world said No every day. *No. Fuck you. What are you going to do about it? Show me the fucking money.* She had been eroded. For a while her arrogance had been a substitute currency. But now even that was gone.

"I think we can help each other," I said.

She knew. She'd felt me catch where Caleb's "Are you—?" was going. Are you still looking for her? We know where she—

"We don't get involved," she said.

But she didn't move. If she'd been alone in the world, if she'd been the lone term on her side of the equation, she would have got to her feet there and then. I felt her reflex to do just that like a small electrical discharge in the air, as if her ghost had stood up and started for the door. Only to be halted. Only to be pulled back. Because there was the child. She had made him. Now there would aways be the child. Now there would always be love.

"Listen to me," I said. "I can give you some of the things you need. Money that will last you . . . Well, not perhaps your entire lifetime, but a long time. Long enough for you to make it into other money. Enough to give you a second chance. In this country I own property in every state. I have places around the world that will be shelter for you whenever you need it. If you want a permanent home you can take your pick." I could feel Caleb letting the vision have its way with him. I could feel her influence on him: Say nothing. Say nothing yet. And I could feel her own desperation. She was like someone who had been tortured with sleep deprivation now standing looking down at the perfect bed, crisp white sheets, soft pillows, unimaginable comfort, rest. All she had to do was lie down in it.

"In return?" she said. Not her voice but her spirit was hoarse. For weeks, months, years now it had been screaming. "Assuming we can deal with the question of why we should trust you."

"In return two things. First, you help me find the person I'm looking for. Second, you tell me where Talulla Demetriou is."

"Yeah, but how *do* we know we can trust you?" Caleb said. He was excited. This was the first thing with any promise that had happened to him for a long time. What *felt* like a long time, to someone as young as him. "We're just supposed to take your word for it? You're going to have to . . ." He looked at his mother. But his mother was looking at me. She sat hunched forward, white wrists bent on her knees. Her cigarette had burned down, but for the first drag, unsmoked.

"Your mother will know you can trust me," I said, smiling at him.

"How?"

I looked back at Mia. She did know. Had come to know, in the last minute or so. Now she, too, through the exhaustion and threadbare hope, was letting a little excitement touch her. Like a shy cat half-accepting the first stroke of an unfamiliar hand.

"I don't make false promises," I said. *I promise to live as long as I can. I promise I won't leave you, angel.* (So she had left me, to leave my word intact.) "But no one trusts promises, these days, do they?" I rolled up my sleeve.

Mia held my eye a few moments. She was old enough to recognise a turning point. And deep enough in misery to take it. It would be a relief to her, to commit to something. For too long now her life had been merely reactive. Her will bristled. Her will needed exercise beyond survival. Lights were on in her eyes whether she liked it or not. The terrible promise of the freedom she'd thought she'd never see again.

She stood, dropped the cigarette on the floor, stubbed it out with the toe of her boot. Walked over to me and knelt.

"Mother?" Caleb said.

"It's all right, *angel moy*," she replied, without looking at him. Then to me: "It mustn't be much. I've already—"

"I know. Take just enough for what you need. Enough to know."

I thought, briefly, of the change this little house had been through in the last few hours. Leath's years made themselves felt for a moment, decades of crammed emptiness. Then Mia took my wrist, put it to her mouth, and bit.

# 48

AFTERWARDS, SHE SAT back, breathing. For a few moments closed her eyes. Caleb, involuntarily, had come and knelt beside her. He took her hand.

"*Mat?*" he said. "Mother?"

"It's all right," Mia said. "I'm fine."

Caleb looked at me. It was the first time he'd been in a room with someone more powerful than the woman who'd made him. And a male, too. He was fascinated by and afraid of adult males. It was his mother's other guilt, that she'd condemned him to a life without a father.

"He's not false," Mia said. "The promise is good."

"Then you'll help me?"

She got, unsteadily at first, to her feet. Caleb took her hand.

"Aren't you forgetting something?" she said.

I looked at her. Probably like an idiot.

She rolled up her sleeve.

In Russian, I said to her: "It's not necessary. I've lived long enough to know."

"That's foolish. I have no love for Talulla."

"Me neither," Caleb said, manifestly trying to convince himself. It warmed my heart. The sweet lawlessness of the affections.

"It's not blind trust," I said, switching back to English. "We were meant to meet. This was meant. I'll drink if it makes you happy, but I promise you there's no need." What could I tell her? That the rightness of this was constellated around the two of them? That from the moment they'd walked in they'd formed an all but visible necessity? That the *story* had grinned and winked with their arrival? "Besides," I said. "You know enough now not to want me as an enemy. No?"

Mia, belatedly, wiped the blood from her lips. "Who is the new girl?" she asked.

"I'll explain on the road," I said, getting to my feet. "We've spent enough time here." I was thinking it would be a squeeze for three in the VanHome's blackout compartment.

The blood was fresh enough in her to read me.

"It's okay," she said. "We have a place nearby."

In the VanHome I got five minutes into Justine's story before I realised both my passengers were starting to look uncomfortable.

Not sunrise. We still had more than an hour.

"What is it?" I asked. I felt the road drop away from beneath the wheels. Lightness. The world tilting away.

"If you want the werewolf," Mia said, "you're going to have to move fast. She doesn't have long to live."

# Part Four

# The Believers

# 49
## *Talulla*

CONSCIOUSNESS GATHERED ITSELF, tightened, struggled up through the darkness.

"Talulla?" a voice said. "There you are. Back with us."

English spoken by an Italian.

I opened my eyes. I was sitting in a leather chair with restraints around my wrists and ankles. A collar gripped my neck and a strap around my forehead kept me looking where they wanted me to look: straight at them. The chair's absolute immobility said it was bolted to the floor. I felt sicker than I'd ever felt before—even when carrying the twins, mid-hunger. I was wet with sweat. My skin ached. Giant nausea. And eclipsing all physical phenomena the grinning face of justice: It's your fault. It's all your fault. You lost your son. You got him back. You should have been content. You should have preserved what you had. But it wasn't enough. Nothing is ever enough for you. You *are* nothing. Nothing but dirty, insatiable appetite. For whatever it is you haven't got. Whether you need it or not.

Facing me, in a small room with bare concrete walls, were three men. The first, nearest me, wearing the lightweight combat gear of the *Militi Christi*, was in his fifties, tall, heavy-limbed, but with a soft, rounded middle and a big, plump, smiling, boyish face. Side-parted glossy brown hair and gold-rimmed glasses. He looked wrong in the outfit the way Idi Amin looked wrong in army fatigues.

"Talulla Demetriou," he said. "My name is Cardinal Salvatore di Campanetti. I'm delighted to meet you. This is my friend and colleague Daniel Bryce, of whom you may have heard."

"How are you feeling?" This—native English, resonant, posh—came from the second guy, of whom I had *not* heard, standing a few feet to the Cardinal's left, wearing an ivory linen suit, sky blue cotton shirt and red brogues that had seen better days. The whole ensemble bore the crumples of a long-haul flight. Late thirties, slight build, bearded, with longish dark hair and an alert, intelligent green-eyed face. It would be unpleasant to see that alert face shut with passion if he was lying on top of you, fucking you.

"What do you want?" I said. I was very tired. My mouth was dry. Whatever drug they'd shot me with still lolled in my bloodstream. I was shivering. It was an effort to stop my teeth from chattering. That said, a curious little sixth sense told me there was a large window directly behind me—which surprised me—and that we were several floors up—which didn't. No sixth sense needed to clock the third guy: none other than the angelic androgyne I'd glanced down at mid-flight from the roof. He was the only one visibly armed: an automatic assault rifle the make of which I couldn't immediately identify. Next to him was a low steel bench with an open laptop on it. Packard Bell logo screensaver.

*What do you want?*

I don't know why I asked. You wake up drugged and strapped to a chair, you already know what the people observing you want—or at least what their want is going to involve, namely your suffering. Disgust was a tidal wave waiting to break over me. The face of the youngster at the door was dewy. He couldn't have been more than twenty-one. If you were this passionate blank-canvas type with a talent—violin, physics, ping-pong—you became a virtuoso or a Nobel winner or an Olympic champion. If you were this passionate blank-canvas type without a talent, you found stamp collecting or Middle Earth or totalitarian religion. I felt vaguely sorry for him, the misdirectedness of him, the huge, pointless, wrong decision he'd made.

"What do we want?" Salvatore said, smiling—not evilly or madly, but with what looked like tired, earned delight. "We want you to work for us. We want you to become the most famous monster in history. Not for your sake, but for the glory of God."

"Okay," I said. My head was a grapefruit balancing on a pipe-cleaner. "When do I start?"

"Immediately," the Cardinal said. "If you're ready. But you're not ready, because you don't know what the job involves."

*The twins, the twins, the twins. Please let them be safe. Please. Please.* You're done with God, but the reflex to plead to something endures. To nothingness, if that's all there is. But the big face of justice stared. You've lost your right to plead. Even to nothingness.

"It's an extraordinary opportunity," Bryce said. "You really will be making history. We all will."

*Where are my children? Where am I? Are the others dead?* No point in asking. They control the information. They give you what suits them. You're living in a manufactured reality. The weight of everything wrong was a crushing atmosphere. I couldn't even panic. I knew if I looked back I'd see all the choices I'd made since the Curse laid out behind me like a battlefield of butchered dead. And only death to show for it.

"Could I have some water?" I said.

The Cardinal, still smiling the well-behaved schoolboy smile, nodded and turned. "Lorenzo? Some water, please."

Lorenzo was the androgyne, who hadn't merited an introduction. He obeyed reflexively. When he opened the door I glimpsed a striplighted corridor, polished vinyl floor, another door opposite, closed. Then for a moment I had to shut my eyes and concentrate on not throwing up.

"The nausea will pass soon," Salvatore said. "We pumped your stomach in any case, so you won't have anything to throw up."

*How long have I been here? Why? WHERE ARE MY CHILDREN?*

Lorenzo returned with a bottle of Evian and a straw. Salvatore brought it within reach of my mouth. He smelled of the fatigues' clean canvas and a boozy cologne. *Wulf* remnants caught chilli olive oil on his fingers, garlic and parsley on his breath. We pumped your stomach. An interesting haul that must have been. I had an image of the Cardinal, latex-gloved, poking through partially digested human remains, dispassionately.

"Here," he said. "Allow me."

It was wearying on top of the weariness to have to recognise that water, when you're thirsty, remains good. The hopeless little universe of your body forced to report: That's good. That's so *good*. Meanwhile resisting the urge to simply ask if my children were dead was like staying underwater even though you were out of breath.

"The symptoms you're feeling are just the after-effects of the tranquilizer," the Cardinal said, when I'd drunk the entire bottle. "I'm afraid we gave you a heavier dose than was perhaps necessary."

Bryce stepped nearer. His feelings were wildly mixed: fascination, desire, curiosity, ambition. No contempt. As with all straight men the first question he asked himself about a woman was whether or not, given the chance, he'd fuck her. Yes, he would, his eyes said—until the memory of what I was got in the way. They'd filmed me changing back, I could tell. The footage was still running in his brain.

"Okay," I said. "Let's hear it." The restraints were an irksome friction at my ankles and wrists. The skin is the largest bodily organ, Mr. Cooper had delighted in telling us in high school, as if he'd invented skin himself. I was very aware of my skin right now. My largest bodily organ, wealthy with sickness, loaded with pain.

"What we're offering you," the Cardinal said, "is the chance to live out the rest of your days naturally, with your children, in peace—or as much peace as your kind can expect."

"Do you have my children?"

I hadn't made the decision to say this. I just found I'd said it. And now it was too late to care whether it was smart or not.

The Cardinal hesitated for a moment—then decided I'd know if he was lying. He gave a little nod and tightened the smile: no secrets between us.

"We have Zoë, not Lorcan. I'm going to give you the facts because they don't, in my opinion, hurt our case."

Bryce, I intuited, didn't agree. An almost disguised flicker in the green roundel eyes.

"The facts are these: Patricia Malloy and Fergus Gough are dead. We have their bodies at a separate facility if you'd like to see them. Robert Walker, Madeline Cole and Lucy Freyer escaped, Mr. Walker with your son. It really doesn't make any difference. It wasn't them we were interested in. None of them has your status. I wonder if you're aware of the extent to which your myth has grown?"

"I want to see my daughter."

"Yes, I know. That's not a problem. But be patient, please. I assure you she's not in any discomfort. The sisters are taking good care of her. If you need a rationale, let me say that her well-being only helps our interest."

It was hard, in my state, to reach out for a sense of my daughter. My body was full of physical events like planets bumping into each other. So little clear space . . .

ZOË? ANGEL? IT'S MOMMY.

Nothing. If she was here she was too many rooms away. I had an image of her in a small cage, dirty, bloodied, straw on the floor, a coven of nuns surrounding her, gawping.

Shut it out.

*Mr. Walker with your son.* Relief surged, filled me like the goodness of the water when I drank it. Unless it was a lie. Another image of Walker and Madeline together on a couch, his arm around her, his nose in her hair. Lorcan on his belly on the floor, looking through the *Illustrated Book of Aesop's Fables.* The big face of justice again, the delighted sneer: Serves you right. This is what you get when you congratulate yourself on being bigger than love.

Bryce stepped closer, alongside the Cardinal. "What we're talking about is a piece of television like no one's ever seen," he said. "Scientifically endorsed, up-close and personal. An inspirational documentary, a fucking landmark."

"A *devotional* landmark," the Cardinal said, quietly. "The power of Christ at work in the most extreme and undeniable way. The conversion of a monster. And her child. We're talking about creating something that will change the religious landscape forever."

I *almost* said: You're not serious. But I'd been in the world long enough. I knew they were serious. The seriousness of madmen is one of the most exhausting realities. Bryce's eyes had livened. I wondered if he was on coke. He looked the type. As Salvatore looked the type not to care if the instruments of his purpose were on coke. Or under-age girls. Or murder. Or anything else. There was only the purpose.

"Every month," the Cardinal said, "you change. You become a monster. Your hunger for killing and eating a human being is unbearable, a compulsion against which no power on earth can be brought to bear."

Theatrical pause. Me filling in the gaps.

"No power on *earth*," Bryce said, and actually gave me a wink. Partly in delight at the prospect of "televisual history," partly in acknowledgement of the Cardinal's religious lunacy. He, Bryce, had purposes of his own. Unrivalled directorial credit and a slice of the advertising revenue. I wondered if he had something on Salvatore that had got him this gig.

"You will pray," the Cardinal said, taking a few paces away towards flushed Lorenzo. "For the strength to overcome the hunger. I will be with you. You will receive the Sacrament. You will have access to a human victim. And you will not touch him. Or her, rather. Sister Carmelina is our first volunteer."

They were still serious. They were still perfectly serious. Through the roiling sickness my strategist flailed for ways of making this work. Assume Zoë's somewhere in the building. Assume they're not lying about the others. Assume—

"I know what you're thinking," Salvatore said, turning on his heel and facing me. "You're thinking there is no such thing as the power of Christ. No such person. No such mystery. No such God."

"I wasn't thinking that," I said. "But since you mention it, yes. The major flaw in this show is that if you put Sister Carmelina or anyone else in with me on the Curse, I'll kill them. And eat them. You can feed me all the bodies of Christ you like. It won't make any difference."

A not entirely comfortable pause. The Cardinal moving his lips around a little, looking past me out the window. Bryce was smiling at me. His lips were very red in his beard. With a haircut he could have played D.H. Lawrence. Lorenzo—the other Lorenzo—was at some edge of himself, as if on the verge of transfiguration. At the thought of the power of Christ, presumably.

"I'll leave Bryce to go over the details," Salvatore said, turning away again and heading to the door, which Lorenzo opened for him. "Your daughter," he said, raising his hand. "I know. Very shortly. When you have your sea legs."

"Now," I said.

"Very shortly," he said. Then something quietly to Lorenzo. Then he was gone.

I looked at Bryce.

"You won't touch Sister Carmelina," he said. "You won't need to. You'll be full."

He took a softpack of Chesterfields from his pants pocket and lit up with a brass Zippo. Exhaled with deep gratitude, looked down at me. "You with me? You'll be full because you'll already have eaten. As much as you like."

The scam penny dropped. The power of Christ—with an insurance policy. What had I been expecting?

"More volunteers?" I said.

"We have an arrangement," Bryce said. "Don't worry. Nobody who'll be missed." A pause. "You don't need me to tell you you don't have a choice."

"Let my daughter go and I'll do whatever you want."

"Not going to happen. Salvatore's wedded to the monster Madonna-and-child thing. It's his *idée fixe*."

"Not that there's any point in asking," I said, "but how exactly does all this square with me living happily ever after?"

He nodded. In terms of our *if*s and *then*s at least, we shared a logical economy. "Lorenzo?" he said, turning to the boy. "Mr. Avery is in the room next to mine. Could you go and ask him to meet me at the car in thirty minutes?"

Very slight discrepancy between the immediacy of the boy's obedience to Salvatore and this, to Bryce. But with a little nod of the delicate head, off he went.

Bryce looked at me. "No need for bullshit, obviously," he said. "The Cardinal's line is that you do your thing—convert, cured by faith in God's grace—and depart incognito. Plastic surgery, new ID, the whole thing."

I raised my eyebrows: How stupid does he think I am?

"I know," Bryce said. "I told him. But you *can't* tell him. He has these idiotic blind spots. Anyway, regardless of the line, the reality is once we've got what we need you'll be killed. Both of you."

To which, the momentum said, there was an alternative. It was unpleasant that we understood each other so well. It created an obscene feeling of kinship.

"So here's what I'm offering," Bryce said. "I'll get your daughter out. Keep her safe. To be returned to you when I've got what I need."

"Which is?"

"Salvatore's thinking's one-dimensional. The fact is half the audience just isn't going to buy the religious angle. The religious angle will *undermine* it. It's so obviously a vested interest. People will assume it's fake. What I'm talking about is the no-holds-barred fully secular version. Not just you. I want 24/7 access to the pack. All of you. You'll be masked, obviously. I don't expect you to kill and eat people on camera with the whole world knowing what you look like. But everything else, completely up-close and personal. It's *Big Brother* with werewolves. Live coverage for a month, leading up to a group kill on full moon. Then I'm gone. You get your daughter back, no one knows what you look like, I make history."

"As an accessory to mass murder," I said. "You're stupider than Salvatore."

He shook his head. "You let me worry about that." Then a flash of irritation: "Do you seriously think I haven't got that covered? Christ."

The choice wasn't much of a choice. But Bryce's project had at least the virtue of me not being in religious captivity.

I managed—just—not to say: You're all fucking insane.

Instead I said: "I want to see my daughter."

# 50

I DIDN'T GET what I wanted for another twenty-four hours. Twenty-four hours of not knowing if she was alive or dead. Twenty-four hours to feel sick with fear and filthy rich with self-loathing. The thing you swore you'd never let happen again. And now here it was, happening again. Congratulations.

They moved me—in wrist and ankle restraints à la Guantanamo and in the mute company of four *Militi Christi*, including beatifically beaming Lorenzo—to a twelve-by-ten cell with an unsurprising thin bunk and a pair of buckets. I was given a litre bottle of water and a ham sandwich I wouldn't have been much interested in even if I was eating regular food, and told to get some rest.

There was no rest to be got. Rest isn't available when you don't know if they've killed your child. Nor had the journey from the interview room to the cell helped me much. Three long corridors, two left turns, striplights and ammonia-scented vinyl floors, half a dozen other cells. I didn't even know what country I was in.

Then Salvatore showed up with a couple more armed guards (silver buzzed my bones from the Uzi magazines), toting a digital camera.

"Put this on, please," he said, hooking a tiny wired earpiece through the bars. "The wire goes down the back of your shirt. The earpiece you can conceal with your hair."

For a moment I sat still on the bunk. He smiled. The same implacable delight. The same patience. The same certainty. The exercise of his will all but visibly swelled him, as if his body were receiving rich nourishment.

"It'll be painless, I promise you."

"My daughter," I said.

He nodded. "After this. Please. The earpiece."

I got up and fitted the device. Awkward, given the restraints.

"I'm going to interview you," he said. "I will ask you just a very few questions. The responses you're required to give will come through our little friend in your ear. Obviously there will be an unnatural delay in real time, but don't let that worry you. Bryce will edit it, he assures me, seamlessly."

One of the guards pulled a chair up for the Cardinal, at a safe distance from the bars.

"Tell me, Talulla, do you believe in God?"

The voice in my ear—female, filled with surprising clipped passion—said: "'Of course not. God's a fairy tale to calm frightened children.'" I hesitated, then repeated it, verbatim, feeling my jaws tightening. It made me weary to see the thinking here: Atheist monster converted to the one true religion. The more entrenched her faithlessness at the start, the greater the miracle by the end.

"So obviously it follows that you reject the authority of the Catholic Church?"

"'Are you an idiot? The Church is nothing. A house of lies.'"

"Please," the Cardinal said. "A little less robotic."

"I wouldn't talk like this," I said.

"Nonetheless, try not to sound like you're reading the ingredients on a packet of washing powder. Now. You reject the existence of God, the mystery of the Trinity, the death and resurrection of Jesus Christ, the power of the Sacraments?"

The voice in my ear actually *laughed*, before replying: "'The Sacraments? Hocus-pocus and mumbo-jumbo. You might as well carry a rabbit's foot or a lucky penny.'"

"You don't think we can help you, then?"

"'I don't need help,'" I parroted. "'And even if I did, there's nothing for me in your sad bag of tricks. If anyone needs help it's you people. You're all fucking lunatics.'"

"I'm sorry you feel that way," Salvatore said. He looked genuinely pained, the genial uncle whose niece's wayward behaviour had let him down. "I truly am sorry. But I'm also filled with gladness." He leaned forward in the chair, clasping his kneecaps. "Because I happen to know that we *can* help you. I happen to know that Christ died for *all* our sins, even yours, and that the Sacraments are real and mighty gifts."

"'You're pathetic. Go ahead. Give me the full treatment. It won't make a scrap of difference.'"

"God loves you, Talulla," he said, frowning at what an incomprehensible contortion this would be for anyone other than God. "And it's our job, as His hopelessly flawed representatives on earth—it's our highest *duty*—to help you to see that. We have a long and difficult time ahead of us. But understand something: I have absolutely no doubt of the outcome."

"Neither have I," my prompter said, with such scorn that I wondered if this role-play wasn't an outlet for some doubts of her own. I wondered who she was.

"Very well," Salvatore said. "Soon, we will begin. But that will do for now." Then, after the guard had switched off and lowered the camera, he said to me: "Not bad for a first attempt. We need to see more emotion, but I know you'll get the hang of it. You can take the earpiece out now."

I opened my mouth to speak but he held up his hand: "I know, I know. Your daughter. Calm yourself. I'm as good as my word. We're taking you to see her now."

She was in a steel-doored white room three times the size of my cell, to accommodate in addition to its infant prisoner, chairs and a table for two nuns. Zoë sat on the edge of the bed in a miniature version of my wrist and ankle restraints, the ankle chain fastened to a steel loop bolted to the cell floor. She had a movement radius of about five feet, marked (the Sisters needed to know if they were anywhere near within range of a scratch or bite) by a yellow chalk semi-circle on the floor. All of this visible to me on a wall-mounted monitor outside the cell door, which was overseen by yet another guard at a fold-out table and chair. (How many guards so far? Four for the move to the cell, two from the cell to here, and this one at the desk made seven. But the air in the facility said more. There must have been fifty or sixty for the assault on the farmhouse. Maybe they were all here? Maybe there were hundreds?)

The nuns were ordered out. I got five minutes.

She'd been holding the tears in—but they came when I put my arms around her, though I had to lift my cuffed hands over her head to do it.

I DON'T LIKE IT HERE.

I KNOW, ANGEL, ME NEITHER. WE'RE LEAVING SOON. VERY SOON.

PROMISE?

Oh God. Oh *God*.

YES, I PROMISE.

I WANT TO GO *NOW*.

NOT YET, ANGEL. BUT VERY SOON. ARE THESE LADIES HORRIBLE TO YOU?

The compact soft warm smell of her hurt my heart. The precise weight and shape of her pressed tight to me. The bravery she'd had to summon so far unravelling now that Mommy was here and she didn't have to be brave by herself.

THEY TELL ME STORIES BUT I DON'T LIKE THEM.

WHAT STORIES, BABY?

ABOUT JESUS IS MY FRIEND. WHO IS JESUS?

You forget they're three years old. You forget all the shapes of the world they don't know.

HE'S LIKE PETER PAN. I'LL TELL YOU LATER.

DON'T GO! MOMMY!

Because Salvatore had opened the door and our bodies knew separation was coming again.

"Let me stay with her," I said, with my back to him. Her tears were wet on my neck. "What possible difference can it make?"

"That's not permitted yet," the Cardinal said. "The environment we're creating for you—the set, I suppose we should call it—isn't quite ready. And in the meantime you and I both know you'll be more biddable if we keep you separate. It's just to ensure your cooperation in this unfortunate interim. I'm sorry, but that's the way it is. Don't make me behave brutally."

Oh, I'm going to kill you, you fucking idiot, I thought. You fucking *nothing*.

ZOË, LISTEN TO ME. I'LL COME FOR YOU. BE BRAVE FOR JUST A LITTLE LONGER. I PROMISE I'LL COME.

DON'T GO! PLEASE!

REMEMBER HOW I TOLD YOU LORCAN HAD TO BE BRAVE WHEN WE LOST HIM FOR ALL THAT TIME? THIS IS YOUR CHANCE TO BE LIKE THAT.

All the engines of her infancy saying No . . . No . . . No . . .

CAN YOU TRY? JUST FOR A LITTLE WHILE?

The two guards were standing over us. The silver in the magazines was making her frown, though she didn't know why.

ANGEL, CAN YOU?

YOU COME SOON.

It was killing her. I could feel the size and threat of the world to her without me in it. She was small and afraid. The impulse to attack Salvatore was all but overwhelming. But it was like pain. There was nothing to do but bear it.

YOU COME SOON, MOMMY.

How could she do this? How could I have given birth to something that could summon this much courage? My heart was breaking. I thought I wouldn't be able to bear it. The inches then feet then yards and walls and closed doors that would come between us. I thought I wouldn't be able to bear it.

YOU PROMISE YOU'LL COME SOON?

I WILL. I WILL, ANGEL, I PROMISE. GIVE ME A KISS.

Her little face was hot and soft, her lips like furled buds. She was scrunching my shirt in her fists.

One of the guards rested the muzzle of the Uzi very gently on my shoulder.

# 51

THAT NIGHT I had the dream about the vampire again, in a more confused form, with the beach and twilight and the extraordinary fucking all mixed together, his dark face repeatedly in close-up saying something I couldn't understand. I felt sick with pleasure yet death was a stink wrapped around it, woven through it. The landscape was remote, otherworldly, like something in an old science fiction magazine, *Weird Tales*. His face kept pushing me right to the edge of waking with what it was he was saying that I couldn't understand, until eventually I woke myself up saying it myself: *I'm coming for you.*

I'd sat up involuntarily on my bunk. My face was full of panic. In the dream I'd suddenly shouted it: *I'm coming for you!* But of course in reality it had been a mumbled whimper. Enough, nonetheless, to bring the guard to his feet. He was a tall skinhead with long wrists and large hands and big, dreamy grey eyes. Not thrilled with this duty, I could tell. Held the automatic rifle a little too tightly. I hoped he hadn't made out what I'd said.

*I'm coming for you.*

Impossible to quell the mix of scepticism and excitement. Scepticism because he had, after all, said much the same before—*I'll see you again*—but two years had passed without it happening, and excitement because my body was alive with the dream's instilled conviction, a whirl of butterflies around my heart. *I'm coming for you.*

Jake and my mother in the afterlife casino were available, of course, smiling and shaking their heads, clinking glasses (a Mai Tai for my mother, a Macallan for Jake) in delighted incredulity and saying: Really, Lu? *Dreams?* Dear oh dear oh dear . . .

But my palms were wet (as, with characteristic contempt for my predicament, was my cunt; the dream hadn't neglected its other business), my blood electric.

The guard was staring at me. A look of fascination that was part fear, part revulsion, part something else. An all but dead aspect of me wondered, wearily, if I'd had my hands down my pants in my sleep.

"What the fuck are you looking at?" I said to him.

He didn't respond, but his knuckles blanched around the automatic. If the weapon had had a voice it would have said, Ow, you're hurting me!

"I never forget a face, you know," I said, scraping the damp hair back off my forehead. "Seriously, we're like elephants."

His lips moved. He was saying something to himself. A prayer, I realised, when he sat down, carefully, and took a rosary of amber beads from his pocket.

Two more days passed. Same dream, every night. Same unhinging response of conviction and self-ridicule. I was allowed a few minutes each day with Zoë, who was miserable, and who had, whether she liked it or not, begun to get slightly interested in the stories about Jesus. Especially the raising of Lazarus and the healing of the lepers and the wedding feast at Cana. I had a disgusted admiration for the nuns, who had simplified things down to a level a three-year-old could understand—albeit with the aid of large picture books they held up for Zoë to look at, from the safe side of the chalk semi-circle.

Every waking minute I thought something would reveal itself that would help. A soft guard. A clue to the way out. An opportunity to grab one of the automatics and take my chances. But the minutes passed, and the math remained the same.

Then, on the third night, Lorenzo came to see me.

The guard he relieved seemed a little confused, but after a quiet confab slouched away down the corridor.

"I don't have much time," Lorenzo said. Italian, yes, but very good English. He was flushed. Sweat freckled the line above his top lip. "You must listen to me. I can help you."

I looked up at the CCTV camera on the corridor wall.

"It's all right," he said. "It doesn't work. None of them do. Nothing in here works."

"Me and my daughter," I said. "Whatever you want, but it's both of us. Got it?"

"I can't guarantee it," he said, with a touching honesty. "But I can get you out of the restraints and I can give you a gun. I can also tell you a way out that will not be heavily guarded."

"I'm not leaving here without my daughter," I said. "Where's her cell from here?"

"Not now," he said. "We can't do it now—"

*"Where is her fucking cell?"*

Lorenzo looked to his left. His nostrils were like two graceful little apostrophes. His day's odour pounded out of him. Clean sweat, Pears soap, a strawberry yogurt he'd forced himself to eat for lunch. He was breathing heavily. "When you get to the end of here turn right. Then third left. Double doors, but they're locked and guarded. You'll never—"

"How many guards?"

"Two. But listen—"

"Through the double doors *and*?"

"Second cell on the left. One guard. But not yet. Please. You have to wait."

"Now. Right now."

"It's not possible now. Please believe me. Tomorrow—"

"What do you want from me. Why would you do this?"

He came right up to the bars. Gripped them with both slender hands. Rested his forehead against them. There was an inner discordant symphony: desperation—but not, as far as I could tell, madness.

"I want you to bite me," he said.

Footsteps.

"Step back," I hissed. "Quick."

He did—just as the previous guard reappeared in the corridor. Not angry, apparently. Smile-frowning.

*"Lui non' c'era,"* the guard called. My Italian covered it—just: "He wasn't there." It didn't cover the second bit: *"Sei sicuro che ha chiesto per me?"*

"Tomorrow," Lorenzo whispered, then turned and hurried away toward his colleague.

# 52

BRYCE CAME TO see me. He looked exhausted. His face was damp and porous, and the pupils in the roundel eyes were dilated. The cream linen suit had been replaced with black jeans and a green cable knit sweater that almost perfectly matched his eyes. The greens and the beard and the longish hair made me think of him in Sherwood Forest.

"I know it's been tough," he said. "But we're almost there."

It was late—or at least I'd decided it was late. The guard Bryce relieved—a slabbily built guy in his forties with a Saddam Hussein moustache—had been yawning, hugely, for the last hour, though for all I knew it was three in the afternoon. No windows down here, no clocks.

"They're moving you both in forty-eight hours," Bryce said. "Four vehicles, a dozen men. It's a two-hour drive from here to the landing field. There'll be a roadblock. Jesus, you've no idea what this is costing me. I get an hour head-start with the kid, then you'll be released. You'll be given a phone and some cash. You keep the phone and wait for my call. I'll contact you within twenty-four hours. We'll arrange a rendezvous then."

*Tomorrow.*

*I can get you out of here.*

*I want you to bite me.*

Tough to keep everything that had just happened out of my face. Remshi's face from the dream swam up. *I'm coming for you.*

It took everything I had to stay in character. "You fuck with me," I said to Bryce, "I'll find you. If I have to come back from the dead to do it."

I was spared the dream that night because I was spared sleep. Aside from my inner strategist going silently insane the effects of not having fed properly were making torturous fiesta in my blood. *Wulf* never goes quietly even with a full stomach. Denied its monthly due it digs in for prolonged and violent outrage. The way it feels is that if someone were watching you they'd see the big shape writhing and straining under your too small skin, threatening at any moment to tear out. But of course that's not what they actually see. What they actually see is a woman glistening with sweat, unsteady on her feet, occasionally doubling up or jerking as if at the mercy of extreme cramp and furious muscular spasms.

Zoë would be feeling it too, although her little belly was easier to fill, and she'd eaten a good few pounds before the assault had interrupted us. I was desperate to see her. I'd have to tell her to be ready. Yesterday I'd felt in her the beginning of resignation: *We're staying here. Mommy can't do what she said. I have to live with these ladies in the black dresses. I don't like it. I don't like it.*

That I'd held her close only confirmed it for her. She could feel my fear. My hopelessness. Today I'd have to do better. Today I'd have to promise and believe it. All night I'd been picturing it. SWEETHEART, WE'RE GETTING OUT OF HERE TODAY.

YOU PROMISE?

And I'd lie. Because what else was there to do with a three-year-old you might be carrying to her death?

YES, I PROMISE.

The door at the end of the corridor opened and Salvatore appeared, flanked by two guards, the nervy skinhead and the bruiser with the Saddam moustache, both armed.

"Talulla," the Cardinal said, smiling, as if my name was the satisfying solution to a riddle. He stood facing me, hands clasped behind his back. He looked larger than usual, big and plump and human. His moony face was roseate, as if with joy. Light played on the lenses of his gold-rimmed glasses. *Wulf*, determined to make its presence felt, breathed deep in me, inhaled his odour of cologne, recently consumed tomatoes, sardines, strong black coffee. His gleaming boots reeked of polish. All this mixed with the guards' smell of sweat and canvas and the guns' stink of metal and rubber and grease.

I got up off my bunk and went to the bars.

"You'll be expecting your daily visit to see your daughter," Salvatore said. "With regret, that won't be possible today."

It was hard to imagine him alone in a room. His faith was a glaze that only ever reflected non-believers. If I thought of him on his own I pictured him shutting down, like an automaton. God only came into play as a Divine extension of himself when others were present. Alone, he'd have no room for God.

"I must say," he said, putting his head on one side like a pleasantly perplexed dog, "your naivety surprises me."

*You might not want this for yourself, but you'll want it for your children.* The distance between me and Zoë was like a spear being dug into my navel.

"Naivety?" I asked.

"Bryce," he said.

Adrenaline loosened my knees.

"*Big Brother* with werewolves," the Cardinal continued. "Bryce has sunk a great deal of money into a new company developing silver-delivery systems." He leaned forward. "Gadgets to kill your neighbourhood werewolf, if you understand me. Worthless, obviously, until people believe werewolves are *in* their neighbourhood. He's not a man of faith, therefore he doesn't believe in the faith-based exposé. Hence the secular—the allegedly 'scientific'—version. He's blind. He doesn't have the faintest idea how many people *already* believe—thanks to whom? Thanks to us! He could have stuck with our arrangement and still made a fortune."

Which was the verbal cue, obviously, because immediately the words were out of his mouth Saddam raised his weapon—not, I now saw, the standard Uzi, but something lighter and longer-barrelled—and pulled the trigger.

The dart hit me in the midriff, and in the three seconds it took for the giant wrongness to coalesce around me I felt the drug start its sweep up my legs—though the darkness seemed to descend from the space above my head. My hands tightened around the bars, but I could feel the weakness like a rapidly escalating argument in my flesh.

"There have been, as you know, other developments," Salvatore said—and brought his right hand out from behind his back.

Holding Lorenzo's severed head.

"The Devil works in mysterious ways," he said.

I sank to my knees.

"Lorenzo's behaviour has been a crushing blow," Salvatore said. "I've

By Blood We Live

had my suspicions, but I have also had my faith. He was dying, of course. An inoperable brain tumour . . ." He shook the head slightly, as if to listen for the tumour's rattle. "And for us there's no greater death than the martyr's—which is what I'd offered him. But one can never overestimate the greed for life. Apparently at any price. Do you think four hundred years of monstrosity is worth the cost of your soul? It amazes me. It truly amazes me."

I felt my mouth opening and closing. No speech. Strength going as if a sluice gate had dropped open.

ZOË. ZOË . . . I'M . . . DON'T . . .

"I'm taking it as a lesson: Never relax. Never *assume*. Have faith, but wear the knowledge of human weakness like a burning jewel in the middle of your brow."

The darkness had weight, now, a soft mass enfolding me. I didn't know if I was still on my knees or had fallen to the floor. The world's solid geometry was coming gently apart, with a kind of tranquil resignation, an uncomplaining relinquishment of the rules. Complete blackout for a moment, then I forced my eyes open again. The cell bars blurred and Salvatore's round-toed boots with their caps of reflected light. *Wulf* thrashing, drowning. The weight of myself pulling me under. *I'm coming for you.*

I'M COMING FOR YOU.

I tried to send to Zoë, but she was too far . . . Too far . . .

Darkness again, my head completely under black water, pushed down by the drug and Salvatore's voice.

"Lucifer deals in the currency of our own complacency," he said. "His greatest achievement is the—"

An explosion in my head cut him off.

In the last uneclipsed segment of consciousness I thought: No, not in my head. An explosion. An explosion . . .

But it was no good. I was going.

I had a confused dream of gunfire and screams and movement, and a voice—not Salvatore's—shouting: "Attack! Sir, we're under—" before a shrill electronic alarm ripped through for a deafening moment, with one flash of blinding light—and the last of my own lights went out.

# 53
## *Walker*

THE HOUSE WAS thirty miles from where we'd been ambushed. When I got there, Lucy had the Angel tied to a chair in the basement. A guy in his mid-thirties, olive-skinned, with short, thick black hair and bad acne scarring. He looked exhausted, and his jaw was swollen, but he was otherwise unharmed. What was left of the bodies of the house's inhabitants— a retired couple in their late sixties—was in a bloody heap in bed upstairs.

"This is where you come in, I'm afraid," Lucy said.

The last twenty-four hours had been a clusterfuck—and now we'd left a trail a moron could follow. I hadn't even seen Talulla and Zoë fall. We were two hundred metres into the forest before I realised they weren't with us. I'd stopped and turned, but Madeline grabbed me:

NO. THE KID. WE HAVE TO GET HIM AWAY.

She hadn't wanted to let it out but I'd got PROBABLY DEAD ANYWAY, since she was thinking it. Lorcan got it, too. I felt it in his grip tightening around my neck.

EASY, KIDDO. SHE'LL BE ALL RIGHT. YOUR MOM'S TOUGHER THAN ALL OF US PUT TOGETHER.

And she's leaving me.

Left me already.

A grenade detonated thirty metres away. They knew we'd broken through. They were coming. I hadn't seen any vehicles (and even if they had them they'd be useless past the trees); they wouldn't catch us on foot. There was no alternative: we turned back, we died. All of us.

So we ran.

The instinct was to stay under cover, but the forest petered out in less than three miles, and, in any case, stay under cover and do what when the moon set? Stroll into the nearest town naked? Again, no choice.

Twenty minutes out of the woods we hit farmland. Sheep scattered, their little hoofbeats and the fruity smell of their shit. Lights on in the farmhouse. Three dogs. Four humans. The dogs came out silently from their flap and looked at us, awaiting instruction. We didn't need them. We did a slow circle of the buildings (two dozen bullocks in a barn huddled close together, eyes rolling), a tractor shed, a Land Rover, a VW and two quad bikes in an open garage with a corrugated tin roof. Only the house occupied. Mom, Dad, daughter, son. Sitting around the table, finishing dinner. A steel coffee pot, big yellow slab of butter. Cold cuts, wine, half a dozen cheeses, a blackberry pie. The son, maybe seventeen years old, looked pissed about something. Everything, I thought. He didn't want this. Farm life. He wanted the city. TV had made inroads. Porn. Girls. Slow Internet that drove him nuts. I thought of Luke Skywalker saying: *If there's a bright centre to the universe, you're on the planet that it's farthest from.* The kid even looked a bit like Mark Hamill. Your mind goes to these places. You can't help it. The daughter, who couldn't have been more than twelve, was one of those rare kids lucky enough to be born into a world that fit her. She loved it, the big dung-scented cattle, the chickens with their weird little personalities, the dust from the straw at harvest like smoke, the thick walls and the open fires and breaking the ice in the water butt in winter. Mom and Dad loved them both—and each other. You could feel it. You could see it in the house's slight untidiness and the girl's ease in her skin and even in the boy's annoyance. Even in his annoyance he admitted their love. The parents still liked fucking each other. There was humour and habit there, in the sex—but still sometimes the quickening of the old fire. They knew it was there, they knew they could rely on it, for the rest of their lives.

We didn't get all this from peeking through the windows.

We got it when Maddy kicked the door down and we leaped in and tore them to pieces and ate them.

Tough not to fuck.

It'd always been there between Madeline and me. She Turned me, after all. We'd kept out of each other's way for that very reason. I knew, she knew, Lula knew. (*It's okay, I want you to,* Lula'd sent me, back at the chateau, before everything kicked off. *I want you to so I can feel better about leaving you for a vampire* is what she meant. I hated her for that. For trying to manage it. For trying to manage *me*. It had never really been love. First it was love minus what she kept for Jake's ghost. Then love minus what the vampire had left her with. Too many minuses. I'd always been making do with leftovers.)

The family looked up at us. Time stopped. There they were, perfected by fear. At your death your life gathers, adds itself up, reaches its last shape. You. Humans. It tips us, that moment. There's the perfect freeze, when you know, and we see you, complete. It's like a shared joke. Like the pause when lovers look at each other because they realise—oh God, oh *God*—that they're both about to come, together. Then the moment's done its work—and we fall on you, and the life goes, in greedy bites and bloody swallows, into us.

It was hot and fast. It was a blur. The first minute or so always is, for me, a car-crash of joy and disbelief, total blindness and 20/20 smashed together like a pair of cymbals.

But that phase passes. You come back to yourself. To the world, and the solid, filthy reality of what's happening. The solid, filthy reality that's better than anything you've ever felt before.

Madeline with her snout in the girl's flank and her ass in the air, legs spread. The smell of her cunt was sly and sweet and full of tortured willingness. And me with a hard-on that could've broken a piano in half. I used to think I liked sex. I used to think I'd had sex as good as you could have it. Then I Turned. You Turn, and it's as if until then you've been fucking in two dimensions instead of three.

CAN'T Madeline—just about—gave me.

I KNOW.

Didn't stop her lifting her head and rolling her shoulder. We were close. We were so close.

THE KID.

I KNOW.

TALULLA.

I couldn't answer. Didn't know what I would've answered. Instead I reached into the son's chest cavity and tore his heart out and bit it in half. Sorry, kid, but that's what mine feels like.

Afterwards we did what we never do. We stayed with the victims' remains. No choice. The situation had everything we needed. It was remote, there were clothes, there was money, there was transportation. I'd never cared much for Fergus, but there was a feeling like a ragged burn in me when I thought of Trish, dead. She'd had so much life in her. I'd liked her in the mornings, sitting big-eyed and hungover, knees hunched up, fingers wrapped around a mug of black coffee, not watching TV or reading a magazine—just blinking, just existing, happily. I could feel the loss in Madeline, too. Big loss. She'd loved Cloquet. And Trish. Even Fergus. They'd made money together, amazed when it turned out they could trust each other. We had no clue what the fuck had happened to Lucy. Reaching out gave us nothing. If she was alive she was out of range. Both of us were thinking the same thing, that the old days were over, that the world was waking up to us, that from now on nothing would ever be the same.

Lorcan curled up on the couch. I could feel the thought pounding in his skull. THEY'RE DEAD. THEY'RE DEAD. THEY'RE DEAD. Mixed in with the swirling bits of the lives he'd just taken in. I'd wondered about this: How did he and Zoë contain experience that couldn't be anything other than ahead of their years? They do what kids do, Talulla had said. Put it aside until they're ready. Like clothes they'll grow into, eventually.

THEY'RE DEAD. THEY'RE DEAD.

I grabbed his ankle and gave it a little shake. It made no difference. He's a tough kid to comfort. He doesn't believe in it. It's like the world declared itself his enemy at his birth. (Which, given he started life as a kidnap victim, I guess it did.) There's no self-pity in him. Just a kind of remote determination. Zoë expects love. Lorcan expects zip. Hard to imagine him growing up and having lovers. Or at least hard to imagine him loving someone.

Madeline and I took turns keeping watch outside, though the truth was neither of us was expecting pursuit. The truth was both of us thought the *Militi Christi* had got—in Talulla and Zoë—exactly what they were after.

The dogs kept us company, wagging their tails.

When the moon set we showered and kitted ourselves out as best we could with our victims' clothes. Nothing fit Lorcan. We improvised. A pair of the girl's cut-offs and a t-shirt, with a string belt. The kid had to

49

go barefoot, but it didn't matter: If we found ourselves on foot, we'd have to carry him anyway. We found the keys to the Land Rover.

Without any hope, I called Lucy's cell phone from the house landline.

She answered after two rings.

She was in a house thirty miles away.

And she had a hostage.

# 54

INCREDIBLY, THEY'D MISSED an exit. From the house's cellar. Double wooden doors completely overgrown with ivy. Lucy had burst up through them and caught two Angels off-guard. She'd ripped the throat out of one of them then turned to see the other—the dark-haired acne-survivor in his mid-thirties—staring in disbelief at his jammed AK-47.

"He ran," Lucy told us. "But he didn't get very far."

He got as far as the tree line, where Lucy had knocked him unconscious.

"No, you see," she said, Maddy and I silently marvelling, "I thought I might need a driver." She'd told us this as if she'd been weighing up how to get home from a flower show.

She dragged him into deeper cover and waited it out. Watched them take down Talulla and Zoë and body-bag the remains of Fergus and Trish. When the unit moved out there were still seven hours till moonset. Cool as you like, she hauled her captive back to the house, trussed and gagged him, then slung him over her shoulders and set off in search of the Fleet-wood.

"Which was, surprisingly, just where we left it," she said. "I did wonder if they'd booby-trapped it or something, you know, but . . . Well, there wasn't much of a choice. I brought him round and put him behind the wheel. Drove the whole way here with my hand around his throat."

Madeline and I listened to all this with increasing incredulity. Didn't it occur to her that the smart thing would've been to drive somewhere remote and wait till she was human again? Lucy looked at us as if we were idiots.

"I hadn't eaten," she said. "I was starving."

So she'd hustled the Angel into the house, re-gagged and tied him, put a cloth shopping bag over his head, then calmly headed upstairs and slaughtered the retirees.

"They were both asleep," she said.

She couldn't interrogate her hostage until the moon had set and she'd regained the power of speech. "Not without some sort of ridiculous version of charades, anyway," she said. At which point, more or less, she'd got the call from me. "I'm glad," she said. "I wasn't looking forward to it. This is where you come in, I'm afraid."

Because you're used to this kind of thing. Former WOCOP. Former professional.

Jilted lover.

"Take Lorcan upstairs," I said.

It didn't take long. I didn't have to hurt him. I didn't want to hurt him. I knew if I hurt him it would be something for my broken heart to do, somewhere for its violence to go. I knew if I hurt him I'd be disgusted with myself.

But I didn't have to. I just had to tell him what I'd do to him if he didn't tell me what I needed to know. I told him I'd Turn him.

"You know what that means?"

"Yes," he said.

We were looking directly at each other. I didn't like him. It was the religion. It was the blazing faith in magic, in a fairy story. What are *we*? she'd said. *We*'re a fairy story. The violence was right there in my limbs, offered itself. I pushed it down. It wasn't that I didn't like him. It was that I didn't want to kill him. It was that I was disgusted with myself for my own useless sadness—and because I knew I'd have to kill him. It should've been clean and easy. You're a monster. You kill and eat a human being every month. What's one religious nut? And a clear enemy at that. But that's not how it works. Full moon and hunger, killing's natural. It's what we are, what we do. It's still chosen, but it's a natural choice. It doesn't carry over. Lose the hunger, lose the moon, lose the fucking *wulf*, it's a different kind of choice.

And I didn't want to do it. A light, carefree bit of myself said: You don't have to do anything. Just walk away. *Walker*. That's what you really do. That's who you really are. What's in a name? Everything.

For a few moments I felt free. I could turn, climb the stairs, say my goodbyes, go. It *was* what I'd always done. Seeing this, I almost laughed out loud.

But it passed, and the room filled up again with sadness and disgust, and I felt solid and exhausted. The overalls smelled of the farmer's sweat. All my past was in the room with me, with us. Sometimes your life comes to you like that and asks why it doesn't make any sense. Why you've made nothing of it but a mess.

Meanwhile the boring fucking logic of the situation wouldn't take its weight off me. There would be no way of knowing if the information he gave up—the location where they were holding Lula and Zoë—was accurate until we got there. We'd have to keep him alive at least till then.

"Well?" I said.

"When I tell you, you'll kill me anyway."

"I can't do that," I said. "Not until I know you've told me the truth. And there's no way of knowing that until we get there."

"*Then* you'll kill me."

It was intimate between us. The problem with these situations is that the frankness creates intimacy. Whether you want it or not. He actually smiled at me, feeling it. I wondered what had happened to make a believer of him. He seemed intelligent. I wondered what it must be like to be an intelligent believer, to see the whole world and everything that happened in it as a series of clues to something grand and invisible, some big story God cooked up in the Beginning. The way she had when she was a kid. The way she'd started seeing it again. Since the vampire came to call. *When he joins the blood of the werewolf.* Funny how making a joke of that hadn't worked.

"What's your name?" I asked him.

He thought about it, decided giving it wasn't going to make things any worse. "Mario Donatello."

"I'll make you a deal, Mario," I said. "If you tell us where they are, and you're not lying, I'll let you go."

He laughed. "Are you serious?" he said. "Do you think I'm an idiot?"

My arms and shoulders were tired. All the goddamned *if*s and *then*s of these encounters. Again I asked myself why I was bothering. She's leaving you anyway.

But there was Zoë.

It's always the innocents that fuck everything up.

I untied his wrists.

"Give me your hand," I said.

He looked at me from under his brows. Wet black eyes. The acne scarring made me imagine him as a teenager, looking in the mirror, miserable. I suppose it sounds nuts to say I felt sorry for that version of him.

"Just give me your hand," I said. "I'm not going to hurt you."

He was sweating. The fear had drawn back a touch to give his excitement and curiosity room. He knew I wasn't trying to trick him. He knew this was possible because of the intimacy, because I had his life for the taking if I wanted it. There's a transparency between you at these moments. Like heavyweights in the ring. Like lovers.

He put his right hand out. I took it in mine, in a handshake grip, held it. Our eyes were locked.

"I'm doing this because I know you know how it is," I said. "I know you'll know if I'm lying."

He wanted to live. He'd thought for a long time he'd take a martyr's death, willingly. But it was there in his face, the realisation that he wanted, above all, to live. I could see all the sunsets and conversations and cups of coffee and crisp winter mornings he was imagining, that he still wanted, that were precious and that he'd never even thought of before, the absolutely huge wasted gift of being alive.

"I give you my word," I said. "When we get there, I'll let you go. You know I'm not lying because you can feel that I don't want to kill you."

We stared at each other. His hand was slightly bigger than mine. (Reminded me of Susie Carter, who I dated for a while when I was young. She was beautiful, but back then her hands were bigger than mine. It was crazy how much it had bothered me. I couldn't stop thinking about it, even when she was doing something amazing to me in the sack.) "You know I'm not lying," I repeated—and I knew he could feel it. It was a joy to him, to suddenly see that he might have all that life he'd been picturing. It was a joy and a shame, because he hadn't known until now his faith wasn't stronger than life.

When I brought him upstairs, Madeline and Lucy looked at me. What the fuck?

"We need him," I said. "Let's go."

In the Fleetwood I gagged him again and tied him to the base of one of the bunks. He was quiet, cooperative. He'd made his decision. He knew his soul would have to deal with the consequences, but for now, God had lost. It was a relief to him. It always is, to find the edge of yourself. To know the exact limit of your strength. It's a relief because not knowing it is an exhausting full-time job.

I called Konstantinov. The two of us had worked for WOCOP together, and eventually found ourselves on the wrong side of the organisation. Three years ago vampires (the same crackpots who'd taken Lorcan) had kidnapped his wife, Natasha, and Turned her. Mike, faced with losing her, had asked her to Turn him. She didn't hesitate. In a movie she'd refuse because she loved him. In their reality she Turned him because she loved him. Because she knew how much he loved her. Because it *was* love between them, as big and dark as Mother Russia. If I'd loved Konstantinov any less than I did I'd have hated him for having that, right now.

"Mike, we need you. Where are you?"

"Polynesia."

"Fuck. *Fuck.* How fast can you get here?"

I could feel him working it out. Night flights only.

"Three days."

Not fast enough.

"You got people we can use here?"

Pause. I knew the answer. Didn't even know why I'd asked. Madeline and Lucy were changing their clothes in the back of the vehicle. Lorcan was going through Talulla's bag looking for his own gear. He'd pulled out a bunch of her things. A white sun-dress I loved her in. Red espadrilles. A denim jacket. It occurred to me I was still in the goddamned farmer's overalls and cut-open sneakers. I was sweating. My hands felt ill. Lorcan tossed out his mom's copy of *Don Juan*. Byron. Who I knew was someone I should know about.

"No," Konstantinov said. "Why? What's happened?"

Lorcan had pulled something else from the bag.

A voice in my head said: See how it all fits together?

Quinn's journal.

The note from Olek slipped from its pages and wafted to the RV's floor.

"I'll call you back," I said—and for a weird moment it was as if all the atoms in everything around me buzzed and glowed. "There may be someone else who can help us."

# 55

OLEK SENT FOUR vampires to meet us two miles outside Caminata.

Only four? Not enough. And "us" was me and Lucy. Madeline was babysitting Lorcan and Mario. And keeping herself out of the way. (*Did you fuck Walker?* I guessed it would be one of Talulla's first questions to her. Hoping the answer would be yes. *Thanks. Take him off my hands, would you?*) A force of six to take on God knew how many.

"Weapons for you. Twenty clips apiece. Heavy, but you'll need them."

This was Alyssia. Australian, human age mid-thirties, bleach blonde with bangs, blue eyes, supple, neatly proportioned body. Exquisitely beautiful hands with perfectly manicured purple nails. She was wearing, as were we, odour-block paste between nose and top lip—some chemical compound only marginally better than the stink of the vamps themselves (and presumably the stink of us to them); we would've looked fucking ridiculous to anybody watching, but without it we wouldn't have been able to get near enough to each other for a conversation. As it was we were twenty feet apart, fighting off nausea.

"There are grenades, tear gas canisters and masks in the bag," Alyssia said. "We won't need the masks. They're for you."

No disguising the slight sneer in that. As in: We don't need to wait for a full moon. We can deal with this shit anytime. (It's one of the bloodsuckers' snobberies, that we're lunar-governed, that we're *part-timers*.) "We go in hard and fast," she said. "If it's human, kill it—right?" This was to her crew. As in: This is not a drinking party. No stopping for a quick cocktail.

The crew, also armed with machine guns and pistols, sort of ummed and grinned and nodded. Clearly no promises. They didn't want to be doing this, every syllable of their body-language said. They had, make no mistake, better, cooler things to be doing. Olek must have some clout, charlatan or not.

"We're not going to be hanging around," one of them said, "any longer than necessary."

I didn't like this guy, Miro. He was a tall and thin-legged Pole with a hairdo like the top of a goddamned scallion and what my mom would've called a butt-face. Which is to say his cheeks were a little too full and his mouth and nose seemed to sit in a vertical groove.

"We don't need to go over it," a third vampire said. "We know what we're doing. Let's just for fuck's sake get on with it."

She couldn't have been more than nineteen when she was Turned—although, as Lula would've said, for all we know she could've got hammered with Shakespeare. A broad-shouldered English girl with long dark hair in a ponytail and big, bored dark eyes. Her name was Eleanor.

The fourth member of the vampire squad, Nils, a Dutchman, inspired confidence, though his stink was worse than the other three put together. He was at least six-four, not gym-muscled but solid-limbed, dense, visibly full of speed and heft. Short blond curls plastered tight over a big, tough-boned head.

"Don't worry about us," he said. "You just worry about keeping up."

It was (obviously) dark. The facility was a quarter of a mile northwest of the rendezvous. Mario had described the layout—though it was plain from his description there were parts he was hazy on. Talulla and Zoë were being held below ground. Sub-level 2, Red Wing, cell numbers 4B and 17A. The numerical odds were stupid, of course, but we had—in the hired vampire help—more speed and strength than could be counted by heads. That, plus our desperation. That, plus my moments of not giving a fuck whether I lived or died.

# 56

IT WAS A BLUR. Like all combat. And yet like all combat weird details stood out. Dandelions brushing my shins on the approach. The Big Dipper tilted and winking over the installation's roof. The moment between the first grenade toss and the explosion, when Lucy cleared her throat and checked the safety on her automatic one last time. The foot of one of the guards I shot, twitching, bootlace coming undone. A crucifix knocked crooked on a bloodstained corridor wall. One of the female *Militi Christi* screaming something in what sounded like Latin. The sound of a bullet going straight through Alyssia's leg, next to me. Making no difference to her whatsoever. When she went ahead of me her ass looked good in the tight dark-blue jeans. Headfuck: attraction and repulsion at the same time—in the middle of adrenaline chaos.

Nothing works in your favour like the element of surprise. Half of them were only carrying side arms—though the shock of discharged silver was heavy in the air, a sickening combination with the nose-paste and the reek and vibe of the vampires alongside us. I'd underestimated the silver, the effect, the buzz in your bones and the fight it took not to run and hide. I'd got complacent. We all had. So used to victims. So used to people not being able to kill us.

I don't know how many we took out. Thirty, maybe forty. The vampires were fast. They made the humans—and us, in human form—look like we were on Valium. Alyssia wasn't confined to the ground. The first time I saw her leap and take twenty strides along the corridor wall stopped me in my tracks like a moron. The boochies were controlled and focused. They could afford to be: there was no ammunition in the place that would do them any harm. It was impossible to imagine any of the humans getting close enough with a stake.

One of the humans got close enough to me, however.

A doorway into a room we thought we'd cleared. One minute I was changing clips, the next his arm was around my throat and a knife—in the stretched moment I had all the time in the world to recognise the model, Sniper Double Edged Combat Blade by Mercworx, we used them back in the WOCOP days—was heading for my throat. I was thinking (there's all this endless time for thinking in these moments) that it wouldn't kill me but it wouldn't be any kind of fun, either—and it would slow my breathing down for crucial minutes.

Which was when I felt it.

Customised steel.

Silver-edged.

When combat brings death close you realise you never thought you'd die. Not this time, you tell yourself, before you go in. This time is always not the time. Has to be, otherwise you'd never *go* in.

I couldn't see him, but the arm around my neck and the hand holding the knife said a big, powerful guy. Dark skin. Soft-haired hands. His body pounded heat into mine. It made me feel like throwing up. It took me to the moment—there always is one—where you ask yourself whether the thing to do isn't just let them kill you, whoever they are. Death does this, asks you if you're sure—you're really *sure*—you don't want it?

My limbs were dreaming. Full of warmth and laziness. With what felt like fucking laughable slowness I got my hands up to his wrist when the knife was three or four inches from my throat. I could feel his big rib cage pressed into my back. It reminded me of. It reminded me.

You *sure* you don't want me? Death said, again. It's probably why she left you. Not man enough.

Suddenly the weight around my neck and shoulders increased. Couldn't stand it. Literally. Dropped to my knees, and the guy holding me went down with me. I heard him make a weird noise. For a second the weight alone felt like it was going to kill me—then the stink of Nils shot through—and the arm around my throat went dead.

I opened my eyes. I didn't know I'd closed them.

The weight was gone. My face was wet. Blood. Lots of it. *Wulf*—of course—leaped up with a deafening reminder that last night I hadn't fed. A useless bulletin—but the Curse can't help it.

Twenty feet away Nils stood looking over his shoulder at me. He had my attacker's severed head in his hands. He smiled and made a little gesture, as in: Jesus, you once-a-monthers. Then he tossed the head towards me, turned and loped off down the corridor.

# 57

OUTSIDE ZOË'S CELL Miro was feeding on one of the nuns. She lay on her back with her skirt up to her hips and her left leg bent and shivering. The bare flesh made it look like pornography. Like someone *dressed* as a nun. Miro looked up at me and grinned. His chops were covered in blood.

"Guard," he said, swallowing. "There, that one. He's got the keys."

One of the guards was dead, throat ripped out. The other was sitting propped against the wall opposite the cell door, holding his abdomen. He was shivering, too. It was a weird little disturbance in the atmosphere, his and the nun's shivering like that. He had the keys—a bizarrely old-fashioned bunch—on his crotch. When I bent to grab them I saw he was holding his intestines in. He looked at me, baffled and pleading.

I took the keys and unlocked the door.

Zoë was standing by her bunk, hands and legs cuffed, on a chain bolted to the floor. She'd heard the commotion. Her face was full of uncertainty—but the relief when she saw me was like stepping from cold into warmth.

"Hold on, honey," I said, when I bent and she flung her arms around me. "Let's get this crap off you."

There were twenty keys at least on the bunch, so we had the horror movie moments of trying a dozen different wrong ones, time simmering, her little body on trembling pause. You tell yourself: Easy. Do it logically. More haste less speed. But my hands were like two birds tethered to the ends of my wrists.

"Where's Mommy?"

"She's here, babe. Hold still. We're going to get her—there. Jackpot."

The chain dropped with a soft growl. Two more wrong keys, then I had her free.

"Come on, jump up. Piggy-back. Hold tight and don't let go, okay?"

"Okay."

Her face was small and warm against my neck.

"What's that smell?" she said.

"New friends," I said. "They stink, but they're on our side."

"Like Uncle Mike?"

Uncle Mike was Konstantinov. He and Natasha were the only vampires the kid had known.

Unlike her mother.

"Yeah, like Uncle Mike. You ready?"

"Yes."

"Keep your head down, sweetpea."

The gashed-open guard was dead. His arms had dropped to his sides and his guts lolled in his lap. Miro was still drinking, though he'd switched his bite to the nun's still-quivering thigh. I stepped over him.

"No rush," he said, barely raising his head. "They're all dead."

He couldn't know that, but there was no sound of gunfire up ahead. Somewhere much deeper in the building a grenade detonated. The explosion came up through the floor like a loud cough. I checked the clip on the automatic, pulled Zoë's legs tighter around me, and set off.

Outside Talulla's cell I found Alyssia and Eleanor with two men. One, a *Militi Christi* guard, was face-down on the floor in an expanding puddle of blood. The other, who looked ridiculous in the combat fatigues, was being pinned against the wall by Eleanor, who had, with one hand wrapped around his throat, lifted him several inches off the ground. At his feet were a pair of gold-rimmed spectacles. And a young man's severed head. There was no visible body it belonged to.

Talulla was unconscious on the floor of her cell. For a moment I thought she was dead. Then the scent and tremor of her life hit me, hit Zoë. In the moment it had taken I'd asked myself whether I'd look after the kids if Lula was dead. And the goodness of Zoë's weight on me said, Yes, I would, somehow. There are these unexpected measurements of love. When you least want them.

"He's in charge, believe it or not," Alyssia said, indicating the guy Eleanor had by the throat, toes typing thin air. The effects of the nose-paste were wearing off. The corridor's confined space was dense with the vampires' reek. Zoë was pressing her nose into my shoulder to block it out. Eleanor was *holding* her nose with her free hand. Alyssia tossed me the keys. "Fast," she said. "This is becoming intolerable."

Fewer keys on this bunch, and the third one opened the cell door. Zoë slithered from my back and rushed to Talulla.

"Mommy! Mommy, wake up. Wake *up*."

"It's okay, honey," I said. "She's just asleep. They gave her sleep-medicine."

"Anyone alive behind you?" Alyssia asked.

"Only Miro."

"Drinking."

"Yeah."

She shook her head. "Asshole. Okay. Out the way we came in."

"Can you take the kid?"

The logistics. I'd have to carry Talulla. The vampires looked at each other. The face of the man Eleanor was holding by the throat was purple. His feet tap danced. Neither of them wanted to get any closer to me *or* the kid. *Carrying* her?

"Jesus, fuck, okay. I'll have to take them both. Fuck."

"All right," Alyssia said, taking fresh scent-block from a tube in her pocket and virtually filling her nostrils with the stuff. "Give her to me."

I liked her. She had a sexy controlled impatience. And her hands were the most beautiful I'd ever seen. Because your mind goes where it goes, regardless, I had an image of her sliding them into her panties, looking at me.

"Fuck," she said. "I didn't sign up for this."

She was spared the trouble. Lucy appeared with Nils at the far end of the corridor. She looked like a miniature person next to him. The pair of them were spattered with blood.

"We good?" Alyssia called.

"Good," Nils answered.

Lucy rushed up and put Zoë on her back. I fireman-lifted Talulla. I wondered what I would have said to her if she'd been awake. I wondered what she would have said to me. Holding her like that, unconscious, elsewhere, it suddenly felt like there wouldn't have been anything *to* say. I realised how much we hadn't looked at each other over the last few months. Or how much she hadn't looked at me.

Eleanor hurled the guy she'd been strangling head-first at the bars of the cell. His body dropped, heavily.

"Well, that's that," she said, bored. "Let's go."

# Part Five

# The Wrong
# Twilight

# 58
## Remshi

THE LOGISTICS, AS always, were wearisome. Daylight. Darkness. We had to make the bulk of the flight in the blackout room, to arrive in Italy after sunset. Mia and Caleb refused to take the bed, insisted on curling up on the floor. There's ivory silk and wool shag-pile in there, mind you, and cushions aplenty from the cabin, so they weren't uncomfortable. Still, I couldn't help feeling a heel.

"You're not well," Caleb said to me, after we'd been up for half an hour. "You don't look right."

We were back in the main cabin. The jet was an hour from Rome. Damien and Seth were in the cockpit. Mia was taking a shower. Caleb was thrilled with the experience, though he was trying not to effervesce. The luxury was a shock to him. The cabin's corpulent cream leather recliners, the cherry woodwork, the blackout room, the dense technology slotted snugly together like a Chinese puzzle. Every fixture and fitting said precision cut and quality finish. You forget these things until you see them through fresh eyes. In their old life his mother had had access to wealth, yes, but not like this. Not comprehensive fingertip control. He'd taken a copy of Browning's *Men and Women* from the shelf (which reminded me of the *Collected Works* I'd never yet picked up from the floor of the study at home at Las Rosas) but he'd done little more than glance at it. He wasn't, his aura said, a reader. I thought of all the textual pleasures he had awaiting him, if someone would only get him started. I resolved to speak to Mia about it in a quiet moment. But at the same time wondered where one *did* start, these days. These days young people found *The Catcher in the Rye* . . . sorta dull, kinda boring. Not to mention the new cognoscenti of all ages, for whom the test of whether a book was worth reading was whether they'd want to be friends with the protagonist.

"You're sweating, in fact," Caleb said.

This was the tone he'd decided on with me: equals. Tangents, blunt observations, non sequiturs. Overcompensated adulthood. I didn't mind. I still felt sorry for him.

"Maybe you need to drink some more? Shall I get you another bag?"

"I'm fine," I said. "Believe it or not, flying's never really agreed with me. Even flying in one of these."

The truth was I *wasn't* feeling well. Not just the effects of the dream, which I'd had again, which I'd been having every night and understood I would go on having every night for as long as it took, but a higher than usual (or comfortable) rate of snapshots from the improbable past, memories that came like rounds of machine-gun fire or occasionally like flashbulbs exploding in slow motion. Botticelli woken by a nightmare of his own discovering me in his workshop studying by lamplight the all but finished *Birth of Venus* and backing away, barefoot in his nightshirt, crying out, knocking over a small wooden table and a vase of irises. I would have killed him to have a moment longer with the image (the smell of oils remains one of my favourites, along with mown grass and a brand-new packet of tea bags and the first whiff of the ocean when you get near enough to the coast) but the thought of cutting off his talent and depriving the world stayed my hand. And the young private in an Ypres ditch, close but not close enough to death, stomach wound bubbling, skin tight and damp in the moonlight, knowing what I was and saying in a voice that sounded twelve years old, Please, sir, can you kill me? I can't stand it anymore. Please, please . . . These were the slow-motion flashbulbs, yes, but the rest was vertiginous, an impossible compression of thunderstorms and dark rivers and neoned cities and constellations and news reports and night-marching legionaries and one of the big moonlit stones of Djoser stained with blood where a slave had dropped from exhaustion and cracked his head and a blind singer in a torchlit Athenian courtyard that stank of vomit and piss and spilled wine draining his own cup and emptying the dregs for the gods and beginning in Greek "Sing, goddess, the anger of Peleus's son, Achilles . . ."

I got up and stretched my legs a little, lifted my arms above my head until the higher vertebrae cracked like a card dealer's riffle. Caleb raised his recliner a few inches. He'd taken his shoes off. Odd socks, one blue, one black. His pale big toe poked through a hole in the right, like a button mushroom. He was at war with how much I fascinated him. I was thinking it would give me pleasure to make him and his mother materially comfortable. I'd give them the house at Big Sur, if they wanted it. It would be nice to have company there when I visited. Without warning my eyes filled with tears.

"Who made you?" he said.

I'd known he was going to ask, sooner or later. The young's natural need for origins. I took the pack of Lucky Strikes from the countertop of the minibar and lit one. I remembered Justine standing here, mixing drinks for herself. She'd bought a book of cocktail recipes in Kuala Lumpur and worked her way through, getting drunker. She'd kept taking them up to the pilots and poor Veejay (who in any case didn't drink) had had to keep politely saying no, thank you, miss, I have to fly the aircraft. I looked at the bar's little horseshoe of bottles. Big jewels: green; gold; sapphire; diamond white. It was a sadness to me that I'd been Turned before the invention of alcohol. I'd watched the Egyptians loosened by beer. The slurred segue into familial warmth—and familial violence. I've many times worked the night shift in bars down the years (saloons, gin-joints, taverns) when things have got lonely. It's always helped, the room's wink and murmur, the conversation, the short stories blooming and fading as customers come and go. The comfort of strangers, as my darling Justine had learned.

"It was a long time ago," I said, turning my back to him so I could dab my idiot eyes.

"You don't want to talk about it?"

"It's a long time since I've told that story. Maybe I've forgotten it."

Caleb didn't say anything. Mia came out of the bathroom, freshly cosmeticised and smelling of Justine's coconut shower gel and Flex shampoo. I'd had Damien pick up clothes for her and her son en route to the airport. Now she was in crisp blue jeans and a white t-shirt. A new short black leather jacket and boots. Purple Converse for Caleb, who had refused a new leather jacket, kept the crash-scorched red one instead. I knew it was a friend to him, gave him a little feeling of fraternal comfort every time he shrugged it on. He'd had too much loneliness in his life already. Too much thinking that he'd fucked things up for his mother.

"You need to take a shower," Mia said to him.

Caleb lit a cigarette of his own, ignored her. There were these little battles between them. I sat on the high stool behind the bar and rested my elbows on the marble counter. There was a pretty red carnelian ashtray within reach, niftily bolted to the surface. I'd been at the lecture William Morris gave in Birmingham in 1880. "Have nothing in your houses that you do not know to be useful or believe to be beautiful," he'd advised the designers. He'd found the maxim written on a piece of paper in the pocket of a blue serge jacket he'd been wearing a month before. Put there by me. I've always had a mischievous habit of planting messages on influential humans.

*Ours is essentially a tragic age, so we refuse to take it tragically.*

*Ask not what your country can do for you, ask what you can do for your country.*

*Coke is it.*

*Do not go gentle into that good night.*

*Fresh cream cakes. Naughty—but nice.*

*Yes, we can.*

I ASKED HIM WHO MADE HIM.

Caleb's gauche mental shield might as well have been cigarette smoke. Mia looked an apology at me. The jet dipped in and out of an air pocket.

"I was made by someone I never saw," I said. "According to this little Oa around my neck, twenty thousand years ago."

Neither of them spoke, though I could feel Caleb's young mind tumbling back towards steamships and Native Americans and then plunging with a shock to movie cavemen, fires, spears, the world alarmingly uncluttered by pop songs and litter. It came as a shock to him, rocks and streams and forests and deserts, a nude world of natural objects curiously untouched by *Mad Men* and Twitter.

CAN'T BE. NO ONE'S THAT OLD.

"I was thirty-nine when it happened," I continued. I put the cigarette down in the ashtray and began making a Manhattan. There would be no takers for it, I knew, but there's comfort in the small ritual actions of the hands. "I'd been out hunting with five of my kinsmen. We knew we were close to the edge of another tribe's territory, but we could smell the boar, and it had been too long a chase to go home empty-handed. There was only an hour or so of daylight left, and we had a ten-mile walk back to our people and the fires."

"What were you hunting with?" Caleb asked. He'd brought his recliner all the way up, and sat now with his knees under his chin.

"Spears," I said. "Bows and arrows. What you'd call slingshots. The ratio of projectiles to dead meat was pretty lousy most of the time. We had a phrase: 'nuts and berries.' It meant the less desirable of two options. It was what we ate when there was no meat."

Caleb, I could tell, wanted Mia to sit down. It was spoiling the act of listening for him, to have her on her feet, implying potential interruption. It was taking a little part of his consciousness away from the story, and he wanted to be immersed. His childhood really wasn't very long ago.

Mia felt it. Gave me a glance of complicity. Took the seat opposite her son, reclined it, laced her fingers on her midriff and crossed her long, slender legs. I felt Caleb relax. Aside from the pleasure of being told a tale he took his emotional cues from her. If she was at quiescent ease, so was he. Which added to her weight of responsibility. It was comforting to be getting all this so quick and easy from them, via mutually lowered guards. It had been a long time since I'd been among my own kind by choice— Justine's recent species-shift excepted.

"We got a boar," I said. "A big one. Probably two hundred pounds if you weighed it today. We trussed it and strapped it to the carry-pole. I can't tell you how the feeling of warmth and goodness used to go between us when there was meat to bring home. Imagining the faces and the kids' bellies stuffed and the women's fingers and lips shining with animal fat in the firelight."

I had to pause. Balance. The memory was the edge of a sheer drop through my time. The fall would be everything. You know, Juss, I sometimes think that if I remembered everything that's happened to me . . .

"But we were attacked," I said. "Twenty hunters from the other tribe. My kinsmen were killed. I was wounded, but I got away. Obviously they took the boar, too."

"Where were you wounded?" Caleb asked.

"Guts," I said. "A spear went straight through my intestines, destroyed my kidneys. I broke the shaft, but when I tried to pull it out I realised the head was barbed with teeth. The pain was unbearable."

"So how come you got away?" Reflex modern teen scepticism: Look for cowardice, lies, trickery. Things aren't what they seem unless they seem shit.

"I was lucky," I said. "We were still in the forest, and darkness gathered quickly. I slipped them and struggled on for what felt like miles. It was so tempting to lie down and close my eyes. I was very cold."

It was a minor, separate fascination to Caleb that I was making the drink as I spoke. Sweet vermouth. Bourbon. Angostura bitters. There were maraschino cherries in a jar on the shelf—but I doubted we had an orange for the peel rub around the glass. Shame. Caleb would've been tickled by that.

"It rained," I said. "By the time I found the cave I was crawling on my hands and knees. I knew I was dying. I was hoping there'd be a big cat inside to finish me off. There was something in there, but it wasn't a big cat."

"Your maker?" Caleb said.

I strained the bourbon, vermouth and bitters over ice into a funnel glass. I was right: we didn't have oranges. It offended my inner bartender, a tiny aesthetic pain. A missing piece. He lied in every word.

"It was a good place to die," I said, sliding the cocktail to my imaginary customer (I pictured a tired midtown businesswoman with fractured blue eye-shadow and a creased pinstripe skirt, shapely, aching calves, coffee breath, the day's migraine of corporate jabber draining away in the first sip of the drink) and leaning on the counter on the heels of my hands. "It would have been a good place to die. The mouth of the cave looked west, out over the tops of the trees. On the horizon the last flakes of sunset like blood and gold. When I heard a sound behind me I thought the gods had answered me. He came close. I felt his breath on my neck. He said: 'Answer me something. Do you want to live?' To this day I can't recall whether I answered yes or no. It didn't matter. He said: 'I've seen this place in my dreams. It's a relief to come to it.' Then he took me in his arms and put his teeth in my throat."

I was remembering the darkening land, those last flakes of light and the night coming down inside me, his drinking to the rhythm of my heart, to what felt like the rhythm of the land itself. It was such a thin, light-aired place between life and death. In it you could see the universe was like a frail smile.

"When he opened his wrist and put it to my lips, I remember I said: 'Why?' And he answered: 'Because someone must bear witness. My time is over. This is the last thing I can do. Now drink.' So of course," I said, smiling, feeling the tears coming again, "I drank."

Caleb had forgotten to smoke his cigarette. It had burned all the way down, and its ash had fallen on the carpet. I could feel Mia trying to make the emotional calculation. She was barely six hundred years old. There was, I knew, a determination in her to pass the thousand-year jinx—but twenty thousand?

"What happened to him?" Caleb asked.

I swallowed the tears. Blinked. Blinked. There's no fool like an old fool.

"I never saw him," I said. "I crawled deep into the cave and slept. When I woke the next night, there were only the remains."

"What remains?"

The other youth demand—for end-points. Prime movers and final destinations.

"Not much," I said. "I couldn't see. It was still dark. Something like wet ash. I left the cave and went out into the night. I had a woman. Children. There was no going back. I knew that from the very beginning."

"And did you have to feed straight away?" Caleb asked—but Mia shook her head.

"That's enough questions," she said. She, at any rate, could see or sense the state I was in. You're a bit fragile . . .

Caleb, snapped out of it, saw what had become of his unsmoked cigarette. "Oh," he said. "Shit. Sorry."

"Sir?" Damien's voice came over the PA. I picked up the phone by the bar.

"Yes, Damien?"

"Sir, we're starting our approach. We should be on the ground in twenty minutes."

I turned to my guests. "Okay," I said. "Seats upright, please. Fasten your seat belts. We're landing soon."

# 59

IT WAS OBVIOUS before the Caminata installation came into view that whatever had happened here, we'd missed it. The air (to noses of our refinement) stank—beyond the quiet base notes of meadow grass, gorse and rain—of explosives and gunfire.

Something very bizarre had happened to me en route.

We'd parked the car a quarter of a mile away on a chalk track that led off a rutted lane and made our way through a thin line of woodland up towards the ridge. A stream ran through a gully some thirty metres into the trees. Mia and Caleb went over it in a single leap, but I found myself compelled to wade. Not just the threatened unsteadiness in my pins (my body had decided to experiment with various anomalies and I'd decided to keep quiet about them) but a *psychological* necessity. A sort of dim curiosity about what the water would feel like, although I had no earthly reason for expecting it to feel like anything other than water. Fortunately, by the time I began to cross mother and son were far enough ahead not to see what happened.

What happened was that after three or four paces, shin-deep, I became convinced that I was treading not on what were obviously—visibly—the rounded stones of the stream bed, but on the heads and bodies of dead people.

I made it to the opposite bank and sloshed out, shaking, wondering not only what new doolally gimmick my brain was trying out, but also why the feel of the non-existent corpses underfoot reminded me of the old geezer I'd seen that night on the drive at Las Rosas, with his crutch and his bloodshot eye and his baffling bulletin that I was "going the wrong way." Him and that wretched horse I'd had to shoot the night I went after Justine in North Vegas. I'd forgotten both of them until just now.

Needless to say I didn't mention any of this to Mia and Caleb when I caught up with them at the edge of the tree line.

Now we lay on our bellies on the ridge with night binoculars trained on what looked like the human equivalent of a smoked wasps' nest some three hundred metres away. Part of the building's roof had caved in. There were detonation scars everywhere. The main doors had been blown clean off. Half a dozen dazed personnel moved around, manifestly not knowing whether to abandon what was left of their post.

"She's not here," Mia said. Grudging satisfaction. She'd pulled her blonde hair back and bound it in a bun as hard as an eight ball, exposing her fine Slavic cheekbones and the superb whiteness of her throat. Had I not come along, she could have had a career as a model. Night shoots only.

"Apparently not," I said. I could feel her weighing up whether to take a feed from the shell-shocked victims still in the facility. They looked in no state to offer resistance. She was at least thirty hours early, but her recent travails had made an opportunist of her. The thirst was lifting its head in her, the red snake waking from a light (always light) doze.

"We need one of them alive," I said.

"They're not going to know anything," Mia said. "She's been taken out by force. I'd say it was her pack, except . . ." She didn't need to finish. I could smell it, too: along with the odour of werewolves was the inimitable perfume of our own kind. Vampires had been here.

"Two different snatch teams?" Mia said. "That's an unlikely coincidence."

"And yet still more likely than ours and theirs joining forces."

"How many do you think are left?"

"It doesn't matter," I said. "Stay here."

I went fast and low between the gorse bushes. I needn't have bothered. *Militi Christi* vigilance had collapsed.

Seventy metres. Fifty. Twenty-five. There were now only two guards outside the building. Take one out, grab the other. I readied myself for the last sprint.

I must have made some sound when I fell, but, either deaf from the explosions or past caring, neither of the grunts heard it. The world swung up and went out. I lay on my side with my left arm trapped under me. Nausea. A rush that dipped me for a second into complete blackness. A moment needed when I came back to organise the rearranged geometry. Grass tickled my face. One huge trodden daisy head beamed at me sadly. I could smell wet earth, rabbit shit, wild rosemary. I retched, thinking, as I retched, of the idiom, *as weak as a kitten*. I thought, Yes, I've never considered the weakness of kittens properly, but that's how I feel, *as weak as a kitten*. Briefly, I felt sorry for weak things everywhere.

Something moved, very fast, over my head.

It was a moment before I could lift my kitten skull (on what felt like its broken kitten neck) to see what it was.

Mia.

She was—even in my state—a joy to behold. She took the last thirty feet in an airborne leap. The first guard—a trim woman in her twenties with a long dark plait—lost half her throat in my companion's single right-hand slash and fell to the floor—or rather knelt, slowly, trying to hold the blood in with her hand, mouth opening and closing. She had marvellously long thick eyelashes. The second guard—a fair-haired, tough-headed guy with a frowning face and a stocky, muscular build—made some vague, slow-motion movements with his hands about his person, in abstracted reflex search for the automatic rifle that was in fact propped against the wall ten feet away, before Mia's high kick—a *gullgi chagi*, to be precise—rendered him immediately unconscious, and nearly took his head off into the bargain. Within two seconds she had him slung up over her shoulder (his weight no more to her than a sack of potato chips) and was heading back to the cover of the ridge.

I heard her dump him on the ground and say to Caleb: If he wakes up, knock him out again.

Then she came back for me.

"What's the matter?"

Good question. I was on my hands and knees, thinking what a distant and futile goal getting to my feet seemed. I had a brief, vivid vision of my old friend, Amlek, the way he'd looked when I found his body one night in Athens, staked through the heart and bound to a wooden post, papyrus scraps driven into his flesh with nails, covered in Greek obscenities. *Names in my ears, /Of all the lost adventurers my peers . . .* The vision vanished.

"Fuck," I heard myself saying, as if from a long way away. "Fuck. I don't . . . I . . ."

At which I was unceremoniously hoisted myself, and carried back to the ridge.

"Caleb," Mia said, "go and get the car."

"What's wrong with him?"

"Just get the Jeep, will you? Do it. Now!"

Caleb (no slouch overground himself) was back within ten minutes. He nosed the vehicle in second gear cross-country with the lights off (he had to perch on the edge of the seat to reach the pedals) though there was no one outside the facility to hear. I wondered if Mia's abrasive visit had been observed, and now the remnant force was indoors, collectively and firmly resolved on cowardice. Or prayer. I had a curious little image of them all kneeling, saying the Rosary in unison.

"It's all right," I said. "It's passing. I can manage."

*It's passing.* Whatever "it" was. The kitten-weakness, the nausea, the dip into the vat of pitch. The vortex of memories. Amlek's corpse. *You don't look well.*

We put the guard in the trunk. I got in the back seat and lay down. Caleb slid over and Mia got behind the wheel. I called Damien. He was at the rendezvous, ready, with the truck. No one likes spending the daylight hours in a freight container, but on the road needs must.

Halfway there (I was feeling better) my phone rang. It was Olly, from Amner-DeVere.

"What've you got?"

"Two hours ago," he said. "LAX. She bought a one-way to New York. Flight leaves in thirty-five minutes. Sorry I couldn't get this to you sooner."

"Keep tracking it," I said. "Get me the next transaction as soon as you can."

"I'm supposed to be going to Napa this weekend," he said. "It's my mother's—"

"Double rate," I said. "You're not going anywhere."

Pause. I could see him doing the imaginary steam-train-whistle-pull celebration. "Roger that," he said.

"As soon as, Olly. Understood?"

"Understood."

I hung up.

"How far are we?" I asked Mia. She was a fast, utterly confident driver. Her white hands looked lovely on the wheel and gearstick.

"Twenty minutes," she said. "Do you want to tell me what's wrong with you?"

I don't know. I don't know. I don't know. Except he lied in every word. And the stream was filled with bodies.

"Do you two have passports?" I said.

Caleb looked at Mia.

"Yes," she said. "Several. Why?"

I thought of the fear Justine was up against. Night flights. The real world. Small windows to get undercover. All the way to Bangkok, the hard way.

"Because we're going to Thailand," I said, redialling Damien's number.

# 60

## *Talulla*

I WOKE UP in bed in my underwear in a room in the Last Resort. So christened by poor Fergus, who would never have need of it again. I remembered Trish getting childishly excited over the architectural drawings. Sweet Trish who always looked too small for whatever motorbike she was riding. And for whatever helmet she was wearing. I know I look like a science fiction dwarf, she said, but I don't want my feckin brains all over the central reservation, do I? Zoë, who had a passion for headwear of all kinds, once put one of the visored helmets on. She was sitting on the floor. When she tilted her head back to look up at us the weight of the thing made her keel over. It was, we all agreed, just as well she was wearing a helmet.

*You might not want it for yourself, but you'll want it for your children.*

I lay there in the first minutes of coming-to with Olek's words running through my head. Jake was dead. Cloquet was dead. Fergus. Trish. I'd been close to death a dozen times or more in the last three years. My son had been kidnapped, my daughter incarcerated with me. WOCOP was gone, but the *Militi Christi* had picked up where they'd left off. I thought of Bryce's *Big Brother* with werewolves format. There would be other shows. Hunting shows. Game shows. Gambling shows. The world was turning its gaze on us. The world was realising that *something would have to be done*. The noose, as Olek had suggested, was only going to get tighter.

"Hey," Madeline said.

I opened my eyes. White ceiling with inset yellowy halogens turned low. I was in a crisply made bed, linen fresh out of the packaging. It smelled of department stores, human civilisation, the old life, mixed with the room's comforting odour of new plaster and paint. Pale oak floor, no windows. (Most of the Last Resort was underground, for obvious reasons.) Skirting uplights opposite. A green leather recliner next to my bed, with Maddy in it. She was, as usual, accurately made-up. She wore slim-line khaki combat pants and a black t-shirt that had belonged to Cloquet. Red flip-flops showing off her pretty feet and scrupulous pedicure, toenails vermillion. She'd caught the sun in Italy. There was a tan line where her watch had been.

"Zoë's fine," she said. "She's here, she's safe. She's playing snakes and ladders with Lorcan and Luce upstairs."

I hadn't known I'd got up on my elbows, my whole body tensed, until I felt it relax now.

"Know where you are?" Madeline asked.

"Croatia?"

She nodded. "Whatever the fuck they shot you with, there was a lot of it. You've been out for two days. We had to tell passport control you were zonked on painkillers. Still cost us three hundred quid. How are you feeling?"

"Thirsty."

There was a bottle of Jamnica mineral water on the floor next to her. She handed it to me. I drank the lot.

"More?"

"In a minute. What happened back there?"

Back there. When I was captured. When I risked my children's lives. Again. Part of the question—oh, *part* of it—was: Did you fuck Walker? I could feel her screening a little for a moment, then giving up. "No," she said. "I didn't."

It was the truth, but it was also an admission of how close she'd come.

"It's fine," I said. "It's . . ." I let it go. "How is he?"

"Physically he's all right. He didn't get a scratch, apart from apparently he nearly got stabbed in the throat."

"How did you find me?"

"Oh Christ, Lu, that's a long story. We had help. Blimey, I don't know where to start."

She didn't have to. The door opened. Walker. Unshaven. In black jeans and a denim shirt. The shit-kicker boots he hadn't worn since the WOCOP days. He looked like he'd lost weight.

An awkward exchange of not quite direct looks between the three of us. Then Maddy got up from the recliner. "Well," she said, "now you've decided to rejoin the land of the living, I'm going to pour myself a bloody huge gin and tonic. We're still waiting for half the furniture, but the booze and fags arrived today, thank God."

# 61

W<small>HEN SHE'D GONE</small>, Walker came and sat on the edge of the bed and put his hand around my ankle through the comforter.

"I'm sorry," I said. The lingering drug had tears ready for me, if I wasn't going to be ruthless with myself.

Walker gave my ankle a squeeze, then took his hand away. I thought: That's the last time he'll ever do that. He leaned forward, elbows on knees. Looked at the brand-new floor. It was all there between us, the innocent reality, that this was us—*us*—and yet this was still happening. All love's details burned bright. Surely they meant something? Surely they were enough? But they came and went and there we still were, with new unfillable space between us. I felt old and tired. Sometimes your coldness thrills you. Sometimes it's just a wearily disgusting tumour. Not for the first time, nor did I imagine the last, Aunt Theresa's voice came back: Talulla Demetriou, you are a dirty little girl. A dirty, *filthy* little girl.

"Thank you for coming for us," I said. The power of plain words. *Thank you.* I swallowed, swallowed, but the tears came anyway. Shocking to feel them hot and intimate on my cheeks. My mother had always grudged her own rare tears. The harder you are the more they undo you. It's the price you pay for *being* hard. I was sick of myself, suddenly.

But not sufficiently. My self always wins. Sits out the sickness, drumming its fingers, until I come back, then says, Right. All done? Can we *continue* now?

"We had help," Walker said. "Vampires, if you can believe that."

"What?"

He told me. Not looking at me. Like a departing employee tiredly running through stuff for his successor.

"Lorcan pulled Quinn's book from your bag," he said. "I wouldn't have thought of Olek, otherwise. Maybe someone's making this shit up after all."

There was a twitch in the ether between us when he went through the vampire character sketches and got to Alyssia.

"Sounds like she made an impression," I said.

He was silent for a moment. Then said: "Don't." Quietly. If he'd said it in anger it would have been easier to hear. I resisted the urge to say (pointlessly), "Don't what?"

He stood up—and when he looked down at me and smiled all the shame and guilt my efficient little self had kept in check rushed up. Into my face, I knew.

"Don't try for a smooth baton change," he said.

The smile was his smile, being used now to express its opposite.

I'm not normally the one who looks away. Even now I almost, out of sheer self-loathing, didn't. Then, with more warm tears, I did. It was a little Pyrrhic victory for him. I felt "I'm sorry" coming up in me again. And him thinking: Don't bother.

We stayed like that, him watching me crying, for as long as we could stand it. Then he took a couple of paces away. The room needed a window for him to go to and look out of. I could feel the grammar of the moment demanding it. But the room was the room. The room was innocent. And designed by us.

"You don't need me to tell you this," he said. "But we got the vamp help because I promised Olek you'd go and see him. That was the deal. That's the story."

We both knew I would go, that I was always going, but nonetheless I said: "You promised?"

"He took my word. Old school. Obviously there's nothing making you go. But since you were going anyway . . ."

I didn't contradict him.

"He didn't seem surprised," Walker said. "Maybe he's in on the plot."

It really sickened him, this idea that there was a shape or purpose to all this. Because if there was then he'd gone through everything he'd gone through according to its design. Was still going through it. I thought of how much we'd loved kissing each other. It was almost an embarrassment, how much just kissing turned both of us on. I imagined myself opening my mouth now and saying: I love you. I do love you.

But I didn't say it. Instead I lay there and he stood there, enduring the pain and awfulness of this. The moment you think is unbearable forces you to disappoint yourself by bearing it. There's resigned laughter available, for the hilarity of your own durability.

"He's in India," Walker said. "I've got the details. He wants you there in time for the next full moon."

As soon as he said "India" it felt like déjà vu. I realised now that when I'd spoken to Olek on the phone I'd imagined him somewhere like that. Somewhere superficially—somewhere *cinematically*—unlikely for a vampire.

"Mike and Natasha will meet you there," he said.

Mike and Natasha. Not him. So it had really begun, the sequence of severances. Well? It was what I wanted—wasn't it?

Walker went to the door and opened it. All our past tenderness rose up in my chest. I was so close to saying, Please don't go. Please let's not do this. Please forgive me. Please, please, please. The thought of how good it would feel if he came and put his arms around me and held me wasn't a thought but a physical sensation, an ache in the space around my body. I imagined myself saying it, heard myself, felt the sweetness that would come to me in his embrace. And immediately it had come so would the knowledge, like a gunshot, that it had been the wrong thing to do.

"It won't be safe for the kids," he said, not looking at me now. "You should leave them here. We'll take care of them until you get back."

"And when I get back?" Sometimes you need every nail hammered in.

Walker turned and looked at me. He looked so tired and handsome. I wanted to get up from the bed and go to him. He didn't say anything. It was as if there was a membrane between us, every moment tearing. We stared at each other. You push it to the absolute brink of finality and there's a pure moment when you know you can pull it back. The huge gift of our past—and the future we could have—was there like an invisible treasure giving off a golden light and warmth.

Then he turned and walked away, and closed the door behind him.

# 62

## *Justine*

Los Angeles to New York. New York to Dublin. Dublin to Istanbul. Istanbul to Delhi. Delhi to Bangkok. All First Class. So I could be off the plane fast when we landed.

The New York to Dublin leg was always going to be tough. Six hours. As soon as we took off I couldn't believe what I was doing. All that resolve about not being stupid. This was the stupidest thing I'd done so far. All the *what-if*s I'd brushed aside came back like a crowd of ugly people around my seat, jabbing me with their fingers. What if there was a problem with the plane? What if we got re-routed? What if we had to circle for ages before we were cleared to land? What if I took too long getting through Immigration? What if there was a bomb scare, or a fire that closed the airport? I don't think I moved for the first three hours. Just stared at my video screen, not seeing anything. The movie's end credits went up and I had no clue what had played. I switched to Flight Map. Distance to destination. Time to destination. That was worse. There was nothing to do except sit there and freak out. They kept offering me stuff. Champagne, food, chocolates. They thought something was wrong with me. Everyone else in First took everything they were offered. I was grateful for the spaces between the seats. I wanted to smoke. Smoking would have helped. Instead I kept getting up and going to the bathroom and washing my hands and face, just for something to do.

Then worse. In the Arrivals lounge at Istanbul one of the TVs was showing CNN with the sound down. Captions in Turkish I couldn't read. At first I didn't know why the footage bothered me. It was just another crime scene. Lights, police cars, yellow tape, people milling around, an officer standing with his hands on his hips and his back to the camera. I couldn't even understand why it had made it to the news.

Until I realised it was Karl Leath's house.

The footage cut away to the news studio. A new blonde anchorwoman

I didn't recognise and three male studio guests, one of whom was a priest. I stood there watching, my hands fat and heavy, waiting for a photo of me to come up. I could imagine the voiceover: "The suspect, picked up on CCTV leaving the scene, is considered extremely dangerous . . ." Any second now. Any second now. My face on screen. My face.

But nothing happened.

They cut back to the studio, and after a couple of minutes of worried-looking conversation, moved on to a story about Justin Timberlake.

Justin. Justine. The feeling of beguilement. The world snickering and dropping a hint.

Stupid, stupid, stupid.

I made it to the airport hotel with less than thirty minutes to spare. If I'd had luggage I'd have been fucked. As it was, checking-in was agony. The sun trying to slow everything down. Two morons from Atlanta ahead of me at the desk complaining about having twin beds instead of a double. The lights in the lobby were Christmassy, reflecting off everything, digging in behind my eyes. I was drenched with sweat, shaking. My hands all over the place when I had to sign. The clerk asked me if I was all right.

But the bathrooms in big hotels don't have windows. The sun hates the bathrooms in big hotels.

I was so fucked-up I almost didn't go on.

But I did go on. What else was there to do?

I searched online for everything I could find on the Karl Leath murder story. As far as I could tell there was no CCTV footage, no identikit or police-artist sketch of Justine Idiot Cavell, no *suspect*. I'd left the gun and my prints all over everything, but since I didn't have a record there wouldn't be a database match. (All the low-life years before Fluff took me under his wing flashed, the miracle of never getting busted for anything. A blessing I never even appreciated at the time. Well, I fucking appreciated it now.)

The Internet was pounding out werewolf and vampire content with a new intensity. What I'd done to Leath was just one of countless cases of what more and more people were seeing as the work of monsters. Not tabloid monsters. *Actual* monsters. The Churches were loud. Twitter was full of people asking how much longer was the government going to sit on its fat stupid ass and Do Nothing. Not so many "exposed hoaxes" as there used to be. A group of scientists publishing as far as they were concerned irrefutable DNA evidence. Monster-deniers were on the same shrinking bit of polar ice as climate-change sceptics.

I must have spent a couple of hours in the bathroom trawling through all this on my phone. I told myself it was necessary. Information gathering. An end to me rushing blindly into things. But I knew what it really was. Delaying tactics. Putting off what I knew couldn't be put off.

Feeding.

When I'd thought about it I'd imagined finding the poorest area. Homeless. Less chance of investigation. Some piss-stinking old guy with a bag and a bottle. But the Internet told me Istanbul's slum districts were fast disappearing. Sulukule, formerly home to the Roma, had been pulled down to make way for fancy new buildings. There was hardly anyone left in Tarlabasi. One barber shop pointlessly still open surrounded by rubble and condemned tenements. I took a cab there soon after sunset, but I couldn't. When it came right down to it I just didn't believe I'd find someone. I stayed in the cab and went back to Taksim Square. I was so insane and freaked out I nearly just took the fucking cab driver when we stopped at a red signal in a quieter street. He was only about twenty, a thin guy with oily skin and a small head and a too-big moustache and an Adam's apple that seemed to move around way too much when he talked to me, glancing up in the rearview. I actually felt myself leaning forward towards his seat, smelling deodorant and some kind of hair product and a samosa or something spicy he'd eaten and breath that was a mix of cigarettes and Turkish coffee. It's possible I would've bitten him if the light hadn't changed when it did. Instead I sat back in my seat horrified that I'd been so close. Was this what it was going to be like? A constant battle with your own loose will? I had a list of Escort Services. Not many supplying male escorts. Male *gay* escorts, yes—but very little for straight women. A sort of religious hypocrisy, I guessed. But the thought of phoning (they all advertised "English Spoken") to find an in-call, going there, being let in, doing what I had to do, getting out . . . I was afraid the calls would be recorded. I'd have to use a card for the agency booking fee. The apartment building might have CCTV. I don't know, maybe it was just the fucking surreality of it, of calling up a company to make an appointment to kill someone.

In the end I just asked the cab driver to drop me at the nearest night club.

"Fuck me, I'm starvin'," the guy said, when we got back to his hotel. "But it can definitely wait. Come here."

His name was Mick. He was English, from Manchester, not bad-looking, in a monkeyish, Robbie Williams sort of way, and enough success with his cheeky-chappie routine and gym-worked body (he was in black Levis and a tight white t-shirt that showed it off) had given him a twinkly confidence I knew would fly with a lot of girls. He and his "mates" were in Istanbul for a "lads' week," but he'd got separated from them on the club crawl. I hadn't had to do much. He was drunk when he hit on me at the bar—"Orright, love? What you drinkin'?"

At first, having to pretend like I was reluctantly interested was awkward and made my face feel swollen. I couldn't concentrate on playing my part. God only knows what I said to him. But after a few minutes a little thirst-pleasure crept in. The thirst gets fascinated by the mystery of everything that's on the inside. The pleasure's like the pleasure of the moments before you unwrap a Christmas present. It feels good to make the suspense last, but the longer you wait the more fascinating it becomes. Talking to him (I said I was only drinking mineral water, but he bought me a Budvar anyway, which obviously I didn't touch) was like holding the gift up to your ear, smelling it, shaking it to see if it rattled. But I knew there was only so long I could stand it. There was a darker edge, too: the pleasure of knowing the most important thing about someone's life when they didn't. The most important thing was that it was going to end. The most important thing was that you were going to take it. It made me feel sick and thrilled. Nothing like the blind need, nothing like the sort of body-reflex that had made me take Leath (his spirit had gone quiet in me, sort of introverted, like a child who'd accepted it was never going to be let out of its room). This was something else: a mix of delight and power and disgust and loneliness. I knew I'd get better at it, at enjoying it. But I knew too that there was a thin line somewhere down the road between enjoyment and emptiness. It frightened me—and suddenly I missed Fluff. You couldn't do this without knowing there were others doing it too. You'd be the loneliest thing on earth. How did solitary psychopaths survive? In a crazy moment (he'd touched me for the first time, put his hand on my hip when he leaned close so I could hear him over the music and his breath tickled my ear) I found myself thinking it was kind of amazing that psychopaths hadn't formed a secret society. Like the Freemasons.

"Where are you staying?" I said, returning the touch.

In the cab, he kissed me. Every instinct screamed push him away.

Every instinct except the one that counted. The new one.

His mouth was hot and soft and through the sour aftertaste of beer the big, pounding fact of his blood came up. I found myself kissing him back, hard, greedily, with desire.

Just not the desire he imagined.

In his hotel room, I said: "I need to use the bathroom. Take off all your clothes and lie down on the bed." I can't believe that's what I said. I could see it sounded robotic to him even through the booze-blur. He gave me a sort of smile-frown (like a bad actor) then (also like a bad actor) a shrug and a raised-eyebrows thing that meant: Okay. Weird. But a fuck's a fuck. Whatever floats your boat, babe.

In the bathroom I took of all *my* clothes and stuffed them into the cupboard under the sink. Then I looked at myself in the mirror. My whole life I've hated looking at myself in the mirror. I've hated seeing my face. Now I looked and saw something new looking back at me: curiosity.

He was lying on his back on the bed, naked, with his hands behind his head. He'd been thinking up something to say to me when I came out, but now that I had, whatever it was, he'd forgotten it. It was interesting to see him suddenly existing without any kind of strategy or schtick. There was a sort of purity to it.

When I climbed onto the bed, on my hands and knees above him, his cock thickened and brushed my thigh.

My teeth livened. My finger- and toenails. The thirst was like a bigger, stronger body inside my own, wearing me like a glove. I had a weird little vision of Fluff talking to someone on the phone, frowning, but it passed.

The blood was like a child reaching out to me. He opened his mouth to say something.

So instead of letting him, I sank my teeth into his throat and bit down as hard as I could.

It was easy to hold him. His struggles felt so slight. I locked my legs around his thighs and forced his arms behind his back. I didn't even have to lift my head, just kept my teeth in him. He weighed nothing. The more he struggled the more his strength went into me. A sort of removed part of me wanted to say to him: Look, don't fight me. It's pointless. Why waste your last minutes doing something pointless?

A very removed part of me, the tiny part of me watching all this on TV.

The rest of me was huge and warm and dark red. His blood went into me and the feel of him under me, straining and utterly without power while I drank, was like nothing I'd felt before. Different from Leath. With Leath the whole thing had had to go through a filter of rage. With Leath I'd tried to erase myself, blot myself out from what I was doing, but the rage had kept forcing me back. This was heavy and sweet. This was as if his blood wanted to come to me, was desperate and full of desire to come to me. It was the joy. Drinking him was a suffocating joy.

The images came fast and randomly. Not images. Understandings. Him three years old sitting on a rug in the middle of a tiny circular train set and his delight going round and round with the clockwork train and his mother, a soft-faced woman with dark hair standing watching him with her arms folded, laughing because his delight was so pure and simple and him loving her and the train and the thing going because he moved the little metal switch and when you moved it back it stopped and when you moved it forward started again and it was as if he had magic in him because it was up to him, up to him the starting and stopping of the train. His face suddenly hitting the damp turf of a soccer pitch and in the blur of the game the good smell of the mud and grass and a sudden glimpse of the world as being made of this stuff with the seas and oceans somehow clinging because of gravity and there was the game going on around him under the white and blue hurrying sky and for a second or two a kind of thrill at nothing, just the reality of it . . . A girl's face close to his and the blondeness and softness and her hot wet cunt tight and good around his cock and the smallness of her in his arms giving him everything with a confused eagerness and his own confusion which was like wanting to split her in half and at the same time worship the softness she gave him and the moment in the bar when Tony had said it's going to kick-off and him feeling his arms and knees filling with adrenaline and suddenly you were in the middle of it and though you were kicking and punching you were removed in a different kind of softness like when he'd had fever and his bedroom had gone strange and the air fat and full of silence and someone breaking a beer bottle and him imagining what the glass would feel like if the guy mashed it in his face you'd have to get plastic surgery and they all kidded him about being a vain bastard and he knew he was but he was fond of himself for it he was fond of his face and body and the good feeling of having shaved and you step out and the city says anything could happen and you think of the colours and lights of the bar all the bars and clubs and the women in them and he knew he could never get tired of women the way they flashed their eyes and it meant yes and he loved the way they rested their handbags on one bent knee to look for something in it and especially that weird way their arms came around their shoulder blades to hook or unhook their bras it looked physically impossible but it was so pretty the way they did that—

STOP.

The heart. You don't let the heart stop. Your own heart warns you.

I rolled off the bed onto the floor and for a few minutes lay there, dazed, swollen, it felt like, not just the blood but all of his life that had gone into me. How would you keep finding room? How? Six months like this? Five years? Ten? *Twenty thousand?* It was impossible.

But Stonk had said: You keep finding room because every life *makes* room. Every life you take—like every book you read, even the bad ones—makes you a little bigger.

I must have lain there like that for fifteen or twenty minutes, listening to the AC's hum. And the compressed loud silence around Mick's dead body. I knew that if I wasn't careful I'd be lulled into lying there all night. Or what was left of the night.

Couldn't afford that. *More* stupidity. I had to get back to my own hotel. There were less than three hours till daylight. I had to hole-up and be ready for the flight to Delhi at nine. It hit me, lying there thinking these things, that thinking these things was already not weird to me, was already normal.

I took a shower. Scrubbed. Watched the water running red around my feet. I thought: This is the first of many times you're going to be standing in a shower, seeing this. I was thinking, too, about the physical logistics of a murder. How long before the hotel staff realised something was wrong in here? How long did a dead body take to start smelling?

My own body felt crazy good. There was live restless strength in my calves and fingers. I wanted someone to attack me on the way home, to give all the power somewhere to go.

I dressed. Used a towel to wipe away everything I thought my hands had touched, which seemed sort of lame since it's all micro-fibres and DNA now. Then, using toilet paper to prevent prints (I congratulated myself on not forgetting this last set—the idiot set—on the door handle), I let myself out and closed the door behind me. If my geography was right, it was no more than a half-hour walk to my hotel. I wanted to walk, to feel the night and the living human beings around me.

# 63
## Walker

SHE'S GONE. IT'S a relief. Endings always are.

I spent the morning and afternoon checking the systems. You give yourself things to do. Couldn't face being with the kids. Lorcan's his usual superior self, but Zoë doesn't like letting me out of her sight. She forgets for a little while—lets Lucy read to her or Maddy try nail polishes and lipsticks out on her—then suddenly remembers and goes: Where's Walker? At least as often as she goes: Where's Mommy?

Mommy has gone to see a witch-doctor, honey. Mommy has gone on a wild motherfucking goose-chase. We don't say it, but it's what we're thinking. Tough to screen it from them. Maybe they know. Kids always know more than you think.

"Would you take it?" I asked Lucy. I was up on the walkway, or rampart, or balcony, checking the gun mountings. They're hidden under concrete flower boxes that'll roll back at the flick of a switch. "If you could go back to being normal, get a fresh start—would you?"

She was leaning against the parapet wall, drinking a glass of white wine. She was barefoot, wearing a pale green summer dress with a print of tiny yellow flowers. Every now and then the breeze blew her hair forwards, made her skirt flap. The sky was crisp and blue, a few white clouds travelling happily. I was thinking: We could hold out for a long time here. But not forever. If they came in real numbers, sooner or later, we'd go down. (And they will come in real numbers, eventually. Of course they will. It's only a matter of time.)

"This *was* my fresh start," Lucy said. "I don't need another one. I don't want another one." She took a sip of her drink. I could smell the grapes in it. It made me want one myself. "But then I don't have kids to worry about," she said. "If I had kids, then maybe, for them."

Lucy's ready for a man. I can feel it. Not me. But it's coming off her. It's in her radius. Our little clan's not enough for her. Why should it be? It's not enough for me, now. It would've been. I tell myself it would've been. With Talulla.

•

Later, in the small hours, there was a knock on my door. I was sitting on the edge of my bed, staring at the floor. I'd just taken a long, hot shower. Shaved for the first time in a week. Cut my finger- and toenails. It felt ritualistic. Like making a commitment to going on. It felt pathetic, too. When I looked ahead into the future I couldn't see anything. The world seemed small. Full of rooms to be alone in. I'd been going, in my mind, to situation after situation—travelling with Mike and Natasha; finding a new crowd; starting an organised force to prepare for what was coming— but all the visions drifted into seeing myself sitting in airport departure lounges, or walking in the quiet, depressing streets of small Mediterranean towns, or in a pick-up, driving through the nowheres of the Midwest. Jake had done more than a hundred and fifty years in that kind of solitary. I couldn't see how.

"Come in."

It was Madeline. I'd known it would be. I'd wanted it to be. Or part of me had. She was in an ivory silk nightie that stopped a long way above her knees. She came over and stood in front of me. For a long while neither of us spoke.

"I'm not the consolation prize," she said, eventually. "This isn't for you. It's for me."

# 64
## Talulla

HAVING ALL THE travel arrangements taken care of made me realise what a fucking horrendous journey it would have been if I'd had to make them myself. Zagreb to Delhi, Delhi to Kolkata, Kolkata—via small, precarious jet—to Bhubaneswar, where Olek's gofer, Grishma (a natty little guy with a small but dashingly dark-eyed and high-cheekboned face) met me with a car. From there what felt like an interminable drive southeast to Jogeswarpur, five miles north of the Balukhand Konark Reserve Forest.

I felt lousy by the time I got there, anyway. Full moon was just over forty-eight hours away and *wulf* was busting the usual tedious moves, the premature lunges and twists, the pointless clawed spasms and swipes. I hadn't slept properly since Zagreb. My eyes were raw. The nerves in my nails throbbed.

Olek's . . . what? laboratory?—was a former ashram on the edge of the reserve, but barring a few weathered statues of the smiling Buddha in the garden, you'd never have known it. The garden itself was spectacular, dense, lush, a sort of willing stereotype of the exotic East, blood-reds and splashy yellows and simmering pinks, though with the exception of bougainvillea, jasmine and oleander I didn't recognise any of the flowers. There were two huge banyans and, dotted here and there, lemon, tamarind, guava and peach trees, all heavy with fruit. Three green ponds with long, fat, drowsy fish—koi carp?—and a paved, semi-circular patio at the front on which a large abstract sculpture—a torqued ovoid with a hole in the middle, in some kind of polished blue stone—took pride of place. The building itself was three large, intersecting, flat-roofed concrete rectangles, with three floors above ground (on arrival there was no telling how many below, but I had to assume at least one) with tinted windows and an iron-railed balcony going all the way around between the second and third storeys. He's dug-in here, I thought. Maybe that's what happens in the end. The wandering stops and you just accept a place as home. No matter how many centuries you have ahead of you. I hadn't noticed any security on the drive in, but that didn't mean there wasn't any.

Grishma looked at his watch. "Mr. Olek will be with us shortly," he said. "Can I offer you anything in the meantime? Tea? Something stronger?"

I'd been led through an entrance hall of white plaster walls and a terra cotta floor into a library of floor-to-ceiling books. Furniture was three green leather Chesterfields, a large glass desk and a white, futuristic recliner, all on three or four big blue and gold-fringed Indian (or for all I knew Persian or Chinese) carpets of exquisitely intricate design. A huge benign asparagus fern on a dark wooden plant stand cast a stretched shadow the full length of the room in the last of the low sunlight. A tall art deco standard lamp stood in one corner, twin nymphs holding a glass globe. There was a book open face-down on one of the couches.

"Just water," I said. "Is it okay to smoke?"

Grishma seemed calmly delighted at the idea. "One hundred per cent," he said, and fetched an ashtray from the hall—a pretty copper dish on an ebony stand—which he set down beside the nearest Chesterfield. "I'll bring your water," he said.

"Actually," I said, feeling *wulf* giving my spine a wrench, "I'll take a scotch as well, if you have one."

"Talisker, Glenmorangie, Oban, Laphroaig or Macallan?"

Not bad for someone who didn't drink.

"Macallan, please. Straight." Here's to you, Jacob Marlowe. It's a library, after all. Sorry I turned out to be such a lousy werewolf. It's your own fault. You shouldn't have died.

Grishma was back in less than five minutes with a silver tray. He turned the lamp on. "I'll leave you now," he said. "Feel free to have a browse in here while you wait."

As in: Don't leave this room, sister.

I didn't. I lit a Camel and picked up the book next to me on the couch. Browning. *Men and Women.* A first edition. Open at "Childe Roland to the Dark Tower Came." I'd read the poem before, in college. For no reason I could think of, it reminded me of the dream. The vampire dream. The only dream I had, these days, these nights. I began reading.

*My first thought was, he lied in every word,*
*That hoary cripple, with malicious eye*
*Askance to watch the workings of his lie*
*On mine, and mouth scarce able to afford*
*Suppression of the glee, that pursed and scored*
*Its edge, at one more victim gained thereby.*

"Marvellous, isn't it?" a voice said.

I looked up. I couldn't have been reading for more than a few seconds, but somehow it was now completely dark outside. The lamp's globe had brightened.

Olek—I recognised the voice—stood in the doorway.

Not what I'd been expecting, since like it or not I'd been expecting Omar Sharif. What I was seeing was a short, dark, plump, thin-moustached man in his mid-fifties (humanly speaking) with skin the colour of milk chocolate, mischievous black eyes and a full-lipped, currently smiling, mouth. His teeth looked unnaturally white. He was dressed in faded black jeans and a white cotton *kurta*. Green suede Adidas sneakers. Big gold and garnet ring on his left index finger.

"To my mind one of the most remarkable poems in the English language."

"I don't really remember it that well," I said.

He came closer, and offered me his hand. At which point I realised what I should have noticed straight away. He didn't smell.

Or rather, he didn't smell of his species. He smelled of patchouli and toothpaste and lemons. He read my face.

"Talulla—I may call you Talulla, yes?"

"Yes."

"And you must call me Olek, of course. No, I don't smell as expected, I know. I'm delighted. I've put a lot of work in on olfactory inhibitors. But we can discuss that later. You don't remember the poem much, you say? Please, please, let's sit."

I'd stood up to shake hands. He waited for me to resume my seat, then sat himself on the industrial glass desk, legs swinging. No socks. Delicate brown ankles.

"I remember it's about a knight looking for the Dark Tower," I said. I was yielding so easily to the casual madness of the encounter I wondered if they'd put something in my drink. "I remember a journey through a kind of nightmare landscape. I remember it's *long.*"

"Do you recall whether Childe Roland *finds* the Dark Tower?"

I couldn't see that it mattered, but I racked my brains anyway. "No," I said. "I don't. Does he?"

Olek smiled again. He had an immensely likeable face. So likeable that if this were a movie he'd have to be a psychotic villain. "I shan't spoil it for you," he said. "You must take that volume to bed tonight and see for yourself."

Madder and madder. Browning for bedtime reading at a vampire's house. In India. Okay. Why not?

"But you'll want to freshen up, perhaps? You won't be wanting anything to eat, obviously."

I stubbed the Camel out in the ashtray. Mentally gave myself a slap.

"Look," I said. "I don't mean to be rude, but why don't you just tell me what I'm doing here?"

"You're here because I have a cure for your condition," he said, not missing a beat. "Or I dare say more importantly a cure for your children's condition. You're here because they're still young enough to slip through the world's tightening net. You saw the footage. Hardship, one way or another, is coming to your species. Most likely to mine as well. Your face is known. Your children still have a chance." He paused. I caught a sudden full stink of vampire.

"Mikhail, Natasha, come and join us."

I looked past him. Konstantinov and Natasha were in the doorway. Konstantinov looked exhausted.

"Mikhail hasn't slept," Olek said. "Despite my best efforts to reassure him he insisted on sitting up all day, staring at the monitors."

It had been almost a year since I'd seen them, but apart from Konstantinov's obvious lack of sleep he and Natasha looked—of course—

unchanged. As, visibly, palpably, was the love between them. Utterly sufficient and self-contained and above any law, human or otherwise. Their love made them their own law. I hadn't realised how afraid I'd been until I felt the relief of seeing them.

"I'll give you a little while alone," Olek said. "Please, Talulla, help yourself to another drink."

When he was gone, Natasha, Konstantinov and I looked at each other.

"Can you stand a hug?" I said.

We embraced, holding our noses, laughing—but the mutually repellent odours were no joke. Rolling her eyes, Natasha broke out the nose-paste. "He offered us something instead of this," she said. "But we couldn't take the chance. Sorry."

They'd been here for two days.

"The place is CCTV'd," Konstantinov said. "And there *were* guards, but we told him they had to go."

"How could you not have slept?" I asked.

"Monitors are downstairs," Konstantinov said. "Underground. I needed to be sure. I'm fine. One day I can manage."

When he spoke, Natasha looked at him with calm certainty. The delight in each other Jake and I had had. As opposed to the almost delight between Walker and me. That would be an awkward conversation to have with these two, I realised, with a small detonation of dread, the one that would begin with one of them saying: How's Walker?

"So what's the story with this guy?" I said, preemptively.

Between them, they told me what they knew. Olek was old. Very old. He was also the nearest the species had to a Chief Medical Officer. "There are illnesses, apparently," Natasha said. "But don't ask me."

"I think you've got to have been alive for a long time to get them," Konstantinov said. "But anyway, he's a scientist. He's *the* scientist. Physically, there's nothing he doesn't know about the species. When WOCOP dissolved, the Fifty Families bought a lot of the research. All of it went through him. He was with the Helios Project from its inception. He says he's retired from that now, but who knows?"

The Helios Project was the vampires' ongoing attempt to find a cure for nocturnality. To which, inadvertently, werewolves had for a while become integral. The virus we had until recently carried had stopped the Curse passing to human victims who survived the bite. But to vampires who got bitten, it gave an increased tolerance to sunlight.

"And the cure for what ails me?" I asked.

"God knows," Natasha said. "He's refused to discuss it. It's for your ears only. The only thing he says is that it's completely unscientific. What does he want from you?"

"I don't know. I really don't. Nothing that I'm going to want to give, I'm guessing."

"Do you remember Christopher Devaz?" Olek said. He was back in the doorway, hands in pockets. All three of us looked up.

Devaz was one of the WOCOP guards I'd Turned when I'd been detained at their pleasure three years ago, a fruity little Goan fattened on maternal love who'd been easy to seduce with a paradoxical (and not wholly invented) posture of moral reluctance and libidinal need. Turned, he'd had no choice but to help me get out come full moon. He hadn't been happy about it, not surprisingly.

"Yes, I remember him," I said. "What about him?"

"Christopher Devaz is no longer a werewolf," Olek said.

I looked at him for signs of bullshit or strategy. There weren't any. He just looked straight back at me.

"Because you cured him."

"Because I cured him."

The terrible thing was I knew he wasn't lying. It didn't help. It made me feel exhausted. Sitting there, it was as if all the miles and hours had gathered on me, suddenly, had hung themselves on me like . . . yes, giant vampire bats. And the tireder I was the more *wulf* tried it on. Watch it, fucker, I thought. There's a *cure* for you here. Apparently.

"Would you like to see him?" Olek said. "He's downstairs."

# 65

THERE *WAS* A laboratory, of course. And two basement levels. Lab on minus one. I only saw part of it. Guessed it occupied the building's entire footprint. Not that what I saw told me much. A wall of bottled and jarred chemicals. Three big refrigerators. A lot of things that looked like slim-line VCRs or DVD players, with, I intuited, technical clout inversely proportional to their number of blinking lights. (In the twenty-first century the gizmos to be scared of are the ones that look like they don't do much.) In addition several desk monitors, a pair of open laptops, shelf after shelf of zip-drives. Cable management and a cloying medicinal smell that whether I liked it or not evoked my high school chemistry lab, my best friend Lauren, and her one-semester obsession with homemade explosives. Two doors led off. Through one I glimpsed more stacked gadgetry and the corner of a brushed steel table.

"Down another flight," Olek said. "I hope you don't mind accompanying me in private for this. But this part is for you alone."

Konstantinov and Natasha had protested, but in the end my own impatience had settled it. The house, they conceded, was empty but for the three of us and Grishma, and whatever it was Olek wanted from me it plainly wasn't my life.

The next flight down took us to a door that opened onto a more complicatedly divided space. Corridors, floors, walls and ceilings tiled white high-gloss. A hospital cleanliness that would have made the sight of two or three drops of blood on the floor particularly ominous. There were none, however. All the doors were steel—one very heavy. The air down here had a failed feel, like the air in an airplane toilet. There was a new etherish smell that made my nostrils fizz and that *wulf* didn't like at all. I thought of the sneezing tracker dogs in *Cool Hand Luke*.

Olek, a couple of paces ahead of me, moved with loose-limbed ease, but I could feel his aura hotting-up. A slight odour of his species crept out of him now, forced by tension, exacerbated by the smaller space.

"In here," he said, opening a door to our left.

"In here" was, in effect, one of the rooms you see in movies (but which I've always suspected don't exist anymore, if they ever did) where a victim gets to look through one-way glass at a line-up of suspects.

"He can't hear us," Olek said. "Or see us, obviously. This is just so you know it's him."

Devaz, on the other side of the glass, was lying in the foetal position on a fold-out bed, staring at nothing. He was barefoot (the pale soles of his brown feet affected me with a curious dreary sympathy) in sky blue pyjama bottoms and a white cotton singlet. He didn't look injured. Just unbearably sad. Aside from the bed his small room was empty.

"He's not in any discomfort," Olek said. "And he won't be obliged to remain here much longer. But I do need to know that you recognise him. Do you need to hear his voice?"

There was an emptiness to the man on the bed that made me strangely angry, although angry at whom or what it wasn't clear.

Olek hit the intercom. "Christopher?" he said. "How are you feeling?"

Devaz had started at the voice, slightly, but he didn't get up. Just curled a little tighter on the bed. I tried to go out to him, mentally. As the one who'd Turned him it ought to have been effortless and immediate.

DEVAZ?

Nothing.

*DEVAZ*. IT'S ME.

Still nothing. I might as well have been reaching out to a bucket and mop.

"Christopher, you'll be out of here in a couple of days, I promise you," Olek said.

No response. Devaz just stared.

"Christopher?"

"Please go away," Devaz said, quietly. "Please."

I did recognise the voice. If it wasn't the real Devaz, it was a very convincing impersonation.

Back in the white corridor, I said: "Okay, fine, it's Devaz. Now what?"

"Now," Olek said, hands in pockets, "we wait for the full moon to rise. At which point you'll see that Christopher is no longer under its spell. You'll see, not to put too fine a point on it, that he's human again. Ergo, the method works."

And makes you suicidal, apparently.

"Now," Olek said. "The method. Follow me."

Back down the corridor to the heaviest of the doors. Vault or submarine-hatch thickness. Numbered keypad entry. Inside, another of the steel tables. On it, a black metal container a little bigger than a briefcase, also with a numbered keypad. Olek tried not to make a show of not letting me see the code and I tried not to make a show of not trying to see it. *Wulf*, to my surprise, had gone completely still.

A small hydraulic hiss and the sound of a precision mechanism—then the case was unlocked. Olek opened it. "Take a look," he said.

The container's interior was foam padded. In the middle of the cutaway was a flat piece of whiteish stone—the sort of thing I imagined the Ten Commandments being written on—with two pieces missing, one from the bottom left corner, one from the right-hand edge. There was a rough circular hole the size of a tennis ball in what looked like its exact centre. It was covered from top to bottom in carved symbols—a script of some kind—and stained with (my nose confirmed the visuals) human blood. Weeks old, the blood. Weeks. Not millennia.

"You'll remember," Olek said, "that along with Quinn's journal went a stone tablet. This is it."

I didn't touch it. I was thinking of all the times I'd seen ancient things in museums. Arrowheads. Pottery. Mummies. Always under glass. Even under glass the objects gave off a calm, clear, mute energy that collapsed the space between your time and theirs, that astonished you with the proof of time itself, that it really passed, that not just individual people but whole civilisations came and went. Millions were born and lived full lives and died and some little bit of stone or clay that had lain untouched through it all testified that there had been a time before any of that had happened. The air around them had a different silence, one that had never been passed through by the racket of modernity.

*. . . but it was not until people returned to the banks of Iteru that*

"You know," Olek said, "I'll be honest with you. I did this as an experiment. I had absolutely no belief in it. It was, as far as I was concerned, risible, pure fucking mumbo-jumbo, contrary to every principle I hold dear. I'd like to be able to take the scientific line and say that just because a phenomenon is unexplained at the moment doesn't mean it's terminally inexplicable. I'm an adherent of Ockam. All things being equal, look for an explanation in the terms you already have. Don't start inventing phenomena to explain a phenomenon. But I have to say, this has rocked me. This has rocked and confounded me. If it's as it seems to be, frankly, it changes everything. I still can't really believe it . . ."

He was off on the little journey of his own amazement. He hadn't been able to leave it alone, since it had happened (whatever it was that *had* happened); he hadn't been able to *get over it*.

I realised that until now I hadn't taken the possibility of reversing the Curse seriously. Or no more than half seriously. It wasn't belief in a cure that had led me here. It was the feeling of answering something calling from behind the surface events. As if something were asking for my help in bringing itself about. As if I was—oh, dear *God*—a necessary part of a story. Ever since the night the vampire came to call. *I'll see you again.* When I opened my mouth to say what I said next, sickness, excitement and weariness rose up in me like a wretched Trinity.

"Not that Devaz is any kind of advertisement," I said, "but how does it work?"

# 66
## *Justine*

ANOTHER NEAR-MISS AT the hotel in Bangkok. I got there less than an hour before sunrise. I was in such a fucking state I gave the cab driver the equivalent of $100 and didn't take the change. Just ran straight into the lobby.

"You don't look well," a voice said, behind me, while I stood in line for the desk, trembling. "Can I be of assistance?"

I turned. A tall paunchy guy in his early fifties in jeans, white shirt and black blazer. Side-parted brown hair and gold-rimmed spectacles. He had a moony face and an annoying little smile—and a padded surgical dressing over his nose. His face was bruised. My first thought was that he'd been in a car crash. Then, somehow, I felt sure he hadn't. I felt sure someone had *done* this to him. With good reason. There was a smell coming off him, too: bitter cologne and some tomato sauce thing he'd eaten recently, and something else it took me a moment to identify: incense.

"What?" I said, while every muscle tightened and my dumb brain still registered the piped hotel music softly filling the air-conditioned space around us, a bad cover version of Fleetwood Mac's "Dreams."

"You seem distressed," he said, looking as if my distress was just about the nicest thing he'd ever seen. "I was just wondering if you were . . . If you needed any help?"

For a moment I stood there, mentally jammed, hands and feet and throat packed with panicking blood. The sun was a big sick smile waiting to break over the horizon. The cells in my face were screaming, silently.

"I'm fine," I said. "Thanks."

I turned my back on him but I could still feel him there, sense him smiling, as if his smile were a tiny fragment of the sun's, one of its messengers that came on ahead of it. If my turn hadn't come I don't know what I would've done, but the businessman in front of me picked up his briefcase and headed for the elevators and suddenly there was the beautiful Thai clerk, a girl who couldn't have been more than twenty, smiling at me and saying "Welcome to the Sofitel. Are you checking-in?" and I had to focus on registering, though my hands were shaking so badly I could hardly sign.

And even then he didn't budge. I could feel him behind me, a sort of smug energy coming off him. I thought again of all the stupid, careless mistakes I'd made since leaving Los Angeles. All I wanted right then was enough time to do what I had to do. It wouldn't need twenty thousand years. Forty-eight hours should be enough.

"Sorry, ma'am," the receptionist said. "I'm getting an incorrect PIN message. Would you like to try again?"

I *would* have turned on him then—told him to back the fuck off, punched him, screamed at him, whatever, I don't know—but his cellphone rang, and he walked away to answer it, talking in Italian.

There was no sign of him when I looked after checking-in (I was so spooked it took me another two attempts to key the PIN in correctly; I knew the number, it was just I couldn't control my goddamned hands) and in any case there was no time. I got to my room on the nineteenth floor, hung the DO NOT DISTURB sign, locked the door, killed the lights and shut myself in the bathroom.

# 67

## *Remshi*

I FLOPPED ONTO the bed, feeling, frankly, terrible.

"What is it that makes you think she's in danger?" Mia said to me.

We'd just checked-in to the Novotel at Suvarnabhumi. Hardly a first choice, but even with Damien's near-infallible jiggery-pokery we were too close to sunrise for anything further afield. It had been a frustrating few days. Commercial airlines would have been faster, but the risks of losing the night—without the jet's blackout-room fallback—were too high. I'd been tormented by the image of Justine going up in daylight flames in her airplane seat, or the back of a cab, or in the lobby of a hotel just like this one. Three days ago Hannah had called with the necessaries on Duane Schrutt. *Duane* Schrutt. The near-misses I'd had—Dale, Wayne—were a minor irritant, a bit of grit in my mind's eye. A minor irritant, I repeat. The major irritant was too major to be described as an irritant. It was more a disaster. A recurring disaster. I'd suffered several more inexplicable episodes of . . . of what? Unconsciousness. Nausea with nothing to throw up. Periods of being—I was tiring of the phrase—*as weak as a kitten*, when the lifting of my hand or the turning of my head called for an energy that felt—in the tissues, the vessels, the bones—like a logical impossibility. I had no appetite whatsoever. The jet's blood-stock was at my companions' disposal. Caleb didn't like it, that I didn't drink. He didn't like it in the way human children don't like the urine-and-Vicks smell of the human old. I told him it was no biggie. I told him that when you got to my age you just didn't need . . . You just weren't that thirsty. I was becoming, I could tell, an alarming disappointment to the lad. I had, however, opened a numbered account in Mia's name in Geneva and transferred five million dollars into it to start her off. (Her only surviving account after Fifty Families ostracisation was, pitifully, a chequing account at Chase Manhattan. You might as well put cash in a coffee jar.) Five million probably sounds like a lot. It's not. Even in human terms, these days, it's not.

This is, after all, the age which spawned the economist's joke: *A trillion here, a trillion there . . . Pretty soon you're talking real money.* I watch people on game shows losing all dignity and restraint when they win *One Hundred Thousand Dollars!* How long do they think that's going to last? They think their lives have changed. They haven't. Not unless they put the lot on a million-to-one shot at the track and it comes in. Then they might find out where their freedom takes them. Then they might find out who and what they really are . . . But, in any case, an indefinite lifespan makes five million nothing, makes five million *change*.

"Did you hear me?" Mia said.

"What? Oh, yes. Sorry. I don't know. She's new. She's . . . There's an emotional investment in the victim. I promised I wouldn't leave her. I just hope we're not too late. She's a bit unpredictable."

Mia stood with her hands in the leather jacket pockets, looking down at me on the bed. She really was extraordinarily beautiful. The cold blonde hair and cold blue eyes and cold white skin and warm red mouth. A shocking, perfect contrast. I thought: Beauty just keeps coming into the world and passing away, coming in and passing away. You can't blame beauty. Beauty doesn't know what else to do.

"What's the matter?" she said. "What is it? Are you in pain?"

You're a bit fragile, Fluff, Justine had said. It felt like a long time ago. Sometimes, when I was forced to consider my sense of time, it was like looking out of a carriage window to see that the wheels were running right on the edge of a sheer and infinite drop. I forced myself to sit up, dried my eyes. Laughed a little.

"I'm fine," I said. "Forgive me. I'm a bit . . . I'm sorry. Kindness hurts."

"Kindness?"

"You and Caleb. You've been very kind to me."

I felt the reflex in her, to reply that I was paying them. I felt the huge, tense, ever-ready reflex, which was to strip away sentiment at all costs. I felt her suppress it—just—with the words on the tip of her tongue. Instead she said, quietly, "I think you should give me your spare room key. In case you oversleep."

*In case you have another episode.* I was thinking of all the old people I'd ever heard say: I don't want to be a burden to anyone.

"You're absolutely right," I said. I gave her the spare. Nowadays a hotel key was a piece of magnetised plastic. It's a mark of the state I was in that that fact made the idiotic tears well again. The thought of the human world moving forward with its shifty bravery, inspired madness, bloody inversions, deafening ignorance. It's hard not to love your species' dedication to craftily making things physically easier, even though you know by now it just leaves more room for getting mentally fucked-up. Corkscrews. Ironing boards. Aeroplanes. Cellphones. You kill me with these things. Walking on the moon! A group of humans sitting around discussing walking on the moon. Knowing the mathematical razor wire it's going to roll them in, knowing the scale, the ludicrous giantness of the undertaking, knowing all this but still assuming it'll get done because the giant undertaking breaks down into a million small things like the manufacture of single tiny components and the necessity of one minus one equalling zero. The labour you lot are willing to put in from there breaks my heart. And then as soon as you've done it you're on to the next thing. Mars. The Genome. CERN. It's a sort of nymphomania or satyriasis of consciousness, a hopelessly promiscuous *carrying on.*

I'll miss it.

At the door, Mia turned. "Are you going to be all right?" she said. "Do you want me to . . . ?"

For a moment I thought she meant, Do you want me to stay here with you? But then I realised she meant, Do you want me to help you into the bathroom?

"I'll be fine," I said. "I'm sorry. You must think . . ."

"I think you say sorry too much."

Don't cry again. Do *not* start that obscene blubbering again.

"Sleep well," Mia said, and a moment later she was gone.

Leaving me to face sleep—and the dream—alone.

# 68

## Talulla

I WASN'T SHOWN or told "the method."

"After you've seen the proof," Olek said. "Believe me, it'll sound too incredible without it."

He was a little tedious. This was his show, so he would have it played his way. He did, however, tell me what he wanted from me. I followed him back up the stairs to minus one, and through the first two rooms of the lab. Another vault door (where the fuck did he *get* these from? did he have them airlifted in?) opened onto a third room, similar to the first, although more obviously the site of physical experiments. There was unfathomable kit here, in glass and steel, but plenty of minimally winking hardware too. Also a single very large—keypad entry, again—refrigeration unit.

"WOCOP, as we know," he said, "is no more. It was always a sloppy, unwieldy organisation—in fact 'organisation' was a misnomer—but in its death throes it was in chaos. Total *chaos*. I don't know whether you know but we bought pretty much all the research material they had, all the science. Outbid the *Militi Christi* on the lot. The Directors were simply flogging everything for cash."

He was turning the gold and garnet ring on his finger as he spoke. It looked very glamorous against his dark skin.

"Their science division was all over the place," he went on. "They'd had so many personnel changes, conflicting directives from the suits, people running for the hills. Murdoch—whom you knew, of course—was operating as a law unto himself . . . Well, I shan't bore you with the details. The long and short of it is that by the time the whole thing fell apart they didn't even know what science they had. They'd spent God only knows how much money and time on lycanthrope research. Which also happens to be one of my areas of expertise."

He hit the keypad buttons and the fridge door gasped open. Colder than a regular icebox, I gathered. The little wisps of expanding air cleared in a moment, to reveal several shelves of black canisters. He beckoned me over. In among the black was a single white flask.

"I won't take it out," he said. "Can't afford a significant temperature drop until we're ready to use it."

Pause. For dramatic effect. He couldn't quite suppress a smile.

"Okay," I said. "I give up. What am I looking at?"

The smile broadened. "Haven't you guessed? It's the virus."

He didn't say anything else. Just let me put two and two together. Then he closed the refrigerator door.

"They had all the bio-chemistry they needed to synthesise it. It was all there in the notes, in the samples, in the data. They were just too dumb to see it. A simple business of joining the dots. I hate to lean on a cliché, but you really can't make this shit up."

I felt tired. My ex, Richard (my *human* ex), was annoyingly fond of the French saying *Plus ça change (plus c'est la même chose)*. The more it changes, the more it stays the same.

"And you want to infect me with it," I said. "Again. Are you serious? Actually, scratch that. I know you're serious. I've got depressingly good at knowing when people are serious."

"Of course I'm serious," he said. "Vampires bitten by a werewolf carrying the virus show increased sunlight tolerance. Do you know how old I am, Talulla?"

"You know I don't," I said.

"I was born as a vampire more than seven thousand years ago. I'm old, even by the reckoning of my kind. I know I don't have much longer. Even in a world as perversely fascinating as this one fatigue sets in. Plus, I know I'm not what I once was. There are signs of . . . Well. Let's just say everything I've learned tells me I'm not going to live forever. Do you read Bowles at all?"

"Bowles?"

"Paul Bowles. The novelist. I saw him in his last days, in Tangier. Charming man. Do you know he and his wife once shared a house in Brooklyn with W. H. Auden and Gypsy Rose Lee? Dalí was there for a while, too. What evenings they must have had! Apparently they took turns cooking. You will perhaps have seen the movie, *The Sheltering Sky*?"

I had seen it. With Richard. In the old life. Debra Winger. Bedouin. Sex. I couldn't remember much more about it. It was a movie that didn't encourage you to read the novel. I was annoyed (why not?) by his assumption that I was more likely to have seen the movie than read the book. Especially since he was right.

"Bowles himself makes a cameo appearance at the end of the film," Olek said, "where he gives a famous little speech in voiceover. It's from the novel, obviously. He says: 'Because we don't know when we will die, we get to think of life as an inexhaustible well. Yet everything happens only a certain number of times, and a very small number, really. How many more times will you remember a certain afternoon of your childhood, some afternoon that's so deeply a part of your being that you can't even conceive of your life without it? Perhaps four or five times more. Perhaps not even that. How many more times will you watch the full moon rise? Perhaps twenty. And yet it all seems limitless.'" He smiled again. To my astonishment, his eyes had tears in them. "I want to see the blue of the ocean again, Talulla," he said. "I want to see leaf-shadows on green grass. I want to watch the sun rise. You will forgive the whiff of portent, but I feel the finiteness of my days."

Well. Surprise. Was there anything other than sunshine a vampire ended up wanting? Is there anything other than what we don't have that we all end up wanting? Who knew that if not me?

"It costs you nothing," he said. "You've had the virus before. You carry it, you bite me. We go our ways. I'll even throw in a shot of the anti-virus, too, so you don't have to be a carrier any longer than you like. Everyone wins. And in return, your children get a normal life, free from persecution. You, too, if you want. Your face is known, certainly, but I know several very good plastic surgeons. The identity paperwork will be your own business, but you have the contacts and the resources for that. I'm offering you a door back into the life you lost."

He sounded eminently civilised. Eminently sane. I wondered again if I'd been drugged, or if he was pulling some boochie mind-trick, since I felt lulled by the simplicity of the equation. I had an image of picking Zoë and Lorcan up from a school in Manhattan. Books. Homework. No more care (except the benign aesthetic one) for the next full moon. No more blood on our hands. Were they young enough to forget? Could I tell them it had all been a dream?

"Why didn't you just use Devaz?" I said. For all Olek's suavity the vision of his other guest's despair was fresh. "You've got your werewolf right there. I'm sure he would've obliged. He's probably broke. He'd probably have done it for fifty bucks."

Olek nodded. "He would have," he said. "When I found him he'd have done it for a pack of cigarettes or a decent pair of shoes. But back then I was still missing several vital pieces to the puzzle. And I'm afraid my curiosity about the cure got the better of me. I can't tell you how much the timing depressed me. But I must repeat, when I tried the cure on Devaz it was in a spirit of complete scepticism. I simply wasn't expecting it to work. Well, that was a lesson!"

The refrigerator hummed. As far as Olek was concerned, he'd said all he needed to say. The opening line of "Childe Roland" came back to me. *My first thought was, he lied in every word.*

"Let's go up," my host said. "I don't expect you to answer until you've seen proof of the cure, obviously. Besides, I don't want Mikhail and Natasha to start worrying I've done something unpleasant to you."

On the last landing before the living quarters, he stopped and turned: "Before we rejoin your friends," he said, "let me reassure you, since you've been too polite to ask, that your feeding needs have been provided for. All you'll need to do is walk fifty metres into the trees beyond the garden. Acceptable?"

Only because it was the simplest thing to do, I nodded.

"Very good," Olek said. "Now, let's rejoin the company."

# 69

ABSURDITY HAS A momentum you can surrender to. As does exhaustion. Olek left Konstantinov, Natasha and me at our leisure to "catch up" (throughout which Walker was the invisible fourth person in the room, loudly not mentioned by any of us; he must have short-versioned it to Konstantinov over the phone—and really, what was the long version?) but by two in the morning jet-lag and tantrumming *wulf* had me at my limit. I gobbled four codeine and took a large Macallan with me upstairs to my quarters. These were a cedar-scented sitting room of dark wooden panelling, Indian silk paintings, a lute, a statue of Krishna, and a bedroom of soothing pale walls with one huge framed mandala over the bed, carpeted with at least twenty more of the fabulous fringed rugs. An en suite with a free-standing tub and a walk-in shower, mosaic tiled in a dozen shades of blue, frangipani incense sticks burning in a tiny brass pot. I was escorted there—with impeccable deference—by what looked like a freshly scrubbed and hair-oiled Grishma, who handed over matching white towels and robe that had plainly never been used before. Sensuous pleasures present themselves regardless of circumstances, and I was tired and unhinged enough to let them in. An hour soaking in the tub to allow the pills and booze to take off what edge they could, then I undressed and got into a large double bed that recieved me like a lover who'd been waiting for my body for a thousand years.

Which was when I noticed the copy of Browning's *Men and Women*, open at "Childe Roland to the Dark Tower Came," on the ebony nightstand.

Everything in me that could send its message sent: *sleep.*

But of course I picked it up anyway.

*My first thought was, he lied in every word,*
*That hoary cripple, with malicious eye*
*Askance to watch the workings of his lie*

*On mine, and mouth scarce able to afford*
*Suppression of the glee, that pursed and scored*
*Its edge, at one more victim gained thereby.*

The speaker is the knight (or "Childe") Roland, last survivor of a gallant band whose lifelong quest has been to find the Dark Tower. Following the satanic old cripple's directions (which he both believes and despises), Roland sets off into a weird landscape of deformity and horrors.

*Yet acquiescingly*
*I did turn as he pointed: neither pride*
*Nor hope rekindling at the end descried,*
*So much as gladness that some end might be.*

It's a long (thirty-four stanzas) journey through a lonely phantasmagoria. Among other horrors, Roland comes across a wretched horse:

*One stiff blind horse, his every bone a-stare,*
*Stood stupefied, however he came there:*
*Thrust out past service from the devil's stud!*

*Alive? he might be dead for aught I know,*
*With that red gaunt and colloped neck a-strain,*
*And shut eyes underneath the rusty mane;*
*Seldom went such grotesqueness with such woe;*
*I never saw a brute I hated so;*
*He must be wicked to deserve such pain.*

Mutilated horses, stunted trees, turf that looks "kneaded-up with blood," a stream the knight's forced to ford, convinced he's treading drowned corpses underfoot. Halfway across he sticks his spear in to test the stream bed:

*It may have been a water-rat I speared,*
*But, ugh! it sounded like a baby's shriek—*

I stopped reading.

I'd heard a baby cry.

Not a cry as in *crying*—but the start-up or preamble to crying proper, the perilously narrow window which, if you can get in—with the feed, the diaper, the lullaby, the kiss—might just stop the real crying from starting.

I sat up.

Silence.

Not quite silence; the bathroom's cooling pipes and the ambient rasp of the garden's cicadas.

But no human sound. No baby.

I was more than willing (more than enough whacked, Macallaned and painkillered) to write it off as . . . As whatever. Aural hallucination. As nodding off. As ludicrous, *Northanger Abbey* paranoia. But in spite of myself I got out of bed and went through the panelled sitting room to the door. Opened it a crack.

Only the low murmur of Kostantinov and Natasha talking downstairs. I listened past it. Sent strained hearing out through the house's packed atoms.

Nothing. No baby.

You dismiss things.

I closed the door and went back to bed. Back to the poem.

It gets worse for Roland, mile after hellish mile all alone. He tries to comfort himself by remembering his virtuous friends—the other knights who shared his quest—but the visions his memory calls up are grotesque and wretched: all his companions died in shame and disgrace.

On he goes, without hope. The whole poem is this going-on without hope. Stanza after stanza. You get lost in it. The landscape gets increasingly hideous:

> *Now blotches rankling, coloured gay and grim,*
> *Now patches where some leanness of the soil's*
> *Broke into moss or substances like boils;*
> *Then came some palsied oak, a cleft in him*
> *Like a distorted mouth that splits its rim*
> *Gaping at death, and dies while it recoils.*

*Was* it a baby?

I seemed to come-to, suddenly. Must have fallen asleep reading. There's a part of you finds it funny, fascinating, consciousness just dipping out and wafting back in like that.

There was that scene in *Dracula*, I thought, when the Count brought the baby for the three vampire women to feed on.

There was the night I held a baby in my big dark cradle hands, wondering if I could kill and eat it.

*The subject is prone to anxiety about infants,* my inner therapist said, bored. Boredom for the therapist is the end-point of all therapy.

I actually shook myself. To wake myself up. I was stupidly determined to finish the poem. (Though the memory of Devaz curled up on his bunk came back, suddenly. Bloomed in my head like a big cold flower. Tomorrow I would have to try to speak to him. How was I only just thinking this? My own dumb belatedness appalled me, though the soothing bedroom said Don't be so hard on yourself. *Had* I been drugged? Everything here seemed out of sync with itself. For a moment I found myself wondering if even Konstantinov and Natasha . . . No. They were all right. The pounding love and pounding vigilance testified. Christ, what was wrong with me? I thought of the way I'd just sat down alone in the library when I arrived, just sat down like a moron and asked for scotch and picked up the goddamned book. As if I was waiting to meet a minor dignitary.)

Roland, utterly hopeless now, crosses the stream to find himself confronted by an impassable mountain range.

> *For, looking up, aware I somehow grew,*
> *'Spite of the dusk, the plain had given place*
> *All round to mountains—with such name to grace*
> *Mere ugly heights and heaps now stolen in view.*
> *How thus they had surprised me,—solve it, you!*
> *How to get from them was no clearer case.*

But I knew. The thing is you know. All readers of this poem know, by the time they get to the mountain range.

> *Yet half I seemed to recognise some trick*
> *Of mischief happened to me, God knows when—*
> *In a bad dream perhaps . . .*

My head felt swollen and hot. *Wulf*, sick of all this reading, had started up again, torn through the scotch-and-codeine gauze and was raking me with foul-tempered kicks and swipes. The nearness of my own dream, my only dream, the dream to which I'd been reduced, was like a deep space very near me—like a vortex opening in the bed: fall through, let myself drop softly through and there would be the vampire, the sex— paradoxically dense and transcendent—the dusk beach and the black water and the handful of stars.

> *Burningly it came on me all at once,*
> *This was the place! Those two hills on the right,*
> *Crouched like two bulls locked horn in horn in fight;*
> *While to the left, a tall scalped mountain . . . Dunce,*
> *Dotard, a-dozing at the very nonce,*
> *After a life spent training for the sight!*

The words wandered, sprouted insect wings, buzzed and whirred away. All the day's separate madnesses I'd absorbed without protest grew back in me to their proper unassimilable size. It was as if I'd let the hours and days put one by one more and more soft heavy things on me, and now was realising too late that I couldn't breathe, that I was suffocating.

You're just exhausted. This is just *tiredness*, Lulu. I imagined my father telling me this. I imagined I was a little girl. I felt small, at that moment, in the big bed. The dream pulling me like a black hole. I was going to go into it. There was no not going into it.

> *What in the midst lay but the Tower itself?*
> *The round squat turret, blind as the fool's heart,*
> *Built of brown stone, without a counter-part*
> *In the whole world . . .*

Of course you know. The whole poem's a piece of escalating déjà vu. Like falling in love. Like *falling* in love.

Roland stands looking up at the Dark Tower—and you realise that until this moment in the poem you've never wondered what the point of finding it is. It's a quest—yes—but what will be gained by its fulfilment? The poem doesn't tell you and you don't ask. When you start reading you sign the contract. Like the contract you sign with life.

And when he does find it? This thing that's all but killed him and sent every one of his companions to their bloody and debased ends?

> . . . *noise was everywhere! it tolled*
> *Increasing like a bell. Names in my ears*
> *Of all the lost adventurers my peers,—*
> *How such a one was strong, and such was bold,*
> *And such was fortunate, yet, each of old*
> *Lost, lost! one moment knelled the woe of years.*
>
> *There they stood, ranged along the hill-sides, met*
> *To view the last of me, a living frame*
> *For one more picture! in a sheet of flame*
> *I saw them and I knew them all. And yet*
> *Dauntless the slug-horn to my lips I set,*
> *And blew. "Childe Roland to the Dark Tower came."*

# 70

# *Justine*

THE WHOLE THING so far had been me catching up to my own stupidity. In the cab from the hotel I realised I didn't even know if he was here. If he was home. I had the landline number. Why hadn't I just called? Because I was scared of hearing his voice? Because hearing his voice would remind me—just like Leath's had—that I was nothing?

But I had his voice in my head anyway. Had had it ever since. His voice in my head and the bump of his heart beating against me. The heart that felt as big as a bull's head.

He lived in a house on a hill fifteen miles southeast of Bangkok. Google Maps got me as far as an aerial shot. I couldn't drag the human figure in for a street view. Satellite showed a red roof and a paved yard—salmon pink—with colourful plants in big tubs. A small pale blue swimming pool. I thought of how every time a TV ad wanted to show you success they showed you someone in a lounger by a pool drinking a cocktail. All the pools in satellite aerial looked like blue mosaic tiles. I thought how I wouldn't ever see a pool in sunlight again. Not in real life. I imagined how weird it must have been for Fluff to have lost daylight thousands of years before there was TV and photography and the Internet. Before proper paintings, even. I'd asked him what it felt like seeing daylight on film. He said at first it was a miracle. He said he cried when he saw his first movie in colour, just sat there with tears streaming down his face. Then after a while it was like breathing recycled air.

The cab dropped me half a mile away, on a road that wound up the hill. It was after two a.m. Sunrise in three hours and fifty-six minutes. I didn't want time. I wanted to have to get in and out, fast. Time was like someone alongside me who could be unpredictable, could nudge me into something stupid. The Thai air was the way I remembered it—soft and crammed and warm—but ramped-up by my new nostrils. Sweating asphalt and the land full of the sweet dense greenhouse stink and somehow no matter where you were the smell of frying ginger and coconut and rice starch and drains. The hill had palm trees growing three or four deep on either side of the road. White gravel tracks led off to each of the couple dozen houses. Halfway up I looked back. There was a floodlit driving range down below I hadn't noticed on the way here. A few guys smoking and laughing and whacking golf balls. They looked a little drunk. I wondered for a moment if he was down there, if he was one of the guys. But when I focused I saw they were young and dressed in the gear, those dumb check pants and v-necks, even the prissy shoes. I couldn't see him in anything except the dark blue overalls that stank of engine oil and cigarette smoke and sweat.

At the wall running around the pool patio I stopped. My hands were shaking. There were two lights on in the house (a bungalow, though it couldn't have been more different to Leath's shithole), one behind the frosted glass window of what I guessed was a bathroom, the other in a bigger room at the other end of the house. I'd kept asking myself what I'd do if there was someone with him. I'd kept telling myself I'd know how to handle it if it happened. Except I hadn't, really. It had just kept going round in my head like clothes in a dryer. I'd just let it keep going without knowing what I'd do. Without really even believing it was possible.

I went over the wall.

That helped. The ease of it. The strength and silence I was still getting used to. That was like a friend that would be with me now, always.

The front door was unlocked.

It led into a small, white-tiled hallway with nothing in it except a wet pair of bathing shorts on the floor. There was a smell of bleach and burnt onions. The room with the sound of the TV was two doors up, on the right.

# 72

HE WASN'T ASLEEP. He was sitting in a rattan chair next to the bed in his underwear, with his feet up on the bed and a laptop on his lap. Details come at you. The first thing I noticed was that the big toenail on his right foot was black. His feet were big and fat. *He* was big and fat. His chest was full of cobwebby dirty grey hair. The room smelled of whiskey and cigarettes. His face had a bulldog underbite (badly fitting dentures) and jowls like pears. His thin hair was grey, swept back, but his sideburns and eyebrows still had black in them. His head seemed huge. There was a drink and what looked like some sort of croissant on a small white plastic table next to him.

I felt the floor pitch under me. Had to grab the door handle to stop myself falling. The noise startled him, violently.

The laptop fell. I didn't look at what was on the screen. I knew what was on the screen. The screen was something I'd fall into.

It would have been comical, the way he tried to pick up the computer and cover the front of his underpants. In the panic he accidentally kicked the laptop further away from himself. It hit the base of the bed and half-shut. He fell on his knees trying to grab it. It was like a fist in my gut, the way a separate part of me could see it would look comical on a YouTube video. There was a book at home in LA. *Ways of Seeing.* There was a sort of exhaustion, if you saw things enough ways.

"What the fuck— What the *fuck*? Who are you? Get the fuck . . . What the fuck do you think you're doing in here?"

"Nothing," I said. It seemed to take a long time to say that one word.

"Who are you? This is a fucking . . . This is a private . . ."

Something about the way I was looking at him. I could feel how still I'd gone. I could feel him suddenly thinking I had a gun. Because there was no fear coming off me.

I wasn't afraid. Only pressed down on again by the temptation like a heavy drug to just lie on the floor and let whatever was going to happen happen. Let it all happen again. The thought of his life, all these years—images came: him pushing a shopping cart around a supermarket, bored; him emptying an ashtray; him lying on a sun lounger squinting at a beer in the sun—and nothing had happened to him for what he'd done. He'd won the lottery. He'd won a fortune. I'd heard a Catholic nun on TV once saying that bearing suffering was the route to grace. Forgiving those who inflicted suffering on you was the route to grace. I remembered Fluff saying: If there's a God he's addicted to faith. Because without evil there's no need for faith. I can't get excited about a God whose divinity depends on a drug habit.

"What are you on, fucking *crack*?" he said. His erection had gone. Now that he stood upright I could see the little pouches of soft fat above his knees. His gut was big and shiny. I could feel the panic in him subsiding. Now he didn't think I had a gun. He just thought I was on something. Yet at the same time, because of what he'd done, because of what he was, because of all the seconds and hours and days and years of hiding it, his mind was still racing over all the possible ways this might be connected to it, might be because of what he was.

The disgust came up again. The disgust which, if I didn't act—

If he hadn't moved, if he hadn't taken a step closer, I might have stayed paralysed.

He went over when I hit him. I don't remember. My feet were off the ground. I felt the air moving under me. A cheap white-framed oil painting of a matador sticking a bull (heart as big as a bull's head flashed, the beguilement) in reds and golds went by. A digital clock with a flickering number nine that reminded me of when you're short of sleep and your eyelid twitches.

Don't drink.

Because I didn't want to know.

My fingernails went so easily through the soft flesh of his throat. I was on top of him. His body was like a tough waterbed. His face came close. I could see the capillaries in his eyeballs. Smell the whiskey dehydration on his breath. I could feel the bull's head heart. The familiarity of it butting me.

Honey, I'm gonna make you so dirty you ain't *never* gonna scrub clean.
Don't drink.

I didn't want to know. I didn't. I *didn't.*

I got a grip on the wet tubing of his throat and pulled. A lot of it came out. His eyes couldn't open wide enough to fit this surprise in. Miles away, his legs were kicking, trying something, some shift of weight. It wouldn't help him. His feebleness brought the tiredness and disgust up in me again. The power I had over him made me furious and empty. I felt my thumbnail go through a big slippery vein. An artery, I guess. Blood went through the air like a Spanish fan. I wanted something, I didn't know what—for it to be more, for it to be enough, for it not to be ordinary. The ordinariness of the facts—the veins, the blood like a weakening water fountain, his fat heels thudding, his face going through all its pointless expressions—just made the fury and emptiness worse. I knew, suddenly, that I wouldn't go see my mother. She'd be just another collection of facts. A small collection. This was what happened, I realised: the ordinariness of the facts shrank a person—or rather, made you bigger, once you could see them, made you bigger than them, made them something you could contain, whether you liked it or not.

Don't drink.

But in the end I had to. You have to. You have to know.

# 72
# *Remshi*

IT RAINED. HARD. One of those absurd South Asian downpours that come like a sudden burst of religious conviction. Caleb had insisted on accompanying us, much against his mother's wishes. Partly out of fascination with my condition.

My condition.

*Twenty thousand years, you think you've seen it all.*

A lesson to be learned in choice of phrase. Because I hadn't seen this. "This" was a farrago of booming symptoms, from the mild—hot head, peripheral vision trippily edged with cut-glass rainbows or fizzing pixels, pins and needles in my hands and feet—to the severe—sudden, coruscating attacks of thirst, hand-in-hand with boisterous nausea at the prospect of drinking. I *hadn't* drunk. Not since Randolf, which seemed an age ago.

All of which I could have borne, had it not been for the continual avalanches of memory. I'm used to flashes, firebombs, fugues of recollection. But these were inundations. *Floods* of memory that rose in me like dark hallucinogenic waters and threatened to cut off my air. Objects, people, places, snippets of conversation, vast, asphyxiating upwellings of unassimilable detail I had nonetheless to assimilate. Occasional thrust-forward pairings—a dusk view from the roof terrace of a Minoan temple I'd been particularly fond of rammed into my mind's eye along with a Salvadoran family living room, all six members decapitated, their bodies like broken mannequins under an ecstatic chorus of flies. The massage room of gold-inlaid ebony at Xianyang Palace, the little masseuse who was Qin Shi Huang's favourite, not only for her manual skills but for her seemingly inexhaustible fund of dirty jokes; this image manacled to a fair-haired drummer boy with a muddy face wandering in tears through the Hastings dead, suddenly screaming at the sight of a crow finnickily plucking out the eyeballs from an archer's corpse. The Paris skyline, moonlit, with the Eiffel Tower half-built—cheek-by-jowl with the face of a Sumerian storyteller, brown and glossy as an oiled saddle, toothless and laughing in the firelight. The only consistent theme was dead friends. I saw Amlek staked in the Greek market square. The viscous black remnants of Mim's corpse surrounded by gawping Hittites in torchlight. The photo of Oscar's head on a pole shown to me by an SS officer in Berlin. Gabil leaving the cave and crawling towards the sunrise . . .

This deluge, yes, the body's logic going walkabout, yes—but through it all the thought that if anything had happened to Justine, if any harm had come to her it would be more than I could bear.

"He should've stayed at the hotel," Caleb said. I was, from time to time, so manifestly elsewhere that he'd started talking about me as if I were deaf.

Mia didn't answer. We'd pulled up in the Damien-sorted Transit van (rudimentary blackout facility; a sheet of hardboard sealing the back off from the windscreen) on the road at the bottom of the hill that led up to Duane Schrutt's bungalow.

"Stay in the van," Mia told Caleb.

He ignored her. Climbed out the passenger door, then stood looking as if he'd regretted it with the rain crashing straight down on him. The boy was woefully skinny. And would never, now, fatten up. The rain woke me, slightly, forced a welcome hiatus. Gold jugs and night skies and *Kojak* and neoned Cadillacs and swarming starlings and slumbering camels and Shakespeare passed out with his (*not* bald) head on a tavern table and the floodlit Statue of Liberty and Farrah Fawcett's smile that always looked a little as if there were two invisible fingers tucked into each cheek, tugging, and wind simmering in dark prairie grass and a Russian peasant village softly illumined by thigh-deep scintillating snow . . . All this and a million things more momentarily subsided. To return, I knew.

"Are you all right?" Mia said. "Can you . . . ?"

Stand. Can you stand. Since I was not, truth be told, doing a very convincing job. I summoned my will. And though summoning it was like trying to lift a piano with broken wrists did, eventually, get vertical. Straightened my spine. Tipped my head back and let the rain fall full into my face for a few moments. It helped. Don't think about it. Concentrate on getting this done.

Don't think about what? Knowing you know something without knowing what it is?

"I'm fine," I said. "Let's go. I can feel her. She's close."

She was in Schrutt's bedroom, hunched up against the wall under a garish matador-and-bull in oils, knees under her chin, arms wrapped around her shins, staring into space. Her face and chest were covered in blood. She looked like something out of a horror movie. A slasher movie, in fact. Which of course was what she was.

"It didn't happen to him," she said, apparently not the least surprised to see us. Her dark eyes were raw and lovely. "I looked in him. It happened to Leath, but it didn't happen to him."

I went to her. No-fool-like-an-old-fool tears welling. Whatever it was (I knew what it was; it didn't need telepathy) it had broken her into enlargement. When I touched her shoulder I felt all her past shrivelling, becoming hard and not quite negligible. Not quite. I was so happy she was alive. I don't know why I'd been so certain she'd be dead. There had been such a feeling of death.

"Come on, angel, let's go. Let's leave this now." It was a pure pleasure, like falling snow in a forest, to find her physically intact. All her precious details. Thank you, I thought. Thank you, thank you.

"I'm sorry," she said. "I'm sorry."

It wasn't addressed to me. It was addressed to herself. To her old self, for whom revenge had not been sweet but a sad education.

I put my arms around her, held her close for a moment. My body's exhaustion and throb were signals coming from a padded cell a thousand miles away.

"We need to get out of here," Mia said. Caleb was, I knew, feeling the awkwardness of his juvenile form afresh. As a vampire he was older than Justine, but he'd always look like a child to her. His energies of self-consciousness were live, a troubled little heat in the room.

"We need to go," Mia said. She was wonderfully calm.

But Justine put her head on my shoulder, and did not cry, and for a few moments there was nothing, just the peace of holding her, alive, close, real. Caleb was poking around the room. He picked up the laptop.

"Don't look at that," Justine said.

"What?"

"Don't. Please. Please leave it."

Caleb looked at Mia.

"Please," Justine repeated.

Caleb put the laptop back on the floor.

"Are you ready?" I said to Justine. Schrutt was still flailing in her. I could feel him. She hadn't needed to drink. She'd drunk without the thirst. The blood, therefore, was fighting her. Sitting still was the worst thing she could do. You have to move. Expend energy to encourage the conversion, to force it through.

"My legs feel weak," Justine said. "I'm sorry, Fluff. All this trouble for you."

I kissed her forehead and put my arm around her waist to help her get to her feet.

Which was when I realised I couldn't get to mine.

# 73
## *Talulla*

MOONRISE WAS CLOSE. I sat on my bed in the paradisal bathrobe, and even its soft fibres were a torturous abrasion. I thought of poor Lorcan and the trouble his body (not to mention whatever was going on in his head) gave him in the lead-up to Transformation. Zoë was, for now, without discernible side-effects or symptoms, but what if that didn't last? As far as I understood it they were the first natural born werewolves in history. What if puberty inaugurated a whole new phase? What if adolescence had a bag of hormonal tricks ready for them that would make my monthly tribulations look like afternoon tea?

*You might not want it for yourself, but you'll want it for your children.*

When I'd asked to speak to Devaz, earlier, Olek had shaken his head. "I'm sorry, but I've given Christopher a sedative," he said. "He's getting cabin fever, poor chap. He'll be awake soon enough."

My strategist was still bullshit-testing his every utterance, but it wasn't any use. Aside from Olek's unreadability, I was finding it impossible to stay sharp. From the moment I'd arrived and sat down in the library it was as if I'd been breathing a tranquilizer that added a layer of numbness with every inhalation. There was a peculiar inevitability to everything I did, as if the air around me was gently coercing my movements, from raising the Macallan to climbing the stairs to labouring through "Childe Roland" last night. I couldn't shake the poem. It was like a maddening soft mental loop: The Dark Tower is the end . . . The point of getting to the end is to realise you've got to the end . . . The quest has no purpose . . . The Dark Tower is the end . . . The end is the fulfilment . . . My first thought was, he lied in every word . . .

There was a knock at the door.

"Are you ready?" Olek asked, when I opened it. He'd changed out of the casuals into a dusk blue linen suit and pale green cheesecloth shirt. Excitement was pushing his odour out again. Less than comfortably bearable, with my girl so close to the surface. He saw me draw back in spite of myself.

"Yes," he said. "I'm sorry about that. I'll meet you in the garden, shall I?"

The door to the library was open. Konstantinov and Natasha were on the couch, listening to Bach's cello suites. She was lying with her bare feet in his lap, his hands caressing her, idly. They had between them that vague, delighted pity for the rest of the world, for not having this love. They both turned and looked at me, Natasha with silent enquiry: You okay?

I nodded. You forget what you're nodding in affirmation of. Yes, I'm fine. Just the usual pre-murder nonsense. I was more than usually divided. The hunger was there, of course, tympanic in the blood, severity doubled by last month's half-feed, and *wulf*'s anticipation was a bump-and-grind go-go dancer under my skin. But my human self was still there, heavy, static, uncharacteristically sick of itself. Conscience was there, too, withered, leprous, dragging itself along in my wake, unable to do anything but repeat that this was disgusting and I should be ashamed—but it wasn't conscience troubling me. It was tiredness. The human tiredness of knowing your life was only going to get harder. Your life and the lives of your children.

In the garden, Olek stood leaning against the big blue sculpture, smoking. He straightened, smiling, when he saw me. The moon was two minutes below the horizon. The bathrobe might as well have been crawling with lice or lined with barbed wire. One of my vertebrae bulged and subsided. The nerves in my fingers and toes coiled and jerked. I staggered two paces—thought I was going to fall—then righted myself.

"You'll find what you need just beyond the banyans there," Olek said. "But there's no hurry. Please take your time." He was full of excitement that manifested itself as rich physical calm. He couldn't keep the smile from his face. He had a terrible seductive self-delighted energy. "When you're ready," he continued, "come back to the house and make your way down through the lab to the lowest level, as per yesterday, and along to Christopher's cell. There you will find me as good as my word. He will be human. All too human, as the phrase is." He dropped the cigarette and stubbed it out with the toe of his shoe. "I'll leave you now," he said.

None too soon.

Ten paces from the banyan trees he'd indicated I tore off the bathrobe and dropped to all-fours. Big red-petalled flowers brushed my shoulders and breasts. The earth was warm and ringing under me. *Wulf* stopped its epileptic burlesque and turned to fluid forces that yanked my bones and rent my tissues. Ran its hand down my spine as with a showy pianist's frill. What felt like two huge bubble-wrap bubbles popped in my knees. The monster's head fought its way jerkily into mine—that moment when you think your skin will tear, *has* to tear—and I felt the skull's blunt compression and leap as the canines burst the gums and my hot tongue swelled. A brief, shocking pain in my left wrist as ulna and radius got out of sync. Then the claws all at once, a collective shout for joy at the ends of fingers and toes. Five seconds for the last expansions, consciousness forced through a dark, tight funnel into shocking rebirth.

You'll find what you need.

And so I did.

He was perhaps nineteen or twenty, naked, slumped semi-conscious at the base of a young tree, around which his hands had been tied. I took him quickly. The drug—and the hunger's urgency—spared him a deal of suffering. It was a wretched feed. Last month's aborted kill had left *wulf* desperate, and the desperation made me rush. Past dalliance, past play, past the all but unbearable delight of making it last, of seeing him seeing it, what was about to happen, what was happening. Instead I slit his throat and dropped like a stalled jet straight down into the blood and meat dark, ate greedily, barely felt the fragments of his life—a fishing boat, his mother's small face and missing front tooth, the warm air flowing over him, coasting down a sun-blasted street on a bike, his hand on a market girl's bare breast, the days and days of sunlight on the water and the slap against the hull and the good feel of the warm wooden gunwale and the wind grabbing the smoke from his cigarette and the thrum of exhaustion in his calves and shoulders and wrists—before the hunger was an aching satiation and I had to stop, stop because soon it would become sickness and part of me wanted it, to push through into disgust, because everything had gone wrong and I was lost and the world was onto us and what do I do except break good men's hearts and fail my children and what am

I other than a dirty, filthy little girl who no matter what she gets is never satisfied?

The sky was clear. The garden winked and glimmered with impassive sentience, spoke the merry silence where God's judgement ought to be. I stood by the sculpture and let the fat moon's light bathe me. *It doesn't wash clean.* Let my breathing slow. Let the taken life find its confused way to the calling chorus of my swallowed dead.

Then I went back into the house.


"Go and look," Olek said, outside the door to the room with the one-way glass. "So you know it works."

It surprised me that he was willing to be alone with me. His species stink, to my nose now, was dark and thick, threatened to unsettle my sated guts.

I pointed. You first. Konstantinov and Natasha were at the top of the stairs, but deep instinct said caution. He understood. Nodded, went in ahead of me. I had to duck my head to follow him. My transformed dimensions made the small room smaller—and jammed his scent up against me.

"As you see," Olek said.

Devaz was sitting on his bunk with his knees up, head bowed. Unchanged. Untransformed. Human.

"How do you feel, Christopher?" Olek said into the intercom.

Devaz raised his head. His eyes were raw, but apart from that he looked completely normal. He shouldn't. He should look just like me. For a moment I wondered if the vampire had found a way of insulating a room against the effects of the moon. But I'd been deep underground myself, on more than one occasion. It hadn't made any difference.

"Let me out of here," Devaz said. He still sounded exhausted.

Olek ignored the request. He released the speak button and turned to me. "Well?" he said. "Are you impressed?"

I didn't respond. Just ducked back out of the doorway. He followed.

"It'll be tedious for you if I explain how it works now. You'll have questions, for which, obviously, you'll require your regular vocal skills. So in the meantime, rest, digest, consider. My home is your home, and your friends are here. Please, after you."

Back in the hallway above ground, he lit another cigarette. "If you prefer to be outdoors," he said, "feel free. There isn't another property for a couple of miles around. You won't be disturbed. And don't worry about the mess. It'll be taken care of. I have some work to do downstairs, but get your friends to let me know if there's anything else you need."

I did spend the night in the garden. Stuffed, objectlessly angry, going into and out of sadness. When I thought about Walker. When I thought about the future. When I thought about my kids.

# 74
# *Justine*

I'D SEEN HIM like this before. After London. After Crete. After Talulla. His head was hot. His limbs felt swollen. His breath stank. In and out of consciousness, and when he was in, making no sense. No strength in him. You could see the effort it was just for him to raise a hand. He couldn't lift his head.

"We have to get him into the hotel," Mia said. "We can't spend daylight in here with him like this."

In the Transit van, she meant, which is where we were. Where we'd had to carry him from Schrutt's villa. We'd pulled over halfway to the airport because suddenly he'd half sat up and seemed to be trying to vomit. But nothing had come up. Just him spasming, like someone was repeatedly punching him in the guts. There were three hours of daylight left. I was getting better at being able to tell without a watch.

"What's happening to him?" I asked. "Is this something that happens?"

Mia shook her head. "I've never seen it," she said. "I don't know any more than you."

It was weird, us feeling each other out, mentally. I'd got enough from Stonker through the confusion of those first moments when they came in—FRIENDS. DON'T BE AFRAID. TRUST—but we were all still testing and pulling back. She'd put a screen up, eventually, but sort of politely, as in, There's enough going on here. Let's just talk. The kid was wide open, but I let him alone. I didn't even know if I *could* screen.

I wasn't feeling good myself. Shouldn't have drunk when I didn't need to. I hadn't needed to. But I'd had to. The air in the back of the van was heated by Fluff's body going crazy. The kid, Caleb, had got out and was smoking a cigarette. He was quiet, freaked out, fascinated. He could feel how new I was.

"He was sick like this two years ago," I said. "When he went looking for . . . He went looking for a werewolf."

"Talulla," Mia said.

"You know?"

She smiled, without any pleasure. "It's a long story," she said. "And irrelevant. Enough that I know who she is."

"He thinks she's . . ." I stopped, didn't know how much he'd want me to say. But her face told me she was picking up the gist anyway. Obviously I *couldn't* screen. She felt me thinking how dumb and fucked-up it was. He thinks she's the reincarnation of his dead lover. I could feel her mental reflex, too, to dismiss it as bullshit. As mumbo-jumbo. As a fairy story. But then immediately the reflex to that, too, as in, Who the fuck were *we* to dismiss fairy stories?

I held Fluff's head in my lap. He was shaking. His lips were moving, but I couldn't tell what he was saying.

"What? What is it? Tell us what we need to do!"

Suddenly he opened his eyes and looked at me.

"Fluff? Jesus . . . What should we do? Do you need blood? Should we get blood?"

He smiled, but like he was seeing something else. Not me. Something miles away.

"Nor hope rekindling at the end descried," he said. "So much as gladness that some end might be."

"What? For fuck's sake, Fluff, we—"

But a spasm took him again, lifted him almost into a sitting position like someone had yanked a chain around his throat. Then he fell back into my lap. There was pinkish snot coming out of his nose. My hands were weak. "Oh God," I heard myself saying. "Oh God, Oh God . . ."

"Listen," Mia said. "Will the pilot take orders from you?"

"What? Yeah. Why?"

"Call him and tell him to make the preparations. God only knows how we're going to get him through the airport like this . . . We'll have to find another way . . ."

"What are you talking about?"

"Are we going to stay here all night?" Caleb said, appearing in the van's open rear exit.

"Get in," Mia told him. Then turned to me. "I know someone who might be able to help," she said.

# 75

## *Talulla*

I SLEPT THROUGH most of the next day, but since there were still three hours of daylight when I woke I went downstairs with the hope of grilling Devaz. Whatever it was that had "cured" him had come at a cost. I needed to know.

No luck. The doors at the bottom of the first flight down were locked. So much for *mi casa, su casa*. The house was quiet. There were no signs of the gore I'd traipsed in yesterday, nor, when I went back out beyond the banyans, was there any trace of the kill. Grishma, presumably, whose absence from the house my nose had noted, despatched to do the unsavoury necessaries. There was nothing to do but wait. I poured myself a Macallan and ran myself a bath. "Childe Roland" hummed a little, from the bedside table, but I felt sick at the thought of going back to it. Even when you knew the ending every reading would be the same hopeless circular triumph of loss. It was in keeping with the place, somehow, no matter how superficially different its landscape. It was in keeping with the sluggish, surreal quality of everything I'd seen and done since leaving the Last Resort. It was in keeping with the dream of the vampire. It was in keeping with me.

Bath and single malt didn't take much of the edge off. *Wulf* was still wide awake, fighting the lunar law, teeth and claws dug into every grudged second, minute, hour. There was a huge, sudden temptation to phone Walker, to speak to the kids. But by the time I left the bath and dressed (jeans, a black cotton t-shirt, a pair of red DMs—impractical footwear in the heat, but the brand-new flip-flops Grishma had left by my bed would be worse than useless if trouble came my way) I felt as if I'd lost the right. Every moment I spent here—this slow-motion vertigo—dragged me closer to inertia—yet there was nothing I could do to pull myself out. By sundown, all I'd done was sit on the edge of my bed and stare at the floor.

When someone knocked at my door, I assumed it would be Olek—or Grishma to take me to him.

It was Konstantinov.

"Put it on," he said. "I want to talk to you."

The damn nose-paste.

"What's the matter?" I said, when we'd applied it. Confronted by him, I was relieved and sad. Because there was no lying to him. He never lied himself. And always knew when you were. He looked at you and your energy for lying just burned away.

"Listen," he said. "I know things aren't good between you and Walker. I'm not asking. It's for the two of you. You go your separate ways, my friendship remains. You'll both have it, always. Understood?"

It was a terrible refreshment, his plain way, the simple words, the absence of strategy. It made you realise how much of your life you spent not being like that. It made you realise what a waste not being like that was. My body, which I hadn't known had been tense, sitting on the bed, relaxed into a kind of pleasant defeat.

"Understood," I said.

"There's a little disgust in you, right now," he said. "It's not for me to tell you not to be disgusted with yourself. That's your business. But don't let it make your decision for you here."

"You think I'll regret it? If I take the cure? If I give it to my children?"

"I think you'll regret it if you make a decision out of disgust. That's all."

And that *was* all. Conversations that would last dreary, punishing hours with other people were over with him in a half-dozen exchanges. Truth forged economy.

For a few strange, purged moments we remained in silence, me sitting on the bed, him standing, dark and still and tall in front of me. He was a blessing in my life. My life was full of blessings. And one curse: That no amount of blessings was ever enough.

He went to the door, opened it.

"He's waiting for you downstairs," he said. "Whenever you're ready. If you need us . . ."

"I know. Mikhail?"

He turned.

"Yes?"

"Do you trust him?"

He shook his head. "I don't know."

"You don't know?"

"I can't read him. At all. I'm sorry. All I can tell you is that so far everything's been as he said it would be. But that doesn't mean much, since we don't know what he *hasn't* said."

Again we paused in silence, as if there were crucial information the room's ether might choose to share with us.

It didn't.

"Okay," I said, getting to my feet, as a knot of *wulf* came undone in my shoulders. "Let's go and see what he has to say."

# 76

OLEK, BACK IN Levi's and a new crisp white *kurta* with a Nehru collar, was waiting for me in the vault. On the steel table, the case containing the stone tablet was open. He was holding a sealed envelope in his left hand.

"In here," he said, "are the remaining pages—bar one, which I shall retain until you fulfil your part of the agreement—from the journal of Alexander Quinn." He dropped the envelope in front of me on the table. "They're yours to read at your leisure, but I can summarise in the meantime. They tell the story, long after Liku and Lehek-shi had gone wherever the dead go, but still a thousand years before the First Egyptian Dynasty, of a *gammou-jhi* by the name of Ghena-Anule, a magician-priest who, for all his magical priestliness, got bitten by one of your ancestors when he was in his early sixties and thereafter devoted his energies to finding a cure for the Curse. He was one of the last of the Maru, and, as far as this record knows, the *very* last of the Anum, those members of the tribe who possessed the ability to travel—transcendentally, one must assume—between the Upper, Middle and Lower Realms. One of the last to be able to hold—as Quinn's translation has it—'converse with the gods.' Feel free, by the way, to roll your eyes at any time. I can assure you that was my reaction. I must repeat: I'm a scientist. I'm not, to put it mildly, in favour of mystical claptrap. You look tired, incidentally. Are you all right? Are you rested?"

I wasn't tired. Or rather, I was, but a sort of dead, claustrophobic energy was forcing its way through the tiredness. The vault was full of it, like a subsonic noise you knew would, eventually, split your head. I was trying to picture Jake and my mother watching all this from their afterlife casino. I was trying to picture them smiling and shaking their heads in loving but pitiful incredulity. But I couldn't. This was a show broadcast on a channel they didn't get. This was their reception turned to pixel-snow and static hiss. This was Jake putting his drink down on the baize and whacking the set with his fist and saying, What the fuck?

*Don't bother looking for the meaning of it all, Lu. There isn't one.*

"I'm fine," I said. "Finish the story."

Olek smiled. I wondered, suddenly, if Devaz was still in his cell. Lingering *wulf* nose reported human presence not too far away, but it didn't smell like him.

"So," Olek continued, "Ghena-Anule begins by petitioning the Upper Realm. These would be the good guys of the cosmogony. This would be, in the moral economy, the appeal to mercy."

He paused. I wasn't looking at him. I was looking at the floor. It was one of those moments—one of those situations—wherein the absurdity of the content vivifies the mundanity of the context, refreshes the humble molecules of walls, floor, table, light. These and the blameless pounding continuity of your own body. Yes, this is really happening, and here you still obscenely are. I was very conscious of the weights of my hands at the ends of my wrists. A vision flashed: Myself, in a cave, transformed—but with my hands missing. Amputated. For a moment I felt the cellular fizz of regrowth—with such convincing intensity that I actually looked at my hands to check it was an illusion.

It was. But it brought the dream back, the vampire's face. I'm coming for you.

Olek's pause, I knew, was to acknowledge our shared understanding of where appeals to Divine mercy got you. Nowhere.

"So," he went on, "Ghena-Anule turned the other way, and began to petition the Lower Realm. Not for mercy, but for a transaction, for a deal. Eventually, apparently, he succeeded." He raised his voice a little: "Muni?" he called.

An elderly Indian woman in thick dark-rimmed spectacles entered, smiling, with a baby-carrier strapped to her front. In the carrier, obviously, a baby. Very small. Weeks old, I guessed. The one that I hadn't imagined hearing the other night. The one I'd dismissed. The woman, in baggy jeans, brand-new Nikes and a blue-and-white floral print smock, had grey hair in a plait that reached her coccyx. Grey-green eyes and deep lines from the curve of each nostril to the corners of her mouth. She smelled of jasmine oil and tobacco—but the baby's odour, of clean diapers and Sudocrem and talc—had the bulk of my attention. The woman seemed wholly at ease. She stood just inside the vault doorway gently moving her hips from side to side, both thin-skinned elegant hands cradling the carrier, smiling.

"Muni doesn't speak English," Olek said. "Not, frankly, that it would make a difference if she did."

The baby's smell had detonated memories of Zoë and Lorcan as newborns, erased the three years between then and now. Three years. Impossible. I thought of Zoë saying to Cloquet one morning: "Your ears look like bacon." It gave me a moment of vertigo. At the same time the vault's subsonic hum went up a notch. The air was warm and pliable. My breathing wasn't clean. I felt crowded. My face prickled. I knew what was coming. The dirty, disappointing things are always a little ahead of themselves, always make themselves known by the opening your brain makes to receive them, a neural pathway that's always been there waiting for the shape that fits. I thought of Christ in Gethsemane, beads of blood on his brow, asking for this cup to be taken from him. Knowing already that it wouldn't be. Couldn't be. The Divine Chomskyan grammar in him had already guaranteed its necessity. I thought of Devaz, lying curled on his bunk, so obviously empty, so obviously at the end of himself.

"A child born on a full moon," Olek said. "Less than three months old. There is a ritual, there are words, which sound, I'll grant you, nonsensical, and which are written on the page I'm holding on to until you've done your part. In any case you speak the words . . . You place the stone on bare earth, you see . . ."

And shed a little of your blood on it, and slaughter the child, and the blood mingles and runs through the hole in the centre of the stone and carries the soul down to Amaz in the Lower Realm, who takes it in exchange for freeing you from the Curse.

Wittgenstein said we don't really ever discover anything. We just remember it.

Which was what this felt like. A drearily dredged-up memory.

Olek laughed, having observed me intuiting it. "Ridiculous, isn't it?" he said. "After all, what is one supposed to believe? That deities—which for starters one *doesn't* believe in—deities from the ancient world are still knocking around up there or down there or wherever in some metaphysical fashion? I suppose there's the notion that these things are outside time, as we understand it, but really . . . I mean, *really*—it's risible. Exactly risible." He was, if his face was any indicator, tickled immensely by how risible it was. "Believe me, you can't possibly hold this in greater contempt than I do. But here's the remarkable thing. It works. Look at Devaz. I can only say to you: Look, please, at Devaz."

Yes, I thought, *look* at Devaz.

There was something still missing. There was something the room was trying to tell me. Or rather the room was trying—with the stone as its little centre of intelligence—to savour withholding.

At a gesture from Olek the old woman, still smiling, still gently rocking the baby, exited. I heard her Nikes squeaking down the corridor.

"What's the catch?" I said. My voice sounded slightly slowed down. Tape running just barely below speed. "I mean, it's hardly a head-scratcher, is it? We kill and eat a human being every month. Babies are . . ." I was thinking of the night, transformed, I held a human baby in my hands, waiting for something inside myself to say: You can't do this. This is too much. Her little head was silhouetted against the moon. I'd waited and waited. "Babies are no exception," I finished.

Olek was watching me. Separate from what he needed out of this his disinterested clinician—his scientist—was fascinated.

Again his answer arrived in me fractionally ahead of him giving it. And I understood how Devaz had ended up in his state.

"You cannot perform the ritual on full moon," Olek said. "You have to be human to do it."

The room's atmosphere emptied. All my muscles relaxed.

And, upstairs, something big crashed through a window.

## 77

I WAS AHEAD of Olek until the second flight of stairs—in spite of the alarm he didn't neglect to lock the case and the vault door behind him—but on the landing he went past me without his feet on the ground. I could hear raised voices, objects being hurled and broken. It sounded like people throwing furniture around.

Then Olek's voice, raised above the racket. "Stop this immediately! Stop! All of you!"

They were in the library. The big window was smashed. The asparagus fern was on the floor in a sad little disgorgement of soil. There were books all over the floor and both couches had been overturned. The stink of vampires almost kept me from entering the room.

Natasha, with a gash in her forehead, was on her hands and knees by the glass desk.

Konstantinov had someone pinned against one of the bookcases.

A young dark-haired woman—vampire—I'd never seen before was struggling to get up off the floor. Her hands and face were bleeding.

Suddenly Caleb—Caleb!—appeared outside the broken window.

"Let her go," he shouted, leaping into the room. "You fucking let her go right *now*."

"Please, Mikhail," Olek said, quietly. "Do let her go. Let us all immediately calm down calm down calm *down*."

A fraught moment of everyone waiting to see if this was sufficient. A piece of glass from the window fell and tinkled.

Then Konstantinov released his victim and stepped back, and I recognised her.

Mia.

"What the *fuck*, if you don't mind, please," Olek said, "is going on here?"

*I'm coming for you.*

"We need your help," Mia said, straightening her jacket, brushing the fierce blonde hair off her face. She and I hadn't seen each other since the uneasy leave-taking two years ago on Crete, though I'd sensed her from time to time, keeping an eye on me, weighing up whether to kill me. I'd saved her life. But I'd also kidnapped and threatened to kill her son. We were, at a distance, peculiarly and mutually fascinated.

"Remshi's sick," Mia said.

"Remshi?" Olek said.

"He's outside." Then to Caleb: "I told you to *wait.*"

"Good Lord," Olek said. "Remshi is here? My good godfathers, how utterly extraordinary! For heaven's sake, tell him to come in."

No one moved. The room was in shock from the violence that had just exploded in it.

"He can't come in," Caleb said, stung by the rebuke and his own (relative) powerlessness and the shock of seeing me. "He can't fucking *walk.*"

*I'll see you again*, he'd said.

Well, I didn't think he was seeing me now, though I was seeing him.

Olek carried him down to the laboratory.

"You're going to have to let me see what I can do for him," he said, when he'd laid him on the brushed steel table. Only the dark-haired girl (holding her nose, occasionally gagging) and I had followed him down, without exchanging a word. "Talulla, my dear, I take it you'll . . . Please don't go anywhere until we've had a chance to discuss things further—yes?"

I didn't say anything, but he could tell I wasn't going anywhere. I was thinking—in the storm of thinking—of poor Devaz. Who'd got his humanness back at the cost of his humanity. Ancient gods or not, something still had a black sense of humour.

"I thought it was your fault," the girl said to me, in the hallway at the top of the stairs.

"What?"

"I thought it was your fault when he got sick like this the last time. Now I'm not so sure."

A sudden stab of her scent made me remember one of the first things I'd discovered about him. On Crete we'd been surrounded by vampires, so it had gone unnoticed, but when he'd sat only feet away from me at our last encounter I'd realised: Remshi didn't smell.

And still didn't. I wondered what it meant.

"Look," I said. "I don't know who you are. Maybe it'd be easier to talk outside. Hang on." I went back into the library, where Natasha and Konstantinov were righting the furniture. I got a tube of the nose-block from Natasha.

"They're in the upstairs sitting room," Natasha told me, meaning Mia and Caleb. "What's the story?"

"I don't know," I said. "Stay put. I need to talk to the girl."

In the garden, I offered her the paste. "It's not perfect," I said. "But it takes the edge off." I applied my own when I saw her hesitating. "Go ahead. Seriously. It's fine. We're all using it."

She put it on, but kept her distance. I sat down on a carved stone bench backed by a huge bougainvillea.

"For starters," I said, "who are you?"

# 78

PARTLY, I COULD sense, because she was ragged with newness and too much too soon and exhaustion and air miles and fear, fear, fear for him, she—Justine—told me everything. Or at least told me so much so disingenuously that it was hard to believe she was keeping anything back on purpose.

"Is it true?" she asked, more than an hour later. "Are you . . . I mean who *are* you?"

The muscles in my back were full of granular crunch. *Wulf*, regardless of plot intrigue, was still fighting every inch of the road back to quiescence.

"You mean am I the reincarnation of his dead lover of thousands of years ago?"

She didn't laugh, exactly, but her face acknowledged that I was acknowledging the ridiculousness of it. Or at least the ridiculousness of the way it sounded.

"I'll tell you the truth," I said. "I don't believe in any of this shit. Afterlife, God, reincarnation, dreams, clues, destiny, magic. A plot. I don't believe the world's got a fucking plot. I really don't. But ever since I met him, ever since those first moments on Crete, and afterwards, when he came to see me . . . Ever since then he's been in my head. Ever since then I've been having this dream." Our eyes met. "I know, a *dream*, right? But anyway I've been having this dream about . . ." I hesitated. Then thought, Fuck it: she's been honest with me. "Oh God, well, it's partly an erotic dream"—she looked at the ground—"but it's mainly the two of us on this beach. Walking along this beach at dusk. It doesn't sound like much, but there's a weird quality to it. I know: It's a dream. Of course there's a weird quality to it. But this is different. I realise I sound like a lunatic, by the way. I'm sorry."

"Do you have a cigarette?" she said.

Two Camel Filters—just two—left in my crumpled softpack. One—just one—tear-off match from an airport bar. We looked at each other. Again, didn't, quite, laugh.

"Thing is," she said, "here you both are."

I was thinking I liked her. I was thinking she was a fast learner. If she survived even another two or three years she'd be a force to be reckoned with. There was damage there, but she had sufficient self-brutality and hunger to make herself bigger than it.

"When I left him in LA," she said, "I wanted him to be free to go look for you. But he didn't do that. He came looking for me. And because of that, he's here. On the other side of the world. In the same house as you."

"Well, if you believe in destiny," I said, "I guess that's what you'd call it."

"Do you?"

I remembered the conversation with Maddy on the way back from Rome airport. *Ever since I met him I've had this feeling that this isn't just all random crap. It's as if someone's watching it all, or making it up.*

"I dislike it enough not to believe in it," I said, thinking: That's the first time I've ever thought that. There was that Forster quote: How can I tell what I think till I see what I say?

"So how come you *are* here?" Justine asked.

Well. Yes.

And though merely opening my mouth to begin felt like a labour against giant exhaustion, I told her everything. Granted there was an uncanny ease between us, but I was so sick of weighing narrative rations by now that I would have told anyone. All of it. Quinn's Book. The myth of origin. The Chinese executions. Salvatore and Bryce. Olek's vampires. The fucking human *world* closing in. You might not want this for yourself, but you'll want it for your children.

"We were attacked by the religious nuts, too," she said. "Back in LA before I left. Mia says it's going to be an all-out war."

"Or all-out primetime entertainment," I said. "Whatever does not kill them makes them make TV shows." I had an image of Zoë and Lorcan pitted against human kids: assault courses; IQ tests; spelling bees; cooking shows. I could see the new version of *Blind Date. One of these three would-be Prince Charmings has a dark secret . . . Will tonight's Cinderella still want to go to the Ball—when she finds out it's on a full moon?*

"So what *is* the cure?" Justine asked. As I'd known she would, since I'd stopped short of the details. I'd stopped short of the details because the cocktail of disbelief and nausea and absurdity and intuitive certainty made me want to go somewhere far away in the middle of nowhere and sleep. I thought of Muni, her calm, smiling physical care for the baby. I thought of Devaz, lying on his bunk, staring into space. Human again.

While I told her the details she stood looking at the ground, frowning, slightly, one arm wrapped around her middle, the other—hand holding the all but untouched cigarette—down by her side. I told her without emotion. Just what I'd heard. Just what I'd seen.

When I'd finished, she said: "You don't believe that." Fast learner was right. I'd known her less than a couple of hours and here were the pronouncements. On me. On what I believed.

"No," I said. "I don't. But I knew without him having to tell me exactly what the ritual was. It didn't feel like an educated guess. It felt like a memory. And there's Devaz. He was a werewolf. Now he's not." As soon as I said this I realised (slow, Talulla, this place makes you so dumb and *slow*) that of course Olek wouldn't let him leave here alive. He was probably already dead. He'd probably already been neatly driven away by Grishma and neatly buried somewhere. It was a strange little fleck of disgust in the mass of disgust. Out of it, I said: "I could give my children the chance of a normal life."

You say these things as an experiment. To see if you believe them. How can I tell what I think till I see what I say?

•

An hour before sunrise Olek surfaced. "He's conscious," he said, "but very disoriented. I've given him a lot of blood, but he's not metabolising properly. I don't know. I've never really seen this before."

Justine and I had come in from the garden. Mia and Caleb, showered and changed, were sitting at the bottom of the stairs. Konstantinov and Natasha were boarding up the window in the library.

"Can I see him?" Justine asked.

"Go ahead," Olek said. "He's very heavily sedated, however. I doubt he'll know you. Mia, Caleb, there's plenty of room below stairs. Please make yourselves comfortable. Do you need to drink?"

"Tomorrow," Mia said.

"Fine," Olek said. "I have everything. Talulla, you and I need to—"

"I need to go to bed," I said. "I'm exhausted."

He looked at me for a moment. Then smiled. He took the envelope containing the remaining pages from Quinn's journal and handed it to me. "Corroborative reading," he said. "Just so you know I wasn't making anything up."

I was thinking: I'll go upstairs, get my things, give it a couple of hours, then walk away from here.

I was thinking this.

# 79
## *Justine*

I WANTED TO stay awake, but I knew I wouldn't be able to. The sun comes and sleep's like the ground sucking you in. Like magnetism from hell.

"I promise you, my dear girl," Olek said, laying out a comforter and pillows on the corridor floor, "I've done absolutely everything I can for the time being. If he makes it through the daylight hours he'll be much stronger. Then we can re-assess. Now you're sure you wouldn't like one of the other rooms? I feel an absolute barbarian letting you sleep here like a little cat, albeit a lovely one, with personality."

"I want to," I said. "I'll feel it if he wakes up."

He squeezed my arm and gave me a neat little smile. He was one of those guys you couldn't tell whether you hated. So polite and charming you thought it had to be a cover for something.

"Of course," he said. "I understand. Well, if you have everything you need, I'll take my leave for now. I'll be one floor below if you need me. Bottom of the stairs, second door on the left. Just knock."

So, I thought, after he'd gone, that's her. *Her*. I guess I shouldn't have felt happy when she told me she didn't believe she was anyone's reincarnation. For poor Fluff's sake I should've been sad. Except of course she *hadn't* said she didn't believe in it. Not exactly. No such thing as destiny. But Fluff had come after me, not her—and it had brought the two of them together anyway. It was impossible to believe it was all part of some invisible scheme of things, like God's plan, like a fucking *story*. And just as impossible to write it off as a series of accidents. Both ideas impossible to believe and impossible to dismiss. Which is what he's told me Christ knows how many times before, about the signs, the connections, the correspondences between things, the goddamned *beguilement*. You have to both believe it and know it can't be true, he'd said. You have to learn how to be the wry servant of two masters. I'd been so annoyed, I'd said: Yeah. I've never known what the fuck "wry" actually *means*.

And now this.

Him. Sick. Again.

I lay on the comforter on my side with my knees drawn up. The house hummed, quietly. I was thinking: Just let him be okay. If you let him be okay . . . If you let him be okay I'll never . . . Just let him be okay and I'll be bridesmaid at their fucking wedding. Please . . . Please . . . Please . . .

You think like this. As if there's someone you can plead with. Even when you know there isn't.

Then suddenly I thought of what my world would feel like without him in it. The cold fact of it. All the countries and faces and skies and cars and TV screens and people. Without him to make it bearable.

And it was like the earth falling away underneath me.

# 80
## Talulla

IN MY ROOM I packed my rucksack.

Then sat on the edge of the bed looking at it.

It was a beautiful morning. The window was open. Blue sky. Furious birdsong. The garden's perfumes. A very slight, sporadic breeze brought, at moments, the faintest whiff of the ocean. It seemed odd to think of it so close. Barely a couple of miles.

I took out my phone. Time difference. They'd be asleep. The kids, at any rate, would be asleep. Walker might be awake.

In bed with Madeline.

I hoped he was. And the hoping put another fracture in my already crazy-glass heart.

*I could give my children the chance of a normal life.*

For Christ's sake, Lulu, I imagined my mother saying, either think it through or shut it down.

My mother. Jake. Cloquet. Fergus. Trish. The dead were an unimaginably long way away. A distance that defined loss. The living were only a little nearer. The distance that defined sadness.

I picked up the envelope, tore it open and read.

It was exactly as Olek had summarised. Of course it was. I hadn't expected anything else. He had no incentive to make it up.

Gods. Souls. Bargains. Sacrifices. A hidden scheme of things.

Absolutely every part of me—except one—rejected it, utterly. The one part of me that didn't was the memory of knowing exactly what Olek was going to say before he said it. The part of me that recognised it, as something I'd known all along. I thought of the Apostles at the Last Supper, hearing for the first time the words that would become the rite of Transubstantiation:

*Take this, all of you, and eat of it:*
*for this is my body which will be given up for you.*

# By Blood We Live

*Take this, all of you, and drink from it:*
*for this is the cup of my blood,*
*the blood of the new and everlasting covenant . . .*

To them it wouldn't have felt like something new. It would've felt like something they'd once known and subsequently forgotten. The neural pathway or soul's grammar would've opened to receive it, to welcome it home in an act of giant, terrible, thrilling recognition. If it hadn't, Christianity would never have got started.

Grishma (presumably) had left a new bottle of Macallan and a clean glass on the nightstand. An unopened pack of Camels, too, next to "Childe Roland." I put the pages back carefully in the envelope, poured a drink, lit up and went to the window.

The chance of a normal life.

Put the all but total scepticism on one side. What sort of normal life? One that would depend on them not remembering anything from the life they'd already had. Was that likely? Certainly not unless I took the cure as well. If I didn't, I'd have to let them go. Elsewhere. Adoption. A brand-new start with human parents. Either way the therapists of ten or fifteen years in the future were looking back to my present and beaming.

At which point I knew, very simply, that even if I believed the ritual would work I wasn't going to do it.

It was a funny, liberating thing to be able to reject what you knew to be true.

*Besides,* Remshi's voice said in my head, *that's not what you were brought here for.*

# 81

## *Remshi*

I WOKE JUST before sundown feeling better than ever. Notwithstanding I hadn't the faintest clue where I was. My opened eyes (I felt not just well, but *reborn*) showed a white ceiling with three fluorescent striplights. My (what felt like virgin) nostrils reported chemicals and processed air. My sentience (washed, primped, ready for devil-may-care action) said wherever I was it was exactly—it was precisely and wholesomely and inevitably—where I was supposed to be. I sat up.

Fine. A laboratory. *Vaguely* familiar. Teasingly filed somewhere in the crammed mental cabinet. The thing to do was not to try to remember it. Think about something else and it would pop right in like magic. I got to my feet. I might as well have been Lash-sated, because even that humble physical action filled my molecules with glee. Look at me! Standing up! A marvel!

A big memory door swung open on a vision of Justine sitting in the corner of a large bedroom, knees up under her chin, covered in blood.

Schrutt. Duane Schrutt's house.

Bangkok.

Mia, Caleb . . .

I stood there for a few moments, following the image-trail backwards. The jet. The devastated *Militi Christi* base. Leath's place in North Vegas. Justine's note. Turning Justine. Near-death darkness. The attack on Las Rosas. Porn king Randolf. The two lost years.

Vali.

Talulla.

Vali.

*I will come back to you. And you will come back to me. Wait for me.*

Perversely, I hadn't had the dream. The beach, the twilight, the someone behind me, the knowing that I knew something without knowing what it was. Nor, thank God, had I woken with *He lied in every word* gadflying around my head.

## By Blood We Live

*What's the last thing you remember?* As I'd trained Justine to ask.

Schrutt's bedroom. Not being able to stand up.

It seemed absurd, given how beautifully I was standing up now. I was the Platonic Form of Standing Up. You could go a long way, my singing legs and spine and head said, before you'd find a better example of standing up than the one we had right here.

In the room next door—more bottled chemicals, fridges, unnervingly thin gizmos—I found Mia and Caleb, still sleeping, spoons fashion, on blankets on the floor, mother behind son, her left arm wrapped around him. He was frowning. Poor lad had a busy dream life, I knew. The stunted subconscious forever wrestling with the unchangeable fact that he'd never be a grown-up, no matter how many millennia he lived. I felt a great flowering of tenderness for them. I must make sure and transfer more money later. I must make sure they had no material worries. The image of the two of them making a home of the house in Big Sur was a warmth and a comfort to my heart.

Justine was asleep, curled up on a comforter in the corridor. She looked beautiful. I put my hand out to wake her—then didn't. There was the loveliness of her, just now, the sweetness of her unconsciousness, but there was, too, my reluctance to disturb my own state of quiet benevolence, my feeling of privileged watch-keeping. If I woke her now there would be questions, her ravenous intelligence and fiery heart; there would be the (albeit joyful) clatter of narrative, of talk, of connecting and making sense. Her energies would wake the others, and the happy problem would be compounded.

Suddenly my own heart hurt. Not cardiologically, but with the need—in spite of everything I'd just thought—to hear her voice, see her awake and animated, in full flight, my little Justine with her smart mouth and her courage and her sometimes terrifying silence. It was a bizarre, urgent upwelling of love for her, for all the ways in which she was precious to me, from the shy, secret way she sometimes took a book from the library to read without wanting me to know, without wanting me to start *asking* her about it, to the speed and obliviousness with which she habitually tucked her hair behind her ear. Her particularity—the uniqueness cashed-out in fingernails, daydreams, coughs, memories, glances, regrets—brought such a surge of need for her that I reached out again to wake her.

But again, didn't.

There was time. There would be plenty of time.

At the top of the stairs a door led into the pleasantly underfurnished hall of what, it was becoming increasingly obvious, was a large and wealthily looked-after house. A memory-bell *tanged*, faintly . . . But no. I knew this place, I really did, but it wasn't quite ready to come clean. There was a last sliver of low blood-orange sunlight running across the oak floor between me and the stairs. It was the flamy centrepiece of the hall's stillness and beauty. And (Berkeleyan idealism notwithstanding) had been here, gradually narrowing and deepening its gash of colour on the oak's golden grain even though no one had been there to see it. I remember thinking a long time ago—perhaps the first time I ever observed the growth rings in a tree-stump—that if there was a Creator then he was a compulsive and promiscuous artist: not content with filling the big canvases of skies and oceans (a different one every day, every millisecond), he must doodle rings in the secret bodies of trees that no one by natural rights should ever even see.

For all its beauty the sliver of light cut off my route to the stairs, but three other doors were accessible without roasting myself, so I went to them and peeked into the rooms beyond, one by one. A kitchen with a big window giving onto a lush—and manifestly not Western—back garden. A lounge, with three huge couches and a wall-mounted flatscreen plus a small walnut coffee table bearing a half-finished game of chess. A Persian rug–strewn library with one boarded-up window and several books scattered on the floor. The books, naturally, called to me. There was an early edition of *Swann's Way*. A *Don Quixote*. A *Northanger Abbey*. An Arden paperback *King Lear*—*O, let me not be mad, not mad sweet heaven*—and (the ether winked) an early hardback—*If I am out of my mind, it's all right with me*—of Bellow's *Herzog*.

The delighted contraries called to me, but I didn't go. As with Justine, there would be time. There would always be time. The upset volumes reminded me of the night we were attacked at Las Rosas. Browning's *Collected Works* would still be lying face-down where it had fallen. It would be a small, distinct pleasure, when we got back there, to replace it on the shelf. I hadn't read Browning in years. But there would be time.

I thought I'd only been standing there a few seconds, but when I went back into the hall the last of the light had vanished from the floor, liberating my passage to the stairs. Time—why not?—to have a poke around the upper storeys. Let the others sleep. I felt such love for them I sent it as an imperative: Sleep. *Sleep*, my darlings. The world—so various, so beautiful, so new—will still be here when you awake. I was deeply happy. Happy in the blood. Happier than . . . than I could remember being for a long time. An unaccountably long time. Not since I was very young.

Not since Vali.

Whose scent I caught, three steps up.

# 82

*I WILL COME BACK to you. And you will come back to me.*

I stopped. Held on to the bannister. Felt the world dip and momentarily fall away. Was it . . . ? Was I dreaming? It wasn't . . .

The years imploded and the blood in my cock stirred. Oh God. (Only with her. *Only* with her . . . ) Oh, you forgot, you forgot how good it was, the sweetness and urgency, the monolithic need . . . Two years since the tug on this leash. Two years for the blood-fish to thaw and flash into life. Two years since the night I'd seen her in the woods at Big Sur—but before that, how many thousands? How many millennia (that epic comedy of impotence) of having to find the sad, forced sufficiency in Everything Else? It comes back and makes a joyful mockery of the supposed enoughness of Everything Else, of the sexless, the unfuckable world. It comes back and the thought of death is terrible. It comes back.

I still didn't know where I was. But what (I could feel my own smile, the warmth spreading in my face and hands and chest and legs) what could it matter where I was, since she was here, since every subatomic particle affirmed in silent song the absolute inevitability of the place? This place, this moment, this joy.

The miles and days fell away from me like a rotten harness as I leaped up the stairs to her room.

I knocked, heart bobbing in my chest like a trapped helium balloon. (*I knocked.* There are doors to be knocked on, no matter your heights. Drinks to spill. Ringing phones to ignore. Keys in a pocket to be fished out and fumbled with. The world grants you the heights, but only to remind you you're never too high for the intractable mundane.)

No reply.

I knocked a little louder. *I will come back to you. And you will come back to me. Wait for me.*

The sound of her getting out of bed. Barefoot footsteps that testified to her exact weight. Vali's weight.

She opened the door.

"I'm not who you think I am," she said.

# 83
## Talulla

"I'm not who you think I am," I said.

But that was the last thing I said for a little while.

I knew it would be. The words leaving my mouth were like a magical formula that let the spell of heavy, alive silence loose. It was as if the rushing mob of questions got to me just as my own doors closed to keep them out. They got so close. Details and specifics (individual faces in the crowd): Are you better? Are you really that old? I've been dreaming about you. What is this between us? How is any of this possible? But the doors, in slow-motion, closed, and the floor seemed to soften and tilt under me, and I was overcome by a great willingness to not speak, to let whatever happened happen.

There was more to it than that. Of course.

I'd been dreaming when his knock woke me. *The* dream. Mercurial sex with him that alternately bloomed and went into darkness, sharpening at moments into distinct images that had the feel of archetypes—my fingers wrapping themselves around his cock; his dark head working between my legs; his hands (the two of us reflected in an oval mirror) coming around from behind me, one caressing my breasts, the other sliding down over my belly to my cunt—but bled into and superimposed on by the image of the twilit beach, the dark sea and scatter of stars, him a few paces ahead, the little rowboat, barnacled and half-buried . . . Strands of the dream had still cobwebbily clung as I'd crossed the blue and silver rug to the door, until I was *at* the door, and opening it, and (knowing it would be him) seeing him standing right there in front of me.

Superficially he was as I'd remembered him. No taller than me, longish dark hair and light brown skin. A black-eyed face full of the ability to stand back from everything—himself included—and smile. Superficially, he was the same.

The difference was he looked absurdly healthy. His skin had a new glister, as unreal as a woman's in a suntan lotion ad. His fingernails shone. But it was the eyes. They had a rinsed, delighted look, a fresh, excited presentness, as if a faint, ancient glaucoma had been removed. I thought of the Johnny Nash song, "I Can See Clearly Now."

For what felt like a long, *long* time we stood looking at each other. Letting what was happening happen, until the silence between us became a solid, seductive, coercive third person. One that would have its way. He stepped close to me and put his hands on my waist, and in what felt like infinitely slow increments leaned towards me and—the increment that stopped time altogether—kissed me.

What I felt—above or beyond or burning deep in the heat that flooded me (one frail filament of self-consciousness like a veil or ghost floating alongside me, negligibly, noted that my cunt was wet and aching, aching)—was joy, *his* joy, pounding out of him, solar, overwhelming, unarguable with. What I felt was that I'd never—not even with Jake—been wanted like this, with a force that was beyond him. It was as if something the size of a universe opened out behind him, that he'd been carrying its weight—that he was bringing all its weight to bear—on this moment, here, now, with me, that I was an inevitable end-point. And that I'd been waiting all my life (All my life? It felt older than that, made my life seem a blink, a heartbeat, a breath, surely there was a time before it?) for exactly this, for his hands and mouth on me and the mass of darkness flowing out from his back like an endless black cloak.

The kiss was an immediately addictive certainty.

Never let me go. Never let me go.

I don't know if that was him or me. Whichever of us it was it wasn't spoken aloud. My negligible filament-ghost was scrambling to re-gather the threads of the negligibly real world—wait, *wait* . . . But we were moving, not, apparently, with our feet on the ground, in accordance with the deep gravity that demanded something to lie down on, demanded him inside me, close, close, as close as it was possible to be, and his body fit mine perfectly, a shape I'd known before birth and forgotten, that defined and perfected my own. The room blurred. From what felt like a long way away I heard myself say Oh God . . . Oh God . . . Reaching in the insistent prosaic realm through clothes and buttons that at every touch threatened to rupture the blur and break the fall into darkness until I felt my bare flesh on his and how was it possible for everything to fall away so fast, so completely my life even my children a million miles away and at the same time the sound Oh God Oh God the sound of someone in the room the sound of someone—

"Oh— I'm . . . I'm sorry."

I'd never known anything uglier and more desolate than the wrenching away at that moment, the all but unbearable reality of having to lift my head and look over his shoulder (already starting to push him from me though my legs were wrapped around him) to see Olek standing in the doorway, his hair still mussed from sleep, his hands patting the air in front of him in apology, a gesture which made me want to kill him.

"I'm so sorry," he said, the cheeky schoolboy smile for once deserting him, leaving a nude, alarming version of his face I'd never seen before. "I was just—"

He didn't get to finish. Remshi had him by the throat in mid-air for a split-second (while I was still registering the loss of his warmth and weight on me) then Olek crashed into the wall.

"*Varmu!*" Olek shouted. "*Varmu va mor! Remshi! Varmu!*"

Remshi was standing over him, hands raised, dark cock still absurdly standing proud from his undone flies. Energy poured off him, packed the room, forced me up against a confused memory of the dream I'd had here, of lifting my arms and seeing instead of my hands two amputee stumps.

"*Manyek da gorgim,*" Olek said, *his* hands wildly placating the air. "*Manyek va fennu da gorgim. Enyuchin, Remshi, enyuchin.*"

For a moment I was sure whatever that meant it wasn't going to make a difference. Violence was right there at the edge of him. If Olek says another word, I thought, he'll rip his fucking head off. (I wondered if there was something between them—a betrayal, a long-held grudge. Then knew there wasn't. It was just my lover's fury at being interrupted. A rage with the same force as the desire. It was nothing more nor less than how badly he wanted me.) Maybe Olek intuited the same thing, since he kept his mouth shut, although his face went erratically through its calculus of submissive expressions, unable to settle on one.

"Leave us alone," I said to him, getting to my feet. I was dressed only in what I'd slept in: panties and the black cotton t-shirt. My panties were soaked, but I didn't care. Superficially there was the detail-sharpening desolation of interrupted passion, of passion's rug being pulled from under it, but at a deeper frequency the knowledge—utterly beyond question—that we were going back there. My whole body screamed to go back there, the known place, the remembered place, the place out of time.

"Leave him," I said. "He took care of you. He probably saved your life."

We knew—we would always know—when we were speaking to each other. I felt his rage drop a little. There were sounds of movement from downstairs. The sun had been down for . . . I had no idea. Time had gone dreamily AWOL. But in any case some of the nocturnal household was up. There would be questions, petitions, explanations, recaps. We'd have no peace.

"Olek," I said. "Get the fuck out. Right now."

He didn't say a word. Just pushed himself upright against the wood panelling, turned and walked out the door. Remshi closed it behind him. His power thudded in my blood. I loved it. In one of Jake's journals it said: *Some men desire weak women. No women desire weak men. Hardly any men understand this, though it's the most useful truth they could possess.*

I pulled on my jeans and boots.

Without a word he came to me and scooped me up in his arms. (The filament-ghost, strengthened by Olek's interruption and the memory of Jake's observation, flashed *An Officer and a Gentleman,* but that was all right. There was room for laughter. There was room for the real. There was room for everything. That came off him, too, that living was the attempt to find room for everything.) All our movements were revelled in by the space around us. The window was open. It was a twenty-five-foot drop from the ledge to the garden. It was nothing.

# 84

WE TOOK THE BMW 4x4 he and the others had arrived in. He drove. Randomly, as far as I could tell. The tarmac road that led to Olek's, then lefts and rights on narrower lanes and tracks that took us into a series of tough-grassed, low-lying hills. We passed a plantation of some sort, though I couldn't make out the odour of the crop. "Tea" my idiot American assumed. In the same way she assumed "jungle" every time the trees and undergrowth thickened. We couldn't have seen more than a dozen buildings, all small dwellings with orange fire or blueish TV light framed in their doors and windows. There was nothing of the sunset left. One thin, rucked band of cloud lay close to the horizon, but above it the stars were out, the big diagram of remote delight.

I think he knew. That I wasn't her. Or that I wasn't straightforwardly her. Not the way he'd imagined. It was why we couldn't speak to each other. The reality now was that there was a momentum at work whether I was her or not.

It was there, between us, that either way this was happening, this was going to happen. He was fascinated, compelled, uncertain of everything except that there was no turning away from this, whatever its ambiguities. I had internal clamour. The crowd of shut-out questions were pounding on the doors. But the expanding moment held them shut. When we looked at each other we smiled. There was still something—the confusion of my identity in his head—preventing him coming to me, fully. It was as if I were surrounded by a skin of soundproof glass. But when we touched—he put his hand on mine, once, while he drove, then had to whip it back to the wheel to compensate for a pothole jolt—the memory of the blurred moments in the room was live and warm in both of us. I felt my life—my children, Walker, the pack, even the ghost of Jake—curving down and away from me, like a planet seen from a spacecraft, shrinking in the wake of terrible acceleration. But there was dark joy in the loss, too, an appalling glimpse of the genuine transience of lives, tiny scraps of paper igniting for a split-second in the void's cold invisible flame—then gone. Millions. Billions. It was *his* sense of time. It radiated from him. I thought: He can't live like this all the time—can he? With this perspective? He can't, surely, live with all he's seen?

*Twenty thousand years, you think you've seen it all.*

They'd been his first words to me, in Alaska, the night I gave birth.

Olek's judgement of the cure for the Curse came back, too: *but really . . . I mean, really—it's risible. Exactly risible.*

And yet here we were. He'd been in my dreams for two years. He'd eaten away at the thing for Walker that was so close to being love. He'd reopened the question of whether there wasn't, after all, a story at work. *Don't bother looking for the meaning of it all, Lu. There isn't one.* When I tried to see forward, past this night, this *now*, it was impossible, produced instead of any vision of the future (going home, abandoning home, killing myself, curing my children, raising a werewolf army) a pleasant feeling of indifference, a darkness you could lean against like a fevered child leans against a cool surface. Being like this, close to him, was a koan of deep calm and near grotesque excitement. The excitement went beyond sex, though there was no arguing with my cunt, which was still wet, which still ached. (For him. Specifically for *him*.) It was the excitement of being part of an inevitability. It was knowing there was no other way than to let this become whatever it was going to become. It was a liberation.

We stopped.

The invisible coercive choreographer took us out of the car and fifty paces up a gentle hill of dry grass crowned with neem and peepal trees. Even the very slight movement of the air was enough to make them simmer. The constellations were huge and benignly indifferent. They'd smile in the same way (who knew if not me?) had we come up here for murder instead of love.

# 85

*WHEREOF ONE CANNOT speak, thereof one must remain silent.*

Except we can't remain silent. That's the real curse.

I remember—I distinctly remember—taking our clothes off. Not each other's. I remember undressing myself and every action feeling like . . .

Like what?

Like it wasn't happening in time. That it had always been happening. That it would always be happening.

I remember—*not* distinctly—spreading the clothes to lie on.

I remember—this is the last thing I can be sure of—his mouth and the weight of him on me. And thinking: Where's the ground?

After that there's only the going into and coming out of darkness. Like a slow heartbeat. Systole and diastole.

In the darkness there's nothing.

Out of it there's only joy.

No. That's not right.

I remember something else.

I remember that at the end—an end that every time we approached it gave us the gift of moving a little further away, so that the pleasure had to keep growing into it, until any further would have been a kind of grief, at which point it yielded itself, and my body came back to me bringing all the bliss the universe had been saving for just this moment, just this one point where the finite met the infinite—at this paradoxical end of unbearable sweetness something went from him into me, and I knew I would never be the same again.

# 86

## *Justine*

I SLEPT LATE. *Hours* late. God only knows why. The feed when I shouldn't have, maybe. I knew as soon as I opened my eyes he wasn't here, though I checked the lab anyway. Mia and Caleb were gone, too. I raced upstairs.

The house was quiet, but I found Olek in the study, reading. The lamps were lit and the wall-mounted TV was on with the sound down, showing a sunlit cricket match.

"Where is he?" I said.

"Ah, you're awake," he said. "You slept very long, my girl."

"Where is he?"

He paused, and though his smile didn't shift I could tell he was put-out by my manners. I wondered how old he was. Whether manners would still matter to me in a thousand years. Every time I thought about the time ahead it was like the last few paces before plunging off a cliff into total darkness.

"He's with Talulla," he said. "They have . . ." he laughed, "gone out."

"Where?"

"I'm afraid I don't know. But I can tell you he was manifestly much better. I do wish everyone would stop being so hysterical."

"What do you mean? Was he all right?"

He closed the book he was reading and got to his feet. I thought: He's only being nice to me because he's scared of Fluff. He'd have ripped my head off by now, otherwise.

He went to the window and looked out. Dawn couldn't be more than an hour away. I couldn't believe I'd slept so long. Almost the whole night.

"Let me give you the full state of play," Olek said. "Your maker has absconded I know not where with Miss Demetriou. You'll have to fill *me* in on what's going on there, I might add. Mia and Caleb fed from my larder when they woke several hours ago and went out to enjoy the night.

I expect them back momentarily. Our Russian lovebirds, infected by the same anxiety that has you in its grip, dashed off in search of Talulla. Now, are you content? Can I offer you anything?"

"Which way did they go?"

He sighed. Put his hands in his pockets. "Second star to the right, straight on till morning," he said. "You know, considering the openness of my home, considering the hospitality . . . Ah, well. I really don't have a clue. They left from Talulla's window, if that's any help, but beyond that I'm no wiser than you. You're very young. I forget. You'll live in a world I can't imagine. How sad everything turns out to be."

I went to the door.

"I wouldn't wander too far, little cat," he called after me. "Sunrise in one hour and thirty-six minutes."

But I was already running.

Not that I knew where to go. I went down the driveway to see if I could pick up his scent—or hers. But they were too long gone. Or I just wasn't good enough yet to catch it.

Then I saw the guy with the binoculars.

He was standing a hundred metres away at the side of the road with his back to me, but even in silhouette he looked vaguely familiar. The shape of his head, the big rounded shoulders. I imagined a paunch. He was wearing dark combat fatigues. He looked weirdly wrong in them. There was an automatic rifle slung across his back, holsters on either hip. As far as I could see he was alone. But seeing had nothing to do with it. I knew there would be others.

It would take a matter of seconds to get back to the house and tell Olek. But for all I knew Olek was in on it. Whatever it was. Whatever this was.

Whatever this was, it was nothing good.

Don't kill him. Get him to talk. You need to know how many are with him, where they are.

Oh God, Fluff, please be all right . . .

Silence was like something that came out of my body. It was so easy to move through the trees without making a sound. In spite of everything there was still the thrill of the huge gap between what I was capable of and what he was. A human. *Humans.* Fluff used to use the word with me as if I wasn't one. As a joke. Not a joke anymore. The darkness was tense around me. Tense because it knew we didn't have much time.

I drew parallel with the armed man. It was as if the jungle was dying to tell him I was there, but knew it wasn't allowed to. I'd reach him in a single leap. I could imagine what it would look like as a scene in a movie. They'd shoot it from the other side of the road: him in profile, looking through the night-vision binoculars; the wall of dark lush trees beyond him; me suddenly bursting out, the curve of my jump, the second of pure silence. Then contact.

It was all there in my haunches and bent knees. The way the distance between us would become nothing. I flexed my fingers.

At which moment he lowered the binoculars—and I saw the surgical dressing across his nose.

It was the guy from the Sofitel lobby in Bangkok.

I guess it might have made a difference if I hadn't hesitated just then, my mind racing backwards to try to make the connection, figure out who the fuck he was, why he was following me or even *if* he was following me—it might have made a difference, I don't know.

What I do know is that I straightened up when I recognised him.

Which meant the first half-dozen wooden bullets went through my guts instead of my heart.

# 87
## *Talulla*

WHEN I OPENED my eyes, the stars were faint and different. Too much time had passed. He was asleep, but woke when I shook him. I watched him go from complete blankness—no idea where he was, when it was, *who* he was—through the shockingly reassembled history. Three blinks, four, five, the last hours coming back to him in a series of explosions. I thought: He shouldn't have been asleep. That's not normal for him.

My voice, when I spoke, sounded alien, as if I were hearing it with my ears blocked. I said: "It's late. We . . . You have to get back."

The gentle abrasions of dressing. I had a humble gratitude for my body, its finite uniqueness, fingerprints, lips, nipples, eyelashes. I thought: That's the gift the void gives you, the knowledge, when you come back, of how good it is to be mortal flesh and blood. We didn't speak. He was busy with his own confused enrichment. It would take three or four more times before we could begin to talk about it, about how it was. The filament-ghost, desperate to resume normality, desperate to establish that nothing had changed, offered things like *So, was it worth the wait?* Or *You sure you haven't been practising?* There would be time for playfulness, for bringing it gently into language, but it wasn't now. Now there was just the big raw darkness, the new reality, the changed world. There would be time for everything. There would be time.

And the fear, like a whispering virus, that I was wrong. That whatever this meant to me it meant something different to him.

On the way down the hill, he collapsed. His legs went out from under him. He got up straight away, with jittery, unnatural speed.

"Are you all right?" I said.

He smiled. Took my hand and drew me gently to him. Put his arms around me. Held me. I didn't know why I was crying. But there was the feeling of fracture in my chest. The mental doors were open again. The whole dreary mob of questions free to enter. Yet now they were, they didn't. They stayed put, staring, confused, as if they'd just received news of their own collective pointlessness. As if the monster they'd come to kill had turned out to be already dead.

"Come on," I said. "We have to move." It pressed on the fracture, that I was the one bothered about how late it was. I knew I could go on getting him to do things, for a while, but not forever. There was a simplicity and calm in him that I worried would get away from me, eventually.

The real world reimposed itself by degrees, via the sound of our tread through the grass, the receding simmer of the trees, the crickets, the soft whir of a bat. (The filament-ghost was waxing, too, a little vengefully: A bat! Ha!) He still hadn't spoken. It was as if some huge, peaceful mathematical problem was working itself out in his head. He didn't have to do anything. Just watch it resolve.

I was thinking I should drive, but when we got to the BMW he took the wheel. I didn't remember the way, anyway, and it was hard to imagine him calling directions out of his trance. The car's interior smelled good, new leather and vinyl and carpet. It said continuity, the human determination to keep making things possible. Which pressed the fracture again, the thought of how long that had been going on, and how the word "human" had separated itself from me. How I'd lost my entitlement to it. There was a sadness to the little facts of the key in the ignition, the sound of the engine starting, the lights suddenly wrecking the privacy of the dust and the tarmac and the pale dry grass.

# 88

## *Justine*

I woke to loud birdsong and the sweet smell of blood. For a moment I couldn't understand the sudden tip and swing and gravity all wrong—then I realised someone was lifting me over their shoulder. When I opened my eyes, not just sight but all my other senses seemed to rush into a kind of focus. Daylight was close. I was looking down past whoever's back and legs these were onto the bloodstained forest floor. A pulled-off human arm lay there. Combat fatigues. *Militi Christi*. I lifted my head (not easy) and looked around. Bodies and body parts. Impossible to tell straight off how many. Half a dozen at least.

"Put me down," I said.

"She's awake," Caleb said.

"I can walk. Seriously. Put me down."

Mia bent forward and I slid to my feet.

"We have to hurry," she said. "You sure you can walk?"

"We have to find him," I said. "He's out there somewhere."

"There's no time," Mia said. Her aura was still thrumming from what had happened. There were two faint pink flushes under her blue eyes. In the seconds when the first bullets had hit me I'd thought: And still you're stupid, stupid, *stupid*. They'd seemed to come from every direction at once. I'd gone into a kind of dream. Killed two of them without even really being aware of it. A confusion with bits of detail. My fingernails going clean through a guy's throat. A young woman's silver crucifix and neckchain flying through the gloom. Caleb's little voice going: Fucking *hell*. The sound of Mia snapping a neck. I'd never seen anyone move that fast. One guy's head had come off with a terrible wet tearing noise, her pale hand wrapped in his hair. The bullets had hurt like hell. A dozen tiny explosions in my gut, three or four in my left leg. I remembered a bolt going like a line of fire through my left arm. The wood in your flesh made your heart suddenly like a buried alive person trying to pound her way out of a coffin.

"Easy," Mia said, when I took a couple of steps and nearly went over. "Easy."

"The guy with the binoculars," I said. "Did we get him?"

"He got in a car," Caleb said. "I said we should've gone after him."

"If they know about us, they know about Remshi. We can't leave him out there!"

"There's no time," Mia said. "Minutes. We go now or we die. And I have no intention of dying."

She was right. The sun was close. I could feel it like a wall of sound, rising. My body screamed the need to get underground. It feels like all your cells or molecules or whatever are pulling, billions of little creatures straining at the leash.

"If they find him, they'll kill him," I said. "In his state . . . In his . . ." But it was no good. Mia was already thirty feet away. Caleb was tugging at my sleeve. His pale hands were covered in blood. I felt sick. The sun was so close.

"Come *on*," Caleb said, pulling me almost off my feet. "Why are you crying?"

I went quicker with every step. My wounds rushing to heal themselves were like things quietly chattering. In spite of everything there was a sort of sick pleasure in knowing that when I woke I'd be good as new. Good as new and wide awake in a world where the only person I'd ever loved might be gone forever.

# 89
## *Talulla*

THE CAR BRAKING woke me.

No memory of falling asleep.

I opened my eyes to see him staring at something up ahead. A person. An old man dressed in layers of ragged clothes, leaning on a crutch, roadside, just at the edge of the headlights' reach.

"What?" I said.

He didn't answer, but I felt his aura gone suddenly rich. The old man—dark-skinned, filthily bearded, with one completely bloodshot eye—shifted his weight onto his good leg and raised his crutch, as if pointing to something. He was smiling. I thought: Does he want a ride? What is this?

But he lowered the crutch, turned, and limped away into the darkness.

"What is it?" I asked again.

"That hoary cripple," he said, and laughed.

"What?"

He sat, smiling, both hands on the wheel, staring out of the windscreen. He looked bright with tiredness.

"What did you say?"

The headlights of another car came bumping towards us. The road was wide enough—just—for it to pass. A Land Rover with mirrored windows.

He hadn't moved. Hadn't looked at the Land Rover. I knew if I asked him he might not even have registered it, though it had gone by with only inches to spare. He was still busy with what looked like a kind of empty delight.

"Hey," I said, putting my hand on his arm. "Are you all right?"

But he just put the car in gear and eased it forward until we were more or less level with where the old man had been standing. There was a narrow road off to the left. The old man had been pointing it out.

"Is this the way?" I said. The fracture in my chest swelled again. I felt afraid, though I didn't know of what. "Is this the way back?" The sky definitely wasn't wholly dark anymore.

"I think it might be," he said. "Yes."

The road wound between shaggy, unidentifiable trees for a couple hundred metres, then narrowed into a sandy track not wide enough for the vehicle.

"This isn't the way back," I said. There was a searing distance and closeness between us.

"It's all right," he said. "It'll be all right."

The smell of the ocean hit me as soon as he opened the door. Not just the smell. I had a sickening sense of its size and depth and darkness. Its weight. I thought of a black, rusty container big enough to hold all of it, how big that would be, how awful it would be to climb up and look over the edge into it. All the billions of fish in there, sharks, wrecks. The tiny fleck of Cloquet's rotting body.

"This isn't right," I said. "This is crazy. Look at the sky." I was full of frantic weakness, legs, wrists, hands. I'd thought the invisible coercive choreographer had drawn off. But it hadn't.

"We need to turn around," I said. "Right now."

But he was already moving.

"Wait. Wait! Fuck."

I went after him. He was following the track, which broke first into bits of knolly, long-grassed turf, then soft sand dunes that eventually flattened into the beach. It was like entering a vast empty amphitheatre. The water was dark in the twilight, though every time a wave broke on the shore its pale foam ruff morphed out of the gloom.

He took his shoes off. Smiled when his toes gripped the sand. "That's good," he said. "One forgets the goodness of these things."

I looked out over the black water. It was lighter on the horizon.

"Let's walk a little," he said. His voice sounded small in the big space of the beach.

"Why are you doing this?" I said, though I thought I knew. Soft invisible weights slipped from me with every step. The lightness when they'd gone would be unbearable. *Unbearable.* There was a line in one of Jake's journals: *The word "unbearable" makes a liar of you—unless it's followed by suicide.*

"I've been dreaming of this place," he said, after we'd walked a little way. The sound of the waves was a steady, benevolent depletion. Every one subtracted something. Repeated, painful acts of mercy. "Being in this place with someone."

The breeze blew his hair back a little. His dark eyes were big and bright.

"So have I," I said, though saying it made my mouth feel defeated.

"I read somewhere that only the dead understand their dreams," he said.

"Why did you say that about the old man? Why did you call him that?"

He shook his head, smiling again. Happy incredulity. At himself. At how he'd missed something so obvious. "'My first thought was, he lied in every word,'" he recited:

*That hoary cripple, with malicious eye*
*Askance to watch the workings of his lie*
*On mine, and mouth scarce able to afford*
*Suppression of the glee, that pursed and scored*
*Its edge, at one more victim gained thereby.*

"I know that," I said. Another soft weight dropped from me. Another mouth-defeat. "It's from 'Childe Roland.' I just read it, here at Olek's."

He nodded. Smiled again. Unsurprised. I looked east. The twilight was paling.

"'Yet acquiescingly,'" he continued,

*I did turn as he pointed: neither pride*
*Nor hope rekindling at the end descried,*
*So much as gladness that some end might be.*

"But of course—"

His legs gave way again. I helped him up. I could feel the warmth of what had gone into me from him in my loins. I wondered if I was pregnant again. The thought hurt me with a stab of premature loss.

"Thank you," he said. "I'm sorry. I'm so sorry."

"Please let's go back. *Please.*"

"What I was going to say was: But of course it's *not* a lie, is it? 'The workings of his lie'? Because the old man really does point the way. The road he shows really does lead to the Dark Tower."

"You don't have to do this."

"In the dream," he said, "I always saw this twilight as just after sunset. Didn't you?"

I didn't want to answer. Every answer, everything I said or did would shed another of the soft weights. Out of disgust, I forced myself. "Yes," I said.

"But that was the wrong twilight, wasn't it? One forgets there are two. One forgets so many obvious things."

Twenty paces on, the dunes and broken turf on our right gave way to dark rock. Cold came from it. Touched all the exposed parts of me from which the soft weights had gone. And there, of course, adding its own innocent portion to the dreary, deadening déjà vu, was the little rowboat.

He went to it and began pulling away the seaweed.

"You don't have to do this," I repeated. Saying it was perverse proof of its own falsehood.

He carried on methodically freeing the boat. "You're not her," he said. "Not literally. But you're the call back to her. That was the part of her message I misunderstood. She said: *And you will come back to me.* That was the important part. The dead can't come to us. We can only go to them."

His calmness made me angry, suddenly. "This is fucking stupid," I said. "You don't have to do this. This is just . . . So you had a dream. So what? Dreams are . . . Fuck."

"Dreams are prick-teasers *non pareil*," he said. "They promise and promise but never put out. A friend told me that, once. He was right."

"So don't do this."

"Listen," he said. "Tell Justine . . ." But his voice faltered a little on her name. "Tell Justine she'll find a copy of Browning's *Collected Works* open face-down on the floor of the library at Las Rosas. Ask her to tell you what poem it's open at." He shook his head. Laughed again. Another belated realisation. "Ask Caleb what poem he was reading in the volume of Browning's *Men and Women* on the plane."

"That's nothing," I said. "That's just what we put on random shit. That's just *us*."

"Tell her the house in Big Sur is for Mia and Caleb. With her. They'll be good for each other. She needs a family. So do they."

"Why are you *doing* this?"

He pushed the rowboat over onto its keel. The oars were strapped to the little seat. There was a fat, slimy rope tied to the bow. He looked at the eastern skyline. I couldn't tell how long till the sun came up. But it couldn't be much longer. Twenty minutes? Half an hour? We could get back to Olek's in that time. I knew we could.

"Justine tried to keep me away from you," he said, "because she thought getting close to you made me ill. Even when she left it was because deep down she knew I'd come after her." He took a moment to absorb the comfort of this fact. It warmed him. A smile without tiredness. "Because she knows I love her. Thank God she knows that." He looked at his hands, which were shaking. "But it wasn't you. I was ill anyway."

"Olek can fix you," I said. "Yesterday you were fucking unconscious."

He began unwinding the rope. "Vali made me promise her something, once," he said. "She made me promise to live as long as I could. How strange that I've kept my promise! I never imagined I would. And now here you are, her message, to let me know she holds my oath fulfilled."

It wasn't easy for him to dislodge the boat. It took three attempts, and each visibly depleted him. I just stood there, watching, helpless.

"You know what my maker said to me before he died? He said: 'I've seen this place in my dreams. It's a relief to come to it.' In my dream of this place I had the profound feeling of knowing that I knew something without knowing what it was. Now I know."

"Please don't go."

He dropped the rope, came to me, took my hands in his. They were full of fluttering blood. "Talulla," he said. "Such a pretty name. I'm glad you're here with me."

"You're going because you think she's waiting for you on the other side," I said. "What if she isn't? What if there's nothing on the other side for you or anyone else? There *is* no other side." But I thought of the way I'd known what Olek was going to say before he'd said it, the picture I'd had in my head, clear as an enamelled Station of the Cross, of the baby, the stone tablet, the mixed blood running through the hole. Down through darkness that wasn't earth or space, that had no relation to time at all. Remembering it infuriated me. Because it didn't prove anything. Of course it didn't prove anything. Except that our imagination had habits. Except that we were inclined towards things. Get a Jungian on the subject. Get a fucking *Structuralist*. God—*gods*—and fairy stories were nothing but disposition plus desire. The desire for the whole bloody mess to be more than a pointless accident, the desire for it to be *for* something.

"You've got nothing," I said. "Just dreams and coincidences. Just something that makes it look like there's a . . . Like there's some pattern, as if life's like a stupid fucking movie or a stupid fucking *book*."

"I'm sorry, I'm so sorry," he said. Then smiled, sadly. "I've reached the end of my psychology."

I wasn't going to help him with the boat. But he fell, halfway to the water's edge. I suppose I must have looked ridiculous, crying, dragging a boat. Still, I went with him, into the surf up to our knees. In spite of everything the ocean's raw fresh smell excited a part of me. The big sky and the deserted beach. I wondered if I would ever have had enough. The world, the things that happened. The people you got close to. The honest warmth of flesh and blood. Both kinds. I thought of how much I'd hurt Walker. I thought of how disgusting it was that Jake was gone. Cloquet, Trish, Fergus. Never coming back. The dead can't come to us. We can only go to them. That's what life is, after a while, I thought. Choosing not to go to the dead.

"This is wrong," I said. "This is just stupid and wrong." It felt stupid and wrong, too, the two of us standing in the wobbling water, the optimistic little boat, the faint line of light on the horizon saying the sun would rise, another day would come, things would keep happening, the fucking world would go on.

But he laughed and took my hands again. "All these years," he said, then seemed unable to find the words. "Life drops terrible hints. We call it the Beguilement. When we drink . . ." He looked up. Hardly any stars still visible. "When we drink, we see so many of them, coincidences you'll say, the connectedness of things. Humans see them, too. It's our shared curse, that these things won't leave us alone. Dreams aren't much. It's not dreams. It's beauty. Metaphor. Love. Mainly love. Love's the big hint life can't stop dropping, the biggest beguilement of all." He looked out towards the burgeoning light. "I was going to say I'm tired of not knowing," he said. "But that's not right. It's better than that. I'm ready to find out. That's not such a bad thing, is it? Being ready to find out? Come on now, don't cry, please don't cry."

But I *was* crying. Not only for him, but for myself, for the mess I'd made of everything, for all that I'd wasted and all that I'd lost. And of course, of *course*, because I *wasn't* ready to find out, couldn't imagine ever being.

"They say your life flashes before you when you die," he said. "That's going to be some flash. It'll probably kill me." He looked at me, smiling, daring me to laugh, and because there's no end to the opposites we can make meet, the grotesqueries and farces we can find room for, I did, with a sort of anguish, find myself laughing.

"Give me a kiss," he said. "One last one. For luck."

I kissed him. Tried to make it last. But you can't. It ends, sooner or later. You love, you lose. That's the trade.

He got into the boat and dipped the oars. Lost his balance for a moment. Righted himself, laughing again. "It must be a hundred years since I've done this," he said.

We looked at each other. Whatever it was that had gone into me from him tingled, fanned out in my blood.

"You should go now," he said. "Please don't stay."

I didn't go. I watched him pulling away, finding the rhythm with the oars. Ten strokes. Twenty. Thirty. I turned, sloshed back to the shore, my jeans and boots soaked, my eyes burning, my chest emptying. The last of the soft weights dropped from me. For a few moments I stood with my back to the water, looking down at the glimmering sand.

Then I turned.

He was much further out than I'd imagined he'd be by now. It had only seemed a matter of seconds, but the little boat was barely bigger than a matchbox.

It was hard to tell at this distance, but it looked as if he was standing up, facing the horizon. I thought, I never said goodbye. Just thinking of the word, "goodbye," imagining how it would have felt saying it, brought tears again. I wrapped my arms around myself.

And watched.

He had a few moments. Perhaps even a minute. Deep red and orange light, low feathery clouds in bloody, membranous flakes, water the colour of mercury, flecked with blue, pink, peach. Not pretty, but spectacular, a terrible indifferent statement of the scale of things out there, the giant heat involved, the vast, soulless mathematics that gave incidental rise to everything we knew here, all our murders and poems, our dreams and epiphanies, our boredom, our love.

I think he saw the first segment of the sun ease up over the water. I think he shouted something, laughing. It might have been: "It's beautiful!"

Then the boat dipped for a second, rose again, and I saw him. A bright tuft of violet-edged flame, a brief, soft flare of brilliance—then he was gone.

# 90

CARDINAL SALVATORE DI Campanetti, with a big surgical dressing on his nose, was waiting for me when I got back to the BMW. He was holding a gun.

"It used to be, in the old days, that only the wolf's head would do," he said. "It was a point of honour with the old Soldiers of Light, to take the monster in its monster form. Even the heathens in WOCOP tried to keep up the tradition. Nowadays we're a little less fussy."

My blood jangled. The sick taste in your mouth and the vibration like a tuning fork in your head.

Silver.

Bullets.

Nowhere to run. Nothing. Now. The reality of my children exploded in my heart. All my life rushed to this moment to see if there wasn't some way, some way to—

Then the Cardinal raised the pistol and shot me in the chest.

I'd never been shot before. It was like I imagined being kicked by a horse would be. I felt myself falling. Just managed to grab the wing mirror and stay on my feet. The pain in my chest was hot and crushing, a detonation of heavy white light filling my lungs and head. I had, what? Seconds? I was remembering—as my eyes, which I hadn't realised had closed, opened again and the big unidentifiable trees swam back in, vivified, outrageously full of detailed life—I was remembering holding Jake in my arms when he died. How long had it taken? I'd felt it in him, silver racing to map the system, veins, nerves, tissues, bones. I'd felt the silver's delight, set free in him to do its thing, like a power cut knocking out block after block of a city's lights. Five seconds? Ten? A minute? I was thinking, too (God being dead, irony still rollickingly alive), that this threw all my big talk of moments ago—of not being ready to find out—in the trash. Finding out didn't wait until you were ready to find out. Finding out found *you* out. I imagined Remshi's surprise, looking back and seeing me so soon on the afterlife road behind him. And of course if that were true, then Vali would be there too, eventually. As would Jake. As would my mother. Awkward disembodied introductions. How ludicrous! The little light dancing part of me laughed.

A second horse-kick. In my gut. Which unstrung my hand's grip on the wing mirror and sent me, by what felt like pointlessly drawn-out degrees, down onto my hands and knees. Small twigs rolled under my shins, a minor but very distinct irritant. I was thinking of Zoë and Lorcan. Good that they were still young enough to forget me. Walker wouldn't abandon them. Maddy wouldn't. They would be all right.

Then I felt it.

Death looking up in the middle of its mardi gras and seeing Life bearing down on it like a tidal wave.

Death trying to recalculate, to assimilate, to grasp.

Reversal.

Giant water hitting giant fire in a deafening inner hiss.

And water always wins.

*Something went into me from him.*

I didn't understand.

And of course did.

I'd known I'd never be the same. Just not in what way.

It was very quiet. I don't know how long I knelt there, staring at the dust and stones of the track. I was aware of the day's heat building, giving its heavy morning intimation of the suffocating weight it would bring by noon. Something in the BMW's still-cooling engine *tonked*, softly. I raised my head. Got up onto my knees. Got one foot under me. Stood.

The Cardinal was, to say the least, surprised. His face had lost its guiding will. I stepped to within arm's length of him. If I simply reached out and took the gun from him he'd be unlikely to resist. I could take the gun, point it at his head, pull the trigger.

And yet I knew I wasn't going to. Not mercy. Disgusted exhaustion. The world's infinite supply of action and reaction, cause and effect, Jake's hated endless *if*s and *then*s. The little boat and the rising sun and the flare of flame had emptied me. I was tired. I wanted to go home.

I got into the 4x4 and started it up.

Because the universe doesn't suspend physics no matter your extremis, I had to go through the farcically cumbersome business of turning the car around in the narrow space. The Cardinal watched all of it, mouth still stupidly open, the gun dead in his hand. I thought, Jake would roll the window down for a parting shot: *My God, my God, why hast thou forsaken me?*

But I didn't even have the heart left for that.

# 91

IT TOOK ME three attempts to find Olek's. Grishma, toting an AK-47, was at the edge of the garden, looking out for me. When I switched the engine off and got out the cicadas went quiet for a few seconds, then started up again.

"Ah," Grishma said. "Ah. Yes. Good. Come in, please come in."

He filled me in on the attack as we went downstairs. With the exception of the Cardinal it seemed almost certain the whole *Militi Christi* squad was dead. Olek (now locked in his most secure room—I assumed weapons, escape tunnels; you didn't make it to his age without covering the contingencies) had nonetheless recalled his security people, who were expected, Grishma assured me, imminently. The others were all alive, all sleeping. Caleb, Mia and Justine covered in blood. Natasha on a comforter in the lab. Konstantinov slumped against the wall next to her with an automatic pistol in his right hand.

"Mr. Konstantinov was keeping vigil for you," Grishma said, head on one side, looking down at Konstantinov as might a proud mother at her wholesomely exhausted toddler. "But it became impossible. He's had so little sleep over the last days."

I felt as if I'd had none myself.

"There is also," Grishma said, as we headed back upstairs, "something I'm sure you'll want to see."

What I wanted was to take a hot shower and get out of there, but I followed him into the lounge anyway.

The plasma screen was on, muted. CNN. Night footage. A derelict warehouse on fire. Armed figures in combat fatigues.

"They've been running this on all the channels," Grishma said, pouring me a Macallan and handing me the glass. "A development. Absolutely a development." He unmuted, just as I'd started to follow the rolling banner: *BREAKING: CHICAGO—MILITI CHRISTI ATTACK ON*

*WEREWOLF DEN ... "TIME FOR DENIAL OVER," REPUBLI-CAN SENATOR SAYS ... TWEET YOUR VIEW ...*

The footage was hand-held, but professional. This wasn't a jittery eye-witness with an iPhone. This was a crew, multiple cameras. This—the filming—had been part of the intention.

" . . . said the attack signalled the start of an open, global action," a voiceover said. "I spoke to Squad Leader Martin Scholes, who had this to say."

Cut to a dark-haired guy in his mid-thirties in black fatigues, face a mess of camouflage paint and sweat. He was breathing heavily. He looked elated. "This is what we're here for," he said. "This is what—" Another soldier, passing, slapped him on the back and shouted: "*Gloria Patri! et Filio! et Spiritui Sancto!*" followed by a whoop and what turned out to be a failed attempt at a high-five. "Sorry about that," Scholes said, grinning, when the soldier had bounded out of shot. "That's . . . You know, the guys have trained hard for this. This is . . . You can expect some high spirits. The point is there's a job needs doing. No one can pretend this problem is getting better. It's getting worse. Someone has to draw the line, you know? Someone has to . . . This is a threat not just to Christians, not just to Americans, but to the human species, to all human life, every-where. If that's not a clear enemy, I don't know what is."

"Numbers so far indicate five lycanthropes dead and sixteen human fatal-ities," the voiceover cut in, as footage switched to the beheaded corpses of two werewolves, lying among still-smouldering rubble, guarded by four young, fully armed *Militi Christi*.

"We're not a political organisation," Scholes was saying, when they cut back to him. "Our goal here is the eradication of this clear enemy by the grace of and for the glory of God. We're not—"

"What do you say to those people accusing the Church of using this campaign as a credibility lifesaver in the wake of the multiple cases of abuse of young children by—"

"That's ridiculous," Scholes cut in as something exploded, off camera, making the interviewer jump into shot. Scholes steadied him. "You all right? That's okay. That's just . . . The point is that's just an example of hatred of the Church. People have always hated the Church. They'll say anything to try 'n' discredit us. Here, look at this. Can you get this in?"

Someone handed him a bayonetted rifle. With a werewolf's head jammed onto the blade. Again, it was obvious the bayonets had been thought through, for just this moment. For maximum visual impact.

"This," Scholes said, "*this* is what we do."

The report cut to Republican Senator McGowan at a press conference. Camera flashes. A thicket of microphones.

"That's a misquote," McGowan said. "What I actually said was that we're going to need more *than* guns, not 'more guns.' We're going to need more *than* guns and silver to defeat an enemy only the most willfully blind members of the administration still refuse to see for what it is. We're going to need faith, we're going to need a return to solid values. And everyone knows in their hearts what I mean by that . . ."

I hit the mute again.

Grishma hadn't said a word.

"Tell Olek I'll be in touch," I said.

"But, madam—"

"Not for what he's selling. But we may be able to work something out. Tell him to give me a couple of weeks." If there was any way of synthesising what I had in my blood, he could be my best shot. Whatever else, he knew his science. Until we had a lab egghead of our own he might have to do. He wasn't going to stop wanting what he wanted, after all. I'd just have to persuade him not to shop around.

In my room, I called Walker.

"Jesus Christ," he said. "What the fuck? Why didn't you call? Didn't you check your messages?"

No. I was too busy reading Browning and getting vampire-laid.

"Are the kids—"

"The kids are fine," he snapped. I'd never heard him this angry.

"I'm sorry," I said. "I'm getting on a flight today. Where are you?"

Pause. Long pause. I thought: Maddy's in the room with him. It didn't matter. It was good. It was right.

"Still in Croatia," he said. "God dammit, Lu. You've seen the footage, right?"

"Just now. I'm sorry."

"Stop fucking saying that."

"Are the kids . . . ?"

"They're asleep."

"That's okay. That's good. I'm sorry." Sorry again. It was out before I could stop myself.

"What the fuck is going on out there?" Then: "Are you all right?"

"I'm fine. I'm . . . I'm fine. I'm coming home."

"What happened with Olek? What about the Cure?"

I thought about it for a moment. The dozen answers.

"Not worth the price of the ticket," I said. "Not for me, anyway. Not for the kids, either."

There was a silence. All the things I felt him not asking.

"You know this is just the beginning?" he said. "You know we're going to have to fight them?"

"I know," I said. "But we'll do it as what we are. You were right. There's no going back. There was never any going back. And if there was for us, there wouldn't be for them. I'll call you from the airport. Please don't worry. Please don't worry about anything. I want you to be happy. I want you to . . ."

*Come on now, don't cry, please don't cry.*

"I'll call you from the airport," I said again, then hung up.

Downstairs, I asked Grishma for pen and paper. I had notes to leave for everyone.

# 92

ON THE PLANE—and in the airport before the plane—everyone was talking about the attacks. Over the last twenty-four hours there had been at least twenty other *Militi Christi* raids on werewolf dens (sometimes an individual, sometimes a pack) in half a dozen countries, and footage was on every available TV screen. There was palpable collective excitement in the lounges. Even the cabin crew were jazzed, bright-eyed, serving their drinks with a new air of purpose. I thought of Jake's diary: *All paradigm shifts answer the amoral craving for novelty.* Well, this was a paradigm shift, all right. Months of rumour and counter-rumour, YouTube videos, conspiracy theories, "hoaxers" and religious fruitcakes—but now the governments of a dozen major powers had come out and admitted it was true. They'd been forced into it by the Soldiers of Christ. This was the *post hoc* scramble to bring it under political control before the holy rollers started to look like salvation. "We've known about this threat for some time," a plummy British general said, on the BBC World News. "We've known, we've trained, we've developed a range of strategies and hardware, but you must understand our primary objective—beyond the obvious one— has been to avoid civilian panic and vigilantism, which, unfortunately, is the likely consequence of some of these precipitate actions. I'd like to take this opportunity to re-state the government's position in the clearest possible terms: Leave it to the professionals."

I was thinking, as we took off, and the lift as the wheels left the runway hit all the passengers as a little objective correlative for the launch into an unknown future, of Olek's words: *Your species—and ours—is living in the last days of its liminality* . . . It was, in the weird way of these things, a relief to me that he was right. Everyone who's lived through a war knows this, the refreshment of the primacy of survival, the new, brutal perspective, the clean, liberating feeling of being able to cut—since you're living with death on your shoulder like a good-humoured crow—through all the usual bullshit and irrelevance, to get to the quick of a stranger—for a fuck or a fight—in moments.

I was thinking, too, of course, of Remshi, who hadn't lived to see it, but who had given me a gift (unknowingly?) that would be crucial in the days and years ahead. If immunity to silver was in me, then we would—oh, make no mistake, we *would*—find a way of getting it into our brothers and sisters. Our children. My children.

And what of the rest? Gods, magical sacrifices, dreams, clues, coincidences, synchronicities, destiny, the occasionally overwhelming intimation that there was a pattern to things, a purpose, a grand architecture, a meaning, a *plot?*

I remembered something I'd read somewhere, though I couldn't recall where. *It's all right to believe in these things. It's just not a good idea to rely on them.*

"Ma'am?" the stewardess said, bending towards me. "Can I offer you another glass of champagne?" She was pretty. Blonde hair pulled back in a French plait, flashy green eyes, red nail polish (*not* "Scarlet Vamp") that almost exactly matched the red of her tight skirt. She smelled of make-up and Dune, though *wulf* knew she'd eaten a chicken tikka samosa and a fruit salad in the last couple of hours. In the moment it took me to say "Yes, please" all her details gathered with a compact precision that gave me a sudden rush of how good it would be to kill and eat her.

After she'd refilled my glass and moved on, I plugged the headset in and hit a radio channel at random. A moment's silence, then the track started. Dylan. "The Times They Are a-Changin'."

Hard not to smile.

*It's all right to believe in these things. It's just not a good idea to rely on them.*

I settled back in my seat, wondering how long it would be before one of the humans on this flight—one of yours, one of you—lost someone to one of ours, one of us. You. Yours. Us. Ours. The days ahead would bring the division out of the shadows and into the light. The Cardinal and his holy soldiers were the vanguard force in a new war. There would be others.

There will be others.

We know you're coming.

We'll just have to make sure we're ready for you.

ACKNOWLEDGEMENTS

My thanks to: Jonny Geller, Jane Gelfman, Kirsten Foster, Francis Bickmore, Jamie Byng, Jenny Todd, Vicki Rutherford, Lorraine McCann, Cate Cannon, Anna Frame, Jaz Lacey-Campbell, Andrea Joyce, Diana Coglianese, Sonny Mehta, Kim Thornton, Ruth Liebmann, Peter Mendelsund, Mandy Brett and Jane Novak. Love and special thanks, as always, to Kim Teasdale.